The Wire

As Bogdan walked across Marchlewskiego Street a tiny Polski-Fiat 126 skidded to a halt in front of him. Inside sat a young overweight worker in dirty blue factory overalls who was close to tears. Neither man knew the other, but the plump figure behind the steering wheel addressed Bogdan like a long-lost friend.

'It's madness, utter madness,' the driver yelled. 'I just escaped in time. . . . They took away my mother, my father and my brother. . . . There's blood everywhere. Out apartment's been smashed up. . . . They'll live to regret this, those bastards. . . . It's war, a state of war!'

He spat in the snow, slammed the door, revved the engine and sped off.

The snowflakes and the silent, muffled sub-zero emptiness closed chillingly around Bogdan. A State of War? What did the driver mean?

NIK GOWING

The Wire

Mandarin

A Mandarin Paperback

THE WIRE

First published in Great Britain 1988
by Century Hutchinson Ltd
This edition published 1989
by Mandarin Paperbacks
Michelin House, 81 Fulham Road, London SW3 6RB

Mandarin is an imprint of the Octopus Publishing Group

Copyright © Nik Gowing Ltd 1988

A CIP catalogue record for this book
is available from the British Library

ISBN 0 7493 0118 X

Printed in Great Britain
by Cox & Wyman Ltd, Reading

This book is dedicated to the Poles
who suffered under martial law. Their
endurance inspired *The Wire*.

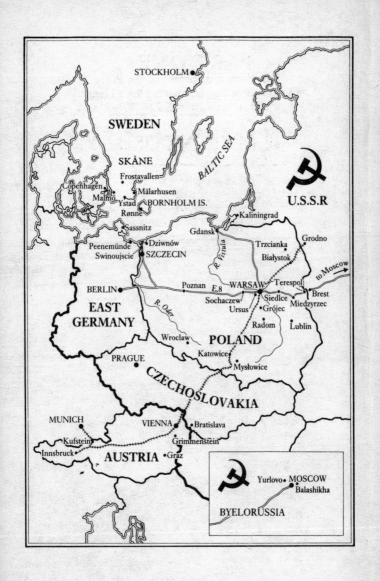

PART ONE

Iron Noose

1

Snow fell lightly on the evening of Saturday 12 December 1981. Poland froze as temperatures plunged to minus twenty degrees centigrade.

'Don't go home!'

The grim warning of the Stalinist years returned.

'Something is going on. Stay out of sight until we know what's happening.'

Like many Poles, Bogdan Miskiewicz was at a party that Saturday night. The swarthy foundry worker from the giant Warsaw steelworks had taken a tram south from the centre of Warsaw to the sprawling high-rise flats in the suburban wastes of Ursynow to celebrate the engagement of two close friends. 'How's Jola?' Every guest asked Bogdan the same question about his wife.

'Fine! Fine!' he yelled each time, his rasping voice competing with the thumping beat from a bootleg tape of the Swedish pop group Abba. But Bogdan's answer was a lie. Jola was ill and alone in their apartment across the city, sweating off a December fever just ten days after the birth of their first child. Yet for these few hours the new father was determined to forget his wife. He wanted a break from the months of strain as a leading figure in Solidarity, the first and only independent trade union in the Soviet Bloc. Tonight Bogdan Miskiewicz wanted fun, music, a girl and a good time.

The engagement party for Jan and Grazina was an oasis amid the hardships of Poland's political and economic crisis. In the finest Polish tradition, vodka flowed and plates were loaded high with cabanos sausages, smoked goose, baked ham and herrings which had been hoarded over many weeks. Like every Pole, the two hosts had 'connections': a friend in a government office who could help them jump queues; a farmer willing to slaughter a pig for a better price than the insulting amount paid by the state; a contact willing to barter finest sausage for black market refrigerator parts stolen from a factory.

Above the shrill dance music and the babble of high spirits there were heavy thuds at the front door. A neighbour complaining about the noise? Grazina shuffled into the hall with her pregnant waddle.

'Is Bogdan still here?' Grazina recognized the young man who stood outside shivering and breathless. It was Bogdan's youngest brother Jerzy. From the state he was in it was clear he must have run some distance.

'I need to speak to Bogdan ... quickly ... May I come in?'. Jerzy gasped through cracked lips as he removed his tattered felt cap and melting ice dripped from his heavy winter clothing. Grazina led him across the tiny hall. Through the dancing bodies in the dingy living room Jerzy spotted Bogdan's tall, muscular frame, a blue check shirt clinging to his torso as he danced thigh-to-thigh with Grazina's blonde sister Anna. Jerzy barged through a dozen clammy bodies to tap his brother on the shoulder.

'Bogdan, I must speak to you.'

The steelworker swung round with a distant expression and peeled his body away from Anna who clung longingly and drunkenly to his crumpled shirt tail.

'What the hell are you doing here?' Bogdan bristled. How much had his brother seen of him and Anna? His sick wife Jola must never learn about this evening of pleasure.

Jerzy pulled his brother out of earshot of the other guests. 'Something strange is happening ... we don't know what ...' Bogdan's bloodshot eyes closed with fatigue as Jerzy yelled to make himself heard above the music ... 'I just met Slawek – you know who I mean – he works at the Solidarity headquarters on Mokotowska Street. He told me they lost all communication with Gdansk an hour ago. The phones and telex went dead: it was just after they heard from the Lenin shipyard that the union's National Commission had voted to call a day of mass protest for next Thursday. They received details

4

of the resolutions then everything died ... Slawek says there've been reports of troop movements. Most of the people still on duty at Mokotowska Street fear the worst.'

Bogdan's mind changed quickly from partygoer to Solidarity activist. 'What about Warsaw? Is the city quiet?'

'No sign of trouble. Took me some time to get the tram down Pulawska Street, but that's not unusual this late on a Saturday night.' In his heavy anorak, Jerzy sweated profusely. 'Slawek told me to tell as many people as I could find. He wanted me to get hold of you first so you could get word to your colleagues at the steelworks then start getting the emergency plan into operation – the food, the printing, the occupation procedures ... everything you prepared last month. Slawek says it may be a false alarm, but after the propaganda and nervousness of the last two weeks he thinks Jaruzelski must be up to something. The main thing now is to go into hiding...'

The vodka had burrowed deep into Bogdan's system. It made Anna's elfin figure look lovelier than ever as she stood alone in the smoky light. It was too good a party to leave. But Jerzy's message sank home and the steel worker's mind began to focus on the enormity of what might be taking place across Poland

Jerzy was impatient and agitated. 'Bogdan! You mustn't hang about!' Bogdan lurched away and kissed Anna as Abba thumped from the cassette deck and his friends whooped and became drunker.

'I wish I could see you later, my dear. Perhaps tomorrow?' Anna did not respond to Bogdan. '... but I don't think it will be possible. If we don't see each other again you must blame Jaruzelski. Maybe that Russian tyrant Brezhnev. Maybe even Reagan and Thatcher. But don't blame me.'

Bogdan pushed through the crush of guests into the pitch black void of the freezing corridor outside the apartment. 'Where's the light?' he shouted.

'Come off it! You should know better than that!' Jan, stood silhouetted in the door holding a whisky bottle.

5

'We haven't had lights for two years now. Where can you get bulbs these days?' he burped. 'Each time the caretaker finds replacements they are stolen by someone to use in their own flat ... But tell me, you bastard, why are you going so early?'

'I have to disappear – just like our parents did under the Nazis. I may not see you and Grazina again for some time. Happy Christmas! Happy New Year! Happy Easter! And happy anything else you can think of ...'

Bogdan's voice tailed off as he disappeared into the gloom with Jerzy, then stumbled through the warren of unlit corridors. His cheeks stung painfully as he stepped outside into the freezing night air. Bogdan had drunk too much and eaten too little, and he knew it. He feared that if he now had to hide without food for several days he would not survive the terrible sub-zero rigours of winter. And how would he survive if he was picked up and detained indefinitely by the dreaded secret police – the *Sluzba Bezpieczentswa* – the SB?

Bogdan told Jerzy he would go home, pick up what he could, then disappear. He would try to keep in touch but he didn't know how or when. The two brothers parted without emotion and Bogdan staggered towards the main road which would take him to the city centre. The crumbling prefabricated apartment blocks of Ursynow typified the Polish planners' dream of urban perfection. But the reality was different for the 18,000 inhabitants. The apartments were small and overcrowded; the buildings were poorly finished and badly maintained; the communal heating system rarely worked; and there were only four shops.

In Pulawska Street, Bogdan stood on the packed ice waiting for the lights of a Polish *Fiat* or a Soviet *Lada* to bear down on him through the snow flurries. The dual carriageway was deserted for many minutes before a *Tatra* truck carrying cabbages spluttered across the traffic lights. Bogdan stood in the middle of the road, violently waving both arms. The driver stood on his brakes and the truck skewed to a skidding, lop-sided halt. Bogdan opened the passenger door and found a large stubble-faced man slouched across the steering wheel.

'Marshalkowska Street?' shouted Bogdan, his chin half-frozen as he shouted above the engine noise. 'Then Marchlewskiego Street to the roundabout where it joins Mariana Buczlka. You know, just before the Powazki cemetery. How much?'

'500 zlotys.' Bogdan clambered into the cab. The driver revved the engine and the truck moved off.

They drove north through a succession of green traffic lights towards the centre of Warsaw, the driver belching and filling the cab with a nauseating smell. Bogdan concluded the driver had been drinking the peasant moonshine *Bimber* – a vicious spirit distilled illegally out on the farms from orange peel and nuts. The man would face an automatic two-year jail sentence if caught driving with alcohol in his blood. But Bogdan had to take the risk.

As they continued north up Pulawska Street the capital lay ominously deserted under the ghostly hue of the amber street lights. Were these really the first signs of a Soviet invasion or State of Emergency which Solidarity had long feared?

For a time during that autumn there had been optimism within Solidarity that a coexistence with General Jaruzelski's Communist leadership might be possible. But Bogdan knew all too well that a clampdown fitted the recent pattern of government panic. Ten days ago, on 2 December, the dreaded ZOMO riot police had made their first public appearance since the birth of Solidarity sixteen months earlier. In their grey paramilitary uniforms they had stormed the Firemen's Academy in Warsaw to arrest and evict striking fire cadets. The assault had brought back terrible memories of the ZOMO's role in the deaths and riots at Gdansk in 1970 and Radom in 1976. Then on 3 December, Lech Walesa, Solidarity's leader, had warned a secret meeting of his fellow union leaders that 'confrontation is inevitable' not because Solidarity wanted confrontation but because union hotheads and radicals had pushed the situation beyond the point of no return. The next day, on 4 December, a bugged tape of Walesa's secret speech had been broadcast hourly on all radio and television channels. It had been labelled 'an incitement to civil war' and had given General Jaruzelski the pretext he had long sought to crush Solidarity.

Ahead, the hard-packed ice left by the snow ploughs shone in the twin beams of the truck's headlights. Bogdan watched a *Fiat* car pirouette outside the giant supermarket on Unii Lubelkskiej Square next to the East German Embassy. But where were the militia Jerzy had warned of? And the army? And the hated ZOMO?

It was a quarter to midnight. The cabbage truck continued north across the city and on across the underpass at Aleja Ludowwej. It was still quiet. The truck slowed for the roundabout on Zbawiciela Square and an empty tram rattled past in the opposite direction.

Suddenly Bogdan froze.

'Don't stop,' he whispered through clenched teeth. 'Drive on normally. Not too fast.'

Diagonally across the intersection forty metres to his right Bogdan saw what he had feared. Six wagons of the ZOMO were drawn up bumper to bumper across Mokotowska Street. In the shadows Bogdan could just make out the grey uniforms standing between the wagons; then the helmets and perspex visors glinting. This brief glimpse was enough to confirm that Solidarity's headquarters was surrounded by General Jaruzelski's security forces.

Bogdan wanted to find out more but he did not dare stop. The truck continued rolling and sliding northwards across the centre of Warsaw, where apart from a queue for taxis there was scarcely a pedestrian or car to be seen. During times of confrontation militia wagons usually gathered in the vast parking lot on Defilad Square at the foot of the Palace of Culture. But not tonight.

Bogdan was confused. Had the presence of the ZOMO outside the Mokotowska Street headquarters been a lone Jaruzelski provocation? Or was there much more which he had yet to see? Where were the large-scale militia and army movements? Or were Jerzy's warnings misguided?

It was five minutes to midnight. Flurries of snow floated in the gusting wind as the driver stopped his truck at the deserted roundabout where Juliana Marchlewskiego Street met the broad avenue coming west from the Gdansk river bridge. Bogdan jumped out, his boots hitting the fresh snow with a muffled crunch. The driver was too drunk to remember to ask for his five hundred zloty fare. Bogdan slammed the door without a thank you.

The steelworker had made the short walk to his apartment a thousand times, but he had never felt as uneasy as he did tonight. Shadows jumped at him from nowhere. A train siren from the Gdansk railway station a kilometre to the east screeched through the early morning silence.

The lobby of the apartment block at 6 Dzika Street was sombre and ill-lit. Bogdan stamped the snow from his feet, tapped one boot against the other to maintain blood circulation, then pressed the lift button. The ageing cage began creaking down. It always took a long time and tonight Bogdan's nervousness made it seem even longer. Only three lifts serviced two hundred apartments. Usually at least one lift didn't work, and the disillusioned maintenance engineer could never get spare parts.

When the lift finally arrived Bogdan took it to the eleventh floor. He knew he now faced a strained meeting with Jola where he would have to explain the enormity of what seemed to be happening. If he stayed with his wife and was captured by the SB, Jola might never know what had happened to him. Therefore he decided it was better to disappear. At least he might then have ways to stay in touch with Jola and their new son.

The tiny one-room flat was dark and silent as Bogdan hesitated on the threshold. He could just make out the overloaded bookcases, the simple Polish furniture for which he and Jola had queued for days, and the pictures of Lech Walesa and other union leaders. As his eyes adjusted to the dark he could also see the Solidarity calendar, the crucifix, and the picture of Pope John Paul II which he had taken during the pontiff's Polish visit in 1979. The apartment did not belong to Bogdan and Jola. It had been borrowed illegally from a friend who had left for Sweden a year earlier and never returned. It had been impossible for them to rent their own apartment. Five years earlier they had put their names on what was already a sixteen year waiting list, but now the list had lengthened to nineteen years and they had no black market zlotys or dollars to bribe a housing official.

Jola lay on the sofa-bed. Behind her in a large cardboard box lay their baby son Miatek, swaddled in a moth-eaten ex-army blanket.

'Jola . . . Jola my darling.' Bogdan bent over and whispered to avoid waking Miatek. 'It's me. How are you?'

Her reply seemed no more than a grunt. Bogdan had to move fast. As he waited for Jola to wake up he packed a holdall with warm clothes, toiletries and the small amount of food he thought she could spare. Then he added the sensitive union documents which he had removed from his Solidarity office six days earlier when he heard Walesa's bugged speech on the radio.

At last Jola spoke and Bogdan began to explain his dilemma. Through her tears she told him that she knew he was right. They had once believed that Solidarity had broken the back of the communist system and that the reforms were permanent. But now they both knew the dream was over and Bogdan would be a wanted man.

'I won't be able to phone or write, darling . . .' he said. 'I shan't tell you where I am. In case the police question you, it's best for you to know nothing of my hiding place or what I'm doing. We can only make contact through friends or reliable third parties . . .'

Jola understood. Bogdan hugged her then kissed his sleeping son. Within half an hour he had slipped away, quietly closing the door on his family and entering the life of what the government now called an 'anti-state extremist'.

As Bogdan stepped into the lobby eleven floors below,

four men dressed in leather jackets brushed past him into the lift. Their hair was neat and short, and all four smoked the best western Camel cigarettes. None of the four spoke or smiled, and on their breath Bogdan could smell the distinctive odour of privileged, high-class vodka. The tallest carried a small Italian-style plastic handpouch attached to his wrist by a thong. Protruding from the unzipped outer pocket Bogdan could just see the top lines of a printed document which proclaimed *State Decree* in bold type.

The steel doors slammed shut. Had the SB agents come for him? Bogdan watched as the lift rose, the tiny light skipping through the floor numbers until it reached eleven. What would Jola have to endure now? Perhaps he should return upstairs to protect his sick wife and baby? Bogdan searched his conscience but his resolve did not change. 'Leave! Go underground!' he told himself.

As he walked across Marchlewskiego Street a tiny *Polski-Fiat* 126 skidded to a halt in front of him. Inside sat a young overweight worker in dirty blue factory overalls who was close to tears. Neither man knew the other, but the plump figure behind the steering wheel addressed Bogdan like a long-lost friend.

'It's madness, utter madness,' the driver yelled. 'I just escaped in time ... They took away my mother, my father and my brother ... There's blood everywhere. Our apartment's been smashed up ... They'll live to regret this, those bastards ... It's war, a state of war!'

He spat in the snow, slammed the door, revved the engine and sped off.

The snowflakes and the silent, muffled sub-zero emptiness closed chillingly around Bogdan. A State of War? What did the driver mean?

2

The call for a nationwide strike came from Solidarity's leaders meeting in the Baltic port of Gdansk. By late evening the decision had been transmitted around the world by the correspondents of international press agencies, newspapers, radio and television.

Jurek Kucharski watched in silence as the National Commission wound up its two-day emergency meeting in the rambling ground-floor hall of the Health and Safety centre at the Lenin Shipyard. Senior union officials sat exhausted at long tables, surrounded by a jungle of waste paper and empty bottles. At a table on a raised platform in front of them sat Solidarity's leader Lech Walesa, who had shot to international fame when he led the first shipyard strikes of August 1980. Alongside him in open-necked shirts, pullovers and scruffy jackets sat the union's twenty-strong governing praesidium, all of them well-known names. On the wall to the left hung a Polish eagle cast in white plaster and to the right stood a two-metre-high bust of Lenin. This ever-present symbol of Soviet vigilance had watched as the Gdansk shipyard workers launched their bold challenge to communist rule in 1980. Now it watched over what would be the final meeting of Solidarity's leadership.

It was a few minutes to midnight. Like the 107 delegates, Jurek Kucharski had heard the rumours of military manoeuvres which had been circulating all day. He had also seen the contents of the urgent telexes sent by the union's regional offices. Up to sixty tanks with Soviet markings had been spotted moving eastwards from Poznan, Leszno and Gostyn; unusual troop movements had been seen in Muszaki, Szczytno and Barto Szyce with one column heading for Gdansk and another for Warsaw; regular troops and conscripts were being

12

reinforced by reservists; and in country districts young peasants had been called up without warning.

Now the lone operator on the shipyard switchboard had taken a new message which he passed to Walesa. Jurek watched the union leader's face turn white as he read the text. Wearily Walesa grabbed the table, kicked back his chair and pulled himself to his feet, inhaling heavily on his usual brand of unfiltered Polish cigarette. He combed a hand through his greasy black hair and grabbed the neck of a microphone stand. His tired, blood-shot eyes peered through the blue haze of smoke and he supported himself on his fingers. Walesa's normal spark and vitality were spent. His head pounded with the strain of sixteen unrelenting months spent confronting the obstinacy of the Polish government and battling to unite Solidarity.

His voice rattled around the loudspeakers and silenced the delegates. 'Phone lines are down ... Telex lines are down ... Communications to Warsaw have been cut.'

Poland's erratic telephone system often failed but this time everybody knew what this news signalled. Soli-darity's leadership had gone further than General Jaru-zelski was prepared to tolerate. Walesa's appeals for moderation had failed. Not only had the union just voted for provocative anti-communist protests and a national strike designed to cripple the country, they had drawn up a list of Solidarity officials who would form a provisional government to replace the country's communist lead-ership. It was one step from treason.

Such was Walesa's anger at his radical colleagues that he had passed the last hours tinkering on a piano back-stage to dissipate his fury. Now he clutched his forehead and struggled to find new reserves of energy before laun-ching an attack on the militants he had spent months trying to restrain.

'Now you have the confrontation you wanted,' he shouted furiously. 'Now you will all have plenty of free time in prison to think about your new government ...'

Walesa had lost. His voice tailed off and he ended with

13

a tired shrug as he slumped into his chair. Confrontation had come a month sooner than he had expected and Solidarity was not prepared. Walesa knew his months of struggle and brinkmanship to ensure Solidarity's survival were over.

By midnight, senior army and militia officers had opened their sealed orders and the machinery of Martial Law was turning with breathtaking efficiency. General Jaruzelski and his fellow generals had conceived the plan in secret over several months. But the strategy had not been finalised until the last few days after a sudden visit by Marshal Viktor Kulikov, the Soviet leader of the Warsaw Pact's combined armed forces. Moscow's patience was exhausted. The Soviet marshal warned the Polish general: 'Either you crush Solidarity or we will do it for you!'

The Soviet move so shocked Jaruzelski that he cocooned himself in his office for several days to work out his response. Now, on Saturday evening, lights burned in all Warsaw's sensitive ministries and at midnight General Jaruzelski told an emergency meeting of Poland's Council of Ministers that he and his new military council had taken it upon themselves to declare martial law. Polish airspace had been closed and civil servants summoned from their beds. In Communist Party offices the *apparatchiks* deemed to have failed in their duties were ordered to clear their desks. From Gdansk to Wroclaw, from Lublin to Szczecin, from Katowice to Poznan, the military and the militia hardware rumbled on to the empty streets. At last the only ideologically wayward nation in the Soviet Bloc was being brought to order.

Behind the ornate stone facade of the Soviet Embassy halfway down the tree-lined hill on Belvederska Street the Kremlin's diplomats and the KGB's agents listened, watched and reported back to Moscow. But under orders from the Soviet High Command, the Red Army's two divisions based among the forests outside Warsaw and at Legnica in south-west Poland remained inside their barracks.

In the West, NATO's monitoring stations and eavesdropping satellites had detected an unusually heavy volume of Soviet signals traffic across Poland to East Germany in recent weeks. But tonight the signals were Polish with no Soviet involvement.

By midnight the Baltic port of Gdansk had been cut off. When Solidarity officials asked the militia commander why, he explained that the city had been sealed 'as part of a regular operation to trap common criminals'. The commander knew that no one could argue.

The meeting of Solidarity's National Commission broke up at half past midnight, and the delegates walked out past the idle cranes of the deserted shipyard ribbing each other about who would be Prime Minister in their 'provisional government'. Only when they were safely inside their hotels near the Central Station did platoons of ZOMO quietly disgorge from the trucks and cordon off the area.

Solidarity's leaders were neatly trapped. High-ranking militia officers moved swiftly along the corridors rousing the union leaders, ordering them to dress, then leading them downstairs to the lobby where their hands were forced behind their backs and they were loaded into freezing militia vans. None of the leaders showed surprise or worry. Each exuded a smug confidence that Solidarity was stronger and more popular than the authorities. Within half an hour the ZOMO platoons and detainees had gone, and once again the grubby streets of Gdansk were occupied only by the biting northerly wind blowing viciously in from the Baltic.

But the security forces had failed to arrest all those who had attended the Solidarity meeting. Jurek Kucharski had watched the ZOMO operation from the shadows of the Central Station beyond the tram tracks. He had evaded capture. Now he had a story to tell Poland and the world. Somehow.

3

In Warsaw, three hundred kilometres south of Gdansk, Solidarity's regional headquarters on Mokotowska Street stood almost empty. Union leaders were in Gdansk and most administrative staff had gone home to enjoy a rare few hours of free time. Only a handful of volunteers remained inside the rambling stone building to assemble information coming from the National Commission meeting and to brief the western press correspondents who had stayed in Warsaw.

Among those left on duty was Andrzej Sulecki, a tall, lean man in his mid-thirties with a trim moustache, black hair, striking Slavic features and the physique of a basketball player. Sulecki had a relatively menial job collating telexes from regional Solidarity branches, preparing bulletins and then dispatching them to the union's fifty-five offices around the country. Although Solidarity's national headquarters was in Gdansk, the office in Warsaw was the union's lifeline to western opinion. Contacts with western diplomats and journalists ensured the vital western support without which General Jaruzelski might have crushed Solidarity much sooner.

It was almost midnight, an hour after the telex connection to Gdansk had failed. With no work, Sulecki decided to leave earlier than he had expected. He clattered along the lofty corridors then down the unlit stone staircase. In the ground-floor lobby he tucked up his anorak collar and pulled on his gloves in preparation for the punishing sub-zero cold of this December night.

Only as he began pushing the frosted glass of the double swing doors did he hesitate. To his right he heard several heavy lorries manoeuvring . . . and then to the left more lorries. He edged the main door open and through a narrow crack counted the lights of eleven ZOMO trucks drawing across either end of Mokotowska Street in the gently falling snow. Unlike Bogdan, Sulecki knew immediately what this meant. The ZOMO assault on the Firemen's Academy ten days earlier had been the dress rehearsal and Jaruzelski's final warning. Tonight was the real thing.

Instinctively Sulecki turned, sprinted past the locked Solidarity shop which normally sold union posters, books and badges, then crashed open the rear doors of the union headquarters. Ahead of him a squad of ZOMO riot police were already fanning out in the dark on Natolinska Street.

Sulecki ran under the wizened branches of the winter trees, across the snow-covered tennis courts and on past the smart post-war blocks of apartments owned by well-to-do Poles. Near the Egyptian embassy he turned and paused for breath. From beyond the trees and apartment blocks came the ominous clanking of weapons and anti-riot equipment being unloaded from trucks. Sulecki's chest heaved with an easy, regular rhythm. During the months of office duties he had always found time to run six kilometres on most days and ten kilometres at least once a week.

Inside the Solidarity headquarters a union sympathiser rushed in to warn the handful of remaining advisers and staff what was happening. But the warning came too late, the building was already cordoned off, and outside, young ZOMO conscripts stood shoulder-to-shoulder in the freezing dark with white, lead-filled truncheons hanging from their waists and perspex riot shields recently delivered from Japan clutched firmly across their chests.

A squad of half a dozen NCOs crashed through the main door. More followed in a second wave, rushing up the long staircases and draughty corridors. Acting like men possessed, they ransacked offices, overturned desks and disembowelled filing cabinets. Then they smashed windows and fractured water pipes to ensure that no early repossession of the building by Solidarity would be possible. But where were the 'massed counter revolutionaries' which weeks of militia propaganda and operational briefings had secretly prepared them to expect? They didn't exist, and even the ZOMO were surprised.

Outside, half a dozen smaller militia vans nicknamed *Nysas* or 'bitches' drew up next to the Solidarity offices. Armed SB officers dragged sacks of documents down the stone steps as colleagues arrested the remaining handful of bewildered union staff and bundled them into the vans.

The end of Solidarity's Warsaw headquarters had been clinical and swift. Within an hour the national union structure so carefully built up over sixteen months had been destroyed.

As Sulecki made his way home, he was surprised by the fact that no red Communist Party flag fluttered from the roof of Warsaw's regional Communist Party offices. He walked briskly down Piekna Street, past the plate glass and bristling aerials of the United States embassy; past the squat, box-shaped Canadian embassy, then the impressive double-winged canopies of the French embassy. Inside each building security guards dozed, but there was no sign that the diplomats labelled by the Polish government as 'imperialist spies and agents' had been mobilised to monitor any unusual developments.

Sulecki mulled over the contradictory signals. Perhaps what he had witnessed at Mokotowska Street had been no more than a localised police action. There were no signs to suggest it was anything more, so he continued to walk on past the empty Polish Parliament building towards the tower blocks on the banks of the Vistula river where he lived in a fifteenth floor apartment with his mistress Magda Gajewska.

Sulecki undressed in the cold and dark, then slipped his naked body between the crumpled sheets. He inched closer, his chest against Magda's back as he begged heat from the woman he had lived with for eighteen months. Magda was thirty and an attractive blonde who was proud of her reputation as an anti-government activist and firebrand dissident. Sulecki warmed his cold hands in his crutch before curving one of them over her breast.

'Any news?' Magda whispered drowsily.

'Gdansk agreed on the national protest strike for next Thursday,' said Andrzej. 'It was unanimous.'

Magda rolled onto her back. 'Excellent.' The blankets slipped and bared her breasts to the chill air. She tucked the pillows under her head and punched one arm defiantly into the air. 'It's what we need. The union has got to convince those pigheads in the Party and the Council of Ministers that they can't treat us like children. They don't take us seriously, but on Thursday we'll show them. Millions will take to the streets. Then Jaruzelski will *have* to talk with us and honour the agreement the government signed with Solidarity last year.'

Sulecki said nothing, either to support Magda or to provoke her. Magda snuggled closer.

'Darling Andrzej ... Something odd happened this evening. Just before midnight I was half-watching an Italian terrorist film on television. It just stopped in the middle, fifteen minutes before it was supposed to end. Then the announcer appeared sounding flustered. All he said was that they were closing down and the film would be shown some other time. There was no late news summary; no national anthem; the screen just went blank ... Strange, wasn't it? Do you think their equipment broke down again? Or perhaps there was a sudden Solidarity strike!'

Sulecki's neutral response was lost in the pillow. He supported Magda on his left arm, as the one-sided conversation petered out, and they drifted into a satisfying sleep.

Suddenly their embrace was blown apart and Magda sat bolt upright. A second crash followed as a crowbar splintered the plywood front door to the apartment.

'Open up!' screamed a muffled voice outside as further blows reverberated around the tiny bed-sitting room. Magda glanced nervously at her watch on the bedside table. It was one o'clock.

Three thick-set men pushed through the splintered front door and took up positions towering over the sofa-bed. Magda had no doubt that they were U-Beks, the colloquial name for SB agents. Even casual use of the name 'U-Bek' revived terrifying memories of Stalin's secret police who had tortured and murdered thousands of Poles in the purges of the 1950s.

In the dark, the three U-Beks hovered over their prey – two naked bodies still only half awake and disorientated. In jeans, denim jackets and anoraks the men looked more like off-duty workers than policemen. They cursorily displayed SB identification wallets but it was a pointless formality. Not only was it impossible to see the cards, Sulecki and Magda knew who the U-Beks were and why they were there.

'Now I know why the television went dead,' Magda mumbled as she fell despairingly onto the pillow. During Solidarity's brief life it had seemed that the SB's techniques of arrest harassment and interrogation had become a thing of the past. But tonight showed that sixteen months had not changed or reformed the secret police.

The voice of the senior officer cut through the atmosphere. 'You refused to answer the door to a functionary of the Polish People's security forces. You refused to respond to our order to open your door.'

He was lying. Neither Magda or Andrzej had heard anything before the SB men smashed their way in. Magda controlled her anger. She knew it was safer to say nothing.

'Get up!' ordered the perspiring officer.

Sulecki rolled towards the packing case which doubled as a bedside table. Calmly he plucked a Marlboro cigarette from a packet given to him by a Western diplomat seeking information earlier that evening. Magda, however, could contain her fury no longer.

'As an SB officer you know the law. It's an offence to intrude into private homes between ten in the evening and six in the morning. Not only have you entered my apartment illegally, you have forced your way in and damaged my property.'

It was an empty gesture which fell on SB ears conveniently deafened by the new and sweeping standing orders drawn up by General Jaruzelski.

'That was the law yesterday, Comrade Gajewska. Today the law is different. This is a state of war.' He waved the decree in a torch beam under Magda's nose. 'Previous laws no longer exist. Your normal rights are suspended. Get dressed and come with us.' Magda knew that to resist would only result in violent retaliation during 'routine questioning'.

Outside the apartment, however, there was no such self-restraint as the shrill voices of neighbours echoed around the stairwell. 'Pigs ... Bastards ... Russian apes' they shouted. The residents had already been alerted by the orange *Fiat* 125 with its special number plates and long floppy radio aerials parked at the base of the apartment block. Now the car had been joined by a 'bitch' wagon.

Sulecki spoke for the first time. '*Prosze pana!* Please allow us the courtesy of dressing in private!'

The Captain's reply was stubbornly unaccommodating. 'You won't be left alone. You might destroy evidence or escape.'

'Evidence of what?' Magda asked defiantly. 'You talk as though we are criminals. What are the charges? What are we meant to have done? Why are you taking us away?'

Sulecki stayed as cool as his reputation. He kissed Magda, then slowly lifted himself out of the confusion of sheets and blankets littering the sofa-bed. He stood naked and shivering as the captain replied to Magda in a monotone voice. 'There are matters to be resolved, questions to be answered. It will be a formality and you will be released in a few hours. You have two minutes to get dressed.'

Neither Magda nor Andrzej believed him, but tired and unarmed, they knew they had no alternative to cooperation. The three agents turned their heads to allow the prisoners to dress in a degree of privacy. The apartment filled with the smell of cheap Polish tobacco.

Standing in the dim light, Magda's skin was dappled by goosepimples and her breasts stood taut in the piercing cold. She felt stress pains in her back as she realised they would have no time to hide all the Solidarity documents. All she and Andrzej could do was grab soap, woollens, gloves, and some Christmas chocolates which had just arrived from friends in Oslo. But as they hurriedly threaded the buckles on their bulging knapsacks, the Captain yanked the bags and heavy clothing from their hands and threw them violently across the room.

'I told you – you will only be away for a few hours. You won't need things like that for such a brief visit. Get out, scum!'

The other two SB men prodded Magda and Sulecki with the crowbar towards the splintered front door like croupiers pushing chips around a casino table. They forced them into the lift, pushing violently as both prisoners defiantly dragged their feet in the hope of delaying enough to be seen by neighbours. As Magda and Sulecki were loaded into the 'bitch' wagon, the chattering militia VHF radio echoed in the empty street. From all over Warsaw they heard radio messages to and from SB agents involved in what was clearly a large number of detention assignments. To Magda it was a return to the terrible political repressions of the Sixties and Seventies. Across Poland hundreds – maybe thousands – of dissidents and Solidarity colleagues were being trawled in by order of a new Military Council which no one had yet heard of.

The mobile cell inside the 'bitch' van was designed to humiliate. Andrzej and Magda sat next to each other on the broken wooden slats of a bench which sagged precariously. Moisture from their breath condensed and froze in icy rivulets on the van's small, filthy windows. Through the steel grilles they could see nothing of where they were going – only a dark blur of occasional blue flashing police lights.

Opposite them in the cell sat a uniformed militia officer with his legs arrogantly splayed apart. He wore the kind of paramilitary uniform not seen for years – a fur-lined combat jacket with battle camouflage, a hat with long

22

ear flaps, baggy blue-grey trousers with bulging thigh pockets, and calf-length leather snow boots. Magda stared at him through the gloom, silently nicknaming him 'Boris' because of the Soviet-like features she could see by the glow of his cigarette.

Boris blew smoke at Magda's face and she coughed. 'Could we open the window a little?' she asked irritably.

There was no immediate response. In his left palm Boris slowly tapped a white truncheon. Then without warning he flicked his right wrist and the lead-filled weapon rose like lightning, striking a painful blow on the underside of her chin. She squealed as blood began dripping onto the bench slats from a cut across her left lower jaw.

'Don't complain,' Boris told Magda sarcastically. 'Enjoy this comfort while you can. It's a lot warmer in this vehicle than where you're going.'

Boris leaned arrogantly towards them, ripped the red-and-white Solidarity badges from their lapels and pulverised them under his boot. Then he reclined again, the truncheon still tapping monotonously, a cigarette stub jammed in his mouth and dripping ash.

'Comrade Gajewska, we've had enough of that fresh air crap from your Solidarity union. Your illegal revolution is over. It is we who will decide what is good for Poland, not revisionist scum like you ...'

He swung the truncheon again. Despite the dark, his aim was just as sharp. But this time the nightstick swished past Magda's bloody face and hit Sulecki's forehead, the blow knocking Andrzej off the bench into the corner of the van.

'As for you, Comrade Sulecki, you'll never see your telex machine again. Your subversive bulletins will earn you a place among those to face trial for attempted treason.'

Sulecki nursed his forehead. He knew treason was punishable by death.

It was clear that the officer was not in the wagon by accident. He was well briefed and must have been assigned there to begin softening them up for interrogation.

'Your involvement in anti-state activity is perfectly documented, Sulecki. We know what you wrote. We have full transcripts from your telex machine just as you sent them: word for word, subversive phrase by subversive phrase . . .'

The van swung on to the hard-packed snow of the yard behind the Wilcza Street militia depot in central Warsaw. Outside Magda and Sulecki could hear engines ticking over and the stern, officious voices of militia and SB officers. Truncheon blows rattled along the steel sides and the side door was wrenched open. Between the tightly packed lines of police vehicles, uniformed and plain-clothes police functionaries were pushing and hand-whipping ill-clothed detainees across the freezing yard into a long police corridor which reeked of sweat, vomit and stale vodka. Magda and Sulecki joined the tail of the queue which snaked back along the filthy wall leading from a makeshift registration desk.

Magda and Sulecki shuffled slowly forward in silence. It was half past one, and processing was already well under way. The volume of well-prepared paper work, the long queue and the huge numbers of militia officers confirmed that this was no chance series of arrests but a brilliantly orchestrated clampdown. Paradoxically, Magda found comfort in the large number of people assembled at the Wilcza Street depot. The squads had brought in writers, film-makers, poets, university lecturers, journalists, artists, television people, Solidarity officials, low ranking union functionaries and political dissidents. Among them were distinguished writers like Anka Kowalska, famous actors like Halina Mikolajska, and even eminent academics invited to Warsaw for the Polish Congress of Culture.

'Clear your pockets . . . check you have nothing incriminating on you . . .'

The whispered warning circulated discreetly from prisoner to prisoner. Deep inside their pockets some detainees tore up scraps of paper. Others even smoked US dollar as if they were cigarettes, fearing that if American currency was discovered in their clothing they would be charged as blackmarketeers or subversive agents of 'western imperialist powers.'

'Name!' The uniformed militia captain did not raise his eyes from the long list.

'Documents!' Magda handed over her green State Security Identity Card. 'Address? ... Personal details? ... Parents' names ... Occupation?'

It was the same old discourteous routine, so Magda gave the same old answers she had given a hundred times during her previous interrogations in the late 1970s. Address: Gornoslaska Street. Occupation: designer at the FSO car factory in Warsaw. It was this sort of humiliating treatment by the SB which Solidarity had been created to destroy. The union had offered a future where people mattered, not ideology; a system where a file number was less important than a person's potential for helping to pull Poland out of its misery and near-bankruptcy. But tonight that flame of hope was being systematically extinguished.

Magda rattled off her personal details in a mocking computer-like voice and as she stepped aside, Sulecki took his turn in front of the desk.

'Name! ... Documents! Address? Personal details? Occupation? Parents?'

Sulecki recited his details. Age thirty-five; farm worker from a village near Sokolka north-east of Bialystok; for the last two years a worker on the production line at the Ursus tractor plant outside Warsaw.

'Empty your pockets. Remove all belts, braces and shoelaces. Everything on the table!'

The captain examined Sulecki's possessions and slowly listed them on the internment paper.

'Sign here!'

Sulecki was not worried. He had cleared his pockets before he and Magda were hauled from their apartment.

'Go!' Without looking up, the captain waved his hand

25

imperiously. Sulecki stepped back to join Magda, and a ZOMO guard swung his white truncheon to prod them both in the required direction.

They each instinctively knew the fate awaiting them. Magda would be consumed by the women's penal system and Sulecki by the men's. It might be months or years before they saw each other again. As they walked along the corridor Magda slowed to let Andrzej catch up. She grabbed his hand and embraced him, her arms round his neck. They were still hugging each other when a militia guard furiously wrenched them apart. 'Move!' yelled the young, stubble-faced conscript, his Polish-made Kalashnikov AK-47 hanging from one shoulder, a fixed bayonet glinting on the barrel.

'*Do widzenia, Andrzej*!' Magda whispered affectionately as a tear rolled down the high cheekbones of her blanched face.

'*Do widzenia, Magda*,' Andrzej reciprocated, his head bowed, his forehead furrowed, his eyes trying to convey the enormity of what he had no time to tell her.

4

Bogdan Miskiewicz scurried south through the centre of Warsaw, his head down, his meagre holdall of personal belongings over his shoulder. It was 1.15 a.m. Within two minutes of leaving the apartment on Dzika Street his nose felt as if it had been chopped off by the punishing cold, his cheek and ear lobes stung painfully, and his dry mouth burned like antiseptic.

Bogdan walked as fast as he dared without alerting any stray militia or SB eyes which might be watching. Each time blue lights flashed through the gloom, he hid in a shop doorway, behind a parked car or in the lobby of an apartment block.

It was a month since Bogdan and a handful of colleagues at the steelworks had read the signs and started to collect secret stores of food, clothing and printing material. They had found safe houses and hiding places, and set up a clandestine network of a few trusted union colleagues to prevent infiltration by SB 'sleepers'. Then eight days ago, following the storming of the Firemen's Academy and the bugging of Solidarity's national meeting in Radom, Bogdan and his colleagues had stepped up their preparations by moving food, documents and equipment to safe locations.

Bogdan hurried south through the empty streets of Muranow, past small stone shrines set in the pavements and walls to commemorate the Warsaw uprising of 1944. Frozen red and white carnations drooped from old glass jars and flickering candles dripped small puddles of frozen wax as they struggled to stay alight in the intense cold.

Bogdan crossed at the traffic lights next to the Warsaw Provincial Court. It was here thirteen months ago, on 10 November 1980, that Poland had witnessed a unique event: the Polish government's legal recognition of Solidarity as the Soviet Bloc's first-ever independent trade union. Bogdan remembered how thousands had packed the street in festive mood as Judge Koscielniak presided nervously in an overcrowded court room packed with senior union figures and cameramen from western and Polish television. Bogdan recalled the euphoria when Koscielniak had anounced his approval for Solidarity to be registered. But few had heard the judge's important qualification: that Solidarity must recognise the Communist Party's supreme right to govern in socialist Poland and must never call a strike. When Solidarity's leaders eventually heard the judge's restrictions they had stormed furiously from the court and threatened a resumption of strikes unless the government honoured the promises it had made to Poland's workers in Gdansk three months earlier.

As he began to confront tonight's new horror of martial law, Bogdan recalled how Poland had faced turmoil in November 1980. The confused government had seemed in a state of permanent shock, reeling from crisis to crisis under the unrelenting challenge of a truly popular mass movement. Party Secretary Kania and Prime Minister Pinkowski had flown to Moscow to consult President Brezhnev. Somehow they had convinced the Soviet leadership that the Polish government could solve the problem themselves without direct Soviet intervention. Then finally, eleven days later, ten million workers had won their unquestioned right to a registered and independent trade union and Lech Walesa had been carried shoulder high down the streets which tonight lay deserted and snowbound.

Nothing stirred on Starynkiewicza Square as Bogdan passed the offices of the communist party newspaper *Trybuna Ludu*. He was now three kilometres from his wife and son. The intense cold had frozen his gloves, packed snow penetrated his secondhand boots, and he had lost feeling in his toes and finger tips. Icicles of frozen sweat hung from his eyebrows and nostrils.

As he reached the open expanse of Wawelska Street alongside the SKRA football stadium, Bogdan paused to catch his breath. Suddenly to the south, from beyond the stadium and the Medical Academy, Bogdan heard the terrifying rumble of what could only be heavy armour coming towards the city up the Zwirki-I-Wigury dual carriageway. He melted into the shadows of the trees in the park running parallel to the road. Nearby, a towering obelisk rose two hundred feet out of the snow, but Warsaw's Soviet War Memorial meant as little to Bogdan as to most Poles. Poland's official post-war history had ignored both the Soviet Union's refusal in 1944 to support the people of Warsaw in their Uprising, and Stalin's decision to let his army watch from a distance as the Nazis demolished Warsaw and slaughtered its population.

'You Russian bastards . . .' Bogdan swore. 'Why can't you leave Poland alone? . . . Bastards . . . Bastards.'

It was two-thirty. Bogdan began to smell the acrid diesel fumes from the barracks a few hundred metres away. He recognised immediately the distinctively sour odour of Soviet fuel which he remembered from his days as a young conscript in an army transport division. Now from the north-west came new sounds: growling engines of Soviet-built turboprop aircraft, and the unmistakeable clattering of Soviet-built helicopter gunships.

Stumbling from fatigue and lack of nourishment Bogdan turned off the airport highway then headed down a path among the skeletal sycamore trees in Mokotow Park. He and his four union colleagues at the steelworks had weighed carefully where to base their clandestine underground operations. They had pinpointed four locations – three apartments in different parts of the city, then this more rural district where state enterprises allocated allotments to workers and privileged Warsaw residents. Here Poles could find a temporary haven from their cramped city apartments by building small summer houses and growing their own vegetables.

In the Rakowiec allotments, Bogdan and his colleagues

believed they would be secure and less vulnerable to searches. They calculated that city apartments would be subject to rigorous surveillance by the militia and SB, but that the security forces, already hard-pressed, would have insufficient manpower to search every allotment shed in Poland. Moreover, they would probably not bother to search locations right under their noses. In these allotments the Solidarity cell would be next to a main army barracks and the air base at Okecie. Behind them were the homes of senior SB officers as well as the exclusive Interior Ministry Hospital for privileged *apparatchiks*.

In the winter murk Bogdan reached a fence and edged his way along the wire until he found a rusting iron gate. He threw his pack over and pulled himself up until he straddled the top of the fence. Dropping over into the snow, he settled on his haunches to listen.

He heard nothing, and seemed safe. Bending double he scampered past broken fences, the remains of storm-damaged trees and the door of a summer hut swunging wildly back and forth in the wind. Finally, a few metres ahead, he saw the distinctive turquoise boarding of the tumbledown sanctuary which he and his colleagues had requisitioned illegally while the owner was abroad on a Polish government contract in Libya. The shed measured four metres by three. It was single storey with a roof covered by felt scrounged from a state-run building site. A small wooden awning at the front gave protection against the fierce heat of a Polish summer, and there were four small windows, in each wall.

The distant sound of military voices and machines continued as Bogdan searched for the key under an oil drum used as a plant pot for summer dahlias. He cleared the snow around the base of the porch, turned the lock and pushed hard. Ice had welded the door to the frame and Bogdan pushed half-a-dozen times before it gave way.

'Oh, my God! . . .'

The wall of musty, dank cold came as a shock. What a

30

hovel! For the first time the Warsaw steelworker was overcome by the enormity of his situation. He might have to live here for months, without seeing his wife and child. Did he have the commitment and mental stability to cope? He dropped down exhausted into an old, moth-ravaged armchair in the corner and could smell the cloud of dust and dirt that he had disturbed. He took an unwieldy Polish-made *Unitra* battery radio from his bag, placed it on a small table and turned it on at low volume. To the accompaniment of a Chopin piano concerto Bogdan pulled two damp blankets over his fully-clothed body and drifted into a cold, fitful sleep.

It was 3 a.m. Already 350,000 militia and 400,000 troops were moving at high speed to paralyse Poland.

5

Magda joined the women internees lined up along one wall of the Wilcza Street militia depot. She recognised most of the faces, some as colleagues and friends, others just as names. They all welcomed her with the same whispered greeting. '*Czesc!*'

Like Magda, three women had blood on their faces. Some, however, were untouched.

'Has anyone had a chance to see their internment order?' Magda asked furtively.

'Yes,' whispered Agneska Szatowski, a tall, slender figure who was the distinguished professor of sociology at the Academy of Sciences.

'What did it say?' asked Magda.

Professor Szatowski spoke slowly as she recalled the wording. 'It was signed by the Warsaw militia commander and said something like ... considering the following citizen might exercise, as long as he remains free, a destructive influence upon his fellow men and cause panic in his surroundings ... it has been ordered by the decree of 12 December 1981, article 42, that the following citizen is to be detained and placed in an internment camp ...'

'Did it say where?'

'Mine said Bialoleka, I think ... Bialoleka camp.'

Every internee was hungry for information. 'What about other details?' asked an unidentified voice.

'Only routine things which the SB have on file anyway – full name, place and date of birth, parents' names and so on.' The professor's cool broke. 'Who the hell do these so-called "representatives of the Polish people" think they really are?' she demanded. '*They* are the destructive influences on our nation. It is *they* who cause panic and *they* who spread lies about Poland. Just look at the newspapers, the so-called 'official' press. Only our Solidarity newspaper reports something near the truth of what is happening.'

As a reflex response to the professor's outburst, the truncheon from a lunging ZOMO officer crashed three times onto her neck and shoulder. It drew screams of agony but no blood as she collapsed among the shivering bodies. 'Get her up!' screamed a militia officer. But as a matter of honour the professor rejected all offers of help and painfully pushed herself up.

'Your ID!' barked the young ZOMO conscript.

The professor held her neck. 'I haven't got it. The captain down the corridor took it an hour ago. He has it with my belongings.'

'Your ID!' the officer repeated. 'No excuses! Every Polish citizen carries an ID. Failure to carry it is a crime under Polish law ... Your card, comrade!'

The 67-year-old professor stared stoically at the young peasant. His bloodshot eyes darted nervously to and fro as he tapped his truncheon against his left palm. The professor – an experienced victim of Polish repression – calmly repeated the excuse.

'The captain has my identity papers. Please ask him.'

The conscript weakened. 'It is also an order that criminals in prisons do not need ID cards,' he stuttered feebly.

Murmurs of congratulation spilled furtively along the line as a shivering middle-aged internee joined the queue and began talking.

'I have some news ...' she said in a low voice as those near her strained to listen. 'Militia surrounded the Solidarity headquarters on Mokotowska Street at eleven-thirty. There were eleven trucks and a dozen vans; more than a hundred ZOMO in full riot gear. Plenty of SB too. My son works at the Warsaw steelworks. He was on his way to celebrate a birthday and saw people being taken away and the police dragging out sackloads of documents. Instead of going to the party my son came home to warn me. Three minutes later we heard the sound of boots running up the stairs. They only came for me. My son's very active in Solidarity but the SB fools didn't recognise him. They pulled me out by my hair and dumped me in a "bitch" wagon.'

Magda looked round anxiously for Andrzej. Her heart began thumping wildly as she took in the implications of what she had just heard from the new arrival. . . . Eleven-thirty? Had she heard correctly?

'What time did you say the ZOMO moved in?' she queried.

'My son said it was eleven-thirty . . .'

Magda slid slowly down the flaking wall of the militia depot and crouched on her haunches. Her brain worked back through the events of that night. Andrzej had returned to the apartment at half past midnight. He said he had come straight home, so he must have still been in the Solidarity headquarters at midnight, half an hour after the militia assault began. Why had he told her nothing then? Had he seen the assault or not? And if not, where was he at eleven-thirty?

Magda was consumed by doubt and suspicion. 'Why?' The question spun frantically through her head.

It was four hours before dawn, the coldest time of the night. In the backyard of the Militia depot ZOMO officers manhandled small groups of shivering bodies into SB cars and 'bitch' wagons. The tumult of police orders and revving engines disorientated the exhausted prisoners who by now simply went where they were pushed. Magda climbed on the first wagon she reached – a high, box-like *Jelcz* truck normally employed to transport militia patrols. In the minute since she had left the relative warmth of the police depot the brutal sub-zero temperatures had ripped through her old jeans and jersey and numbed her gloveless hands. Her stiff fingers grabbed for the climbing handles and she placed a boot on the bumper.

'You comrade . . . down!' The major's sharp command reverberated around the grimy stone walls. 'What the hell are you doing? Don't you understand simple language, you stupid bitch?'

He grabbed Magda by the neck of her pullover, pulled her back on to the snow and shoved her violently towards a group of women who were cuddling each other to preserve their body warmth.

'Get in!' The officer's riot helmet and perspex visor glinted like electric sparks in the dim light as he waved his Kalashnikov. The four women obeyed and squeezed into a smaller blue-and-white *Suka* van. The rusting door slammed, then the vehicle lurched out of the crowded police yard and rattled into the city.

It was too dangerous for Magda to reveal her private thoughts to those with her. Who among them might be an SB infiltrator or provocateur? Even the integrity of known 'activists' was now suspect. Magda pummelled her fist on to her knee in despair. 'They cannot and will not destroy us. Crushing Solidarity will be like trying to crush a giant magnet. If they smash the magnet into ten million pieces it won't destroy the magnetism. It will creat ten million smaller magnets instead.'

The three other women silently smiled support for each other in the dark. Magda could not see them and they could not see her, but each of them knew they were not alone.

After an hour, the van slowed to a crawl, and a heavy gate squeaked outside. The van crawled forward and the unseen gate closed behind them. Where were they? The *Suka* slid to another halt and this time the driver got out. Voices conferred in the snow, then a cacophony of truncheons and hands thumped the steel sides, and a male voice laughed. The rear door swung open. Facing the women were the stern faces of two militia guards, two more ZOMO officers and a female prison official. 'Out, comrades!' she snapped.

The four women helped each other hesitantly out of the wagon, their stiff bodies stooping with cold and fatigue. None of the officers helped. Instead they watched the women walk painfully in single file down a path of packed ice under the light of a single bulb hanging from a tree. Magda could just make out the silhouettes of long, low buildings. Perhaps they were part of a barracks. 'May I ask where we are?' she ventured. There was no reply. She tried again, 'May I ask where we are?'

'Silence, you whore,' the ZOMO guard bellowed. 'You are forbidden to speak. No questions! Be thankful you are here, and not being taken elsewhere.' He pushed the barrel of a sub-machine gun into the small of her back.

The squat brick buildings were dark and empty, the corridors long and institutional, the walls and ceiling filthy. Whoever had once been here had departed many years earlier. The women shuffled forward. 'In! ... All of you!' The heavy wooden cell door slammed behind them. The key turned, and outside the sound of heavy boots disappeared down the corridor.

Magda, Anna, Irena and Renata – part union colleagues, part strangers – stood alone in a freezing cell which stank of stale urine. The cast iron radiator had frozen and burst, and there was no other source of heat. In the corner stood a rusting zinc bucket for the toilet. For the four of them the authorities had provided six scraggy, horse-hair palliasses but no beds, bed clothes, blankets or pillows. A black rat fled from beneath one palliasse and snow blew through the ten broken window panes.

Irena touched a wall and squealed in pain as her skin fused with the ice. Had she left her finger on the plaster any longer it would have welded to the frozen brickwork.

Renata Chajewska, a founder member of Solidarity at the *Polcolor* television factory south of Warsaw, burst into tears. 'I cannot believe human beings would do this. They want to extinguish all ten million of us. They want us to die in disgrace and squalor like animals,' she wept.

Renata's tousled hair, bruised face and bowed head all bore witness to her plight. 'I didn't even have the chance to say farewell to my family. They just took me as I emptied the dustbins into that stinking rubbish chute in our building. The bastards. Big men, foul language. They bundled me into a car, and here I am. My husband Tadek

36

won't know what's happened. Nor will the boys. Tadek will go to the police eventually but they'll say nothing of course. "Who?" they'll ask, "Renata Chajewska? Don't know her. Don't waste our time."'

A key turned in the lock and a woman prison officer walked in. She was large and wore no make up.

'Comrades ... I cannot apologise for your conditions but I can give you an explanation. We were not told until just before midnight – only five hours ago – that we should expect arrivals.'

The prison officer seemed as nervous as the four women because to be seen talking to them was tantamount to fraternisation. 'These rooms have been empty for months. I can't even remember when we last used them. That's why conditions here are so bad.'

The lady officer had heard many rumours that night, and she too wanted to know what was happening. Magda, Anna, Irena and Renata told her about the midnight police raids, the beatings, the blood, the processing by the militia and finally the internment orders. The woman officer gasped with horror. 'We'll try to do our best for you,' she whispered, 'but it won't be easy. We tried to get more materials from the store when we were told you were coming. But it was closed. The phones are dead and our vehicles have been requisitioned ... I'm sorry.'

The officer could see the women were not the 'counter revolutionary criminals' her superiors had warned them to expect. They were frightened women as confused as her.

'One question, if I may,' asked Magda through her chattering teeth. 'Where are we? Where have they brought us?' Magda clasped both arms tight across her green jersey and her freezing, limp breasts.

'This is the Olszynka prison, or rather the old barracks alongside it.' The officer would say no more. She bowed her head, then turned on her heel and closed the cell door gently behind her.

Magda and Irena wore only flimsy clothing but Anna had a sheepskin coat and Renata wore a heavy army-style winter coat. Having looked for vermin droppings they laid three of the six palliasses across the middle of the floor. With their thicker clothes Anna and Renata lay down on the outside with Magda and Irena sandwiched in the middle.

With teeth chattering they tried to doze but could not. It was almost six o'clock. The first light of Sunday was still two hours away.

6

The Militia had crammed so many internees into the overcrowded *Jelcz* truck that Sulecki could not count them. He stood with his feet apart, struggling for balance among thirty or forty men standing crushed like cattle, their manacled hands hanging in front of their chests or resting on their laps.

On a seat in front of Sulecki, in a tatty greatcoat with his head bowed and his arms handcuffed, sat Professor Pilubicki, the eminent psychologist from Warsaw University. Next to him, in a frayed denim jacket, faded cords and a woollen cap stood Henryk Adamczyk, a union activist in his mid-thirties who ran Solidarity's printing press at Mokotowska Street. Beyond him swaying in the gloom, Sulecki could see the tall, elegant figure of Kris Sadowski from the union's international relations department. Alongside him stood Jerry Krawczyk, in charge of investigating workers' allegations of injustice and exploitation.

The *Jelcz* had been travelling for half an hour. Suddenly the engine cut out and the truck slid to a violent halt, propelling bodies forward towards the cab. 'You fuckers!' screamed one furious voice. 'You arseholes!' screamed another. 'You can organise a military intervention but you can't drive a pig truck.'

There was movement outside: excited male voices, boots running across the snow, a dog barking. The truck's large rear door swung open, the wind crashing it against the steel sides. Sulecki tried to work out where they were. It appeared to be a prison compound, but between the lorry and the main building thirty metres away stood forty ZOMO and militia officers with their riot gear and truncheons ready for 'sport'. Half of them stood to the left and half to the right, with the gauntlet to be run down the middle.

Those internees beaten in police custody during the sixties and seventies knew what to expect. There was no time to brace or prepare any protection. The heaving mass of men piled out, stumbling down the vertical iron steps. As they staggered forward the 'gladiators' swung their white, curving nightsticks. One truncheon felled the silver-haired Professor Pilubicki. Handcuffed and next in line, Sulecki bent down to drag him up. 'Get up professor!' he screamed as blood poured from Pilubicki's head. 'Don't give in now! It's too soon.'

The professor found reserves of energy to struggle halfway to his feet, his limp legs desperately scrabbling for grip on the ice, one arm pulled along by Sulecki, one hand on the snow.

'I'll make it ...' Pilubicki gasped. 'I'll make it.' The security forces had spent years trying to break the professor but he had never submitted to their determined harassment and dirty tricks. 'When I die, it will be from natural causes, not as a martyr at the hands of you monsters,' he croaked.

The *Jelcz* was finally empty, and the alley of sweating ZOMO faces was enveloped in a steaming cloud of freezing breath as a wooden door burst open onto the compound and a militia major stood silhouetted against the corridor light.

Professor Pilubicki stepped forward defiantly. 'Major! I assume we will be treated as political prisoners under the Geneva Convention ... ?'

The major stepped forward and stared menacingly half a metre from the professor's face.

'Comrade,' warned the major, 'in this war there are no political prisoners. Just criminals!' He turned to read the internment list.

'A. Sulecki ... Z. Sikorski ... A. Kmiecik ... S. Gruszewski ...'

Sulecki felt the prodding muzzle of a Sudarev PPS-43 in his back and stepped forward, relieved to be spared another moment in the freezing courtyard. In the deep shadows ahead he heard the first cell door crash shut and a key turn. A ZOMO captain grabbed Sulecki's arm and swung him hard against the sweating damp on the tiled wall to carry out a body search. Then the captain released his grip and pushed Sulecki back into the group of internees. He pushed them inside the nearest cell and crashed the door shut with the sole of his snow boot. The key turned and the twelve internees stood beneath the single light bulb hanging from the dripping ceiling.

Henryk Adamczyk, the Solidarity printer, paced out the cell. 'Six metres by three,' he shrugged. 'Eighteen square metres and six bunks between us ... one-and-a-half square metres and half a bunk each. All of it rent free from the government with no need to go through the state renting agency.' But Adamczyk's sarcasm did not amuse his colleagues.

Sulecki passed round what was left of his packet of Marlboro cigarettes and a voice whispered from a lower bunk opposite. 'Does anyone know where we are?'

There was a long pause of sniffing and chattering teeth which was muffled by the stinking bedclothes. 'Bialoleka, I think. Bialoleka camp,' came a lone voice.

Quartz watches on the internees' wrists buzzed in unison. It was six o'clock on the morning of Sunday 13 December – what would become an unforgettable moment in Polish history.

7

It was not yet dawn in Warsaw. But in Moscow, two hours and a thousand kilometres to the east, the sun was rising as the KGB and the Soviet military command monitored with satisfaction the signals traffic and intelligence reaching them from Poland. In the West, however, there were still few suspicions of anything unusual happening inside Poland. Outside the Soviet Bloc the full extent of events in Poland would soon be known to only one person: the Polish Pope, John Paul II.

Shortly before 2 a.m., an aide to Poland's ambassador in Rome telephoned the Vatican and awoke the duty priest on the switchboard.

'His Excellency the Polish ambassador requests an urgent audience with the Holy Father. Please put me through to the appropriate official.'

The priest protested. 'Impossible. It is two o'clock,' he snapped. Each week the Vatican received hundreds of requests to speak personally to the Pontiff. Many were cranks, but others did have to be acknowledged personally.

'It is a matter of extreme urgency,' the Polish diplomat insisted. 'Events of the greatest importance are taking place in the Polish People's Republic even as I speak. His Holiness would expect to be told.'

It was rare pressure for a Saturday night, but the middle-aged priest from Perugia did not panic. 'I will speak to Cardinal Casaroli. He will call you back. Your number, please.'

Cardinal Casaroli was Secretary of State to the Holy See, the only official with direct access to the Holy Father at any time. As number two at the Vatican, Casaroli's responsibility was to build bridges with the predominantly atheist countries of the Soviet Bloc.

The balding, slightly-built cardinal replaced his night shirt with a crumpled black cassock and sat at his desk under the ornate ceiling in his study. He told the switchboard operator to connect him to the Polish ambassador. 'Good morning, your excellency. What is your request?'

In broken Italian, Ambassador Woytaszek outlined details of the cable he had received just before 1 a.m. from the Foreign Ministry in Warsaw for passing on to the Holy Father. Before the ambassador could finish, the cardinal realised the situation was so grave that the call must be transferred immediately to the Pope.

'Please wait a few moments, your excellency ... I will wake the Holy Father.' Cardinal Casaroli's soft-spoken voice betrayed no hint of panic. He hurried down the enormous, elaborately decorated corridors to Pope John Paul's residential quarters where he nodded to the Swiss guards on duty, knocked twice and spoke to the Pope's personal secretary Stanislav Dzlwisz who in turn roused the Pontiff. The switchboard operator transferred the ambassador's call to the study where the Holy Father sat next to a window overlooking a sleeping Rome.

'Good morning ambassador.' They spoke Polish, the Pope's deep Silesian accent booming through the silence as Cardinal Casaroli picked up a second earpiece to listen. Ambassador Woytaszek's message was uncomplicated, and it was the telephone call Pope John Paul had long dreaded. At that moment General Jaruzelski's new Council of National Salvation was imposing what Woytaszek called 'temporary and limited emergency measures' in Poland.

Pope John Paul recoiled in horror. He knew time would show the measures to be anything but 'temporary and limited'. But like the rest of the western world the Polish pope was powerless to intervene.

8

Throughout the night convoys of militia and army vehicles sped to the centre of Warsaw and the factories in the suburbs where Solidarity's power was concentrated. Meanwhile in the allotment hideaway Bogdan sat slumped in the old musty armchair trying to sleep as his radio played classical music.

'It is six o'clock. This is Polish Radio, Warsaw calling. Today is Sunday, 13 December 1981 ...' The gravelly male voice of Polish Radio stirred Bogdan from sleep. 'A special day in the history of our state and the life of the nation has begun. In a moment General Wojciech Jaruzelski, Prime Minister, Minister for Defence and First Secretary of the Polish United Workers' Party will address the nation.'

The martial chords of Poland's national anthem were followed by the solemn, unemotional voice of the Polish leader.

'Citizens of the Polish People's Republic! I turn to you today as a soldier, and as head of the Polish government ... I turn to you on matters of supreme importance. Our country has found itself on the brink of an abyss. The achievements of many generations and the house erected from Polish ashes are being destroyed. The structures of the state are ceasing to function. . . .'

Bogdan had never seen the general in person. But he could imagine the ramrod-stiff, balding figure sitting at a desk wearing his usual immaculately-pressed, slightly oversize khaki uniform along with his tinted, steel-rimmed spectacles.

'.. Strikes, strike alerts and protest actions have become the norm. Acts of terrorism, threats and moral mob trials and also of direct coercion abound. The fortunes of underground economic sharks are growing ...

44

Chaos and demoralisation have assumed disaster proportions ... It is not days but hours which separate us from a national catastrophe ... Further continuation of the current situation would inevitably have led to catastrophe, to complete chaos, to poverty and famine. In this situation failure to act would be a crime against the nation. It is necessary to say 'enough', to prevent, to block the path to confrontation which the Solidarity leaders have openly anounced...'

The General declared that martial law had been operative since midnight but added that it was not a military coup. The new Military Council had not replaced normal government ministries. It would be dissolved when the situation in Poland was 'normalised and stable.' The General's monotone voice announced the internment of Solidarity leaders and the simultaneous arrests of former national leaders now living in disgrace like Edward Gierek, leader of the Polish Communist Party between 1970 and 1980. Jaruzelski also said the battle against black marketeering, embezzlement and negligence would be 'ruthlessly stepped up'.

After twenty-five minutes, General Jaruzelski ended as unemotionally as he began. A heavy gust of wind shook the ramshackle shed, and Bogdan shivered in a cold sweat. He bent down, folded back a scrap of old carpet and loosened floorboards one by one. From beneath them he carefully removed thick straw insulation and a dust cover to reveal a small Japanese photocopier which had been donated to Solidarity by a western company two months earlier. Bogdan rummaged deeper to find paper and printing fluid.

'We will not give in,' the steelworker muttered to himself. 'We must fight. God give us strength.'

Now Bogdan knew this was war.

9

'Communists must be prepared to make every sacrifice, and resort to all sorts of cunning schemes and stratagems, to employ illegal methods, to evade and conceal the truth'

LENIN

It did not seem like a day for war as the sun crept slowly into the crimson dawn sky and new snow refreshed Warsaw's tired winter landscape of slush and dirty colours. Those Poles who had failed to switch on their television or radio that morning ate their breakfast in ignorance. Others walked their dogs, tobogganed with their children or made their way to Sunday mass unaware of the morning's terrifying developments. It was, though, only a matter of time before they met military or militia patrols, or tried to telephone and found the line dead, or turned on the radio for the weekly mass to find an announcer listing the new restrictions of martial law.

Army vehicles now controlled every major intersection, and all traffic entering or leaving Warsaw was being stopped. On kerbside billboards, special gangs began pasting up declarations of martial law which had been printed in the Soviet Union, proving that the state of war must have been in preparation for many months. All trade unions were now 'temporarily' suspended. Army commissars would run trams and buses, railways, telephones, mines, ports, refineries and vital industries, with staff subject to military discipline. Jail sentences for organising a strike would be five years; for sabotaging industrial equipment they would be ten years. Sentences for threatening state security would be even more severe. Travel between different regions was now forbidden without a permit. Everyone had to return to the city or village where they were registered, and travel would be further restricted by petrol rationing. All private and public gatherings of more than three people except religious services, were now illegal, and public entertainment like cinemas, theatres and sporting events had been banned to prevent the formation of spontaneous political gatherings. The use of printing presses was now illegal, and all firearms and radio transmitters had to be surrendered to the militia.

By mid-morning, the Soviet news agency *Tass* had blandly reported Poland's clampdown. And like obedient Soviet puppets the state press and radio stations in East Berlin, Prague, Budapest and Sofia repeated the same message without comment.

In Moscow, one of the most senior members of the Soviet leadership reviewed developments in Poland with contempt. The head of the KGB, Yuri Vladimirovich Andropov, disapproved violently of the way the Polish crisis had been handled by President Brezhnev and the ageing cronies of his Old Guard leadership. Andropov was a brilliant figure in the finest tradition of the Soviet *Cheka*, the secret police organisation of the 20's and 30's which had preceded the KGB. Now Andropov, who had a ruthless reputation as KGB Chairman, was determined to impose his own solution on Poland in secret and without Politburo approval.

On Andropov's orders the four most senior generals of the KGB's First Chief (Foreign) Directorate assembled for an unusual Sunday breakfast conference. The giant crescent-shaped office building, hidden from public view in the birch forests south-west of Moscow, was a stark contrast to the KGB's forbidding headquarters alongside the old Lubianka prison at Dzerzhinsky Square in the centre of the Soviet capital. The concrete, aluminium and plateglass headquarters of foreign operations symbolised the KGB's change of image under Andropov from a security organisation made up of crude, ideologically-motivated hardliners to a sophisticated intelligence organisation employing three quarters of a million of the

Soviet Union's brightest brains.

It was 10 a.m. Across a large mahogany desk the heads of the Foreign Directorate's three sub-directorates faced one of the KGB's two first deputy chairmen, General Dimitri Fedorovich Semenov. Deputy Chairman Semenov was a Chekist trained in Stalin's era who had risen to the highest KGB echelons just one level down from his patron Andropov. As a veteran spymaster, Semenov controlled three directorates, three services and eleven departments – an empire which coordinated all Moscow's non-military subversion and spying operations outside the Soviet Union. The general was an overweight chain-smoker with two gold-capped teeth and a shirt collar one size too large which allowed him to button it a comfortable inch from his neck.

Semenov came quickly to the point.

'Are we all familiar with the latest information from Poland?'

The four generals relaxed. Each officer had a red file bound in the organisation's traditional style, with the yellow sword, red hammer-and-sickle and black dagger of the KGB insignia neatly embossed on its cover. Each file contained up-to-the-minute intelligence briefs on overnight developments in Poland.

'For once we have heartening news from Warsaw. And about time too. But do Jaruzelski's measures go far enough?'

General Semenov looked over his thick bifocal spectacles as his three colleagues munched slices of *Omul*, the Siberian salmon delicacy rarely available in Moscow. 'That is the question I have summoned you here to discuss. Has Jaruzelski's Polish domestic solution been thorough and decisive enough? Has it penetrated close enough to the root of the Polish problem – the failure to crush counter-revolution immediately it arises? Comrade directors, our Chairman, Yuri Vladimirovich, believes last night's operation in Poland has not gone far enough and is never likely to. Jaruzelski may have complied with Brezhnev's demands but he has ignored KGB advice.

He has shied away from the necessary brutal solution demanded here at KGB Centre and at the Defence Ministry. That's why the Soviet Chief of Staff mobilised military reservists here in Moscow last night. Didn't you see the units converging at assembly points in the city in the early hours?'

Semenov went on to speak with unbridled contempt for the Polish leadership. 'Our warnings have had no effect. All we've had is bullshit and Polish window dressing. Jaruzelski and his friends failed to listen to Comrade Brezhnev when they were ordered to visit the Kremlin. They took no notice first of our esteemed ideologist Comrade Suslov and Foreign Minister Gromyko when we sent them to Warsaw to straighten things out. Jaruzelski's army gang arrogantly gave us assurances that they were getting things under control. Yet there have been strikes, marches, sit-ins, and every possible challenge to authority.'

The General's eyes moved to a bowl of fresh tropical fruit flown to Moscow on the twice weekly Aeroflot flight from Cuba. He began peeling a banana, a rare sight in this nation of shortages.

'Comrades, you know our saying: In a field of wheat only the stalk whose head is empty of grain stands above the rest. Well that is the way with Jaruzelski. Compared to other leaders of our fraternal socialist allies he is soft. His Soviet credentials are perfect, of course – years of military and ideology training in Moscow. But in the end he is a Pole, not one of us. This morning was Jaruzelski's last chance. Brezhnev gave in to him, but our own Comrade KGB Chairman was furious. Yuri Vladimirovich believes that Leonid Ilyich sold out to the weak-willed bathchair revolutionaries he keeps around him inside the Kremlin.'

General Semenov tapped his file impatiently.

'And worse still, it seems Comrade Jaruzelski has left the door open for Solidarity to re-emerge. In view of this, the Comrade Chairman has authorised me to activate a first contingency stage of the operation we agreed seven months ago. Today Yuri Vladimirovich formally raised the matter with Comrade Brezhnev on our confidential *Kremlevka* phone circuit, as well as with other members of the Politburo. But the Comrade Chairman's proposal was rejected. Even so, such is our Chairman's commitment to ensuring the security of a fraternal nation that he has authorised us to proceed entirely on his own initiative and with the utmost secrecy under my command. He has ruled that there will be no more referrals to our collective leadership in the Politburo because Brezhnev is a lost cause. It is on that basis that I ask for your full and loyal cooperation...'

The Head of the KGB First Directorate inelegantly stuffed a sturgeon canape into his mouth, then poured a cup of Lipton's English Breakfast tea, the kind only the most senior *apparatchiks* could buy from the Communist party privilege shops.

Only General Zuyenko, head of Service A, the Active Measures department, dared to speak.

'Before we proceed, let us all be clear on one vital point. Why is our Comrade Chairman so concerned about Poland?'

Semenov looked at Zuyenko across a small switchboard and eight telephones which covered one side of his desk.

'Poland is the worst example of how Brezhnev plumps for the weakest option. He vetoed the only solution which would produce the dramatic discipline needed in Poland – intervention by fraternal forces of the Soviet Union. Last April, the old man even sacked six army generals and reposted hundreds of other officers when he discovered they'd made unauthorised preparations to enter Poland. Comrade Generals! Someone has to return the Polish people's revolution to the disciplined path from which it has deviated.'

General Semenov paused. 'Let me take you back a year to when dear Leonid Ilyich was dropping his cutlery and eating food with his fingers on that embarrassing visit to India, and to when our Comrade Chairman and Marshal Kulikov took the opportunity to call up reservists and put twenty-six divisions on "Red Alert" along the border with Poland. Military intervention worked in Hungary in 1956 when as ambassador in Budapest our Comrade Chairman called in the Soviet troops. It also worked in Czechoslovakia in 1968. But it never happened in Poland. And what stopped it? Of all people it was General Jaruzelski! Poland's Defence Minister, someone renowned for years as a reliable and a leading figure in the fraternal alliance of the Warsaw Pact. Jaruzelski warned us: "If you invade I will order the Polish Army to resist." And faced with that threat, Brezhnev gave in. The Soviet troops never crossed the border, and our Comrade Chairman has never forgiven Jaruzelski for that. The Polish general is a shrewd bastard and a true match for the Comrade Chairman. That's why he has to be disposed of.'

General Semenov lit a Marlboro with his gold lighter. 'By removing Jaruzelski now our Comrade Chairman will provoke a crisis and achieve three goals ...' Semenov counted them on his fingers. 'One: it will show how martial law has failed to extinguish counter revolution as Jaruzelski promised ... Two: it will show how Jaruzelski has failed to impose the sweeping reforms, discipline and controls demanded by the Soviet Politburo and unequivocally promised to us ... Third and finally: it will create the lawlessness necessary as a pretext to move Soviet forces into Poland.'

General Semenov was still not sure that Zuyenko and the other two generals had accepted the explanation.

'The operation must remain highly classified among us four, and no one else. Above all, no word must leak to Warsaw: not to our agents there, or to Ambassador Aristov.'

General Semenov turned to his friend and long-time colleague General Martynov, the powerful head of the KGB's 'S' Directorate, who was responsible for the activities of thousands of undercover KGB 'Illegals' planted abroad.

'Vasili Pavlovich, the plan is to activate our Illegal in

Poland. From today the Illegal's usefulness inside Solidarity is finished and our agent has another operational purpose: to liquidate Jaruzelski. The Polish leader must be disposed of by someone seen publicly as an embittered Solidarity activist. The liquidation must be devised so as to achieve our operational aim: the replacing of Jaruzelski with a tougher leader who will respect fraternal policies agreed here in Moscow. We must portray Jaruzelski's removal as a covert terrorist operation orchestrated by the United States, with the aim of destabilising Poland.'

'But why implicate the United States and Reagan?' interjected Martynov, somewhat puzzled.

Semenov flicked urgently through several sheets of telex paper. 'From these cables we know that the American President is exploiting the Polish crisis for his own political ends. He wants to show that communism is collapsing, and with it the Soviet Union. Look here! One of our most highly placed agents inside the CIA has just confirmed to us that three weeks ago Reagan had on his White House desk full details of Jaruzelski's secret plans for martial law. They were leaked by Colonel Wladyslaw Kuklinski, a senior Polish staff officer involved in Jaruzelski's planning. Kuklinski was a CIA agent. Knowing this, as we now do, we have to ask the question: if Reagan knew everything about martial law, why didn't he reveal the plans publicly to embarrass Jaruzelski? Why did Reagan not try to catch Jaruzelski out and make it impossible for him to deploy the Polish army and militia last night? Why? Because it suited Reagan's anti-Soviet policies that martial law went ahead. And that's why our operation must vindicate beyond doubt the Soviet Union's propaganda position all along – that the ranks of Solidarity contain forces which were backed by Washington and intended to overthrow the Polish state.'

General Semenov removed his spectacles and smiled. 'Do I yet have your full commitment, Comrade Generals?'

The three generals remained judiciously silent. Each knew it would be unwise to disagree with Semenov and thereby their ultimate boss, the Comrade Chairman of the KGB.

Semenov snapped his file shut. 'Thank you comrades. We shall proceed with this operation immediately. I estimate preparations will take at least a month, possibly two. The Comrade Chairman wants perfection. He wants a foolproof cover with no possibility of Western fingers being pointed at Moscow.'

'Code name?' prompted Martynov.

'*Amber Monkey . . .*'

'*Amber Monkey?*' queried Martynov.

'Yes, Comrade Vasili. "Amber" is a prehistoric, fossilised yellow resin dragged up from the seabed which then drifts onto the southern shores of the Baltic. That's how the Comrade Chairman views Jaruzelski in Poland – fossilised, dragged up and drifting. And for monkey read Brezhnev.'

The generals smiled benignly. Only General Martynov, who was responsible for running KGB Illegals throughout the world, seemed uneasy.

'I regret, Dimitri Fedorovich, that there is one major problem.'

'Yes?' Semenov raised one silvery eyebrow.

'We have lost contact with our Illegal. All attempts to reach our agent by the normal radio communication have failed. We do not know if the functionary has been picked up; neither do we know a point of contact to which we can pass the Comrade Chairman's new orders.'

Semenov tightened his jaw. 'What chance is there that the agent will reveal anything under interrogation by the SB?' he snapped irritably.

'Knowing our agent, none, Comrade General.'

'Can we be sure?'

'We have to be. I have every confidence.'

Semenov was nervous because he did not know the Illegal personally and was relying on second-hand assessments. 'Our agent must be traced, if not by the SB then by our own forces inside Poland.'

'But patience is needed, Comrade General. The

country is in turmoil. The agent may be in hiding. I ask for forty-eight hours. At this moment we have no need to act hastily. We have time.'

General Semenov considered Martynov's suggestion for several minutes. 'Very well . . . forty-eight hours.'

Semenov's warning was clear but unspoken. Each of the generals knew that the personal price they would pay for failing to reactivate the Illegal would be high. Yuri Vladimirovich Andropov never tolerated incompetence, especially from his closest and most trusted *Chekist* colleagues.

10

Deep drifts of fresh snow at the Rakowiec allotments
sparkled in the first light of that cloudless December
Sunday. Inside his shed Bogdan checked the makeshift
power cable which he and his Solidarity colleagues had
laid to pirate electricity from a street lamp outside the
football stadium two hundred metres away. An electrician
colleague had cannibalised the junction box at the base
of a street lamp. The cable had been hidden by digging
a thin trench across two paths and carefully replacing the
grass.

Bogdan screwed a small light bulb into the socket and
threw an old bakelite switch. The bulb glowed. Then he
replaced it with the plug for the Japanese photocopier
and threw the switch again. The machine's orange
'power' light glowed in the dark of the under-floor hiding
area. Then Bogdan heard the hum of the ventilation fan
as the printing mechanism warmed up. At least the copier
worked but Bogdan decided to wait until another underground colleague was there to help him lift it out of the
hideaway.

Bogdan took the small spirit stove from the corner
cupboard and lit it, keeping the flame low to conserve the
small amount of fuel which had been stored over the
past few weeks. His stomach rumbled with a mixture of
hunger and fatigue so he took a small tin of goulash
from the cupboard, opened it with his army knife, then
balanced it precariously over the stove to be heated.

As his tired eyes wandered across the snowscape
Bogdan remembered the document which gave secret
Solidarity advice on how to respond to a state of emergency. Jurek had hidden it in a gap above the second
rafter. Bogdan moved the stool across, hauled himself up to
roof height and eased the document out. Then he took

the steaming can of goulash from the stove and slumped into the filthy armchair.

As he scooped up lumps of prime German beef in his grubby fingers he read the flimsy paper which was headlined '*Principles of opposition in the event of a state of emergency*.' It had been printed by a Solidarity branch in the hardline mining region of Katowice and was approved by the union's national headquarters in Gdansk. It urged Solidarity members to protect their leaders and not to openly form strike committees. They should remember the well-established principle of underground conspiracy: 'Know only what you need to know and no more.' Members were instructed to work as slowly as possible without provoking a confrontation; to be alert for provocateurs and informers; and to give every help possible to the families of those killed, injured or detained.

As Bogdan's tired mind tried to absorb the details, General Jaruzelski's war was no longer a series of fears, radio announcements and distant sounds. Suddenly the war was right there on the doorstep of his underground hideaway. Beyond the huts and fruit trees of the allotments Bogdan was alerted to a rush of movement outside. He pressed his face to the frozen condensation but did not dare scrape a hole in the ice. A Soviet-built *Gaz* jeep had stopped in the middle of the four-lane airport highway and a staff officer jumped out. A dozen conscripts and junior officers in battledress followed from under the camouflaged canvas canopy of a *Star* personnel truck, the noise of their heavy boots clattering like machine-gun fire on the ice. The captain stopped all traffic, questioned drivers and diverted them away from the airport road. Then through the allotment fence Bogdan watched a long tank barrel swaying above the hedgerow as the driver coaxed an ageing T-54 onto thick snow on the central reservation where it rocked to a violent, shuddering halt.

Bogdan was watching the scene nervously, his breath misting up the window, when feet stomped unexpectedly on the verandah outside. He swung round and edged towards the dirty windows at the rear of the shed. The ice around the ramshackle door cracked like gun fire as it swung open. Only then did Bogdan recognise the heavy, moth-eaten coat and woollen ski hat of his Solidarity colleague Jurek Kucharski. Jurek grinned broadly and wished Bogdan good morning in hushed tones for fear of attracting the attention of soldiers outside.

'*Dzien dobry Bogusz.*'

It was ten o'clock. Jurek's bloodshot eyes were sunk deep into his pale skin and betrayed the toll of a night without sleep. '... Or rather not such a good morning, Bogdan. Didn't expect to see you here. Thought you'd have a hangover after drinking the night away at Jan and Grazina's party. When did you arrive?'

Bogdan's foundry colleague at the Warsaw Steelworks always had a sense of humour and the threat of a national catastrophe did not seem to have lowered his spirits.

Bogdan began explaining the events of the early hours as Jurek unbuttoned his heavy coat, removed his ski hat and gloves and dumped his rucksack in a corner.

'I saw it all happening in Gdansk at one o'clock this morning,' said Jurek. 'I escaped by a matter of minutes. Hitched a lift in a tiny *Fiat* 126. Took me six hours to do the journey. Who said it was a state of war? We saw only two tanks and one APC in 330 kilometres. No one showed a gram of interest in us.'

Jurek dunked a piece of bread in what was left of Bogdan's goulash. 'I got to my parents' apartment just after seven this morning. No sooner had I taken two sips from a mug of coffee than the SB burst in. There was no time to hide in the loft. The bastards threw me against the wall, seized my father and dragged him out screaming. I don't think they realised who I was. Their documents probably only told them to arrest my father so they ignored me. I could hear dad shouting as they hauled him down the staircase. It was just like the days before Solidarity. The moment I heard their van drive off I ran home to my wife and baby. I got there at eight. Only then did I hear the news officially on the radio. I was out of the flat in less than half an hour. I walked here from

Vilanow. Must be ten kilometres but I didn't come direct: I dodged around the road blocks and took the back streets.'

'God, Jurek, you were lucky to make it from Gdansk! Have you seen how many army and militia are on the streets now?' asked Bogdan.

Jurek chewed on a lump of cold sausage. 'Plenty. More than you could count.' He took food from his knapsack and laid them on the table. 'I managed to get to Zbawiciela Square for a quick look at the union headquarters. It's cordoned off, but there's a crowd of two or three hundred. I saw them jeering at a couple of army and police patrols walking by. Then a dozen ZOMO charged thirty people singing the national anthem. They ran up Aleja Wyzwolenia. A couple were caught and beaten up. Those ZOMO bastards!'

'What's the atmosphere like elsewhere?'

'Calm at the moment, but boiling with anger. Everyone wants to protest or strike or demonstrate. But without phones and free movement they can't organise themselves. For the moment people seem content to jeer at the patrols, but I'm sure there'll be trouble later on. People need guidance. Let's do a quick leaflet and get it out on the streets to show the authorities that Solidarity is still around.'

'But we have no authority from the union's officials,' said Bogdan.

'Forget that! This is war. Just get on with it. We'll worry about the damn niceties when it's over.'

Jurek threw a pen onto the table and grabbed a scrap of damp paper from an old Solidarity notebook. With his hand shaking, Bogdan wrote the draft of their first underground communique.

'This attack on trade unions has as its aim the liquidation of our union. It contradicts our statute. We must respond with a general strike.'

Signed by the Provisional Coordinating Committee for the Mazowsze region of Solidarity.

Jurek took a fresh sheet of paper and copied the text in tiny block capitals. To save paper he planned to fit ten copies of the communique onto one sheet. Together, he and Bogdan lifted the copier from its hiding-place. Bogdan switched on the machine, and within seconds the green light had scanned the text and produce a crisp copy of their first underground bulletin.

'We'd better print fifty,' said Jurek. 'Five hundred leaflets in all! Should be enough for Mazowsze Head-quarters and the main industrial enterprises like Ursus, the steelworks and FSO.'

Within a few minutes they had a pile of communiques, each measuring just ten centimetres by six.

'Let's take half each and distribute them in the city centre,' suggested Jurek. Bogdan scotched the idea. 'That's crazy! There's no point us both risking arrest. I'll take them into the city and pass them on. You stay here to brief Henryk and Adam if they turn up.' Bogdan pushed the illegal leaflets into a shoulder bag. 'Tell them we'll all meet here at eleven this morning.'

Jurek didn't seem to care that his colleague had taken the initiative. Bogdan pulled the door firmly behind him and crunched through the snow towards central Warsaw. The prospect of fighting a military regime that was backed by tanks and armour petrified him. But Bogdan would not back out now.

11

Dot matrix printers in the underground communications room of the Soviet embassy on Reisnerstrasse in Vienna chattered their normal Sunday morning stream of signals traffic from Moscow. The volume of messages coming from the Foreign Ministry's Stalinesque skyscraper near the Moscow River never abated, even at weekends, although signals traffic on Saturday and Sunday tended to be the less urgent material.

But not today. Suddenly KGB Centre at Dzerzhinsky Square was demanding urgent action for a vital project. A cipher clerk ripped from the machine a 3-ply telex containing a 'Priority Action' coded order from General Martynov, head of the Illegal's 'S' Directorate in Moscow. Within thirty minutes Major Konstantin Voroshilov, number three to the KGB Resident in Vienna, had returned to his second floor office in the heavily-guarded embassy compound to read it.

A brief phone message from the embassy duty officer had interrupted the major's regular Sunday morning ride in the snow-covered vineyards of the Doebling hills north of Vienna.

The KGB major was not the dour, archetypal Soviet usually posted abroad. He was a suave international diplomat with the veneer and trimmings to match: Rolex watch, tailored western clothes, gold cufflinks, Pall Mall cigarettes and Monsieur Rochas aftershave. Voroshilov was a product of the new-look KGB masterminded by Andropov who would look at home in Hyde Park, the Bois de Boulogne, or on Fifth Avenue in New York. Voroshilov had been in Vienna for thirteen months and was officially described on Vienna's diplomatic list as a trade attaché. But Voroshilov knew as much about Austrian-Soviet trade as a peasant from the Soviet Asian republic of Uzbekhistan knew about the West.

The brief signal from Moscow lay on his desk already decoded. Two pairs of embassy eyes had already scanned the message but only Voroshilov had even a vague idea what the five words '*bring me the Amber Monkey*' might mean. The timing and urgency suggested they were connected to General Jaruzelski's overnight declaration of martial law in Poland. Voroshilov's technical boss, the ambasssador, had already ordered embassy security agents to mount a comprehensive surveillance of the Polish emigré community in Austria. KGB Centre in Moscow had also assigned its Vienna-based agents to the Sudbahnhof to mingle with Polish refugees who might arrive from Warsaw or Katowice on the Chopin Express due at 9.25 a.m. Other agents had been despatched to Traiskirchen refugee camp nineteen kilometres south of Vienna to gather information on dissent and subversion among the Polish refugee population.

Voroshilov changed into a casual blazer. Then he donned a Russian foxskin hat and an English Burberry raincoat, and slipped quietly through the heavy oak side doors of the consulate next to the embassy. Outside, he passed the permanent armed Austrian police guards, their deep green uniforms, red collars and red arm flashes vivid against the grey carpet of frozen slush which covered Reisnerstrasse. As it was Sunday the rusting *Ladas* and *Volgas* of Soviet diplomats were gone and the street was deserted. The only person Voroshilov saw was an elderly Viennese lady pulling a black poodle.

The Austrian capital slowly stirred from its Sunday drowsiness as he made a bracing fifteen minute walk past shuttered shops to the six-storey building which housed the office and shopfront of the Soviet state airline Aeroflot on Schubertring, the tree-lined avenue encircling Vienna's inner city. The KGB major had not telephoned in advance as it was forbidden to jeopardise operational security. But Voroshilov expected to find the airline's deputy station manager Aleksander Firyubin in his office updating his weekly reports of aircraft intelligence and security activity at Vienna's Schwechat airport.

Voroshilov pressed the bell twice. As he waited, a lifesize cardboard cut-out of a fresh-faced Aeroflot stewardess in a blue uniform smiled at him from inside the spotless windows. Within a minute Firyubin's plump, ungainly figure appeared. Flamboyantly, he swung open the armour-plated glass door and let a cutting blast of freezing air into the lobby.

'Konstantin! What a pleasant surprise.'

Firyubin nodded to the lone Austrian police guard pacing outside who paused briefly to watch the two Russians. Voroshilov and Firyubin took no risks and said nothing of consequence until the office door was locked behind them and they had climbed slowly up the curving staircase to Firyubin's office on a balcony above the VDU's and ticket desks. A lithograph of Lenin and a giant colour poster of Red Square loomed over them as they sat facing each other in the frugally-furnished, Soviet-style office.

'Business or pleasure?' enquired the Aeroflot deputy manager. 'On second thoughts a silly question. On a Sunday morning it must be business ...' Firyubin's red face chuckled conspiratorially and he shrugged. Although he 'worked' at Aeroflot and not the Embassy, Firyubin was a KGB colonel and therefore senior to Major Voroshilov.

'Coffee?'

'No time, Aleks. We must get on with business.'

Voroshilov produced the narrow strips of telex paper from his inside pocket and placed the decoded message on the walnut table top. Firyubin squinted as he raised the paper to eye level and silently read the five words *bring me the Amber Monkey*.

'No problem,' he sighed, apparently unmoved by the brevity. Moscow Centre had cabled him four days earlier with full details of the action he should take when he received a message including the words 'Amber Monkey'.

Voroshilov, however, remained curious to know exactly what or who the 'Amber Monkey' was. He and

Firyubin had become personal friends during their Vienna postings, yet there was an edgy silence.

'I will act immediately. Please inform the Centre accordingly. I take it that is all?' said Firyubin.

The KGB colonel threw a dead Sobranie cigarette accurately across the room into the waste bin then produced a virgin bottle of chilled *Stolichnaya* vodka from his fridge. But by the time the bottle was empty and Major Voroshilov had stumbled from the Aeroflot office he had still failed to prise from Firyubin the secret of Amber Monkey.

Inside the Aeroflot office, Firyubin locked his desk and filing cabinets, bolted a succession of office doors behind him, then activated a range of alarms and security devices before wishing the shivering Austrian police guard 'Good day!' and slumping into the driving seat of his rusting *Lada* car. It took the KGB Colonel just ten minutes to circle the Belvedere gardens, pass the Sudbahnhof, then speed through Matzleinsdorfer Platz before heading out of Vienna on the autobahn towards the southern city of Graz. Within an hour he had reached the nondescript village of Grimmenstein where he found the modest, country-style inn he was looking for down a side road opposite the white-walled Nestlé milk plant.

Gasthof Netter was of Tyrolean design, with a long, sloping roof and beige-rendered walls. It was one of hundreds of privately-owned guesthouses which had become state-subsidised sanctuaries for refugees seeking asylum in Austria and a new home in the West. Those like Gasthof Netter were always short of regular hotel trade in winter so the international refugee commissions were happy to disperse refugees from the overcrowded Traiskirchen camp near Vienna.

From inside a window on the Gasthof's top floor Firyubin could hear a cassette or record playing traditional Polish accordion music. As the KGB Colonel stamped the snow from his boots and stepped across the threshold he tasted instantly the inn's cheap, musty atmosphere. In the lobby a dozen Poles, Rumanians and Czechoslovaks sat chain-smoking cheap high-tar tobacco. The grim faces eyed Firyubin suspiciously as he walked in. Who was he? One of them or a secret policeman of one of the regimes they had left behind the Iron Curtain? Or perhaps a city entrepreneur looking for cheap labour? Austrian businessmen regularly came to places like Gasthof Netter to hire refugees as illegal labour.

'*Bitte. Wo ist Herr Rybicki?*' Firyubin spoke fluent German with a near-perfect Austrian accent. He smiled in an unsuccessful attempt to break the ice. Two Poles briefly exchanged words, then one stepped forward.

'*Arbeit? . . . arbeit?*'

Arbeit – Work – was the only German word the Poles knew. They wanted to earn a few schillings, but Firyubin understood them in another way. He thought '*arbeit*' meant that Rybicki was away working.

'*Wann kommt Rybicki?*' insisted Firyubin pointing to his watch. '*Wann . . . kommt . . . Er?*' he repeated, slowly enunciating each word.

The two Poles shrugged their shoulders. Perhaps they knew. Perhaps they didn't. Firyubin realised he would have to be patient and wait. He thanked them, repositioned his Fedora and gloves, then stepped back outside into the chill evening.

To refugee officials and the Austrian police Emil Rybicki was just one of 27,000 Polish refugees housed in Austrian camps that night. But to Firyubin he was a Polish KGB captain, one of Moscow's directly employed KGB agents inside Solidarity, who until four months ago had worked as a coalminer in Silesia. Then in August, just before the union's first congress in Gdansk, Moscow Centre had suddenly ordered Rybicki to 'defect' to Austria in order to infiltrate the Polish exile community. Rybicki had been instructed to maintain deep cover and had been left to use his own ingenuity.

Emil Rybicki had disappeared on 26 August carrying a modest battered suitcase and a canvas grip. He had boarded the overnight Chopin Express through Czechoslovakia to Vienna, where he was taken, like every new refugee, to the former Soviet barracks at Traiskirchen which was now used as a reception centre. By the time he was moved to Gasthof Netter four months later Rybicki believed his refugee cover was safe. Lengthy screening by Austrian counter-intelligence had never revealed his clandestine meetings with Soviet agents in Vienna. To deepen his cover, he had joined the daily scrum for places in the early morning job market where refugees lined the main street of Traiskirchen, arms outstretched like hitchhikers, while black market employers cruised up and down looking for casual workers.

Colonel Firyubin lit his twelfth Sobranie cigarette in an hour and paced slowly up and down on the narrow pavement alongside the Nestlé factory. If he waited much longer he feared he would create suspicions among the refugees or the residents of Grimmenstein.

Time and the cold began to blur the KGB Colonel's memory. He stood under a street lamp and took a small colour photograph of Rybicki from his jacket. It was at that moment that he noticed the yellow post bus pulling away from the stop fifty metres away at the end of the road, then a scruffily-dressed man beginning to walk briskly towards him. Firyubin made no move. As the figure approached he appeared to be in his mid-forties and dressed in a leather cap, torn blue anorak, dirty woollen jacket and faded labourer's jeans. Firyubin was sure it was Rybicki, but he still had to be absolutely certain before making his move. Then the distinctive high cheekbones and deep hollows in his lower face seemed to confirm it.

'Emil ...,' Firyubin whispered as he inhaled heavily on his cigarette. '... Emil Rybicki?'

The man stopped, clearly shocked at being recognised by an unknown, well-dressed figure whom he had never met. He stared closely at Firyubin's face. Stumpy features; heavy arching eyebrows; drooping, mean mouth; a non-committal, remote expression. The man had to be Russian.

The Polish-born KGB captain answered carefully in

Polish, his tone suitably suspicious and probing. '*Tak, jestem Emil Rybicki.*' Yes, I am Emil Rybicki, he said.

Firyubin broke into Russian and bridged his KGB identity card across the palm of his right hand. Rybicki calmed noticeably. Instead of turning up the steps into the Gasthof, he gestured for them to walk on away from the main road and towards the fields behind the builder's warehouse at the end of the street.

'Comrade Rybicki I will be brief. This is your assignment. Immediate action. You will already have heard the news about Poland. It's not unexpected I am sure ...' Rybicki nodded unemotionally. '... You must leave here as soon as you can pack your bags. But you should expect to return to resume your cover as a refugee ...'

Firyubin and Rybicki stopped walking and stood in the pitch dark by the red-and-white barriers of an automatic railway crossing. Firyubin began to relate the orders he had kept sealed in the Aeroflot safe for the past eight weeks. 'Moscow Centre wants you out tonight. Here are ten thousand Austrian schillings and four thousand Deutschmarks. You will also need this documentation: an Austrian passport we have arranged for you. Please note the name. Klaus Heller. You should expect to be away about a week and no longer than two.'

A local freight train en route from the Hungarian town of Szombathely to Vienna rattled past. By the time the red lamp on the final wagon had passed two minutes later the conversation was over. The two KGB officers shook hands curtly with no hint of cordiality.

Back in the lobby of the Gasthof the undercover KGB Captain greeted his fellow refugees with a sullen, unemotional '*Dobry wieczor*', (Good evening) then pushed through and up the stairs. In the spartan surroundings of his shared room he carefully packed the possessions which had come with him from Silesia. Outside, the dank corridor remained silent. Rybicki turned off the ceiling light and silently opened the first floor window, ensuring no loose snow or ice crashed from the ledge to the path below. There was no one in the narrow street. He gently dropped the small suitcase and canvas bag into a snow drift, closed the window, checked he had left nothing in the room, then stepped into the corridor.

Rybicki sauntered through the lobby and into the street, where he stood on the main road through Grimmenstein awaiting the bus to Vienna and the start of his journey beyond the Austrian border.

12

Bogdan felt the eyes of the army road block watch him from the moment he walked through the allotment gate onto Raclawicka Street. But he hoped the conscripts were there to interrogate drivers and protect the airport road, and that a youngish man heading away from them on foot would be of little interest. However, he could not be sure and he knew he was taking a big risk.

In his leather shoulder bag Bogdan carried the five hundred tiny protest leaflets. He boarded a tram and sat facing forward on a single, slatted seat near the rear door. Ageing pneumatic arms slammed the doors shut, then the red-and-cream tramcar lurched forward clanking northwards along the badly-laid tracks towards the centre of Warsaw.

As the motor whined and the tram picked up speed, Bogdan stiffened. Two SB officers were working their way back towards him, examining documents, and everything from shopping and sports bags to bunches of flowers.

Bogdan swallowed hard as he clutched the bag holding the illegal leaflets. It was the longest forty-five second ride between stops he could remember.

As the tram slowed, the SB men were still two passengers in front. Bogdan stood up. Calmly he prepared to get off, but the older SB man raised his blue anorak arm and caught Bogdan's wrist.

'Your ID!' he barked.

From his top pocket Bogdan produced his internal state passport. The tram doors were already open and letting in a swirling draught of bitter December air. Bogdan stood on the lower step. His mind panicked, but he felt that his actions were well controlled and betrayed no guilt. 'May I get off? Or should I come further with you?'

The SB man did not reply, but waved Bogdan out of the tram. Bogdan allowed himself a few seconds for his nerves to calm as he watched a column of ZOMO vehicles prowl slowly eastwards through the modern underpass on Aleja Armii Ludowej. Then he swung north, his feet crunching the frozen snow until he came to Constitution Square a block away from the Solidarity headquarters. Here the usual red-faced peasant women in their heavy wool and sackcloth coats blatantly ignored martial law and sat hunched over their bunches of flowers – the traditional Christmas roses, gladioli and sunflowers grown in hothouses.

But things were far from normal outside the Solidarity headquarters on Mokotowska Street. Two lines of ZOMO still faced a crowd of three hundred people taunting and singing the national anthem, their fingers parted in a V-sign, their hopes still high for Solidarity's survival. Men bared their heads as they sang, clutching their cloth caps or woollen balaclavas in their hands. One old lady ignored any thought of danger. She stood a step in front of a ZOMO officer arguing openly with him. 'Think of the disgrace you are bringing on your parents and family! ... How can you do this to your fellow Poles?' she yelled, her chin and hands shaking as she crushed a plastic bag between her fingers. But the ZOMO officer stared blankly, pretending to ignore her. Behind the lady the crowd murmured its congratulations and continued to stand rock-solid, shoulder to shoulder. The cover was ideal for Bogdan. He dipped into his shoulder bag and began distributing the strike leaflets, passing round small piles of ten or twenty to hands eagerly stretched out towards him. 'Pass them on,' he whispered. 'We must resist ... Don't give up ... We can win ... We will not be beaten.'

Bogdan knew the risk but after careful examination he had not been able to identify anyone who might be a security agent.

Suddenly a voice cut through the crowd's taunting of the ZOMO. From behind the riot shields a commander addressed the crowd with a bull horn. '*Disperse! . . . Disperse . . . You have one minute.*'

The crowd ignored the order. The scores of functionaries stood erect as statues while beyond a fully laden water cannon revved its heavy engines and the target officer ensured the piping system had not frozen in the sub-zero temperatures.

'*Disperse!*' yelled the commander again.

A young tractor mechanic from the giant Ursus tractor factory a few miles outside Warsaw, grabbed Bogdan's arm. 'Bogdan, I have some news . . .'

Bogdan recognised him as Ryszard Zablocki who had been involved in the union's secret preparations for a State of Emergency. 'Preparations for an occupation at Ursus are already underway. Several men are inside the plant. Others are trying to get in. Members of the Committee for the Defence of Workers like Professor Lipski will help organise it. We will not give up without a struggle.'

As Zablocki spoke the ZOMO line behind the crowd split in two and opened a clear line of fire for the water cannon which now sat dead centre on Mokotowska Street.

'The ZOMO will have to blow up the factory to get us out,' added Zablocki, 'I heard the same about Huta Warszawa; they won't produce steel there tomorrow. They'll have to kill workers first.'

The ZOMO commander stood clutching his bullhorn. The old woman returned to kneel in front of him and kiss the dirty ice.

'Jesus, Mary mother of God, I pray for your help in Poland's hour of need . . .'

The commander ignored her. He snapped an order and the first rocket-like blast of freezing water knocked over a dozen men, women and children standing on the pavement near the Czechoslovak embassy. Bodies slid like dolls along the ice and came to rest in a haphazard pile caught by the red and white chains of a traffic barrier.

Sodden, dazed, bruised and bloodied, the demonstrators managed to pick themselves up, but within seconds they began to shiver violently as the water froze and tufts of wet hair became clumps of heavy ice.

None of the remaining demonstrators wanted to suffer the pain of their compatriots. So, as a second line of water bent menacingly towards them, they scattered, a lone western television crew filming as they struggled to keep their precarious balance on the ice.

While the ZOMO's solid line of riot shields re-formed and began to move forward, Bogdan slipped away back under the arch on Koszykowa Street towards the peasant flower sellers on Constitution Square. His shoulder bag was empty and his first instinct was to head home north towards his wife. But within a few steps he realised his error. The SB would still be watching his flat and tailing Jola. He had warned her he would not make contact so he turned sharp west instead.

The lonely walk back to the shed at Rakowiecka took Bogdan half an hour, and waiting to greet him was Jurek, sombre-faced.

'They've got Walesa,' he said. 'They've captured almost all the union leadership in Gdansk. No one's safe, but there's a rumour Bujak and Lis may have escaped.'

Bogdan tapped his boots against the door frame to remove surplus snow. Then he peeled off his layers of thick winter clothing. 'How do you know all this?' he demanded, lowering himself into the musty armchair.

'Henryk met a courier from Gdansk an hour ago. Jadwiga, remember her? Reliable woman. She'd just arrived by car. Said she passed at least two army columns heading north: tanks, self-propelled guns, the lot. Four road blocks as well. But they weren't looking for her. She was heading for Warsaw.'

Bogdan grabbed a hunk of bread and sausage as Jurek continued, 'Jadwiga left Gdansk at nine this morning. She said tanks were lined up everywhere, especially around the gates to the shipyard. Paratroopers had secured the yard. There was no opposition.'

71

Bogdan choked on the crust. 'Any more news?'

'Walesa's home is under guard. He was seized at three this morning. The rumour is that they threatened to hack down his front door with crowbars if he didn't agree to leave. The head of the Party in Gdansk and the district governor came for him. Then he was taken away by helicopter.'

'Any word about where he is?'

'He might be in Moscow for all we know.'

Bogdan sighed to release the tension. 'So we have no leaders and the union has no head. But Solidarity is more than just the National Praesidium and Walesa. There are plenty more to take their places. They cannot kill all of us.' There was an edgy silence.

'Where is Adam? Did he arrive?' asked Bogdan.

'No sign of him. I've heard nothing.' Jurek handed Bogdan a tiny crumpled pellet of paper which had been screwed up to make sure it reached Warsaw undetected by car searches. 'Jadwiga brought this.'

Bogdan flattened the many folds of the paper. The typed document was a brief Solidarity communique from the Lenin shipyard in Gdansk, dated that day, 13 December, and signed by four national leaders who had apparently escaped arrest and gathered secretly inside the shipyard overnight. The leading signatory was Miroslaw Krupinski, one of Solidarity's two deputy leaders under Walesa. It read:

'Today a state of war was declared in our country. At the same time a mass arrest of leaders and activists took place. Our reply to the attempts to use force is a general strike. Let us preserve discipline and calm. Let us avoid unnecessary conflict. Our weapon is dignity and organisation. Our strength is Solidarity with all the Polish working people.

'That is what we must work for,' said Jurek.

Bogdan nodded agreement. '. . . We mustn't give up. But we must realise that it'll never work. In the end the system and the authorities will get us before we have a chance to get them.'

Bogdan tossed cold tea bags out of his mug and refilled it with boiling water from a saucepan. Without warning the music coming at low volume from the radio stopped to be replaced by the nervous voice of the Roman Catholic Primate of Poland, Archbishop Josef Glemp. The military announcer said the sermon had been recorded earlier at the Jesuit church in Warsaw's Old Town.

Bogdan was enraged and dumbfounded. 'I don't believe it ... Surely Glemp's not sold out to the regime! This broadcast must be on Jaruzelski's orders.'

The archbishop spoke in a guarded, low key tone. His voice was bland and unemotional. '... Opposition to the decisions of authority under martial law could cause violent coercion, including bloodshed. Authority has the armed forces at its disposal ... We can be indignant, and shout about the injustice of such a state of things, and protest against the infringement of civil rights and human rights. But this may not yield the expected results. ... Do not start a fight of Pole against Pole. Do not give your lives away, brother workers, because the price of human life will be very low. Every head, every pair of hands will be essential for the reconstruction of Poland which will come, which *must* come, after the State of War...'

Bogdan and Jurek heard rustling as the Archbishop gathered his text, then the fidgeting of the tightly-packed congregation. Bogdan drew breath in the freezing gloom.

'Can you see Glemp being jailed like his predecessor, our dear Cardinal Wyszynski, who spent three years in jail because he wouldn't compromise. It's extraordinary. Glemp has just let Jaruzelski off the hook instead of condemning him. Perhaps we should now call him "Comrade Glemp",' said Bogdan bitterly. 'He is wrong. We must not give up. We must go forward and fight, whatever the risks.'

Through the ice on the windows, and across the snow-covered allotments, Bogdan watched the blue lights of four militia wagons screaming down the airport highway

73

towards the city. A large, black, Soviet-built *Zil* limousine was sandwiched between the second and third vehicles, followed by *Tatras* and *Volgas* belonging to the SB. As the convoy of vehicles sped through the army road block, the frozen soldiers sprang to attention and saluted.

'When I was at Mokotowska Street I heard rumours that the Warsaw Pact commander, Marshal Kulikov, had been here supervising all the preparations for martial law,' said Bogdan, his breath freezing as it hit the shed window.

'So . . .?' asked Jurek.

'I fear Kulikov has just returned.'

13

Andrzej Sulecki lay shivering and wrapped in a single blanket on his top bunk in cell 24 at Bialoleka Camp. He stared upwards, the smoke from his last Marlboro cigarette curling towards the window a metre from his head.

Through the open rusty grille on the cell door he heard the hacking coughs of those already suffering from the intense cold. From across the yard a man wept uncontrollably and Sulecki could hear a cellmate trying to console him.

Then came crisis. On a bottom bunk alongside the latrine bucket, Pilubicki, the elderly professor who had been beaten when he arrived in the freezing yard a few hours earlier, suddenly yelled. He clutched his chest and his frail body tossed under the blanket. Jerzy Krawczyk, a medical student, leaped from his bunk and knelt alongside the professor who was now gasping for breath.

'Water, water ... Get me water please!'

Krawczyk held the professor's left wrist and loosened his shirt and trousers. 'His pulse is erratic ... He's got acute chest pains ... It's a heart attack.'

Henryk Adamczyk, who ran the printing press at Solidarity's headquarters, began hammering on the cell door. 'Guards! Guards! We have a heart attack in here. We need a doctor ... Cell 24 ... Urgent.'

The words reverberated down the tiled walls of the long dark corridor. From a distance came a reply. 'Silence or we'll come and shut you up.'

Adamczyk rattled an aluminium mug back and forth across the wire grille in the door. 'Guards! Don't fool around,' he appealed. 'We have an old man in here having a heart attack. He needs urgent medical attention. Bring us the camp doctor.'

'*Silence!*' the guard roared again. 'He'll have to wait. Today's Sunday. The doctor is off until tomorrow.'

The professor lay on his side, his tongue hanging from his mouth, his eyes closed, his lined face white.

'He's still alive, but he needs attention fast.' Jerzy Krawczyk spoke passionately and the internees around him joined in. '*Bring ... us ... a ... doctor! Bring ... us ... a ... a doctor,*' they yelled in unison.

From the guard room came the sharp, rapid steps of military boots. The internees stopped their shouts and stepped back towards their bunks. A senior officer turned a key and another wrenched the door open to reveal eight ZOMO, militia and prison officers staring threateningly.

'Everybody out! Line up outside! Move! Fast! This is a routine search. We have reason to believe you have hidden subversive, anti-state material ... Out! Out!' the lieutenant roared.

The prisoners did not move.

'You can't be serious,' said Jerzy Krawczyk. He pointed to the frail, hunched figure curled below him in the shadows. 'I am a doctor. This man is dangerously ill. He's just suffered a heart attack. He needs medical care urgently. It you don't call the camp doctor he'll die, and you, lieutenant, will have on your hands the first death under martial law.'

There was silence, perhaps a moment of hope. Krawczyk took two steps towards the officers.

'Perhaps you don't care if anyone dies?'

The ZOMO lieutenant took no notice. '*Out! Out!*'

'Bastards,' spat Krawczyk.

The eleven internees filed out and Professor Pilubicki was left wheezing, the prison blanket rising and falling erratically. Outside, the internees were pushed into line against the corridor wall. Two ZOMO officers stood guard as inside three senior, middle-aged prison officers ransacked the cell. Indifferent to the professor's plight, they threw cushions and blankets onto the floor and turned over mattresses. One officer tore from the wall a small wooden crucifix which an internee had smuggled into the camp. A ZOMO boot crushed it. A young conscript tipped the contents of the latrine bucket over the floor. 'Nothing here,' he reported.

The ZOMO lieutenant swung on his heels and glared at the internees in the corridor. 'It had better stay that way.' He stepped forward provocatively, grabbed the stub end of the Marlboro cigarette from Sulecki's mouth and crushed it between his fingers.

'What about the professor?' Adamczyk asked.

'Don't try that trick on us, again, comrade. You call that old man sick? A heart attack? It's just a bad cough. He'll get over it. I've seen plenty like him.'

Adamczyk refused to accept the lieutenant's indifference. 'He needs hospital attention and intensive care. There is a State of War. We demand the rights of prisoners of war,' he screamed into the officer's face.

The lieutenant smiled. 'Prisoner of war, comrade? There's no such thing in Poland. Everyone detained here is a criminal, and that includes you.'

From behind, two truncheon blows caught Adamczyk in the neck and loins. He crumpled, the whites of his eyes rolling as he fell, his head whipping down against Sulecki's boot.

'Get that rat inside!' the lieutenant ordered.

Sulecki and Krawczyk picked up Adamczyk from the floor, his feet dragging behind as the cell door slammed shut. There was a numbing silence.

Jerzy Krawczyk took it upon himself to mount a bedside vigil for Professor Pilubicki perched on the edge of his bunk. But in the early hours Krawczyk dozed off, no longer able to fight off sleep. With no one monitoring him, the semi-conscious professor rolled onto his back, his tongue partially blocking his throat, so that when the second heart attack came he choked on it. By the time Krawczyk leaped to his aid it was too late. Frantic attempts in the dark to revive the professor with mouth-to-mouth resuscitation failed, and within five minutes he was dead, his arms lying symmetrically across his chest, his shock of white hair splayed like a fan on the mattress.

77

It was an undignified, avoidable end to the life of this distinguished Solidarity adviser and intellectual.

It was 3 a.m. on Monday the 14th.

The internees left Pilubicki's body to lie peacefully covered by a blanket until reveille at six o'clock. Only when a camp officer slid their breakfast of stale half-loaves of bread, cubes of white margarine and black coffee across the filthy floor did the internees announce his death. Sulecki and Krawczyk stepped forward.

'Please ask the camp priest to visit us to give the last rites to the professor,' said Sulecki.

The ZOMO corporal was unmoved. 'There is no camp priest. What do you think this is, a holiday home? If the bastard is alive he doesn't need a priest. If he's dead it's too late.'

Twenty minutes later two officers brought a dog-eared, canvas stretcher. As they pulled the prison blanket across his pallid face an internee threw a Solidarity badge onto his chest, leaving the union's famous logo with the red brush strokes and Polish flag clearly visible.

Who had dared to throw the badge? The two officers paused, their frightened eyes scanning the internees. There were no obvious clues, so silently they carried the professor's body from the cell and a third officer closed the door behind them.

It was 8 a.m., as the sun rose over the fresh snow in the Bialoleka compound, when two burly officers returned to drag Jerzy Krawczyk away. He demanded to know why he was being seized but the officers ignored him. An hour later Krawczyk returned, the guards dragging him by his armpits along the corridor, his feet struggling to keep pace. As the officers flung the door open he collapsed among the internees, his head hanging loose on his chest like a rag doll, his beltless trousers around his knees.

'Holy Mother of Mary,' said a young steelworker as he crossed himself. Sulecki and others quickly pulled Krawczyk's cold limp body onto his bunk. They wrapped him in blankets and Sulecki used cold tea from the enamel prison pot to poultice the swollen mess of dried blood and bruises on his face.

'. . . It was either the governor or one of his deputies . . .' Krawczyk spoke with difficulty, his swollen lips catching on his teeth as he spoke in broken sentences, pausing frequently to draw breath. 'The bastard never introduced himself. He knew who I was. It was all to do with the professor's death. He said I had questioned *his* orders in *his* camp. He said *he* made the decisions on whether internees are alive or dead, not us . . .'

Krawczyk winced. 'At that point he went berserk . . . he lunged towards me and beat me across the face with his pistol. I think I blacked out. When I came to I was sitting in the chair opposite him across the desk. I had a pen in my hand. He kept shouting at me "Sign, Sign! There at the bottom." I had no idea what he was talking about, but I didn't sign.'

The internees sat hunched on their bunks listening.

'It was a typewritten document but it came off a stencil printer. I remember him calling it a 'Declaration of Loyalty' – a promise to respect the laws of Poland. I told him I would sign no such document until I could study it in detail. I told him I couldn't see the point of the document as I hadn't broken any Polish laws and had no intention of doing so. I asked to look at it. It said that I agreed to act in accordance with socialist laws, guided by the principles of the Polish constitution and by loyalty to the socialist state . . . You know the usual sort of crap . . . Then it said that Solidarity leaders like me had defied the laws of the Polish constitution and instigated counter revolution, and that Solidarity had tried to overthrow the State. The document said that by signing I renounced membership of Solidarity. By then it was all clear. If I didn't sign I would never be able to work again and would be prohibited from applying for jobs. He said that if I did sign I might be able to return to medical school. But then if I ever became involved in activities which contravened the new laws of Poland, they would have the pretext to arrest me. They could charge me with breaking signed promises, and either way I would lose.'

Sulecki intervened, 'You didn't sign?'

Krawczyk shook his head, his face grimacing from pain. 'Because I refused to sign he hit me round the shoulders with a truncheon. Then he started on a different track. He wanted to know about my work in Solidarity ... He asked me where I worked. I told him I worked in the Intervention Commission ... He asked me who I worked with. I told him I worked alone. He didn't like that. He asked me what I did. I told him that was a confidential union matter. "Oh," he said, "what union?" Solidarity, I said. He said that it couldn't be confidential because Solidarity no longer existed under the State of War. Again ... and again ... and again ... he ordered me to tell him about my work. I refused ... so the bastard struck me with the truncheon again. Finally as the two goons began to drag me back here he said: "You'll be back tomorrow and every day until you sign." I know he means it, but he won't get my signature.'

'Nor mine,' said Sulecki.

'Nor mine,' said Adamczyk the printer.

'Or mine,' said several voices in the cell.

They were brave words, but during a State of War they were irrelevant.

14

Immediately curfew ended on Monday morning, Magda Gajewska's widowed mother began queueing in the winter darkness outside the police depot on Wilcza Street. It was twenty-four hours since Magda had disappeared. By 7 a.m. her mother was standing with the anxious relatives of many other Poles who had disappeared since Saturday – young husbands, elderly men, expectant mothers, pensioners – all of them, standing in a shivering queue shifting from foot to foot to keep warm, watched by two plump ZOMO officers carrying sub-machine guns.

The previous day, when Mrs Gajewska heard the declaration of martial law, she had taken a bus from her small, state-owned flat in the northern suburb of Zoliborz to Magda's apartment down by the Vistula river. She arrived on Sunday afternoon, twelve hours after the SB hauled away both her daughter and Sulecki. Mrs Gajewska wept when she saw the splintered door. Inside, books and shelves had been pulled from the alcoves; pictures and photographs hung askew on the walls: clothes lay strewn across the wooden floor; the settee lay on its back and the armchair on its side. In the kitchen bottles of spices, coffee and preserves had been knocked over, and the small dining table lay upturned. A few hours later the frail old woman returned with a hammer and nails, determined to patch up the front door and give Magda's possessions protection, however limited.

Now Mrs Gajewska was determined to discover Magda's whereabouts. Only at eleven o'clock, after she and the other relatives had been waiting four hours in the driving snow on Wilcza Street, did the militia guards allow them into the relative warmth of a small waiting room. The walls were stained with cigarette smoke and the air hung heavy with the stench of stale tobacco.

It was a further two hours before they were summoned to face a militia captain who sat at a desk shuffling paperwork. Mrs Gajewska clutched her daughter's birth certificate as she stood unintimidated in front of his desk.

'I have come to ask you where you have taken my daughter Magda Gajewska; aged thirty; registered as resident in this city of Warsaw; employee of the FSO car factory.'

The captain stooped arrogantly over his ink jotter. He seemed more interested in the police radio chattering from a corner of his office than in Mrs Gajewska's request for information.

'. . . Your officers took my daughter from her apartment on Gornoslaska Street early yesterday morning. Where is she?' Mrs Gajewska's manner was persistent and defiant despite her fears of retaliation.

The captain showed no sign of emotion. 'I have no record,' he muttered without looking up.

'But your officers took her away. They had orders. You must have a record.'

'. . . According to my records we have no information . . . Next!'

In disgust, Mrs Gajewska turned on her heels. She would return tomorrow and every day until she received firm news of Magda. But in her heart she feared that to the Polish authorities, Magda Gajewska no longer existed.

15

Emil Rybicki propped himself against the chest-high bar of the stand-up buffet at Vienna's Südbahnhof and ate a *brötchen* for breakfast. It was 6 a.m. The Polish KGB captain had arrived at the station by bus from Grimmenstein shortly before midnight carrying his battered suitcase and canvas bag, and had then spent the night on a railway bench among the empty baggage trolleys. As Rybicki munched his bread and sipped fresh-ground coffee with a schnapps chaser, the first commuter trains were already disgorging workers and businessmen, many of them clutching newspapers which carried the vivid first pictures of troops and armoured vehicles on the streets of Poland.

The Chopin Express from Warsaw was due at 9.25, and even at this early hour television crews and journalists were staking out positions to meet the train. Yesterday's arrivals had faced newsmen who were acting more like wild animals. Any passenger with news from inside Poland had been set upon.

Rybicki's intention today was to show to any western intelligence agent on duty that he was a refugee anxious to hear from Poles any crumbs of firsthand news. When he felt he had been there long enough to leave the right impression, he deposited in a left-luggage locker the small battered suitcase of personal possessions which he would need on his eventual return to Austria. Then he fought his way through the commuter bustle and took a No. 18 tram to the Westbahnhof where he stood in the shafts of sunlight streaming through the tall station windows, his eyes scanning the vast tiled concourse. His SB and Moscow training made him alert to the possibility that he was being watched. He had the same instinctive feeling as during KGB training operations when up to six agents followed him incognito on the Moscow underground in order to trap him.

Rybicki walked across to the enormous timetable gantry. By juggling the train times he was able to change his travel plans so he could spot any agent tailing him. Instead of catching the 7 o'clock express direct to Munich via Salzburg he went to Platform 6 for the 7.20 to Innsbruck. Taking this route he could double back on his tracks at Innsbruck and be able to cross-check the passengers in each direction.

Rybicki climbed aboard the orange-and-cream coaches of Austrian State Railways and sank alone into a corner seat in the compartment. The clear winter sun shed its early morning haze as the train headed west towards the 9,000 ft peaks of the Salzkammergut. After his freezing night on a station bench Rybicki dozed for much of the time. Between each station a jovial conductor with a beaming Tyrolean smile checked the tickets, followed by a young buffet car attendant ringing a small mountain bell to offer sandwiches, soft drinks and coffee.

In Rybicki's semi-consciousness, each mountain village and town merged with the next. The towering, majestic beauty of peaks like the Hundstein and Schmittenhöhe was lost on him. At the junction town of Wörgl, Rybicki could have left the train to take the next express, which would have doubled back heading northeast towards Kufstein on the West German border. But such were his fears of being tailed that he did not dare take it. Instead he stayed on Express 162 heading away from Kufstein and then spent the 35-minute run into Innsbruck surveying all the passengers on board. He started at the locomotive then methodically made his way through the eight carriages towards the rear, making a mental note of each face to cross-check on the return run into Germany an hour later. He scrutinised perhaps fifty faces: farmers, workers, women on shopping trips, and the suntanned faces of the season's first skiers.

It was 13.20 when train 162 snaked into the ugly marshalling yards of Innsbruck. In the twenty-five minutes before the express to Munich, all the KGB captain had to do was buy a new ticket. When the train arrived on its journey north from the Dolomites, Rybicki had to fight his way through the congested corridors to find an unoccupied window seat. Then as the train rattled down the Inn Valley, Rybicki's mind wandered to his home in Myslowice: to his peasant father and mother still tending their five cows and ten pigs on the ten hectares of a small farm. Rybicki believed his parents knew nothing of his true career as a Soviet secret policeman. Being passionate activists in rural Solidarity they would have disowned their son had they discovered he was an agent working for the KGB.

Rybicki dozed as the train slowed in the marshalling yards of the Kufstein border crossing, the wheels biting for grip on the rails as they screeched to a halt. The KGB captain got up to stretch his tired limbs and stood at the open window fingering the two passports inside his jacket. Colonel Firyubin had supplied him with fake Austrian documents in the hope that he would be treated as one of the tens of thousands of Austrians who regularly cross into Germany perfectly legally.

Doors slammed ominously and walkie-talkies came closer. It was five past three as Austrian customs and passport officers barged their way down the crowded corridor. If Austrian counter-intelligence had suspicions about Rybicki they would stop him now. But the border between Austria and the German Federal Republic was not like a border post in the Soviet Bloc, and the three officials pushed on without even a glance into Rybicki's compartment. Fifteen minutes later the green carriages began moving slowly down the platform, then they crawled across the invisible frontier into West Germany, as alongside the track Rybicki watched the tarmac on the border road change abruptly from light-grey to dark-grey and the roadmarkings change from Austrian yellow to West German white. With relief, he pushed the fake Austrian passport deep into his breast pocket among the thousands of Austrian schillings and Deutschmarks, then slipped into a comfortable slumber again with the sun burning fierce on his face as the train sped north.

Munich Hauptbahnof an hour later was quite unlike the sombre, downtrodden Polish railway stations Rybicki knew so well. Even after four months in Austria, successful, capitalist, West Germany mesmerised the KGB captain. On the concourse he passed brash adverts for cars, low-tar cigarettes and Bavarian beer. The tantalising aroma of freshly baked croissants drifted through the confusion of people waiting to greet friends and relations. And there were no queues!

Colonel Firyubin had booked Rybicki into a small, medium-priced hotel near the apartment of the man Rybicki had come to meet. The wait for a subway train heading north revived his earlier fear that he was being tailed. But if he was, then the tail was as cunning and invisible as the brilliant agents from the KGB's Seventh Directorate who had trained him in evasion techniques at their villa on Zubovskaya Street in Moscow.

After alighting at Theresienstrasse, Rybicki walked to Steinheilstrasse, a side street in a middle-class residential district. The Hotel Königswache lay sandwiched between blocks of Bavarian-style apartments in a long terrace. Rybicki checked in as Klaus Heller, an Austrian electrician, and he asked for a room at the front. The second-floor room was a typical businessman's billet, and the net curtains made it ideal for undercover observation of the first-floor apartment opposite. In one corner was a tiny writing table and telephone, in another a fridge with a colour TV on top.

Rybicki fell exhausted onto the bed and dozed until six o'clock, when he rolled over, turned on the radio and switched his mind to German. Poland was top of the news bulletin:

'All direct communications by phone and telex to Poland remain cut. The situation is still unclear, but sketchy reports from travellers and diplomatic missions in Warsaw suggest the army and security forces have a tight grip. In his final dispatches before lines were cut by the Polish authorities, Reuter correspondent Brian Mooney reported that strikes had begun in at least four major factories in Warsaw....'

'Predictable capitalist propaganda!' snorted the hard-line KGB captain as he turned off the radio and fell back onto the bed. He inhaled deeply on a cigarette and played with smoke patterns rising to the ceiling. From his jacket pocket he removed the two passport-size black-and-white photographs which Firyubin had given him in Grimmenstein. One was a head and shoulders shot, the other a group of middle-aged men clutching wine glasses at a reception. Rybicki carefully examined the portrait. It showed a man in his mid-forties with receding black hair. He wore bi-focal spectacles with heavy black frames, and had the strained features of a man suffering from stress. 'Vulnerable' was the way Colonel Firyubin had described him last night, and this picture certainly suggested it.

Rybicki turned the photo over to read Firyubin's hand-written notes on the back.

'Henryk Tarnowski.
Aged 45. Married. Two children. Confirmed dissident and counter-revolutionary. Active KOR and underground University. Registered as living in Lublin 1936 to 1978.
Trained as historian. Degree Warsaw University.
1959–75: Employed as lecturer at Catholic University of Lublin.
Part-time journalist producing seditious articles.
1975: Suspended from University for subversive activities. Employment card withdrawn.
1975–77: organised illegal opposition groups.
1977: arrested for anti-state activity. Sentenced to five years jail.
1978: left Poland with family 'of own free will'.
1979 to present: duty sub-editor and commentator in Polish service, Radio Free Europe, Munich.
Home address: 10 Steinheilstrasse, Apt. 8

1981: Polish authorities prepared unpublished case against Tarnowski for treasonable activity in Munich for broadcasting material designed to threaten the security of the Polish State.'

Rybicki opened his wallet, looked up a number, then picked up the telephone and dialled. A voice answered in a European-American accent.

'Radio Free Europe, can I help you?'

Rybicki responded in heavily-accented English. 'Herr Tarnowski, please.'

'One moment, sir.' Rybicki waited thirty seconds on a dead line. 'Herr Tarnowski is not here at this time. Can anyone else help? Would you care to leave a message?'

Rybicki did not want to betray his identity, nor did he want to leave a hint that an inquisitive Pole was trying to contact Tarnowski. 'No thank you. When can I next reach him? When is he on duty?'

Rybicki's English slipped easily into the colloquialisms he had learned during the intensive KGB language courses ten years earlier.

'Herr Tarnowski is on duty again at eight o'clock in the morning.'

'Thank you kindly. I'll call again tomorrow.'

Outside, Steinheilstrasse was dark as local residents began returning home from work. Rybicki had twelve hours to finalise his strategy. He took a sheet of rough notepaper from his bag and began to write down the message which Firyubin had ordered him to memorise. Already Rybicki's two-day growth of beard reinforced the image which Moscow wanted him to create – that of a Polish refugee carrying information smuggled from Solidarity's new underground operation in Poland at great personal risk.

Rybicki knew that by the morning his strategy must be perfect.

16

Six prison officers and the deputy governor of Bialoleka
came for Sulecki at sunset. In the twelve hours since the
removal of Professor Pilubicki's body the inmates of cell
24 had eaten nothing but a greasy, un-nourishing breakfast. The officers stepped into the cell with handcuffs
jangling from thick leather belts. They divided into two
groups: three officers to either side and the deputy
governor between them with a slip of paper in his black
glove.

'Will the following enemies of the Polish State step
forward. A. Sulecki, J. Krawczyk, K. Sadowski. Collect
all personal items and belongings.'

The deputy governor folded his orders and pushed
them into his outside breast pocket. He showed no sign
of interest or emotion as he watched the three men gather
up their meagre personal effects. Krawczyk stood resolute
in the middle of the cell and faced the deputy governor
just as he had during the confrontation over the removal
of Professor Pilubicki's body. 'Where are we going?
Where are you taking us? We are prisoners of war and
we have a right to know.'

Krawczyk spoke purposefully. He knew that their survival might depend on his prising from the governor in
the presence of other internees details of where they were
going.

The deputy governor stared ahead. 'All I can say is
that you will be taken to another camp. Those are my
orders.'

The prison officers assembled Sulecki, Krawczyk and
Sadowski at the end of the corridor near the latrines.
They were forced to stand against a tiled wall, their
hands and legs spreadeagled, with a package of personal
belongings at each man's feet. For an hour they waited

in the bitter cold, during which darkness engulfed the camp. A second even more painful hour passed as they tried to exercise fingers and toes, and shook their heads periodically to maintain circulation. More internees arrived under escort, and within an hour a total of twenty Solidarity activists were lined up. Some were young workers and some grey-haired intellectuals. But Sulecki, Krawczyk and Sadowski knew none of them.

A body-search came almost as a relief because it allowed the internees to relax their positions. Every luxury or potential weapon was seized, then the internees were manhandled into the yard and half-thrown up the steel steps of a *Star* personnel transporter.

At the top another officer roughly grabbed their armpits to pull them on board. Each man was slotted into an individual mini-cell which measured one-and-a-half metres square, with a tiny wooden bench big enough for one backside and just enough ceiling space in which to stand up. The only ventilation came from a small communal skylight which the guards had left open to let in the sub-zero air for maximum discomfort.

In quick succession the cell doors were kicked shut. Sulecki, Krawczyk and Sadowski sat passive and sub-missive as a large officer in paramilitary fatigues stamped along the tiny gangway between the cubicles. Outside each cell he paused for several seconds and stared inside. Then he grated his keyring along the wire grilles of each door so that the 'rat-a-tat-tat' cut through the atmos-phere. 'Twenty-two on board,' he yelled to the deputy governor.

Through the steel bulkheads the internees could hear a muffled conversation. 'How long will it take to the border?' said one voice.

'In these conditions, six hours, sir,' said another, pre-sumably the driver's. 'There's pack ice on the road and fresh snow blown into drifts against the trees and fences. It would only take three hours normally, but we'll have to cut our speed.'

'So what time might you be at the border point?'

'Not before four in the morning, sir. Probably more like five. Maybe even later.'

'I'll phone ahead. The Soviet authorities will expect you. You're to report to the militia depot in Terespol on your way back for further orders. It's unlikely you'll return here.'

The internees strained to listen. 'The bastards. They're taking us to the Soviet Union,' muttered Jerzy Krawczyk. 'We'll vanish into the prison camps and psychiatric hospitals of the Gulag.'

No one answered him. There was a stunned emptiness. Then they felt the wagon shake as the guards clambered on board and let in an unwelcome rush of freezing night air. Someone banged on the wagon's sides.

'Go! Safe journey!'

The engine turned over, and the *Star* growled across the ice in a motion which would remain unchanged for many hours to come.

'We're not alone,' warned Sulecki. 'Listen outside! They're taking no chances. We're being treated like VIPs.' Sulecki's sharp ears had detected the engine and rattling bodywork of a second, smaller wagon in which alsatian dogs were barking.

Sulecki tried to examine the flashes of towns, villages and open country as they slipped past. They were, indeed, heading due east away from Warsaw along the E.8, the main route from Berlin to Moscow. He knew well the road and the chequerboard of small peasant farms and glasshouses. After two hours the prison wagons stopped to allow the guards to stretch their legs. But the internees were left incarcerated, with no attempt to give them food or water even though they had not eaten or drunk anything for fifteen hours. They had to urinate or defecate in a bucket, and even with the freezing air coming through the skylight the air was quickly fetid from the stench of body odours.

Onward again. The monotonous sliding of the wagon and the variable pitch of the engine began to take their toll. Krawczyk and Sadowski dozed, their heads nodding limply on their shoulders. Meanwhile in the rear compartment the guards defied regulations and opened a bottle of their privilege vodka. Within half an hour they had drunk and sang their way through two bottles of best Wyborowa. Slowly, they too were overcome by the droning rhythm of the prison truck.

As the headlamps of the *Nysa* van following them seemed to draw closer there was a violent jolt. Then a rip of steel and a wrenching of bodies as Sulecki hurtled forward off his tiny bench and upwards towards the roof. He felt as if he had been shot in the back at close range. He flew and then crashed, his head rasping across the wire grille on the cell door, his shoulders crunching like shingle onto the bench. The *Star* wagon began skidding along on its nearside, the steel wall grating through a mixture of ice and snow like a snowplough. It thumped upward, then downward onto its nose, then upwards again, rolling and cartwheeling at the same time as voices screamed and vodka bottles smashed.

Through the skylight poured a mixture of ice, marsh reeds and branches, the snow forcing its way through the widening splits in the roof's steelwork. In what seemed like slow motion Sulecki caught staccato glimpses of guards being flung round their rest area. Then the internees began to experience the same uncontrollable tumbling as rivets popped, bodywork buckled and the cell doors jumped from their locks and swung wildly open.

The prison wagon ended up motionless and upside down. Sulecki lay crumpled untidily, his body and legs above him, the cell floor looking down on him through a subterranean gloom. He was shocked but conscious as he heard the first groans and cries of pain and suffered the smell of upturned latrine buckets which mingled with the stench of stale coffee and vodka. His disorientated, half-numb mind took some minutes to realise that the prison wagon had crashed.

Sulecki slid his legs and trunk slowly down the back of the cell until he lay horizontal. He paused to listen for signs of life. There was nothing. He pulled himself up, found his tiny bundle of belongings and began crawling, edging his way forward across the inside of the upturned roof. Now he could make out the motionless bodies of internees and guards where they had been thrown by the force of the accident. He hunted for any familiar faces or signs of consciousness. He heard Krawcyk groan beyond an impenetrable wall of twisted steel bars. Then he saw Sadowski crushed between two other bodies in the gangway.

Sulecki knew he could not linger and help. His instincts screamed at him, 'Out! Get out while you can. . . . !'

He clambered over silent bodies towards the rear of the wagon. Outside in the moonlight, he could just make out the escort *Nysa* also upturned ten metres away and halfway down an embankment. A guard dog on board whined but only a knocking noise inside the van gave the vaguest suggestion of life.

Around Sulecki, the flat, snowbound Polish countryside near the Soviet border lay hostile, silent and black. Thirty or forty metres above him to his left he could just see the raised line of the E.8 road. Behind, beyond the crumpled *Nysa*, was the cold blue-grey reflection of a frozen river. To his right was a shapeless, black void – probably a dense wood or forest.

'Anyone there? Anyone there?'

A frantic male voice cut the chilled silence from the embankment. Sulecki did not reply. Above him he could just make out the shape and two red back lights of an articulated lorry reversing towards the crash site. On its side was the word 'PEKAES', the name of the Polish state transport firm.

Sulecki tried to guess what had happened. As the prison wagon and the *Nysa* had driven east, the lorry must have been driving west towards Warsaw. For some reason it had forced the prison wagons off the road. Perhaps because of ice, perhaps because one of the drivers was driving too fast for the conditions. Now Sulecki understood the frenzied state of the lorry driver. An accident involving militia wagons would have the gravest consequences for him. As the driver clambered down through the snow, Sulecki tried to move away from the road towards the trees. In a metre of thick, soft snow it was a punishing task. He was weak from hunger and fatigue. Each step was a fight in the sharp burning cold and after fifty metres he halted. All he could make out behind him were the black outlines of the two wagons in the snow and the lorry above on the embankment.

Sulecki made a crude calculation. From the position of the moon and the road he must be heading south. He knew he must keep moving, otherwise he would be overcome by hypothermia if he stopped or collapsed. He gasped for breath, the dry air rasping his parched throat as his rapid heart beats echoed up his wind pipe.

Sulecki had won his freedom. Yet at this moment he was threatened not by the militia, the SB or the army, but by the ferocious sub-zero cold of a Polish winter. Already his eyebrows had grown heavy with ice, his trouser legs had frozen rigid, and the iced pleats of the denim creaked as he moved. His ankles and hands were becoming numb as fresh snow crept inside his ankle boots.

Where was he? He guessed thirty to forty kilometres from the Soviet Border. To reach Warsaw undetected now presented him with be a formidable challenge. As he paused and gasped yet again, delirium began to take a hold. Had Sulecki not heard a train clattering towards him from the east he would have stumbled onto the railway line. As it was, he stopped in his tracks.

From his right, from the direction of Warsaw, came the faint squeaking of metal on metal. Fifty metres away and silhouetted against the snow he could just make out the spindly shapes of the two red-and-white barriers of a level crossing being lowered by a railwayman winding a large wheel. The steam locomotive drew nearer, wheezing as it climbed through the fields, two white lights creeping across the flat snowscape and creating a rainbow of ice crystals in the snow crust. Three hundred metres away now. He could smell the brown lignite coming from

94

the twin stacks as the burning ash and cinders sparkled like a halo of glow worms. The giant 4–8–2 steam locomotive thundered past, the snow vibrating as Sulecki watched the driver and his mate highlighted by the red glow and sparks from the fire.

Then, as suddenly as it had appeared from the white emptiness of snow, the freight train was gone and Sulecki stood alone twenty metres from the railway track and fifty from the gatekeeper's cabin. The warmth from its smoking chimney lured him. He tried to move but his body would not respond. Finally he summoned the strength to drag his legs towards the railway track which he knew he had to cross, and at last he stood on the compacted ice and snow of the road. It felt as if a giant block of concrete had been removed from his ankles. Within seconds Sulecki became light-footed and light-headed. The snowscape turned before him. The whites of his eyes rolled, and his body finally succumbed to the paralysis of hypothermia.

No longer could Sulecki remember why he was there, or how he had got there, or who he worked for, or what he had planned. He collapsed onto the road, the momentum of the fall making his body slide a couple of metres across the ice. His eyes froze shut as if bonded together with glue.

It was 3 a.m. – the coldest hour of a Polish winter night. Sulecki lay on a remote country road, the temperature at minus fifteen degrees centigrade and the heat from his body draining rapidly.

17

In Munich, Tuesday the fifteenth dawned foggy and freezing. Fearing he would oversleep, Emil Rybicki had slipped the night porter an extravagant twenty Deutschmarks the night before to ensure he was brought a tray of hot food at six o'clock sharp. When it arrived, the KGB captain settled behind the net curtains, turned out the light, and by the light of the street lamps started eating a hearty central European breakfast of ham, two eggs, cheese and a large flask of coffee, while across at No. 10 Steinheilstrasse the first-floor windows of apartment 8 remained dark, with no signs of life.

The previous evening, the telephonist at Radio Free Europe had told Rybicki that Tarnowski would be on duty at eight o'clock. That meant he would probably have to leave home sometime after a quarter past seven. The fake Solidarity document Rybicki had prepared overnight was tucked in his back pocket and his forged Austrian passport was hidden in a cupboard. He had carefully cultivated the image of a penniless Polish refugee with an urgent mission. His clothes were unkempt and his beard grew like harvest stubble. A Solidarity badge was pinned on the lapel of his shabby jacket, and in his canvas bag he carried the typical possessions of a devoted union activist: recent bulletins, booklets, handbills and a notebook with names and addresses of Solidarity activists in Silesia.

The light in apartment 8 came on at five to seven. Rybicki could just make out the shadowy forms of two adults and one child moving through the flat from bedroom to bathroom, then back to the bedroom and on to the kitchen.

Tarnowski appeared at 7.30, briefly standing in the doorway as he put on his gloves. It was not a clear view, but the receding black hair and heavy spectacles matched the two pictures he had studied the previous night. The dissident Polish broadcaster had the typical dowdy appearance of the average Pole: black plastic peaked cap, an overlong brown anorak with the waist cord drawn tight, dark grey trousers and black plastic shoes. Under his left arm he carried a brown document case.

From inside the hotel Rybicki watched Tarnowski turn right along Steinheilstrasse and disappear. He slid the breakfast crockery into the corridor, hung the 'Do Not Disturb' sign on his door, grabbed his canvas holdall and slipped downstairs to the hotel lobby. He waited a few seconds until the receptionist's back was turned, then slipped out, following fifteen to twenty metres behind the lone, hunched figure which strode northwards. Rybicki watched him buy newspapers from a self-service stall, then walk on to the No. 53 bus stop on Schellingstrasse. Tarnowski took his place at the rear of the queue and lowered his eyes hungrily to read the front page news on events in Poland. Rybicki slipped in alongside, and they both boarded a bus.

'Lerchenfeldstrasse!' the bus driver's muffled voice announced ten minutes later over the PA system. The doors hissed open and Tarnowski pushed himself through the commuters onto the newly salted pavements. The KGB captain slid after him, shadowing Tarnowski as he strode briskly along the web of asphalt paths cutting through the dirty blotches of old snow in Munich's famous English Garden. Tarnowski's walk to Radio Free Europe would take no more than eight minutes. Rybicki drew level with Tarnowski and began speaking in Polish.

'Mr Tarnowski? ... Mr Henryk Tarnowski? ... '

Tarnowski swung his head sharply and looked at Rybicki who now walked alongside him to his left. Was this the assassination attempt by the Polish secret police which Tarnowski had feared for more than three years? All exiles from the Soviet Bloc lived in fear, especially those with high-profile jobs like Tarnowski's. In February a mystery bomb had damaged one wing of Radio Free Europe. In July a Romanian commentator at the radio station had been stabbed twenty-six times in a murder attempt. And there had been many other unexplained attacks on RFE's Eastern European staff.

It took the Polish dissident a moment to weigh up Rybicki's unkempt appearance, then he replied, also in Polish.

'Yes?'

'We don't have much time ... I have some important information.' Rybicki touched Tarnowski gently on the shoulder and tried to slow the pace.

Tarnowski noticed the Solidarity badge and warmed to the familiarity of the Polish voice. 'This is most unusual ... How can I help you? Who are you?'

The two men shuffled past the English Garden's mini waterfall and empty park benches.

'My name is Emil Rybicki. I am a coal miner from Myslowice in Silesia ...' Guardedly he took his Polish passport from his breast pocket and opened it at the page which identified him. He also produced his Solidarity membership and subscription card. 'I was a founding member of the Solidarity chapter at the Myslowice mine. Four months ago I left Poland. I was sick of the system. I could see no possibility of things changing. Since I defected I've been in Traiskirchen camp near Vienna waiting to be accepted as an immigrant to Australia...'

Tarnowski's first impulse was to believe Rybicki. 'So what are you doing here if you should still be in Austria?' Tarnowski asked.

'I'm here illegally. I have no West German visa.' Rybicki waved the flimsy green Polish passport again. 'I took the risk because I've got an important message. I hitch-hiked here from Vienna and no one checked me at the border. I have to get back by tomorrow so the camp authorities don't realise I have been away.'

Rybicki was lying. He knew the story contained holes, but he hoped Tarnowski would be sufficiently seduced by the fake Solidarity message not to bother checking on him.

'A Solidarity courier arrived at Traiskirchen early yesterday morning. Somehow he got through Czechoslovakia. Before he was taken to the camp "cooler" for processing he slipped me this message.'

Rybicki pulled the folded communique from an inside pocket. 'The courier told me he'd travelled all the way from Gdansk – some 900 kilometres. He was at Solidarity's National Commission meeting on Saturday night. Bujak and Krupinski gave him this message with instructions to get it to the West for transmission back into Poland.'

Tarnowski was impressed by Rybick's command of information. 'How can I help you then?'

'The courier told me the leaders have no means of communication in Poland now. But they urgently need to get over a simple message: that Solidarity survives underground. They want it broadcast on Radio Free Europe so that Solidarity members with short-wave radios inside Poland can hear it and pass on the message...'

Rybicki paused and waited for Tarnowski's reaction. The two men had almost reached the four-metre high electric fence and rocket-proof wall which protected the whitewashed buildings and red roofs of the Radio Free Europe compound. A duck quacked on the bank of the stream. Another flapped and dried its wings. Tarnowski felt in his trouser pockets for a packet of cigarettes, then thoughtfully lit one for himself. Finally he nodded and pointed to the paper in Rybicki's hand.

Rybicki, however, insisted on speaking before he showed it to Tarnowski.

'The courier told me that the underground leadership want this broadcast continuously every hour for twenty-four hours. In that way as many Solidarity members as possible stand a chance of hearing it.'

'That won't be a problem. We've boosted the signal to Poland. We now have ten short-wave frequencies and one medium-wave frequency around the clock. So what does the communique say?' Tarnowski was becoming impatient.

Rybicki unfolded the creased green paper and passed it to Tarnowski, who muttered the words as he read.

'The underground leadership of the coordinating commission of the Independent Trade Union NSZZ Solidarity announces its existence. It confirms it survived the decimation inflicted by the Polish security forces on the night of Saturday 12th and morning of Sunday 13th December 1981. We are working towards a coordinated policy of resistance which we will announce in due course. Until then members of NSZZ Solidarity should activate all previously sanctioned methods of passive resistance in places of work. They should also plan for the overthrow of General Jaruzelski and his puppet régime whose sole interest is the enforcement of Soviet wishes without due consideration for the genuine interests of the Polish people.

Signed: the Temporary Coordinating Commission NSZZ Solidarity, Gdansk, 13th December.'

As a relatively junior KGB officer Emil Rybicki was just the postman, so he had no idea of the significance of the communique or the secret message it contained. But to the KGB Illegal planted by Moscow Centre inside Solidarity some time ago, the last sentence calling for the overthrow of General Jaruzelski corresponded exactly to the phrase finalised by General Semenov's Illegals Directorate in Moscow six months earlier.

To Tarnowski, however, the hawkish instructions in the communique were out of character, because Solidarity leaders had always promoted passive resistance. But the message appeared to be one of the first authentic communications to reach the west, and he concluded that RFE must broadcast it without question. Tarnowski folded the paper. 'May I keep it?' he asked.

Rybicki waved his hand in agreement. 'Of course.'

Tarnowski relied on his Polish instincts to overcome

his early doubts. 'Come inside for a coffee,' he suggested, as the rat-a-tat of a woodpecker echoed around the park.

'A kind offer ...' Rybicki bowed his head, 'but no thank you. I have to protect whatever position I may have in a courier network. I can't afford to be seen by the secret Soviet agents who we all know work in RFE.'

Tarnowski fully understood. The answer was the typical reaction of a suspicious Solidarity activist and it added to Rybicki's credibility. Tarnowski tried another tack. 'Perhaps I can contact you again? We need people like you. From inside Traiskirchen you would be invaluable to us. We would pay too. Good money. I'm sure you need it. Perhaps we can talk over possibilities?'

With no guidance from his controller, the KGB captain hedged his bets. He didn't want to jeopardise his cover, but neither did he want to create doubts in Tarnowski's mind. 'Give me your home phone number,' he asked, although he knew it already. 'I don't want to meet here again, and I don't want to come to your home. Suggest a meeting place.'

'The Jasmine cafe at the corner of Augustenstrasse, five blocks north of the Hauptbahnhof.'

Rybicki had to keep his options open. If RFE did not broadcast the communique he would have to discover why. 'If I decide not to return to Austria immediately I'll call you at RFE. I'll say "This is Emil, can we meet?" and that will mean we'll rendezvous in the cafe at six tonight.'

Tarnowski looked at his watch. It was well past eight o'clock and he was late for work. They shook hands hurriedly and Rybicki headed back down the path towards the 53 bus stop near the Bavarian National Museum. Their meeting had been easier than expected: short and efficient, the kind of operation they dream of at KGB Moscow Centre. Neither Pole had noticed the close-circuit camera focused on them from under the eaves of the RFE building. The United States propaganda machine had watched a small cog in the Soviet disinformation machine at work. But how much, if anything, had the CIA discovered?

By 9.15 Rybicki was back in his hotel room. He ordered coffee then dozed with half an ear on his new Japanese shortwave radio. The ten o'clock RFE update on the Polish situation came and went with no communique from the Solidarity leadership'. Rybicki knew he had to be patient and wait. Only if no communique was broadcast by mid-afternoon would he begin to worry. Then at eleven o'clock he heard the familiar words.

'. . . They should also plan for the overthrow of General Jaruzelski and his puppet régime whose sole interest is the enforcement of Soviet wishes without due consideration for the genuine interest of the Polish people.'

Rybicki stubbed out his twelfth cigarette in two hours, inhaled deeply on a thirteenth and gazed down satisfyingly from his hotel room into Tarnowski's empty apartment.

18

At the headquarters of the KGB's First Chief Directorate in Moscow, First Deputy Chairman Semenov sat with his back to the three generals he had summoned to his office. He gazed across the snow-covered birch forests of Tëpplystan towards the jagged concrete skyline of Moscow's high rise suburban sprawl which poked through the freezing December mist.

'Still no news?' he barked.

'Nothing,' said General Martynov, head of the Illegals 'S' Directorate.

Semenov swung his black leather chair around. '... Nothing?' he repeated, staring at Martynov. He did not address Martynov by his usual patronymic, Vasili Pavlovich. Instead he used the official form of address to signal his anger. 'Comrade General Martynov, with your thirty-two years experience as an officer in the Committee for State Security I need not remind you that the Comrade Chairman has a formidable reputation for rewarding operational success – and punishing failure.' Semenov leaned forward and tapped his fingers impatiently on the desktop.

'I find it incredible that *none of you* can report conclusively on progress and that our agent has disappeared. You have to discover the facts. We need our agent out ... and we need him *fast!*'

Martynov played for time. 'You must have trust, Comrade General. Our Illegal is a fine agent: resourceful, cunning and a ruthless tactician. We will receive details soon, I am sure.'

Martynov paused, then risked addressing his superior officer informally. 'Dimitri Fedorovich, I request you suspend jamming of all foreign radio stations beaming into Poland for twenty-four hours. Today we expect confirmation of the success of Comrade Rybicki's mission to Munich. We will only know he has succeeded when our radio monitoring department picks up the text of the fake Solidarity communique being broadcast over Radio Free Europe. But if our jamming operations at Kaliningrad, Tashkent and Smolensk continue then neither our Illegal nor our monitoring agents can be guaranteed to hear it.'

General Martynov went on to detail the plans made to contact the Illegal in Warsaw. 'A number of Soviet lorries from the *Sovtransport* enterprise will be parked next to the Palace of Culture in Warsaw. They will be part of our 'fraternal aid' to Poland in its hour of need. Lorries from the German Democratic Republic, Bulgaria, Czechoslovakia and the Mongolian People's Republic are already in Warsaw. The driver of one of them is a senior officer from my directorate, Comrade Major Petrovsky. In line with your instructions no one at the Soviet Embassy in Warsaw knows anything about his assignment. Petrovsky will return to Moscow and report directly to us here as soon as my Illegal makes contact with him.'

Semenov was not convinced by Martynov's assurances. The general stared out through the smoked-glass windows towards the traffic of the six-lane Moscow ring-road which was just visible through the trees. Then he thumped his desk.

'Order our KGB liaison officer at the Polish Interior Ministry to make discreet enquiries. Just give him the agent's name and last known address in Warsaw, but give him none of the background to *Amber Monkey*. And warn him about the need for absolute operational secrecy. Not a word must leak to the Polish Interior Ministry.'

Semenov raised his index finger to emphasise his final point to Martynov. 'I want facts Vasili Pavlovich, not speculation. And in the end I want *Amber Monkey*.'

Semenov's finger stabbed the table as his voice swelled to an angry crescendo. Martynov nodded. The head of 'S' Directorate knew he had no alternative.

19

Pain shot through every limb and muscle in Sulecki's thawing body. Hypothermia had numbed his primary senses, and only now did they begin to return. Sulecki sat in a high-backed wooden chair with his body limp. He could still smell and feel and hear, but he could not see. He could smell the heavy fug of an unventilated room. He could feel the warming glow of the cast-iron stove hitting his chest and legs. He could hear wood crackling and water boiling as well as the clatter of saucepans.

'Any sign of life?' The voice was rough and male.

'A bit more,' said a woman. 'He's breathing, but only just. His limbs are warmer. He may pull through.'

Slowly Sulecki summoned the energy to force open his eye lids, first the right eye, then the left. He began to see the smoke-stained timber boarding, the crumbling ceiling, the dishevelled settee, the plain wooden chairs and the large beech table.

Sulecki tried moving his fingers and arms, then his legs and toes. He moved his head, first one way then the other. He discovered he was swathed in several blankets, his feet were bound with sacking and his head was covered by a large woollen hat which smelt of manure.

Slowly he remembered internment and the van ride; then the crash, the escape and the struggle through the snow. He remembered too that his mind had gone blank.

'Hallo...'

The peasant figure spoke in a deep grating voice. He towered above Sulecki in a leather jerkin, grey *kuczma* hat and filthy breeches. The big hands, the smell and the appearance suggested a farmer. He looked about fifty years old with black curly hair, a storm-lashed face and a weather-beaten line across his brow which marked the limit of his hat.

'You made it, then. You're lucky to survive.' The farmer pushed a rusting thermometer in front of Sulecki's face and pointed to the minimum and maximum markers. 'It was down to minus eighteen outside last night. Normally, that's low enough to kill anyone in a few minutes.'

Sulecki's face creased with pain as he tried to speak through his cracked lips. Eventually he managed it quietly and slowly. 'Thank you,' he winced as he stretched out his hand to shake the farmer's. 'Tell me what happened.'

The farmer loaded logs into the enamelled stove.

'We found you at half past three this morning. You were on the track by the railway crossing, almost stiff with ice. We thought you'd gone. We shouldn't really have been out because it was the middle of the curfew. But we'd been invited to a party at a neighbour's and we don't worry about the militia and army out here in the country. They can't police everywhere.'

The peasant farmer spoke in a country drawl, running his sentences together and clipping his words. 'Out cold, you were. When we got you back here we found you were breathing. So we propped you up in front of the fire. How d'you feel now?'

'I'm getting the feeling back in my hands and feet,' said Sulecki. 'I think I can feel everywhere else.'

'What's your name?' The farmer's style was blunt. 'We couldn't find any documents on you. You had no ID card, no wallet, no nothing. Were you mugged? Were you dumped? What . . . ?'

Sulecki drew breath as he calculated how much he should say. On the walls he could see posters of the farmers' union Rural Solidarity but nothing relating to the Communist Party or the State. He decided to play it straight without revealing too much.

'I have no passport because the Interior Ministry have it . . . I was interned. I've just escaped from a prison van after an accident.' Sulecki slowly recounted the details of his internment and his work in Solidarity. 'They were taking a group of us to the Soviet Union. A freight lorry forced the prison wagon and the escort van off the road. We crashed down an embankment. I managed to get away, and I walked – south I think. Then ... well you know the rest.'

'You really think they were taking you to the Soviet Union? Bastards!' said the farmer clearing his throat and spitting. Until yesterday we hadn't seen a single militia man round here. Then a couple of hours ago that changed. ... Perhaps they were looking for you.'

The farmer's wife listened as she cooked breakfast on the stove. The invigorating smells of farm eggs and home-smoked *cabanos* sausage drifted round the kitchen. Sulecki clutched a glass beaker of steaming coffee in his limp hands and sipped, the dregs lying thick and heavy on the bottom in Polish-style. As the three of them ate they talked of Rural Solidarity and the peasants' problems; of the hardships in the countryside; of the shortages; of the bribery and corruption and the thriving black market; of the State's failure to honour its contracts with farmers and the farmers' way of retaliating by refusing to sell meat or crops to the State.

Now Sulecki guided the conversation to more pressing matters. 'I can't stay here. I must go back to Warsaw. My work is there in the underground...'

'But you're not fit to go. How will you get through the road blocks and military checks?' the farmer insisted.

'I'm fitter than most people, and now I've had a good meal. All I need is warm boots, a heavy coat and a solid pair of gloves. Can you help me?'

Sulecki's intentions clearly worried the farmer. 'You're crazy! You'll be safer hiding here.'

But Sulecki was insistent. 'What's the best and safest way to get to Warsaw? You must help me ... It's for the sake of Solidarity.'

The farmer stroked his weather-beaten chin. Like every peasant he was conservative by instinct. 'Things are getting hot round here ... You mustn't risk the main roads to Warsaw.'

He got up and crossed the flag-stoned kitchen to a faded, smoke-stained map of eastern Poland on the wall. It had been printed in 1951 but the roads and tracks had not changed because there had been little investment in the region for years. 'We're here ...', said the farmer, his oil-stained fingernail pointed to the village of Dolha, east of Miedzyrzec. Sulecki's calculations had been right. They were twenty kilometres from the Soviet border and 110 kilometres from Warsaw.

'You must take these back roads towards Lukow and south of Siedlce.' The farmer's hand swept west again along the railway line from the Soviet Union. Sulecki nodded a sort of agreement. He still felt light-headed. 'So how do I do it? I don't have a car.'

'... And I can't help you,' said the farmer. 'I can't risk taking you in mine. It's too dangerous. Martial law means we have to stay in the place where we're registered, and that means here.'

'What about a horse with a trailer?' asked Sulecki. 'Couldn't we do it that way? You could take me.'

The farmer gazed at the map again. He ran his finger westwards and slowly shook his head. 'It's a long way ...'

'But I must get to Warsaw by tomorrow morning,' pleaded Sulecki.

'There's only one answer then,' said the farmer. 'You must use the *kulig* – my sledge. We could cut across the fields on the side roads and tracks, avoiding the main roads.'

The farmer's finger tracked west across the map, horizontally along the thin blue line of a river sandwiched between the E8 and the railway. 'We'll keep north of the river, past the village of Trzebiesow, then well to the north of Lukow. We can keep heading due west. This marshy area near Olszyc will be frozen, and much easier for the horse than going through snow. My cousin Edward has a small peasant farm near Sloczek Lukowski. You can rest up there. He's active in Rural Solidarity too. I'll persuade him to take you nearer to Warsaw. He'll know the best route.'

Sulecki threw up his hands euphorically. 'Let's try it. When can we leave?'

A peasant farmer was not used to such persistence and urgency. 'I need at least an hour, perhaps two,' he said reluctantly. 'I'll give the horse extra oats and barley.'

The farmer shouted to his wife to prepare a hot meal and extra clothing. Sulecki wound two blankets around himself, pulled the woollen hat hard down over his face and followed the farmer into the yard where the cart ruts were frozen into erratic, jagged corrugations.

It took half an hour of heaving and clunking for Sulecki and the farmer to replace the *kulig*'s wheels with the wooden runners required by Polish law in winter. Then they loaded the bundles of kindling wood which would be used to illuminate the *kulig* on the roads. The farmer pitchforked trusses of hay on board for the horse, then loaded a box of smoked pig sausage, bread and raw bacon for themselves. Finally, back in the timber-framed farmhouse Sulecki and the farmer sat down to steaming bowls of white beetroot and a long, fat *kielbasa* country sausage from which they carved great hunks.

'We must celebrate your arrival ... *and* your departure,' said the farmer. He plucked a chilled bottle from inside a pile of snow on the kitchen doorstep and poured transparent liquid into tiny toasting glasses. From the sharp, stinging odour Sulecki knew this was not normal vodka but moonshine.

'*Bimber*,' said the farmer. 'Very special. *Real* alcohol. It's illegal of course although made of potatoes, almonds, acorns and rye. We even found some orange peel!' He proudly listed the ingredients. '*Na zdrowie!*' he toasted. 'Cheers, and good luck! Here's to Solidarity.'

The glasses clinked as Sulecki and the farmer tilted back their heads. '*Na zdrowie!*'

The glasses clinked again, and, as tradition demanded, Sulecki took his turn to speak. 'My deepest thanks. Without you both I would not be alive ... To you and to our union . . . !' Their glasses clinked a third time.

'You still haven't told me your name,' said the peasant.

'Andrzej . . .'

'Andrzej who?'

'Just Andrzej . . . It's a state of war. We are friends. We don't need surnames,' said Sulecki evasively. 'And you? Your name?'

'Jan. Just call me Jan . . .'

The vodka bottle was two thirds empty and Sulecki politely shifted the subject of conversation. 'Perhaps we could listen to a western radio station to find out what is happening. It's just coming up to eleven o'clock. It should be news time. How about Radio Free Europe?'

The farmer leaned over and switched on the old Grundig short-wave radio which he had bought proudly ten years ago with dollars sent to him by a distant relation in the west.

The voice being relayed by RFE's transmitters at Holzkirchen south of Munich spoke of strikes and resistance in Poland; of atrocities and thousands of people being interned; of killings and army brutality. There was news, too, from some Solidarity leaders in hiding underground. Forty-eight hours after leaving Gdansk a handwritten communique had reached RFE. It announced the formation of an underground Solidarity leadership and talked of coordinating a policy for passive resistance. It also asked Poles to 'plan for the overthrow of General Jaruzelski and his puppet regime, whose sole interest is the enforcement of Soviet wishes.'

They were the precise words which Lieutenant Colonel Andrei Igorovich Sulecki of the KGB had long waited to hear. He had memorised the phrase many months ago on the instructions of Moscow Centre. Now Lieutenant Colonel Sulecki, one of 'S' Directorate's most talented and highly-decorated Illegals, had been reactivated inside Poland.

20

Andrzej Sulecki was not the 35-year-old, disillusioned farm worker he had always claimed to his friends in Solidarity. Lieutenant Colonel Andrei Igorovich Sulecki was forty, and a hand-picked high flyer from the KGB's Balashikha training college thirty kilometres east of Moscow. As an Illegal in the Eighth Department of Directorate 'S' within the First Chief (Foreign) Directorate, he had been trained in the ruthless techniques of sabotage, destabilisation and assassination.

Sulecki had been assigned to Warsaw two years earlier, in November 1979. At the time, Moscow Centre had been deeply concerned by reports from Poland of growing popular discontent, and at the behaviour of the corrupt government of Edward Gierek. In theory, the KGB should have had the greatest faith in the fraternal security services of the Polish militia and the SB. But in practice, Dzerzhinsky Square trusted nobody – even those trained by the KGB.

Assigning Sulecki to Poland as an Illegal was a prime example of Moscow Centre's suspicions towards its 'fraternal Polish ally'. By November 1979 Poland had become an unprecedented problem requiring unprecendented measures. Sulecki's credentials for the operation were impeccable. He was a Russian born to Polish parents who had been marooned in the part of eastern Poland annexed by the Soviet Union after World War II. Sulecki came from Grodno, a farming town which had been in Polish Byelorussia before the war. Although still Polish in many ways, Grodno was now a Russian city twenty kilometres inside the Soviet Union.

Sulecki had first come to the KGB's attention twentyone years earlier. Like every bright provincial teenager in the Soviet Union, nineteen-year-old Andrei Igorovich had nurtured ambitions of leaving dull and grimy Grodno to work in Moscow. Unknown to him it was the KGB's clandestine sponsorship over several years which had enabled him to achieve that ambition.

In 1962 the Personnel Department of the First Chief Directorate had secured Sulecki a rare place with other high-flyers at Moscow University's prestigious Institute for International Relations. And with that University place had come the highly-prized *propiska* – the blue visa stamp which was dreamed of by most Soviet citizens and which allowed Sulecki to move from the provinces to the privileged lifestyle enjoyed in the Soviet capital. Thus, in 1962 and without knowing it, Andrei Sulecki had been snared unwittingly in the KGB's web and the die for his career was cast. Using their cover of academic posts at the Institute, senior KGB recruiting officers then spent three years secretly watching and assessing Sulecki because in the best Chekist tradition every high-flying KGB candidate had to be ideologically sound.

Preparation of each KGB 'Illegal' was a costly, time-consuming investment. Only an exceptional person would ever qualify, and no avenue for cross-checking was ignored. While at Moscow University, senior agents monitored Sulecki's personal views, his Marxist-Leninist loyalties, his work, his attitudes and his strength of character. They had also examined his relationships and his indiscretions. And throughout his three years in Moscow, Sulecki had known nothing of this painstaking surveillance until in 1965 the KGB made their first formal approach to him. The invitation to join came in a brief meeting with three men described to him as university officials who worked from a campus office he never knew existed.

'Comrade Andrei Igorovich Sulecki, esteemed graduate of the University of Moscow...! Please accept an invitation for graduation to the most honoured and privileged ranks of the Union of Socialist Soviet Republics ...'

By this time KGB personnel officers always knew their

future agent better than the prospective agent knew himself. They would never have made a recruitment offer had there been the slightest risk of rejection or of their years of undercover surveillance being blown. Sulecki had readily accepted the offer and within six weeks, Andrei Igorovich had 'disappeared' to be consumed by the KGB machine.

As a new 25-year-old trainee Sulecki had vindicated the Centre's six years of investment. He shone in the first year of routine training given to all agents at the college known to outsiders as the 'Diplomatic Translators' School'. Like all KGB recruits he was pampered with unlimited supplies of privileged goods and food he had never seen before – smart foreign clothes, western whisky and cigarettes. The KGB systematically bought his total loyalty by laying on lavish parties which often turned into orgies with young women willingly drafted in from the Young Communist League.

By the age of twenty-six Sulecki had acquired a pseudonym and been confirmed as a member of a department then known as Department 'V', the *Destivitelni Otdel* – the anonymous KGB section responsible for sabotage and assassination. For five years he trained with other crack agents in the KGB college on Metrostrojevskaya Street and at the Balashikha training complex where he learned then perfected techniques of subversion, precision shooting, close combat and murder. Then he went on to the Foreign Intelligence School at Yurlovo where he acquired the KGB's indispensable conspiratorial mentality in line with the Leninist principle that 'Whatever serves to advance communism is moral by definition.'

By early 1971, Sulecki was living alone in a run-down KGB safe apartment a mile from the Kremlin. He had been forbidden to contact the Centre for six months. Officers from the Seventh (Surveillance) Directorate trailed him everywhere – on the subway trains and buses, in the shops, and in cinemas and cafes. In return Sulecki had been expected to demonstrate his subversive abilities by identifying and outwitting the agents without acknowledging he had ever been aware of their presence.

In late 1971 Sulecki was assigned to a new safe apartment attended by a middle-aged KGB housekeeper. For six months he endured further screening and tutoring twelve hours a day, six days a week without leaving the apartment. This different form of enforced isolation was designed to keep Sulecki away from the main stream of KGB agents. As a handpicked Illegal he must know nothing about his colleagues, and they should know nothing about him. If his responsibilities ever became known, his value to the KGB would be destroyed immediately.

In 1972, at the age of thirty-one, Major Sulecki had qualified as a fully-trained KGB Illegal in one of a small group of elite agents who belonged to a secret KGB Department which Western intelligence mistakenly believed had been disbanded. In fact Department V had merely been renamed the Eighth Department of Directorate 'S'. On the personal direction of Chairman Andropov, Sulecki had been forbidden to use his Department V qualifications for seven years following the defection in London in 1971 of the senior KGB agent and saboteur Oleg Lyalin who had blown the cover of Department V. So for seven years Major Sulecki had been posted to Soviet embassies in Asia, Europe and Central America, then to covert training assignments in Vietnam, Lebanon, Egypt, West Germany and Nicaragua before being recalled to Dzerzhinsky Square in August 1979 for promotion to Lieutenant Colonel at the unusually early age of thirty-eight.

It was then, on Chairman Andropov's instructions, that the Eighth Department of Directorate 'S' began to reassert itself worldwide. Within two months KGB Illegal Sulecki was heading west from Moscow with a new identity – that of a 33-year-old factory worker travelling home to Poland.

The Lieutenant Colonel had left Moscow's Byelorussia Station on a crisp, blustery November evening. Everything about him had been meticulously groomed to be Polish. His name had been modified to 'Andrzej Sulecki', he carried a Polish passport and zlotys, and he wore distinctly Polish clothes.

Andrei Igorovich Sulecki was now officially Andrzej Sulecki. Forged KGB documents described him as a Polish peasant's son 'brought up on a farm in north east Poland' not far from his true Soviet home in Grodno. Polish employment papers organised by Moscow Centre had officially sanctioned his transfer from work on his father's farm near Bialystok to a job as trainee technician at the Ursus tractor factory outside Warsaw. Thus, within six months, tractor worker Andrzej Sulecki had shed the image of a simple peasant and by April 1980 had infiltrated the dissident workers' movement to become a willing underground activist. It was at that time that he also took up with his mistress, Magda Gajewska.

It was in this way that by the start of the historic strikes at the Gdansk shipyards in August 1980, Sulecki commanded wide access to workers' tactics and intelligence. And by the spring of 1981 the KGB Lieutenant Colonel had become a telex operator and a key member of the administration at the union's new Warsaw regional offices on Mokotowska Street.

In the second-floor telex room Sulecki had been in a position to know who in the union did what and who wielded power. From telexes and gossip he knew the identity of Solidarity hotheads who believed Poland should break with the Soviet alliance, and he also knew the identities of Westerners who pledged money and equipment. In addition, he knew who among the union leaders, staff, drivers, printers and messengers were Polish secret policemen planted to push the union towards extremist policies.

Now, on Tuesday 15 December 1981, in the kitchen of a peasant farmhouse located among the frozen wastes of eastern Poland, Lieutenant Colonel Sulecki had finally received his long-awaited re-activation order from Moscow Centre. The Solidarity communique was repeated hourly on the radio and it made Jan the farmer grumble about dangers and trouble which lay ahead.

'Those hothead Solidarity leaders must be out of their minds ordering the overthrow of Jaruzelski,' Jan complained. 'If they carry out what that communique demands then the Soviet tanks will stream across the border, and over all our farms here. If they do that there will be war.'

Sulecki, pale and exhausted, did not respond. Instead, he changed the subject.

'Can we get going, Jan? We ought to get as far as we can before it's dark and before the temperature drops too low.'

Jan grabbed the remaining half bottle of *Bimber*. He knew it was illegal to drive even a horse-drawn *kulig* with alcohol in the blood, but both he and Sulecki needed fortification on the long journey across the snowbound fields where they assumed there would be no militia to breath-test them.

Jan's farewell to his wife was matter-of-fact – as if he was going no further than the nearest ploughed field. 'Don't worry. I'll be back in a day or two; maybe a little more.' He made no attempt to kiss her.

Outside, the sun was well up: a brilliant, glowing white ball in the southern sky. In the snow-covered farmyard the farmer hitched the chestnut gelding's harness to the *kulig*'s single shaft. The horse stood under a webbing rug, each outward breath producing a plume of steam, the long winter hairs shuddering in the Siberian wind which blew gently from the Russian Steppes.

Jan clambered aboard and Sulecki sat alongside him on the simple wooden bench perched high above the *kulig*'s ski runners. Each man wrapped himself in multiple layers of blankets, coats and leather. As Jan's dumpy wife waved silently from behind the frozen condensation on the farmhouse window the *kulig* scraped and clunked its way out of the farmyard across the rutted mud. It might take eight hours to reach Jan's brother's farm fifty kilometres to the west, and from there another twenty-four hours to Warsaw.

For Sulecki, time was at a premium. Having re-activated him, Deputy Chairman Semenov of the First Chief Directorate and General Martynov of the Illegals 'S' Directorate would now expect a response.

For Sulecki, Warsaw suddenly beckoned frantically.

21

The black, rusting *Volga* saloon car carrying sealed orders from General Mironenko at Moscow Centre turned through the gates of the Polish Interior Ministry on Warsaw's Rakowiecka Street just after midday on Tuesday.

For the Polish military guards, the arrival of a car with Soviet number plates was just one of dozens of daily courier runs between the Soviet Embassy and the Ministry. They allowed the KGB driver to walk unchallenged into the warren of lofty corridors and up to·a third floor office. Inside sat General Yevgenni Klimanov, an overweight, pear-shaped KGB officer who was the eyes, ears and mouthpiece in Warsaw of the First Chief Directorate's Eleventh Department.

Moscow put the highest priority on close liaison with the security services of its fraternal partners. As Eleventh Department's resident liaison officer in Warsaw, General Klimanov was normally based at the Soviet embassy on Belvederska Street. But during final preparations for martial law, Moscow Centre had commandeered space inside the Polish Interior Ministry. KGB headquarters at Dzerzhinsky Square had insisted it must know at first hand the fullest detail of what was happening at the Polish Interior Ministry during the State of Emergency.

Klimanov sat behind a cluttered desk, his tiny round spectacles balanced precariously above his puffy nose and cheeks as he read General Mironenko's cable from Moscow. The text was unsigned, but reference codes confirmed it came from the highest ranks. It ordered Klimanov to discover confidentially and within four hours the present whereabouts of someone described as 'A. Sulecki, a Polish citizen, last known to be living at an apartment block on Gornoslaska Street in Warsaw and possibly now interned'. As was normally the case, there was no clue as to why Moscow Centre wanted the information, but Klimanov knew that an order to him personally meant the matter was of the utmost delicacy.

The KGB general swept his fingers through his silver hair and ordered his adjutant to plough through the voluminous copies of Polish internment records which had been delivered to him twice daily by the Polish security forces since Sunday morning. Then he summoned his Soviet driver, grabbed his fur-lined coat and drove across the city in a dirty-grey *Volga* fitted with Polish number plates for undercover work.

It took eight minutes to reach Sulecki's apartment block on Gornoslaska Street. General Klimanov took the lift to the fifteenth floor and forced open the apartment door which had been splintered by the SB crowbar and patched up by Magda Gajewska's mother. From the unmade bed, stale food and upturned furniture he deduced that the apartment had not been occupied in the last few days, and that the occupants had probably been forced to leave in a hurry. Time was pressing, so Klimanov made a rapid search among the piles of Solidarity literature. To official Soviet eyes it was all evidence of subversion but gave no specific clue as to the present whereabouts of 'A. Sulecki'.

Klimanov drove back to the Interior Ministry. His adjutant greeted him with details confirming the internment of A. Sulecki early on Sunday morning. But Sulecki's current whereabouts were not documented. By four o'clock that Tuesday afternoon – the deadline set by Moscow – General Klimanov had drafted what he knew to be a skimpy and unsatisfactory reply, but he still sent it by car to the KGB's secure communications centre at the Soviet Embassy.

By this time, however, General Klimanov's enquiries had also alerted the Polish security apparatus. At three o'clock, General Wladek Siwinski, one of Poland's six Deputy Interior Ministers, had received information from two plainclothes SB officers who had been on routine surveillance duty outside an apartment block near the Vistula river awaiting the return home of an escaped internee named Sulecki. At one o'clock that afternoon, the two officers had seen a grey *Volga* draw up. The only passenger was seen to get out and walk into the building. One SB officer tracked the unidentified man to the fifteenth floor where he was seen breaking into the apartment once occupied by Sulecki. The man had stayed inside for fifteen minutes before returning to the *Volga*. The SB officers then tailed the car, which, to their astonishment drove straight into the Interior Ministry.

They cross-checked the numberplate on the *Volga* and discovered that the passenger was General Yevgenni Klimanov, liaison officer in Warsaw for the security organs of the USSR.

Deputy Minister Siwinski was taken aback by the suggestion of high-level KGB interference in a routine Polish surveillance operation. What the hell had the KGB general been up to? What was Klimanov poking his nose into? And why was the KGB general so interested in someone called Sulecki, an internee who could not be a significant 'counter-revolutionary' because until today Siwinski had never heard of him?

As well as being Deputy Interior Minister the lean, balding Polish general was also the powerful head of the SB security police. A career policeman from the coal town of Bytom, and a Communist Party hardliner with strong Moscow connections since World War II, Wladek Siwinski had a reputation for using the harshest and most uncompromising tactics. For years he had maintained close, friendly working relationships with every KGB liaison officer posted to the Polish Interior Ministry, and his relations with Yevgenni Viktorovich Klimanov were no exception. But in the end Klimanov represented the interests of KGB Moscow Centre at Dzerzhinsky Square, not the interests of Polish security, which was why Siwinski did not pick up the phone and challenge him directly to explain today's behaviour. Instead Siwinski again telephoned the officer in the SB's Department 5 who had reported sighting General Klimanov at Gornoslaska Street

'I want that apartment taken apart,' Siwinski ordered. 'I'm not interested in the normal counter revolutionary papers and other Solidarity crap. There must be something more there, but I don't know what. I want you to supervise the search personally...'

Three hours later Siwinski's outside office buzzed through on the intercom. It was six o'clock. 'Deputy Minister! The head of Department 5 to see you.'

Siwinski ordered him in. The Lieutenant General in charge of the SB's surveillance department entered carrying a battered canvas bag. Siwinski cleared a place among the files piled high on his desk. The Lieutenant General laid down a weapon and a black metallic box with a tiny lightweight cable attached.

'Comrade Deputy Minister, in the ventilation duct above the corridor outside the apartment we discovered two items of interest. First this American-made high velocity Smith and Wesson revolver with fifty rounds of ammunition ... Secondly, and perhaps more significant, this small micro-chip, multi-channel radio transmitter/receiver also made in the United States.'

'Anything else?' asked Siwinski, showing no signs of surprise.

'No, nothing.'

'Thank you for your efforts.'

The Deputy Interior Minister signalled the Lieutenant General to leave. The evidence now laid out before him was damning. Whoever had hidden the equipment – presumably this character Sulecki – must have connections with the American security or intelligence services. Sulecki must be a Solidarity activist who was also backed by America and probably sponsored by the CIA. If so Sulecki must be a prime example of American efforts to destabilise Poland – American efforts which Soviet and Polish propaganda had long warned about. But what was KGB General Klimanov's connection with Sulecki? That was what bugged Siwinski. If the KGB suspected that Sulecki was a CIA hit man, then why, during a maximum security operation under martial law, had they not shared what they knew with Polish security?

The Deputy Interior Minister leaned from his chair, grasped an internal phone and waited for a response from his secretariat.

'Captain, I want the file on Sulecki. Interned 13 December, then escaped. First name Andrzej. Last known address Gornoslaska Street in Warsaw.'

22

By the afternoon of Tuesday the fifteenth Mrs Gajewska had still failed to trace her daughter Magda, despite queuing twice daily at the militia depot. Magda herself had shivered for three days at Olszynka camp in the forests east of Warsaw. Her face had become pale and drawn, and her once beautiful blonde hair was filthy and matted. Sitting on the floor and pacing the cell, she had become increasingly tormented as over and over again she weighed the behaviour of her lover Andrzej the previous Saturday night.

'Why?' she kept saying, '. . . Why? Why? Why?'

She had asked the question a million times since Sunday morning. Why had Andrzej not told her about the ZOMO assault on the Solidarity headquarters which he must have seen? Why had he withheld such news when he returned on Saturday night and crawled into bed alongside her? Why had her lover and confidant misled her?

The order to leave Olszynska came without warning that afternoon. The senior prison officer read from a clip board. 'M. Gajewska! You are leaving.'

Magda burst into tears. She hugged Anna, then Irena, then Renata. 'But why only me?' she enquired.

'Orders,' snapped the buxom guard impatiently.

Magda could hear other cell doors slamming open and other names being read out. She stared at her three colleagues. Was she going somewhere better or being shipped to somewhere worse. 'If I'm freed I'll contact your families. If I stay inside and you are freed, please do the same for me . . .'

They nodded. 'Of course. Goodbye Magda.' And within seconds Magda was being marched along the corridor with three internees from neighbouring cells. Each was well-known – Halina Sadowska the actress, Anka Pinkowska the poet and founder of KOR, and Teresa Jaworska the novelist. Magda, merely a Solidarity activist from the FSO car factory, felt honoured.

On board the *Nysa* van the women had to guess their route by looking through the skylight at the apartment blocks and tall buildings which they rattled past. They reckoned they were heading towards Warsaw's western suburbs and suddenly the growling rotors of Soviet-built helicopters confirmed it. This was Bemowok military airfield, out among the concrete apartment blocks of Chomiczowka. On city maps it was shown as lush green parkland, but the local residents knew otherwise. The four women died a thousand deaths. No one had ever heard of prisoners being shipped by helicopter. Were they going to be tortured and thrown to their deaths in the way American GIs had treated the Vietcong in Vietnam and the Soviets their rebel prisoners in Afghanistan?

The militia wagon halted and the side door slid open. 'Ladies,' said a smiling army colonel. 'I apologise for the wait and the delay. I hope you are not too uncomfortable in there. I have some chocolate and I am sure you need it. Share it among yourselves.' The officer handed them a bar of Hungarian chocolate. 'This way please. To the helicopter . . .'

The transformation in the official attitude took the women's breath away. Two conscripts in heavy greatcoats even carried their meagre possessions out across the tarmac. On board the camouflaged Mi-8 chopper the four women joined ten more internees who were mostly professional men and women.

'Miatek, what are you doing here? . . .' 'Tadek, where did they pick you up? . . .' 'Professor Witkowski, what a surprise!' Joyous shrieks echoed around the cabin until the thundering revs made conversation impossible.

By mid-evening the internees had arrived at a 'holiday camp' belonging to a factory in Jaworno near Katowice among the mining towns of Silesia. As a holiday home the camp was poor, but as a prison it was luxury. Without any explanation the internees were now being treated like government guests. It seemed that intellectuals like Magda were the privileged few who had been singled out for preferential treatment.

But Magda's new prison 'luxury' did not diminish her anguish. She had to discover the truth about her lover, Andrzej Sulecki.

23

It was Tuesday midday, and in Munich, Rybicki dithered. After working through his options he decided to call Tarnowski at Radio Free Europe. Without consulting Moscow Centre, the KGB captain was taking up Tarnowski's suggestion that he become a 'refugee source' for RFE at the Traiskirchen camp. He thought it would improve his cover in the West.

Rybicki dialled the radio station from a public telephone booth. The connection to Tarnowski took a few moments. Their conversation was brief with no hint of recognition, just the staccato six word message. 'This is Emil. Can we meet?' As agreed in the English Garden that morning they would meet at six o'clock in the Jasmine cafe.

That afternoon, as Rybicki dozed in his hotel room his bedside telephone rang unexpectedly. The shrill ringing alarmed the KGB captain because only Colonel Firyubin knew where Rybicki was. But as his heart raced Rybicki assured himself that it must only be a routine enquiry from the reception desk. He pulled his arm from under the duvet and fumbled for the receiver.

'Herr Heller?...' It was the hotel reception.

'*Ja*,' Rybicki mumbled.

'Sorry to bother you. It's front desk...' It was the voice of a man Rybicki assumed to be the manager. 'We have a small problem with your hotel registration, Herr Heller. I do apologise. It's just a formality, sir. The police have just called and asked us to check the number of your passport. The number we gave them does not seem to exist. They wonder if we logged it incorrectly in our registration book. Could I double check the numbers again with you?'

Suddenly Rybicki was wide awake, but on the phone

he still feigned drowsiness. He knew his cover story and forged Austrian passport would not survive interrogation by the BND, the *Bundesnachrichtendienst,* the West German intelligence service. '*Moment, bitte.* I've just been asleep. Give me a moment to wake up ... Er ... Do you really have to bother me now? Can't it wait?'

'I really am terribly sorry,' the manager repeated. 'Perhaps you would be good enough to come down to the desk when you can and just give us your passport for a few minutes. Then we can clear the matter up.'

Rybicki sighed ostentatiously. 'OK. I'll come down to see you when I get up. But it'll be an hour or two because I've been working and I need rest.'

'Thank you, sir.'

Rybicki dropped the telephone receiver back onto its mount, sprang out of bed, dressed quickly, then pushed the Solidarity documents and his few belongings into his canvas bag. Rapidly he cleared up the room, vacuuming it with his eyes just as the Balashikha training college had taught him. He pocketed the paper from the waste bin and picked up the visible grains of Munich mud which had dried on the carpet. Then he wiped the water glass, furniture, telephone and door handles to ensure there were no fingerprints when the police came to search the room. He scanned the street below: there was no sign of anyone loitering and no police car. But what about downstairs in the hotel lobby? He doubted police suspicions would have yet got that far.

The deep carpet on the landing outside Room 208 deadened the sound of Rybicki's departure. When he reached the ground floor, instead of turning right to the lobby he turned left and walked through two heavy fire doors into the back yard next to the restaurant.

Ten minutes after the manager's phone call 'Klaus Heller', the scruffy electrician from Austria, was turning south down Luisenstrasse and heading for Munich's Hauptbahnhof, a fifteen minute walk away. The neon street lamps picked out a man in leather cap, torn blue anorak, filthy woollen jacket and dirty faded jeans. But with so many Turkish *Gastarbeiter* in Munich no one took any notice of such a scruffy figure.

As Rybicki walked he weighed up the risks of the routes back to Austria. Pockets bulging with Deutschmarks and Austrian schillings meant he could affort a direct flight back to Vienna. But he was sure there would be individual passport checks at Munich and Vienna airports and German passport officials might have been alerted to look for the name and the Austrian passport. It was therefore a simple decision. His escape had to be by the direct Vienna express that evening where he hoped the border checks would be as cursory as they'd been on the train from Innsbruck yesterday.

At the station Rybicki bought an Austrian newspaper and propped himself against an upturned barrel outside a kiosk selling beer and wurst. It was just before six o'clock and the station announcer advised travellers that the 18.30 express to Innsbruck, Milan and Rome would leave from platform 10. Half past six? The announcement momentarily reminded Rybicki of his planned meeting with Tarnowski which should have been taking place at that moment in the Jasmine cafe. But Rybicki no longer cared about the grubby little exiled dissident from Radio Free Europe. 'Fuck him,' the KGB captain thought to himself, 'he'll have to stew. He's done what Moscow Centre wanted.' Rybicki poured his beer, sipped at the sagging froth, and dipped his white sausage in a curling blob of mustard on the cardboard plate. Names on the giant timetable board revolved high above him. 'Rosenheim, Traunstein, Freilassing, Vienna.'

Tomorrow Munich and Tarnowski would be no more than fading images in Rybicki's KGB career.

24

General Siwinski propped himself against his office
window and looked out at the decaying grey facades of
post-war apartment blocks on Warsaw's Rakowiecka
Street. The security file on Andrzej Sulecki contained
three closely-typed pages of computer notes from the
Polish Interior Ministry's National Security computer
in Gdynia. The details dated from Sulecki's childhood on
a farm in north-east Poland and had been revised several
times over the years. The eyes of the Deputy Interior
Minister scanned the most recent entries once again.

The latest print-out classified Sulecki with the letter
'N', which signified that he was considered a dangerous
threat to state security. His record at Ursus revealed his
dissident interests, but the details of his year at Solidarity's Warsaw headquarters shed little light on his
activities. But more intriguing to the SB general were
the mysterious gaps and unusual inconsistencies in the
records of Sulecki's earlier years. Where, for example,
were the full SB details about Sulecki's childhood on the
farm at Trzcianka near Bialystok? And why did Sulecki's
record highlight his competence rather than his ideological and reliability record at school? The Polish general
noted the dates, codes and official initials entered during
that period. Then he turned to the giant wall map of
Poland and pinpointed Trzcianka forty-five kilometres
north of Bialystok near the Soviet border. The nearest SB
and militia depot to Trzcianka was at Sokolka. Siwinski
turned to his militia adjutant.

'Captain ... Get me the MO Colonel in Sokolka near
Bialystok. I want him and no one else. If he's not there,
find him.'

The general stared through the window at a column of
military vehicles which growled through a thick cloud of

diesel fumes past the Interior Ministry. The phone rang and the general began scribbling.

'Yes? Name? Put him through ... Comrade Colonel Moszczenski? This is Deputy Interior Minister Siwinski. I'm personally checking details in a particularly important case. I have one query. The initials Z.K. occur in a set of criminal records dating from 1979 relating to a period spent by the suspect in Sokolka district. I'd like to know the name of the case officer.'

The militia colonel paused, 'I don't recognise the initials and I've worked at Sokolka for 21 years,' he told Siwinski hesitantly. 'Can you wait a moment? I'll check with my major. Or shall I call back?'

'I'll stay on the line.' As Siwinski waited for confirmation he scanned Sulecki's record yet again.

'No!' the colonel in Sokolka responded a minute later. 'The initials "Z.K." mean nothing. I can confirm that no one with those initials has worked here.'

General Siwinski persisted with other possibilities. 'What about "S.K.", or "S.F."?'

'No! We're a small rural depot. I know everyone. No one of those initials has ever been posted here.'

'Not even temporarily?'

'Any reports by officers posted here for a short time are, as you know, always counter-signed by permanent officers, Comrade General.'

'I see. Thank you very much.'

Siwinski crashed down the phone. His doubts about Sulecki seemed increasingly justified. If 'Z.K.' was a set of forged initials belonging to a non-existent militia officer then he must assume that the records of Sulecki's earlier life on the farm near Trzcianka had been doctored. If so, by whom? Apart from closely screened militia and SB personnel, who else had access to the Interior Ministry's vaults and computer? And who outside the Polish security forces knew enough to tamper with the complex procedures to forge records?

Despite circumstantial evidence from the revolver and the radio that Sulecki had a strong American connection, the Deputy Interior Minister had never been briefed about any CIA ability to penetrate the Gdynia national security computer. That meant there was a more frightening possibility. General Siwinski knew that only one organisation had unrestricted access to the state security computers in all countries of the Soviet Socialist alliance.

The KGB.

25

The wooden runners of the *kulig* swished between drifts of virgin snow and windblown ice. For six hours there had been no sign of the ZOMO, the militia or the army and it did not seem like war. Sulecki was experiencing winter in Poland at its most beautiful. There had been rare glimpses of movement from animals, and wolves occasionally howled menacingly among the trees, but essentially he had been alone with farmer Jan in an empty and breathtaking winter snowscape.

They sat alongside each other on tatty sheep skins and huddled in their heavy clothing, Jan holding his whip in his right hand as his left foot periodically pumped the primitive braking mechanism which dug a metal spoke deep into the snow. Without any sprung suspension on the *kulig*, each rut and snow hummock jarred against their spines and back.

The journey towards Warsaw had already taken longer than Jan predicted. They had travelled for three sessions of two hours. Between each they had taken half hour rests, sheltering in a deserted barn or forest while the gelding was fed from the hay piled at the rear of the sledge. By nightfall only the few last drops of *Bimber* helped both men withstand the punishing night temperatures as the sledge cut the image of a tiny, slow-moving dot on an enormous blue-white frozen carpet under a moon which was almost full.

The *kulig* reached Edward's modest farm just after seven o'clock that evening. As Jan and Sulecki stumbled into the kitchen unannounced, Edward and his wife were doubly surprised – firstly to see anyone, and secondly because Jan had managed to get there at all through the rumoured road blocks.

The four of them ate in their sweaty clothes alongside

132

the giant log stove in Edward's rambling kitchen which doubled as both living and sleeping quarters during the winter. Blood returned to the travellers' cheeks as they hungrily spooned up bowls of *krupnik*, a thick broth of barley, beef and vegetables. Soup was followed by huge slices of boiled carp, the seasonal fish delicacy which Edward had been saving for Christmas. But tonight's celebration took on a special importance: it might be the only time the two cousins met that winter. Edward had been unable to buy vodka so they drank moonshine which he kept in a secret cache under the floorboards. As the glasses clinked and the drink flowed the three men began confronting the problem of how to get Sulecki to Warsaw.

'One of our neighbours had to go to Warsaw this afternoon,' said Edward. 'His mother's been seriously ill since before martial law. I saw him just before you arrived. He got there – and he got back. He said there were hardly any patrols and he wasn't stopped until he got to the city boundary. He drove north from Otwock along the east bank of the Vistula. There's a big road block halfway up, just by the canal in Zbytki. A couple of APCs, a large military tent, jeeps and militia cars. Plenty of barbed wire rolled across the road and up over the dyke. My friend said they're building a permanent barrier and they'll be there some time.'

'So how did he get through?' Sulecki asked.

'Showed his documents, of course, and they were in order. Answered a lot of questions. You know the sort of thing. And he said it was the same coming back. He said there were road blocks, tents and concrete tank traps on the Lazienkowski and Poniatowski bridges across the Vistula... But that's the second line of checks and they don't take so much notice. You have to slow down: they point a Kalashnikov at you, glance inside the car if they can, and then just wave you through. They don't check your documents or even your name. It seems to be the same whichever bridge you go across...'

Sulecki stroked the brittle stubble on his chin which was still sore from the intense cold. 'Remember... I have no ID documents. Knowing that, would you still be willing to help me, Edward? Would you take the same risk with me in your car?'

There was no hesitation in Edward's reply. 'Of course. You've come as far as this and you can't go back now. Besides, you're a good friend of my cousin Jan...' Edward slapped Jan heartily on the back. 'We're all fighting the system and fighting the authorities. If we don't try to win, we never will.'

'Thank you, Edward...' Sulecki knew he should make a gesture in return. 'Your favour to me will use up most of your petrol ration. So when we get to Warsaw, I'll try to arrange to have your tank filled. I know a man who works at the petrol station on Wawelska Street just by the football stadium. He'll give you some petrol on the side if he knows you're a friend of mine.'

Edward nodded with appreciation as Sulecki refocussed on the trip ahead. 'Here's my suggestion. We'll leave here at three tomorrow afternoon... We'll stop just beyond the British Embassy Country Club on Romantyczna Street about a kilometre south of the roadblock. I'll get out and check that the road and the area around are all clear. Then I'll clamber up the dyke and down onto the Vistula river beach. It'll be after sunset by then so I can use the darkness as cover to get round the end of the barbed wire. In the meantime you drive on through, and I'll meet you again the other side. You can park behind the trees in the sailing club on the dyke. You know where I mean?'

Edward nodded. 'I'll do it,' he said with the fire of a challenge in his eyes. 'It's worth the risk, and I'm happy to play any games against those bastards.'

Their business was over, and they talked until three in the morning. That night the four of them slept in the kitchen wherever they collapsed from the effects of a fine dinner and excess *Bimber*. For a few hours they all forgot the pressures of martial law, even the KGB Lieutenant Colonel.

But throughout the *kulig* ride and their long evening

together Jan had listened and watched and made a mental note. He had come to distrust Sulecki.

And Sulecki knew it.

26

In the dark of Tuesday evening Bogdan swung open the allotment shed door and knocked the snow from his boots. It was just after seven o'clock, and the main radio news was due at half-past. Jurek sat wrapped in blankets preparing the next underground bulletin. He looked up from the typewriter.

'Did you hear that communique from Gdansk,' Bogdan asked breathlessly as he kicked the door closed. He flung his gloves and hat excitedly onto the table, spraying Jurek with loose snow. 'It's being broadcast on Radio Free Europe. The underground leaders in the shipyard want us to fight Jaruzelski and his army. Jesus Christ! Bujak and Krupinski want us to overthrow the regime!'

Jurek was as astonished as Bogdan by the order from Gdansk. 'They want us to fight T-55 tanks? But with what? Our secret plans were to ensure Solidarity's survival. We made no preparations for war. We have no arms, no guns, no explosives, no ammunition. So how do they expect us to fight? They're mad!'

Bogdan paced the shed and agreed. 'The military are already accusing Solidarity of hatching an armed plot. They claim they've found caches of arms: grenades, ammunition, explosives, steel bars, even an anti-tank shell. But when have any of us ever seen anything like that? Who in the union ever bought and kept such things so secretly? It's trumped-up propaganda.'

Both men's eyes were dark with exhaustion. Long hours of anxiety had sapped their energy, but the enthusiasm which drove them in the first hours of martial law had not evaporated.

'Anything more from Gdansk?' asked Jurek.

'The rumour is anything from forty-seven to sixty factories on strike, and conflicting rumours about

136

Walesa – that he's interned, dead, in hiding, held in a *dacha* near Warsaw, and even that he's negotiating with the Government... With telephones down and everywhere sealed off who knows who or what to believe? I don't.'

'They're picking everyone up,' said Bogdan. 'Even former prime minister Babiuch has been arrested with twenty-one other Party *apparatchiks* of various ranks.'

'But Jaruzelski's only doing it to save face,' said Jurek. 'He wants to give the impression of balance. But soon those old government cronies will all be free, because if they charge Babiuch they'll have to charge everyone in power. They're all corrupt and crooked.'

Bogdan took the small saucepan outside and scooped up fresh snow for boiling. 'They've broken up the occupation at the Swierczewski precision instruments factory. The workers blocked the entrance with a crane. They put up appeals for a strike demanding an end to martial law and the release of colleagues seized on Sunday. It didn't work. The ZOMO just bulldozed their way in. End of strike. End of occupation. And more Solidarity people arrested.'

Bogdan tipped instant coffee into a stained mug. 'Our network's getting smaller, Jurek. They're closing in.'

'I don't believe it. You must have some good news?'

Bodgan peeled off his top layer of clothing. 'I called in at St Anna's church. I met Father Bardecki.'

'You idiot!' snapped Jurek. 'Are you crazy? You know the SB are watching all the chuches. It's the first place people on the wanted list will go for help. The SB and militia have every church staked out. The goons are inside and outside recording and taking photographs. How do you know they didn't follow you?'

'I checked of course,' said Bogdan arrogantly, hurt that Jurek was insulting his intelligence. 'The risk was worth it.'

There was an uncomfortable silence full of mistrust. Bogdan broke the ice.

'Father Bardecki was in a desperate hurry. He was

collecting things to take to internees. I told him what we were doing – I know we can trust him. The Episcopate have set up an aid centre at St Martin's Church to organise help for internees. It's in the rooms off the church cloisters. They've begun drawing up lists of who's been detained and where they're being held. It's going to be a long job but they hope to have it done by Christmas. They've started to collect packages: food, cigarettes, clothes, toiletries, anything internees need in this terrible cold. And they're trying to arrange visits to camps. But that's a long way off yet. They want no publicity, just a line or two saying they exist so that people will call by to find out more.'

Jurek warmed the frozen ink in his biro and began details of the St Martin's operation for the next bulletin.

Bodgan poured the boiling water from the saucepan onto the coffee. He sat and sipped from the mug, both hands clutching it in an effort to get some heat into his numbed fingers. It was 7.30 and he turned up the radio.

In contrast to the earlier news on the Western radio stations, the army newsreaders of Polish Radio reported that the West was reacting with indifference to martial law.

'Bullshit,' snapped Bogdan. 'The BBC and RFE say there have been crisis meetings of NATO in Brussels, urgent discussions between Western Foreign Ministers and fears among international banks that Poland might soon default on its 27 billion dollar debt. There's also. . . .'

Suddenly Bogdan jumped to kill the radio. A floorboard creaked and both men held their breath. Someone was standing outside the allotment shed. There were no lights to show the shed was occupied. Bogdan feared their voices had betrayed their presence.

The footsteps crunched again, more hesitantly on the threshold of the shed this time. Then a gentle knocking on the door: five light taps. Outside, a hand tried the door handle. Then the shed door creaked open, and ice and loose snow blew off the architrave onto the floor.

'Bogdan, you there?' The door creaked open wider,

letting in the faint light from the street lamps. 'Bogdan, it's me, Sergiusz.'

Bodgan recognised the voice as that of Sergiusz Marwinski, a workmate at the Warsaw steelworks. Bogdan lunged forward, hauled Sergiusz into the shed, and pushed the door shut as fast as he could without slamming it.

'What the hell do you want? How did you know we were here?' Bodgan was furious that someone had discovered their hideout. He stood six inches from Sergiusz's face, his eyes blazing anger.

'It was a hunch,' Sergiusz replied calmly. 'When you were drunk one night a couple of months ago you told me you'd found a shed in these allotments. You didn't say why. But I put two and two together. I didn't know which one – I've been trying them all for the last hour.'

'And who the hell d'you think might have been watching you? What about all the footprints you'll have made in the snow?

'Don't worry, Bogdan,' said Sergiusz in a consoling tone. 'It's snowing again. There'll be a heavy fall tonight to cover my tracks, and by early morning no one will ever know.'

Jurek glared furiously at Bogdan. 'This was meant to be a secret hideout. Why couldn't you keep your bloody mouth shut?'

Sergiusz perched nervously on the edge of the rickety table alongside scattered sheets of unused photocopy paper, then he brushed melting snow from his thick greatcoat.

'Bogdan, you may be angry, but I know you'll forgive me. Your baby's well but Jola collapsed last night.'

Bogdan stiffened. 'How d'you know? How do you of all people know? You hardly know Jola.'

'Her brother Woytek's a mate of mine,' Sergiusz explained. 'We used to play football together in Zoliborz. He must have known you worked at the foundry with me, and he came to see me at home this morning because he was upset about Jola.'

139

Bogdan sat down heavily in the dog-eared armchair. 'You'd better tell me everything. How bad is she? What's wrong?'

Sergiusz unbuttoned his great coat. 'Woytek put it to me like this. Before all this blew up, Jola was used to you being away for long periods doing work for Solidarity. But under martial law she doesn't know where you are, or how to contact you. She's living on her nerves. She's got no idea whether you're dead or alive and she desperately needs to talk to you because she's worried sick about Miatek. Woytek said it was only by chance that he called round to see her just after she'd collapsed. He tried to get an ambulance, but with the phones down he had to walk the streets looking for one. It took an hour and a half and when it got to your apartment the orderlies said Miatek and Jola weren't ill enough for hospital treatment. So they walked out. They didn't even leave any sleeping pills to help her relax. You've got to try and make contact, Bogdan.'

Bogdan held his head in his hands as Sergiusz sipped a steaming mug of coffee. 'But I can't go and see her at home. The SB came for me on Saturday night. I'm on the internment list and I'm sure they're watching the apartment. A friend told me he passed the building the other day. There was a brown *Polonez* with two SB aerials in the car park outside and two plainclothes cops inside. I'm flattered that they think I'm so important.'

Jurek intervened with a solution. 'You must meet somewhere else; somewhere with plenty of people so you won't be too conspicuous.'

Both men considered the suggestion for a moment.

'What about the cafe at the junction of Marshalkowska and Krolewska?' said Sergiusz. 'It's a small cramped place halfway down, among the secondhand kiosks near the old bookshop.'

'I know it,' said Bogdan, 'but it's too public. Listen Sergiusz, go and see Jola. Tell her to leave the apartment at six o'clock sharp tomorrow evening. She'll have to leave Miatek with neighbours. Tell her she must walk

140

south down Marchlewskiego Street on the eastern side of the pavement, then on past the courthouse towards the Hala Mirowska. I'll watch her come out, check she's not being followed, then meet up with her among the shoppers outside the food hall when I'm sure everything's safe. Tell her she mustn't make any move towards me if she sees me.'

Sergiusz wrapped his red-and-white Solidarity scarf tightly around his neck then hid it under the turned-up collar of his great coat. 'Sounds fine to me. Woytek told me she didn't want any visitors. He said all contact must go through him. I'll give him the details. He was interested to know where you are, by the way. I said I didn't know. Shall I tell him?'

'No way,' snapped Jurek emphatically. 'The safety of too many people is at risk. And don't you dare tell anyone else either. You must forget everything you've seen here. Understand?'

'Six o'clock', Bogdan underlined, 'and tell Woytek to give Jola all my love. Say I miss her and that I can't wait for tomorrow.'

Bodgan felt the goose pimples sweep across his back then up his arms and neck. He had not forgotten the miserable state in which he had been forced to leave Jola, and he was still touched by guilt. As Sergiusz turned to the door Jurek's deep whispering voice cut through the fetid air. 'And Sergiusz,' he interrupted, 'don't ever show your face here again. Now piss off!'

Woytek's messenger left in silence.

27

By Wednesday morning Deputy Interior Minister Siwinski had two new priorities to add to the enormous security pressures of martial law. First he had to track down Sulecki to find out who on earth he was. Secondly he had to confront KGB General Klimanov about his apparent interest in Sulecki. Although the Polish secret policeman was determined to take the initiative it was the Soviet KGB officer who made the first contact.

'Ah! Comrade Wladek...!' Klimanov's telephone manner was courteous but insistent. 'May I have a moment of your time?'

The SB general's response to such a high ranking KGB officer always had to be positive. 'Yes of course! Come along to my office, Yevgenni Viktorovich,' Siwinski replied, speaking the fluent Russian he had perfected at staff college in Moscow twenty-six years earlier. It took four minutes for the KGB general to walk the length of the third-floor corridors to Siwinski's office. Klimanov sat down across the desk opposite his Polish counterpart.

'This visit is only what you might call an "informal call", Wladek,' he began in a conversational manner. 'It's off the record ... you know what I mean. As an old friend I just wanted to warn you that Moscow Centre is twitchy – very twitchy. They are watching everything here and they don't like what they see. Your crushing of the counter revolution is not as determined and successful as our comrade General Jaruzelski promised it would be.'

'Give us time, Yevgenni Viktorovich!' sniffed Siwinski. 'The state of war has been operating for just four days. In that time my SB and militia forces, and General Jaruzelski's defence forces, have brought a large percentage of this country under our total control. There is now no trouble or resistance in Warsaw and most other Polish cities. The subversive actions of the last sixteen months are over for good, I can assure you. . .'

The KGB general interrupted Siwinski in mid-flow. 'But what about Gdansk? Seven thousand workers are barricaded in the shipyard and threatening to blow it up. In the coalmines of Silesia 5,000 miners are refusing to leave their pits and 2,000 men are occupying the Katowice steelworks. Where is this total control you boast of?'

The Polish Deputy Interior Minister leaned forward to pick up a file of cables. He spoke confidently. 'Well, Yevgenni Viktorovich, your information is out of date. I have good news for you. Let me go through some of those places Moscow Centre is so worried about.' Siwinski opened his file. 'First Gdansk. By dawn this morning the army and security forces had crushed the gates of the Lenin shipyard, broken up the workers' sit-in and occupied the premises. Several hundred deviants were expelled from the yard and forced to run a gauntlet of stones and missiles thrown by loyal members of the shipyard workforce. Crowds outside were dispersed using tear gas. Tanks and heavy armour have taken up defensive positions and the shipyard management have taken control again under military supervision.'

'We'll see if it lasts . . .' the KGB general broke in sarcastically.

'As for Silesia . . .' Siwinski read another telex and pointedly ignored Klimanov's remark, ' . . . the occupation of the Lenin steelworks in Krakow was ended peacefully last night. The Wujek mine is now under siege. None of the miners will escape.'

But the KGB general would not be hoodwinked. 'And what about the occupations at the Piast and Ziemowit mines . . .?' Klimanov snapped back.

'I assure you our competent defence and security organs are working with all speed to end such resistance. We don't envisage prolonged problems.'

But Siwinski's bland reassurances fell on deaf Soviet ears. 'The fact is that as you yourself have just confirmed, Comrade Wladek, there remains trouble, and Moscow

Centre is not pleased. Your forces must be ruthless and uncompromising to eliminate all threats to socialism in Poland. If you and your colleagues fail ... well ... I need not elaborate on the consequences.'

Siwinski calmly plucked another cheap Polish cigarette from a crumpled packet in the breast-pocket of his shirt, but the KGB general had not finished. 'One other question, Wladek. What's the latest count of internees?'

Siwinski leaned forward and rummaged through another file. 'At 17.00 hours last night the figure was three thousand eight hundred and sixty. It will be slightly higher today after overnight detentions.'

'But how many suspects are still at large and yet to be captured: thousands?'

Siwinski resented Klimanov's implied criticism of Polish failure. 'Not thousands, perhaps two or three hundred.' He sat back in his chair. 'You're a professional policeman, Yevgenni Viktorovich. You know every big operation takes time and manpower. And you know that we'll get them all.' Siwinski paused and drew heavily on his cigarette. He saw a chance to find out what Klimanov knew of the mysterious Sulecki. 'But let me ask you something, Comrade General. Are there any names on our internment lists for which Moscow Centre expects what one might call *special* attention?'

The question seemed to strike no particular chord with Klimanov. 'No! They're all shit-stirring counter revolutionaries, and they all deserve the harshest treatment and conditions. And as you know, in due course Moscow Centre will expect the leaders to face trial as criminals.'

Siwinski tried again. 'Are there any names which you personally say must have the harshest treatment?'

'Walesa. Lis. Bujak. Kuron. Jaworski. Geremek. All the big fish, of course – but you know who they are. You have all their criminal records.'

'And Sulecki? ... Andrzej Sulecki?'

Siwinski cast the bait. He waited for the KGB general to bite.

'Who? ... Sulecki? ... Who's he?' replied Klimanov

innocently. Siwinski knew he could never confront the Russian directly about his appearance at Sulecki's apartment the day before, but he made certain he sounded surprised by Klimanov's negative response.

'I was sure you'd know the name, Yevgenni Viktorovich,' he said in mock astonishment. 'Sulecki is a real prize. My officers searched his apartment yesterday and discovered piles of subversive literature. In a ventilation duct in the lobby outside they also found an American weapon, fifty American-made high-velocity bullets and an American mini-radio with the ability to receive and transmit. This is evidence of contact with American influences, and we conclude that must mean the CIA ...'

Siwinski tossed the three page computer printout of Sulecki's background across his desk to Klimanov.

'This is Sulecki's record from the computer in Gdynia. Most of it's been checked and significant parts before 1979 are false. Sulecki never lived on a farm at Trzcianka, and he did not spend his childhood there. Neither did he work there before coming to the Ursus tractor factory in Warsaw in 1979. Our enquiries lead us to suspect that the computer has been doctored by an unauthorised outsider and that Sulecki is not who these records say he is.'

Klimanov examined the paperwork. As he knew nothing about Sulecki – apart from the fact that Moscow Centre had sent a cable expressing interest in him – his response had to be vague and suitably diplomatic. 'So if Sulecki is not who the records say he is, who is he then? Where did he come from? And where is he now?'

Klimanov's question surprised the Polish Deputy Interior minister. All along he had assumed that having been at Sulecki's apartment yesterday the KGB general must know more than he was letting on now.

'We don't know, Yevgenni Viktorovich. He was interned on Sunday morning, but while being transferred to another camp the prison wagon carrying him was involved in a road accident. This dangerous criminal escaped and now we have no trace of him.'

Klimanov already knew about Sulecki's internment,

but he made a mental note about the escape so he could cable the new information to Department Eleven at Moscow Centre as soon as his meeting with Siwinski was over. 'And what efforts are you making to find Sulecki?' Klimanov added.

'Every effort, of course. But in this state of war there are limits to our resources, so you must realise that we do have other priorities as well. But we have had round-the-clock surveillance on Sulecki's apartment on Gornoslaska Street in case he returns...'

The Polish general had taken as many risks with his Soviet counterpart as he dared. Having turned the knife, he paused, watching Klimanov realise that Siwinski's surveillance team must have seen him entering Sulecki's apartment the previous day. For the first time the Polish SB general detected a hint of discomfiture in the KGB general. Klimanov began to wonder whether Siwinski had set him up.

Klimanov stood up, half leant across the desk towards his old colleague and said: 'This Sulecki affair, whatever it is, is clearly an internal Polish matter. But you should not underestimate the wrath of your fraternal colleagues in Moscow should you allow such a damaging CIA plot to succeed.'

Siwinski stiffened and clenched his teeth. After the KGB general's frosty departure, he took up his favourite position by the window and stared down at two militia APC's thundering through the slush on Rakowiecka Street. Then after a couple of minutes he returned to his desk and began sketching a flow chart of links in the Sulecki case.

The probability of Sulecki being an undercover Polish operative for the CIA seemed clear. But why did the KGB have such a special interest in him, and why had Klimanov refused to acknowledge this interest? An alarming scenario began to germinate in Siwinski's mind. Could it be that his first assumptions had been wrong? Could it be that Sulecki worked not for the CIA but for the KGB? Was it conceivable that Sulecki might be an undercover KGB sleeper in Poland disguised by Moscow to be a CIA agent? And if so, what on earth was Moscow Centre up to? And why concoct such a convoluted strategy?

From his years of experience, Siwinski knew that every complex KGB security operation was always supported by enormous resources and levels of personnel. If that was true in Sulecki's case, then what Siwinski had discovered so far might only be the tip of a KGB master plan of enormous importance to Moscow Centre. The possible ramifications frightened even a policeman of General Siwinski's eminence and experience. As head of the Polish SB he wanted clear answers to straightforward questions. If Sulecki was just a Polish CIA agent then the course of action was clear: eliminate him. But if the KGB was behind Sulecki then Siwinski faced a terrible conflict between his duty to Poland and his duty to his supreme ideological masters at Dzerzhinsky Square in Moscow.

Siwinski feared that soon he must make his choice. It confronted him with an appalling dilemma.

28

By ten o'clock on Wednesday morning Jan was out in his
cousin Edward's frozen farmyard preparing the *kulig* and
gelding for the return journey to his farm near the Soviet
border. Both his departure and his farewell to Sulecki
were unemotional. Jan had rescued Sulecki and saved his
life yet they embraced only briefly, touching cheek to
cheek three times as was the Polish tradition. Within
a minute, Jan had mounted his *kulig* and disappeared
from Edward's tiny farmyard. The hunched figure with
the long whip trailing in the breeze did not bother to
wave to the three faces watching him through the kitchen
window.

Three hours later Jan was dead: a crushed, frozen
corpse, lying trapped in a mush of bloodied snow under
the upturned *kulig*. Sulecki had decided he could not risk
betrayal by the man who during the previous evening
had made clear his dislike for him. The KGB officer's
gratitude for being rescued two nights earlier was out-
weighed by the threat to his own security. So in the first
light of dawn, the Lieutenant Colonel had secretly sawn
through the runners of the sledge with a hacksaw blade.
But before his death, Jan had honoured his duty as
an informer by calling at a rural militia depot to
report both his suspicions and what he knew of Sulecki's
future plans.

It was three o'clock that afternoon when Sulecki and
Edward eventually left the farm in Edward's Polski *Fiat*
500 – a small, box-like, bubble of a car with scarcely
enough room for a tiny back seat. The two men sat
cramped and a little nervous for the slow grinding drive
to Warsaw. Despite the risk of being stopped by patrols
they kept to the main roads where the snow was packed
and conditions were better.

By five o'clock the sun had gone and the slush had frozen into lethal ruts which threw the tiny *Fiat* this way and that. They had passed the vandalised apartment blocks in the suburb of Otwock and were now on the southern outskirts of Warsaw approaching the first road-block. Five hundred meters short, Edward turned east off the road and into a copse of silver birch trees. The *Fiat* rattled as he negotiated the fresh snow on a farm track running parallel to the main road.

Halfway along, Edward stopped the car where it would be hidden between a haystack and wooden cabin. Sulecki donned his gloves, thick scarf and grubby hat. 'Wait for ten minutes after I've gone,' he told Edward. 'Then drive up to the road block.'

They synchronised their watches. It was twenty-five past five.

'Wait in the car park of the sailing club until a quarter past six', added Sulecki. 'If I haven't found you by then you must assume I'm in trouble. But don't try anything clever.'

The KGB Illegal heaved himself through a snowdrift then across a tiny wooden bridge over a frozen stream and up onto the dyke running the length of the Vistula. He slid down the slope on the river side. In front of him in the half-light of dusk lay the snow-covered sand flats and two hundred metres beyond he could see the outline of the Vistula, the blocks of ice moving slowly downstream towards his right. Beyond the river shone the orange glow of the southern suburbs of Warsaw and the red air-traffic warning lights on the towering chimneys of the Augustowka power station.

Sulecki paused, crouching on his haunches and breathing uncomfortably. After two days' internment, a brush with death and two days travelling, he was in terrible condition. His legs ached. His back had stiffened. But this was the kind of situation Moscow Centre had trained him for so he plundered his last reserves of energy and began slowly heading downstream, his eyes and his ears alert for the faintest hint that he was being watched. It

149

took him twenty minutes to scramble to the barbed wire barrier which rolled out from the dyke across the shore into the river. Sulecki paused. Still there was no sign of life. Then, from beyond the dyke, he heard a sudden confusion of voices and activity. He dropped to the sand. He waited for a rush of activity on top of the dyke then torch beams frantically trying to pick him out. They never came.

Sulecki waited two minutes. There was still a commotion beyond the dyke. He speculated that the guards must have found someone during a check, perhaps a courier carrying illegal Solidarity documents. The noise suggested there was a struggle.

Now was the time to take advantage of the unexpected diversion. Sulecki ran at right angles to the dyke and towards the river, out across the sandflats among the reeds and the small frozen pools. He felt exposed but could only hope that the darkness hid him. After four hundred metres the end of the barbed wire lay piled in a disorganised heap in the frozen, stagnant water at the edge of the Vistula. He leaped and hopped between the slow-moving blocks of ice at the river's edge. 'One ... two ... four ... eight ... nine.' Sulecki counted them under his breath like a child counting stepping stones. It took just thirty seconds to negotiate the ice floes around the end of the barbed wire. The cold and the anxiety seemed to stifle his breathing. 'Always breathe! Deep! In and out with purpose!' the KGB training officer at Balashikha always yelled at his recruits. 'Stop breathing and you starve the brain.'

A minute later Sulecki was running diagonally back towards the dyke and away from the northern edge of the barbed wire. Was his silhouette visible against the lights of the apartment blocks beyond the dyke? Surely yes. His legs began to tire. He faltered but managed to reach the shadows in the lee of the dyke. He checked his watch: it was twenty to six. He had made it, just. He staggered to the *Fiat* which was hidden as planned behind the ice cream kiosk in the car park of the sailing club.

Edward greeted Sulecki coolly. 'The militia officer at the checkpoint knew everything, Andrzej. He knew I was coming. He'd been expecting me for some hours. They knew the car. They had the number. They even threw a few details of my Solidarity activity at me. I couldn't believe it ...'

Edward steered the *Fiat* onto the road along the east bank of the Vistula and they headed north 'And they mentioned you, Andrzej,' he added ominously.

'Mentioned me?'

Sulecki was visibly shaken.

'By name? It's not possible.' The KGB Lieutenant Colonel swung his head towards Edward in disbelief.

'I was only saved when a *Lada* reached the road block. There were six people on board. It was bad enough for the car to be overloaded. But to be overloaded and have a driver who's pissed out of his brain is a double crime. So the militia forgot all about me and a young army conscript waved me through. It was a close call, but remember Andrzej, they knew ... they knew.'

Edward was shaken by the close call. He drove in silence under the spindly concrete arches of the new Lazienkowski bridge. Traffic was light, and as they approached the roundabout next to Warsaw's main sports stadium he spoke again, this time thoughtfully.

'How could they know? Who could have told them? Only four of us knew. Me and you, Jan and Yvonna.'

'What about Jan? Do you trust your cousin?' asked Sulecki pointedly. 'Are you sure he's not a part-time wire – an informer bought off in return for some favour or other?'

'Impossible,' snapped Edward outraged by such a suggestion. 'Jan has always been one of the best. He let his farm go so that he could devote himself fulltime to Solidarity.'

'Unless the militia or SB paid him so well that he didn't mind if his farm went to ruin ...' Sulecki intervened with a devilish tone.

'Andrzej! If he was a spook would he have hidden

you? Wouldn't he have handed you over to the militia straightaway?'

Sulecki had an answer. 'But there again, why was he so confident about being out with me on the *kulig* in the early hours during curfew?'

'Crap,' said Edward decisively. 'Crap', he repeated.

At the city end of the Poniatowski bridge the army conscripts standing by their camouflaged tents and rusting braziers waved the *Fiat* through the tank traps and barbed wire unchecked. After four days away from Warsaw, Sulecki was struck how the tanks, APC's, AK-47's and steel helmets, had become moulded into the contours of city life.

'Turn right up Marshalkowska, then right again. I'll get out by the Centrum department store,' ordered Sulecki. 'I can melt into the rush-hour crowds.'

The atmosphere between Sulecki and Edward had turned as chill as the weather. Edward nodded silently, leaving Sulecki to speak. 'I apologise if I upset you, Edward. Think whatever you want, but remember I'm grateful to Jan for saving my life *and* to you for taking risks to bring me here.'

For a rare moment this was not the voice of a KGB officer, but the human side of Sulecki, the toolmaker's son from Grodno.

Edward eased the *Fiat* against the pavement in Widok Street just as Sulecki requested. They waited for a six-man army patrol with fixed bayonets to walk slowly past, then Sulecki eased his body from the seat, crouched through the doorframe and shook Edward's hand. 'There's only one other possibility to explain what happened at the roadblock. Your farmhouse must be bugged, and they listen all the time.'

Edward shivered. He wasn't important enough for such costly electronic surveillance and Sulecki knew it. 'They watch everyone', added Sulecki, 'not just the big fish. So for the sake of Solidarity, be careful.'

Sulecki forgot his original promise to buy Edward petrol. He slammed the door, and limped away towards the shuttered hot-dog kiosk opposite the Palace of Culture.

It was six o'clock, and the KGB Lieutenant Colonel moulded unobtrusively into the crowd of sombre-faced Christmas shoppers.

29

General Klimanov's 'Maximum Priority' cable from Warsaw reached the Eleventh Department at KGB Moscow Centre late that Wednesday afternoon. When it arrived, General Mironenko, the head of Department 11 was at Dzerzhinsky Square headquarters in the city centre receiving a delegation from the *Khad*, the Afghan secret police.

Within twenty minutes of being told of the cable's arrival, Mironenko had made his apologies and been whisked by high-speed KGB *Zil* limousine to the First Chief Directorate building in the south-western suburbs where he personally witnessed the decoding of the message. Only then did Mironenko agree to forward the text to Semenov, head of the First Chief Directorate, who then arranged a secure telephone conference of the four senior generals involved in *Amber Monkey* – himself and Mironenko in their offices at the First Directorate, Martynov at Dzerzhinsky Square, and Zuyenko by radio telephone to his *Zil* parked at the VIP area at the south side of Vnukovo airport outside Moscow.

'Comrade Generals!' Semenov began, 'I've brought you together because I've received a cable from our liaison officer in Warsaw. You'll remember Comrade Klimanov reported yesterday that he had discovered no details of Sulecki's whereabouts. Well, this morning he's reported a meeting he had with Polish Deputy Interior Minister Siwinski. Klimanov says the SB general confirmed new details about Comrade Sulecki. I can now report that our Lieutenant Colonel is free. He escaped from internment and is on the run from the Polish security forces. That is the good news ... But of great concern to all of us must be the additional information which General Klimanov says the SB have about Sulecki.'

Semenov reported to his generals the SB's discovery of Sulecki's American weapons and radio transmitter, and how they had also deduced that Sulecki's computer records had been forged.

'As a result,' Semenov continued, 'our two-year investment in Sulecki's deep cover as an underground Solidarity activist may be on the point of being blown. What Comrade Klimanov has discovered in Warsaw vindicates all our planning: the SB think our Comrade Lieutenant Colonel is a CIA agent just as we intended. On the other hand, as a suspected CIA spy he could now be shot. Sulecki must be warned of this new danger. He must avoid re-arrest at all costs.'

General Zuyenko swore. 'Damn those ruddy Poles!' General Martynov, head of the Illegals 'S' Directorate, tried to address the danger to Sulecki. 'The question is how do we warn him? As the SB have seized his radio receiver-transmitter we can only hope he will follow the operational rules and meet our back-up courier, Comrade Major Petrovsky, in Warsaw.'

Semenov interrupted. 'Is Petrovsky on-station yet?'

'I have no reason to think otherwise,' Martynov assured Semenov.

'Petrovsky has a radio?'

'Affirmative, Comrade General, but only a receiver.'

'So what do you suggest?'

'A coded sound loop on Sulecki's dedicated KGB frequency so that when he eventually tunes to his frequency we'll be sure he receives our warning.'

'I have one other critical question, comrades,' said Semenov. 'Does Klimanov's new information constitute such a grave threat to *Amber Monkey* that we should consider abandoning the whole operation?'

Semenov was flying a provocative kite to test the response of his colleagues. 'Does Sulecki sit tight or should he be ordered out of Poland? If so does he come to Moscow or go somewhere else? And if Sulecki leaves Poland do we have a substitute Illegal who could take over *Amber Monkey*?'

As head of 'S' Directorate, General Martynov had responsibility for all Illegals. 'I reject that,' he said determinedly. 'There is no replacement for either Sulecki's experience, operational calibre or underground cover in the Solidarity network.'

'What about pulling him out of Poland until the heat dies down?' asked Semenov.

Again Martynov resisted such an idea. 'Why leave Poland, when his target, Jaruzelski, is sitting right there in Warsaw? What's the point?'

Semenov accepted Martynov's argument. 'I suggest we tell Sulecki to use his ingenuity. He must find his own way to lie low until the four of us agree it is safe for *Amber Monkey* to enter its final phase.'

General Mironenko, responsible for liaison with the security services of communist countries, was concerned by such a prospect. 'We must be more specific about what we expect of him. There must be no ambiguities.'

The capabilities of 'S' Directorate were being challenged but General Martynov would not entertain such doubts about his agent. 'Lieutenant Colonel Sulecki has years of operational experience. He is one of our most resouceful operators. He has been taught to work through all possibilities on the ground in Poland, and that is what he will do. He doesn't need us breathing down his neck and checking his every move. Trust him!'

None of the generals could reject such an expression of confidence in Sulecki by the senior KGB officer who knew him best.

'Strategy approved, Comrade Generals?' asked Semenov impatiently.

'Approved!' chorused the other three voices down their respective telephone lines.

'Vasili Pavlovich! Spare no effort to contact Sulecki. No effort at all.'

30

Bogdan's parting words to Jurek at the allotment shed were to expect him back by midnight.

It was now getting on for six o'clock. As Bogdan strode up Juliana Marchlewskiego Street feeling vulnerable and exposed, he was surprised by what he saw. Life in Warsaw seemed to be continuing just as the Military Council had planned it would. In the shops people still haggled over shoddy goods and a few emaciated meat carcasses. They even argued with the military patrols. But the lined faces and blackened eyes betrayed the true hardships and private crises in each family: the missing workers who had never come home; the husbands, sons and daughters who had not been seen for several days, and the enquiries at militia depots which had continually gone unanswered.

As arranged, Bogdan arrived at the apartment building on Dzika Street at two minutes to six and hid across the road behind a parked truck. Four minutes later, the main steel-framed door to the apartment building crashed shut, and he watched Jola emerge wearing the heavy green coat for which she had queued for two whole days during a July heatwave. Bogdan hurried from shadow to shadow, keeping his distance, continually observing the area behind his wife and checking she was not being followed by the SB. So far there was nothing suspicious.

But Bogdan was puzzled. If Jola was as ill as Sergiusz had claimed, how could she walk so fast? Or had her 'serious illness' merely been some kind of excuse? Ahead on the pavement he heard the rasping boots of an army patrol. As they passed he feigned interest in a pensioner sitting on a stool selling firelighters. Then he set off after Jola who by now was two hundred metres ahead.

He pressed the pace across General Swierczewskiego

Avenue and past the City courthouse, and by a quarter past six they had both reached the Hala Mirowska, the giant food and market hall. Jola walked more slowly now as if she knew she had to allow Bogdan to catch up. The Christmas crowds began thinning as street vendors loaded their trucks, and peasants returned their highly priced chickens, geese and vegetables to the baskets and sacks in which they had been brought from remote country villages that morning. Jola stood in the shadow of the cast iron awning at the entrance to the foodhall. She was a lone, sad figure stamping her feet to keep warm. Bogdan paused twenty metres away and surveyed the wide concourse. He bent down as if to examine the soles of his boots, then he rotated his eyes around the pavement, first to the left, then to the right. Once, twice, then a third time for absolute assurance.

Only when he felt there was no threat did Bogdan stand up and edge towards Jola. Now he could clearly see her drained, pale face. With no make-up the deep furrows stood out starkly. She looked ten years older than her twenty-seven years, but she still retained her beauty. They stood a step apart, the closest for five days.

'Darling Jola,' Bogdan whispered. 'I'm right here, but don't kiss me. It's too dangerous.'

Jola smiled warmly, conscious that a more emotional greeting might betray them.

'How are you? How's little Miatek?' asked Bogdan.

She nodded slowly, as if to say they were fine.

'You look better than I expected. Have you recovered?'

Jola looked blankly at her husband.

'Somehow Sergiusz Marwinski from the steelworks found our secret hideout last night,' Bogdan continued. 'Jurek was with me. We were bloody furious because the location was meant to be a secret. Sergiusz told me your brother Woytek had called on him at home yesterday morning ...'

Jola nodded. Then as Bogdan detailed Woytek's message about her illness, her expression changed to one of incomprehension.

'Darling Bogusz! My brother told Sergiusz what?' Jola asked incredulously. 'I never told Woytek anything of the sort. I'm fine. Can't you see? So's Miatek. Life's not easy, but then it's the same for everyone. My mother's been round every day to look after Miatek while I go and queue for food. But not today, I didn't want anyone to know about this meeting. .... Why on earth did Woytek tell Sergiusz that extraordinary story?'

Around them city workmen swept rubbish and rotten food into piles. Bogdan's mind raced. He was sure he had not misunderstood Sergiusz who he trusted implicitly. Sergiusz was a brave, resourceful steelworker colleague who had taken many risks as a Solidarity activist. Bogdan stuttered, searching for words. 'Then if you're not ill, darling – and I can see you're not – why are you here?'

'Because Woytek told me you'd begun to crack up. He said the strain of avoiding the militia and army every day was getting to you. He said you felt terribly guilty about leaving us, and that you needed to see us – for comfort if nothing else. .... But I just don't understand. You look fine. You sound fine. What's wrong, Bogdan?'

There was a dreadful silence broken only by the clatter of stalls and the swishing of brooms. The same terrible fears dawned on both of them. Such was the horror of betrayal that neither of them had noticed the approach of two men who now stood menacingly on either side of them. They wore ordinary worker's clothes but their demeanour immediately confirmed who they were. They clamped their hands on Bogdan's upper arms and the steelworker winced with pain. 'Citizen Bogdan Misckewicz. By order of the Warsaw Militia commander under Article 42 of the State decree of December 12th ...'

Bogdan stared at Jola in horror.

'It was Woytek! Your brother!' he shrieked, his voice echoing under the awning of the food hall.

The SB man on the left quickly put his gloved hand across Bogdan's mouth. Bogdan watched as Jola's face turned grey and she gave the faint hint of a nod – an acknowledgement that Bogdan must be right about Woytek. The two SB men rapidly pulled Bogdan away trying not to create a public scene.

'But I never knew, darling,' Jola cried, desperate for Bogdan to know that she had no part in this terrible betrayal. 'I promise you! Woytek never told me! Never, darling! Trust me!' she yelled.

Bogdan believed her. He knew from her eyes that she was telling the truth. 'The bastard! Your brother is one of these men ... A spook ... a bloody SB man ...'

Again Bogdan was forcibly muzzled by the large, dirty hand of the SB officer who was dragging him backwards. The second SB man blew a whistle, and from a road alongside the food hall roared a rusting blue and white *Nysa* wagon. The van's sliding doors crashed open. The SB men threw Bogdan onto the fouled floor in the rear cell and locked him in. Bogdan hauled himself up to the tiny window. Through the grille he could still see Jola standing alone.

The van edged forward, its high-pitched horn wailing as it bumped across the pavement. In the dusky, meagre light of the street lamps Jola could just make out Bogdan's face at the window. Through the grime she saw his finger slowly make the sign of a cross. Then she saw him blow her a kiss as his face faded and the wagon picked up speed rattling away through the frozen slush.

31

By Wednesday evening it was four days since the SB had dragged Sulecki and Magda from her apartment. Now the undercover KGB officer knew he must try to return to collect his radio and revolver from their hiding place in the ventilation duct before he could proceed with the next part of *Amber Monkey*.

Sulecki's walk to Gornoslaska Street took longer than usual. He carried no ID card or work permit so he had to zig-zag down unlit side streets and back alleys to avoid the patrols and road blocks. When he reached the apartment block he lingered for several minutes next to the building site opposite, surveying the two rows of parked cars. Most were still hidden under several days of snow, and it was clear that few had been driven since the declaration of martial law on Sunday.

But one car stood out: a black *Volga* parked in a shadow beyond the building's entrance, the sweeping lines of its vulgar chrome trim picked out by the street lamp directly above. The double aerials at the rear betrayed its identity, as did the idling engine, the white plume of exhaust fumes and the silhouettes of two hunched figures in the front. Periodically Sulecki saw the tiny orange glow of burning cigarettes behind the windscreen, then a finger of blue smoke trickling out through a gap in the driver's window. It was clear the two men in the *Volga* were there to watch, wait, report and then pounce when their prey arrived.

Sulecki shifted from one leg to another to keep warm. The apartment building had only one entrance, and Sulecki did not dare to approach it. Even if the SB men were waiting for another resident in the block they might still demand to see his papers. And despite his agility and KGB training he could not clamber in through a side

161

window to the building either, not without a high risk of being seen.

Sulecki's priority was to avoid detection. He had only one option. He would have to abandon the shortwave radio and revolver and use other methods to contact Moscow Centre.

Sulecki retraced his zig-zag tracks around the snowy backstreets to the city centre. Even on this route he had to avoid army and militia patrols by darting into the courtyards or alleys of old buildings.

It took him forty-five minutes to reach Marshalkowska Street in the centre. He arrived outside the Forum Hotel as a young garlic seller folded his small steel fishing stool, and nearby a chestnut man doused his brazier by throwing handfuls of snow over the coals. Underneath the towering Palace of Culture, Sulecki wound his way through a fleet of buses parked on the vast expanse of Defilad Square. The stepped skyscraper had been Stalin's post-war gift to the Polish people. What many people disparagingly nicknamed 'Stalin's erection' now dominated Warsaw as a permanent, much-resented reminder of the Soviet Union's millions of roubles of 'fraternal assistance' since World War II. It was here on Defilad Square in 1956 that the first leader of Poland's new Communist party, Wladyslaw Gomulka, had addressed half a million people as he fought off a challenge to the communist system in many ways identical to the new challenge by Solidarity.

Tonight Soviet freight lorries stood in line along Defilad Square with a token militia guard at each end. Moscow Centre's standing order to Sulecki had been to make contact with a KGB officer who would be disguised as one of the lorry drivers. So the Lieutenant Colonel rapped on the window of a truck nearest the edge of the parking area. The half asleep, unshaven face of a driver scraped a hole in the frozen condensation inside the cab window. '*Da?*' he growled.

Sulecki did not reveal his true nationality. He motioned to the driver to open the door, so they could

162

talk. 'I am looking for Comrade Driver Petrovsky. D'you know him?' he asked in perfect Polish.

The Soviet driver did not understand. He shrugged and stroked his stubble with the shaking hands of a man sleeping off a vodka hangover. Sulecki repeated his request, this time speaking Russian with a fake, broken accent.

'Fuck off you Polish arsehole,' the driver swore as he slammed the door shut.

Sulecki stepped down from the running board and moved to the next cab where the reaction was the same. Each of the Russian drivers had been warned that Poland remained a dangerous country where counter-revolution was rife and where everyone's safety was threatened by a 'mass hooligan element'. Sulecki wondered how long he could continue this search without being spotted by one of the many militia patrols. He squeezed himself deftly between the trucks, crawling under the trailers or diving under the wheel axles to avoid being seen from the front. The growl of the refrigeration units drowned his footsteps. At the twenty-fifth lorry he tried, the driver opened the cab door dressed in a black leather jacket and cowboy-style shirt. He was a barrel of a man built like an ice-hockey goalkeeper: a bruising Goliath with a chubby, pock-marked face, a nose like squashed plasticine and a worker's close-cropped haircut. Sulecki continued to speak only Polish or broken Russian.

'I'm looking for Comrade Driver Petrovosky. D'you know him?'

This time the driver responded with a broad grin which exposed a collection of gold fillings. He grabbed Sulecki by the arm and pulled him in to the passenger seat alongside. 'Make yourself at home, Comrade. I'm pleased to see you and I know Moscow will be relieved. They were getting a bit agitated, to say the least.'

The driver dug his right hand into the left breast pocket of his jacket and with the dexterity of a magician flicked open his KGB ID card across his left palm. His name, major's rank and small photograph confirmed his identity and Sulecki acknowledged the details with a nod. He unbuttoned his anorak and removed his hat and gloves as his stomach turned with the clammy smell of sweat and body odours in the cab.

'Glad to see you,' said Sulecki. 'Or perhaps relieved is more the word I was looking for, Comrade Major.' Sulecki wiped away the melting icicles which had been clinging to his hair. From an old Nescafé tin on the bunk at the rear of the cab Petrovsky produced a bottle of *Stolichnaya* vodka drawn from the KGB's privilege shop before leaving Moscow. 'It's been on ice for two days, sir ... for you, of course.'

The Major's words were mocking, Soviet-style flattery, but he did have a vested interest in the *Stolichnaya* too.

'I know that under the new regulations it's forbidden to drink on duty, Comrade Colonel, but I'm sure that in these dreadful conditions you wouldn't say no. It'll help bring back some warmth.'

Sulecki smiled, the scabs on his frost-bitten lips opening raw. 'On such occasions, rules are sometimes made to be broken, Comrade Major. After all there's just me and you, I take it. No comrade agents from the Surveillance College in Leningrad tucked away in the trailer, I hope!'

They both chuckled as Petrovsky pulled two glasses from his shoulder bag and a package wrapped in newspaper. He balanced the glasses on the dashboard, and then opened the newspaper to reveal half a loaf of rye bread and a plastic box containing *zakuski*, beetroot salad, shining balls of black caviar on boiled eggs, a dozen pickled cucumbers and several herrings in brine. As Petrovoksy poured the vodka Sulecki tapped the back of his neck in the traditional Russian prelude to a toast.

'To the Operation,' said Sulecki.

'The Operation!' Petrovosky echoed.

Both men drained their glasses in one gulp. Petrovosky tore off a wedge of bread to absorb the alcohol and Sulecki sank his teeth into a slice of herring. 'What messages and information do you have, Comrade Major?' he asked.

'Very little. They just asked me to make contact with you, Comrade Colonel. I'm a one-way messenger. When I left they were shitting themselves to know where you were. They'd had no radio messages, and you hadn't responded to their activation order either.'

Sulecki was still eating, and in no hurry to respond. As Petrovosky took out a small pad of notepaper, Sulecki began his response.

'First, tell the Comrade General that I did receive the activation message broadcast through Radio Free Europe. Pass on to him my apologies. Tell him that there was a good reason for my inability to make immediate contact. Last Saturday night I was interned as an enemy of the Polish State. I eventually escaped and arrived in Warsaw this very evening. I returned to the apartment to try to retrieve my short-wave radio, revolver and ammunition, but there were SB officers outside the building on surveillance duty. I wasn't prepared to risk my Polish cover so I didn't try to go in. Instead I headed here to make the agreed rendezvous with you, Comrade.'

Petrovosky's shorthand held up well. 'Fine, Comrade Colonel. I've got all that.'

'My first priority is to get a replacement radio receiver-transmitter. Do you carry one which you could let me have, Comrade Major?'

'No, Comrade Colonel, all I have is the usual radio facility built into this truck.'

'Damn!' said Sulecki in frustration. 'What kind of facility?'

'Normally Moscow Centre uses this truck for sensitive long-distance surveillance runs through the NATO exercise areas in Western Europe. The agent-driver would only need to receive messages, not transmit them. So it only has a receiver.'

'Only standard wavebands and frequencies?'

'Yes, Comrade Colonel.' Petrovosky burrowed under the bunk, opened a plastic panel and removed a false bottom holding the first aid kit. 'The micro-receiver is in here. The aerial system is built into the supports and

165

bulkheads of the superstructure so it can't be detected.'

'Headphones?' asked Sulecki.

'An earpiece, Comrade Colonel.'

'How do you tune it?'

'It's digital. Just punch in the frequency and it holds automatically. What frequency do you want?'

Sulecki shook his head. He would never reveal the personalised frequency allocated to him by Moscow Centre for this operation. He waved Petrovosky away and stretched himself under the bunk, inserting the earpiece in his ear. He punched his personalised frequency on to the tuning pad and after eight seconds the signal steadied.

The monotonous voice of Moscow Centre's tape loop was distant but audible as it droned through an unending list of numbers grouped in fours. Any instruction would be in one of two codes which Sulecki had memorised before leaving Moscow in 1979. The female voice spoke slowly and precisely in short staccato bursts. Firstly he awaited the identifying code-word which confirmed that the message was for him. Then he began listing the numbers. The twenty-six word message took Moscow Centre four minutes to transmit and took Sulecki fifteen minutes to decode.

'*Your identity threatened*,' it read. '*Suspend operation temporarily. Take precautionary measures to protect existing cover. You have full authority for any self-generated contingency plans considered necessary ... You must re-base current location and reactivate operation within twelve weeks.*'

Sulecki de-tuned the radio so that Petrovosky would not discover his frequency, then he turned it off. Only when it was clear that Sulecki had finished did Petrovosky break his silence.

'Success, Comrade Colonel?'

Sulecki remained impassive. He scarcely nodded. 'Vodka!' he demanded imperiously as he burned the decoded message and kicked the ash out of the cab. From the lower level of vodka in the bottle Sulecki could see that Petrovoksy had been drinking while he was on the radio. The Major dribbled onto his notepad as Sulecki began to dictate.

'Having heard the radio message, I understand the new deadline and conditions. You should rely on me to succeed. Do not try to make contact. I have no radio receiver-transmitter, no revolver and no ammunition, and in the current circumstances it would be a high risk for me to carry any of these. But in due time I will expect you to arrange delivery and I will endeavour to inform you of my new whereabouts. Be assured I will uphold the expectations and traditions of Department 8 of Directorate 'S' in the First Chief Directorate of the KGB. Signed.

'Now Comrade Major, move your fat arse. It's Wednesday evening and I want that message in Moscow on the Chief Director's desk by Friday morning. Right? Did you get all that, Major? Answer me!'

The speed of the dictation had sobered Petrovosky a little. 'I have it all,' he assured Sulecki as he smiled benignly through a haze of *Stolichnaya*. 'I have every word, Comrade Colonel, and the operation will not be jeopardised. My written confirmation of our meeting will be in Moscow by Friday morning.'

Sulecki jumped down from his side of the cab, crawled under the trailer, emerged the other side and pulled open Petrovosky's door.

'Out you bastard! Out!' he yelled.

Sulecki had forgotten the Polish militia patrols prowling Defilad Square as he yanked the major's limp body violently from the seat. Although Petrovosky's drunkenness was typical of millions of Russians and thousands of KGB officers, it posed a threat to a highly sensitive operation.

Sulecki leaned forward and hand-whipped Petrovosky's face a dozen times. 'If you don't pull yourself together I'll report you. Consider your career at risk, Petrovosky. Be warned!'

The combination of threat and harsh temperatures seemed to have the desired effect. Petrovosky shook his head and rubbed his hands across his face.

'Re-read your notes to me,' ordered Sulecki.

Petrovosky took out the pad and slowly deciphered his shorthand. It was perfect.

'You're a bloody drunkard but a fine agent, Comrade Petrovosky,' said Sulecki. 'You like your drink and you like your work. I like your style. Now get in and piss off back to Moscow Centre!'

Sulecki pushed Petrovosky's backside into the cab and jumped down. 'And what about all the fraternal food aid you brought to Poland in the convoy?' he asked sarcastically.

Petrovosky looked down arrogantly and grinned. 'There's nothing in the trailer. We off-loaded the food in a Polish army barracks on our way here. I came in to Warsaw empty. These lorries are just for show: for Polish television.'

Petrovosky slammed the cab door shut and turned the ignition. The roar of the Soviet engine reverberated round Defilad Square. The major gave Sulecki a clenched fist sign for good luck and Sulecki acknowledged. As the KGB Illegal slipped away between the other Soviet trucks, the lorry's headlights conveniently blinded the Polish militia officers sitting in a van under the trees.

By the morning Petrovosky would be in the Soviet Union and Sulecki would be in hiding.

In the Solidarity underground.

32

Sulecki walked east through Warsaw's empty streets and faced up to the prospect of further prolonged isolation from Moscow. His brisk walk to the Square of the Three Crosses, halfway between the Communist Party headquarters and the Polish Parliament, took ten minutes. Even at this late hour traffic swirled round the one way system encircling the towering, golden dome of St Alexandra's Church. As cars, buses and army trucks roared past, Sulecki could hear the faint sound of the church organ and the congregation singing vespers. He took advantage of a break in the traffic to hurry across the road and up the dozen steps which led to the huge oak doors.

The large congregation had already begun drifting away after the eight o'clock mass, the grim-faced men replacing their hats and *kuczmas*, and the weepy, red-eyed women pocketing their rosaries. Sulecki pushed open the smaller side door and edged himself forward through the stream of worshippers. The smell of incense was overpowering and Sulecki, the atheist KGB agent, felt uncomfortable in this alien world of prayer and worship. He moved along the white stone walls towards the wooden confessional boxes where he joined a queue of elderly women, middle-aged office staff, and young workers with their wives. They all stood beneath a statue of the Virgin Mary, posies of fresh flowers strewn around her feet, weeping men and women kneeling in silent prayer in front of the small altars of the ante chapel.

Eventually it was Sulecki's turn. He stepped forward, brushed aside the crimson curtain and sat on a stool in the dark confessional. Through the carved oak grille he could see the eyes and mouth of the priest.

'May God be with you,' whispered the cleric as his index fingers made the sign of the cross in the half-dark.

'Please speak, my son.' The priest's voice was solemn and expectant: a sympathetic tone designed to encourage Sulecki to speak openly.

'Father, I have sinned.' Sulecki whispered with conviction. 'My name is Andrzej Sulecki. I lived in an apartment on Gornoslaska Street. I was a telex operator at the Solidarity Headquarters in Mokotowska Street.' Sulecki heard the priest's robes ruffle, and as he related details of his internment, escape and return to Warsaw he saw him open a small notebook and bend his head closer. 'I need help, father. I'm on the run. I have no documents, no home, no food. But I'm no criminal. I was a lowly worker for Solidarity. My ambition was to get the best for the people of Poland. Now the security forces have been ordered to punish me for it.'

Sulecki bowed his head and clasped his hands tightly. He feigned fear and anguish, and his voice quavered. 'I ask God's assistance. Who can help me and hide me? I want to help whatever is left of Solidarity. That's my duty, and my wish. Can you point me to them?'

The last of the congregation was leaving the church, the echoes of their footsteps breaking the silence outside the confessional. 'You said your name was Sulecki, Andrzej Sulecki? A telex operator at Mokotowska Street?' From the tone of the priest's voice Sulecki was sure the priest was taking more than a passing interest. 'My son, we in the church have a duty to help you. You are not the first to come to me.'

The priest was taking a risk. Without corroborating Sulecki's identity as a Solidarity worker he had openly voiced his support for Solidarity and the illegal underground. For Poland's Catholic Church, and for the priest personally, it was a dangerous gamble which played directly into the hands of the security forces.

'Brother Andrzej . . . go straight to St Martin's church in the old town. There Archbishop Glemp has set up an aid centre for internees . . . The authorities are, of course, offering no help to those interned.' There was bitterness in the priest's voice. 'At St Martin's, priests and vol-

170

untary workers are compiling lists of names of internees and where they're being kept. It's still in its early stages, but they are collecting food parcels and other comforts – and money too. The priests and nuns can maybe offer you shelter, or point you to someone who'll hide you.' The priest's voice quickened. 'Now go, my son. If I spend too long speaking to you the duty SB man behind you in the nave will get suspicious.'

'Thank you, father. I am indebted.' Both men made the sign of the cross, then Sulecki rose from his knees and left. In case he was being watched he dropped a 200 zloty note into the offertory box, bought a tiny wooden crucifix, then walked past a sidesman extinguishing candles and emerged from the church into a gentle night wind which blew fresh snow. Silently Sulecki congratulated himself. After the traumas of recent days the undercover KGB officer felt a renewed self assurance.

Half an hour later at St Martin's church, Father Janusz Bardecki bowed his head and swept his arm in an arc, inviting Sulecki to follow him through the velvet draught curtain into his office. The priest turned up the volume of the old radio perched on a shelf in his cluttered office, cupped his hand around his right ear, pointed to the ceiling and shrugged his shoulders to warn Sulecki that his study was probably bugged. Both men leaned towards each other, their foreheads almost touching. In a low whisper Sulecki related his story, and as he talked, a nun scurried in and out interrupting the conversation to give the priest freshly typed documents requiring his signature.

'You must be patient,' said Father Bardecki, his bald head shining under the desk lamp as his tired, bloodshot eyes stared at Sulecki over heavy, black-rimmed spectacles. 'Don't leave here tonight. There's a high chance you'll be picked up. We're watched all the time. Our information is that the SB want to break up our relief operation – but so far the Interior Ministry has ordered them to hold off because they want the church to promote calm and respect for the new laws. That's why you'll be safe here for the moment.'

Father Bardecki rose impatiently from behind his desk and began ushering Sulecki out. 'I have no more time to spend with you now – there are too many pressing cases to deal with. I've hardly slept for four days.... Follow me, please! We'll talk again later.'

The priest bustled across the cold flagstones, his cassock flowing around his ankles. Outside he caught the attention of a passing nun. 'Come with us, Sister Janina!' When the three were out of sight and ear shot of the two suspicious men in the reception area Father Bardecki turned to the nun. 'Now, Sister Janina. Please find this brave man a bed for the night.'

Sulecki followed her through a long, dimly-lit passage along one side of the cloisters. Stacked against the walls were boxes of aid addressed to different internment camps. Some was donated by Poles, the rest had just arrived in Poland from the West.

'All we can do is prepare these boxes at the moment,' said Sister Janina with a pained smile. 'We still can't deliver them. A committee from Archbishop Glemp's office is trying to visit the camps but Jaruzelski's security forces are worried we'll use visits for political purposes. We think we'll eventually convince them, but it'll take time. I just pray that people won't die before we reach them.'

Together Sulecki and Sister Janina climbed a narrow flight of curving stone stairs. As they reached a door in the attic the nun picked up a black rubber torch from a small alcove. She raised the heavy latch then slowly pushed back the oak door. Sister Janina swept the room with the torch and Sulecki counted half a dozen camp beds. He heard breathing and snoring and could see faces and tufts of ragged hair protruding from under the rag-tag of blankets and sleeping bags. Sister Janina pointed the torch at the last unoccupied camp bed behind the door.

'That's yours,' she whispered. 'It's not luxury. But it's better than nothing. Goodnight and sleep well.'

'Thank you, Sister,' said Sulecki.

The nun bowed her head gracefully and disappeared. The door squealed shut. In the dark Sulecki undressed and slipped naked between the sheets as he shivered and wriggled to shake off the cold. From outside across the narrow cobbled streets of the Old Town came the single toll of a muffled bell at St John's Cathedral. It was 1 a.m.

'Hello!'

The whispered greeting came from the bed crammed hard up against Sulecki's. 'What's your name?' said the anonymous voice.

'Andrzej Sulecki. What's yours?'

'Janusz Krupinski. Welcome, Andrzej! Welcome to the underground.'

33

Bogdan sat alone, shivering in the stinking, unheated interrogation room at the Mostowski Palace, the dreaded SB headquarters nicknamed the Lubyanka of Warsaw.

It was late evening and Bogdan had been left alone for several hours. He knew that isolation was the first stage of the SB's deadly game designed to break him. The single light bulb had been unlit when two SB men threw him into the cell at seven o'clock. He had tried to turn it on, but there was no switch. Instead, every thirty minutes the light suddenly went on and off, controlled from an outside switch by an unseen SB officer whose boots clunked threateningly up and down the corridor at regular intervals. Periodically in the courtyard below Bogdan heard vehicles roar in, then the sound of doors slamming and the screams of people being manhandled into the building.

'That bastard Woytek,' Bogdan kept mumbling to himself. How long had he been one of 'them'? Had he joined the SB willingly or under pressure? And more important, how long had he been in a position to betray Bogdan and his Solidarity colleagues, and what had he passed on?

Bogdan was already tormented by the need to warn Jurek. He had told Jurek he would return to the allotment shed by midnight. Would Jurek now realise the danger? And if he did, how could he know that Woytek was the traitor?

Alone, cold, and isolated Bogdan knew he was powerless to warn anyone. He began to fear his own weaknesses and confront the forbidding psychological wall which faced every political prisoner around the world. He stood up and began shuffling slowly around the tiny floor space.

He knew that if he did not conquer The Wall, then the SB would conquer him.

The moment curfew ended at 6 a.m., Jola left the apartment carrying Miatek across her chest in a sling. When she arrived at the Wilcza Street militia depot there was already a queue. As she moved forward towards the scruffy desk with its two large piles of paperwork, the militia lieutenant did not raise his head.

'Miskiewicz, Bogdan,' said Jola in a firm voice, her hand stroking the back of Miatek's sleeping head.

The lieutenant scanned down a ten page list of internees. 'Miskiewicz has not been detained. You'll have to look for him elsewhere.'

'But, Comrade lieutenant,' said Jola 'I know he was detained. I was with him when two SB men took him away in one of your "bitch" vans. It was at seven o'clock last night outside the Hala Mirowska on Marchlewskiego Street...' Jola leaned forward. 'I know, lieutenant. *I was there.*'

The lieutenant laid down his pen. He said nothing, but his eyes threatened everything. Jola recoiled, realising the danger of militia reprisals. 'I'll return tomorrow,' said Jola a touch defiantly.

As she walked away, an elderly woman grabbed Jola by the arm. 'Don't despair, my dear,' said Magda Gajewska's mother. 'They took my daughter on Sunday morning. I know they came, but this beast still denies it. Today's my fourth visit. I come here every morning and so must you. You must never give up.'

The two women smiled supportively at each other. Jola resolved to return again tomorrow and every day until they told her where Bogdan was.

Had he known, Bogdan would have been proud.

34

The first trams and buses of Thursday morning clanked through the frozen slush lying below the windows of the Mostowski Palace, the former aristocratic mansion which had once been the residence of a Tsarist police chief.

Bogdan dozed uncomfortably on the floor, half propped up against the wall and half slumped in the corner. He wrapped his arms around himself and pulled his winter clothes tight. A key turned loudly in the lock. The door swung open and Bogdan slid himself awkwardly up the flaking plaster until he sat bolt upright, his bloodshot eyes staring ahead.

The steelworker knew he was at his most vulnerable. Three SB officers wearing leather jackets and neatly-pressed corduroy trousers towered above him. The man Bogdan assumed to be a captain settled onto the lone rickety chair behind the tiny desk. He threw down Bogdan's identity card and registration papers, then added a file bulging with official paperwork. Bogdan got to his feet. Upside down, he could just read the capital letters handwritten in black felt pen.

'H.3823 – 9/80. MISCKIEWICZ, Bogdan.
PLACE OF WORK : HUTA WARSZAWA.'

The existence of the file was no surprise. Like every leading Solidarity activist, Bogdan assumed that since the birth of the union sixteen months earlier, the SB would have logged his activities, bugged his meetings, monitored his speeches and listened to his phone calls.

Bogdan remembered the advice and warnings from old dissident hands who had been interrogated frequently in the years before August 1980. The objective for any SB officer was always to disable his captive psychologically and if necessary physically. He will make you feel guilty

176

when you aren't. He will say almost nothing and want you to do all the talking. He will control your food, your light, your exercise – everything that happens to you. In time your powers of reasoning will fade, but you must yield nothing. The more you give the more he wants and expects. Stonewall. Say nothing that can be turned against you. Overcome your fear and you will win.

Bogdan steeled himself.

'We know everything. We know all about you ...'

It was the classic opening designed to give the false impression that the SB officer had interrogated Bogdan's friends and received from them valuable and com-promising information.

The SB officer spoke softly. 'How is Jola? I hope little Miatek is recovering. I'm sure they'll want to know where you are. We'll tell them nothing, of course. It's not my job to make things easier for you or your family. You are an enemy of the state. A counter-revolutionary. As a leader of that pig-shit organisation Solidarity you have undermined the established Socialist order and plotted the overthrow of the Polish United Workers Party. You will be punished accordingly.'

Behind him Bogdan could hear the heavy, erratic breathing of the two other SB men and could smell the stale alcohol on their breath. He found the silence between the captain's sentences more threatening than his words.

'Of course we knew that you were going to Jan and Grazina's engagement party last Saturday night.' The captain paused for effect. 'But at that time we decided not to bother with you. We knew you would be of more use to us after martial law started. If we'd caught you on Sunday, then under this internment order you'd have had some sort of political status. But now you're a crimi-nal, and we can put you away for a long time. Much tidier than internment, don't you think?'

It was crude intimidation, but Bogdan knew that not everything the captain claimed so confidently was true. Why had SB officers come to the apartment at one o'clock on Sunday morning if they knew he was at Jan and Grazina's party?

'Sergiusz told us everything. The hideout. Where it is. Who set it up. Where you got the money. Then there's the printing press, and which Western spy organisation it came from. And we also have copies of the bulletins you've been producing. Here!' The captain opened up the top cover of the file and produced a crumpled copy of *War Weekly No. 1*. 'You see there's no point trying to lie. You've committed a crime under the statutes of martial law.'

The captain produced another sheet of paper which was half-filled by closely typed lines with a militia stamp and signature at the bottom. Then he laid a cheap biro on top.

'Why not make things easy for yourself by confirming everything for us in writing, just as we have discussed.'

And then after the stick came the predictable carrot – the possibility for Bogdan to sell-out. 'You can expect a jail sentence of at least ten years imposed by a military court. As a criminal you will be crammed five to a cell with convicted murderers and rapists, and there'll be no remission. But by agreeing to cooperate, that ten year sentence could be reduced to three – maybe less if you tell us enough.'

Bogdan had already decided he would not confess or sign. Determined to stand by his decision, he waited for the next move, wearing his composure like a mask in the hope of not betraying his terror.

The captain tried again. 'Think of your family. We have evidence of complicity by your wife too . . .'

Bogdan knew that was a lie.

'If you don't sign we'll arrest her and fix it so she gets ten years too. That means, Citizen Miskiewicz, that your young son will have to spend the first ten years of his life in an orphanage. Could you endure that, knowing it was your stupidity and refusal to admit your crimes which destroyed your family?'

The captain advanced the paper and pen across the table again.

Bogdan shook his head. 'I am unable to sign any paper or cheap confession which will compromise and discredit me.' He stared straight ahead at a paint blemish on the wall behind the captain. As a result he did not see the captain's faint nod.

Hands clasped Bogdan's neck. They began shaking it violently from side to side and pressing hard on his windpipe. He gasped and tried to yell, but the noise became an anguished cough as he crumpled at the knees. From behind one SB man thrust his knee into the small of his back. His head jerked backwards as he jacknifed over the policeman's knee, a pair of SB hands still clasping his throat. The few seconds of torture seemed to last for hours. Then starved of oxygen, he fainted.

The two SB men hauled Bogdan up, his head gyrating like a rag doll. One of them opened the door and threw a bucket of freezing water over the prisoner. The shock revived him.

In satisfied silence the captain waited for Bogdan to compose himself, then slowly he laid out sheets of paper face down on the desk in front of him.

'Citizen Miskiewicz, your resistance is futile. I have here fifteen statements from colleagues of yours in the Solidarity union.' The captain turned over the sheets in quick succession. Each was covered with varying amounts of handwritten script in different styles.

'Marek Borowski, your assistant at the Warsaw steel-works office ... Jozef Morawiecki, senior printer at the Warsaw union headquarters ... Arkadiusz Sobanski. Do I have to go on?'

Bogdan, bedraggled and shivering, was still alert enough to reject the confessions as frauds. It was inconceivable that so many friends and union colleagues would have coincidentally betrayed him.

The captain walked slowly around the desk and stopped in front of Bogdan, their faces almost touching.

'You are scum. You are vermin. You are unworthy to

have the honour of Polish citizenship.' Saliva frothed in the corners of his mouth, and with each word he drew back his jowls and cheekbones. 'The price you will pay for your anti-state activities will be pain, humiliation and degradation. And at the end we'll tell your wife to pick up the emaciated body of her husband who has "mysteriously fallen from the top floor" of an apartment building. You must understand, Citizen Miskiewicz. We mean what we say and we do what we threaten. There is no way you can win.'

The two SB officers knew what their chief now expected of them, the captain did not have to give a signal.

The tall man with the build of a seventeen-stone boxer clamped his arm round Bogdan's neck, jerking his head and body viciously upwards until his feet left the ground. Bogdan screamed, every muscle and sinew stretched by his full body weight. What he was experiencing was as ghastly as death by hanging. His eyes closed and sounds around him blurred as the SB men tossed him high and he gasped for air.

As Bogdan slipped into semi-consciousness and the torture continued, the captain tidied his papers and walked out before turning into the corridor and flicking off the light switch. It was the sign for the two SB men to let Bogdan's body crash to the concrete. They straightened their jackets, walked out and slammed the door leaving Bogdan lying motionless on the cold, tiled floor.

35

It took three bursts of knocking to rouse Jola from her trance-like state. The distraction came as a welcome change to her chainsmoking and weeping. Was it a friend or relation at the door? Or someone with news of Bogdan? Jola did not consider any other possibility, but facing her in the doorway stood two swarthy men, one thin and badly shaven, the other small and stocky. They pushed their way in.

'Who are you? What do you want?' screamed Jola, shivering from fear.

'Just stand there and shut up, you bitch! We've come to check up on matters relating to certain criminal and subversive activities of your husband. I'm sure I don't have to explain.'

Jola stood frozen in shock as the men separated to each side of the room and went berserk. With giant sweeping movements they pulled books, files, boxes and papers from the shelves. They wrenched posters from the wall along with two prized paintings which had been wedding gifts. Against a background of Miatek's screams they kicked over the furniture and smashed pots of flowers. In the kitchen they hurled food against the wall and emptied onto the floor spices, preserves and dried mushrooms for which Jola had spent hours hunting or queueing. They ripped open soap powder sent specially from the West, then ransacked the chest of drawers, trampling clothes under their filthy snowboots.

Jola's restraint snapped. 'I want to see the Public Prosecutor's warrant. By law there must be a warrant for all searches!' The men ignored her.

Jola screamed, but was forcibly silenced by a large hand which was covered with warts. After five minutes the ransacking was over. 'Where is my husband?' yelled

Jola. 'You must know or you wouldn't be doing this dreadful thing.'

'Never heard of him,' taunted the taller man. The short man opened the door clutching a large sausage stolen from the kitchen. 'Remember ... You were out when this happened, and you never saw us. If you say anything, you can be sure we'll find out and then we'll be back to finish the job.'

The door slammed shut.

Jola shook her head slowly back and forth. She could not comprehend the horror of what she and Bogdan were having to endure.

36

Father Bardecki despaired.

'They won't even let archbishops and bishops travel freely between cities. They say the security risk is too great. Human rights? Dignity? The Polish military code shows no respect for such things.'

Father Bardecki stood among the aid packages piled like bricks in the library at St Martin's. After five days of martial law, he and his nuns were still struggling to discover the whereabouts of hundreds of people who had disappeared from the Warsaw area alone since Saturday night.

Upstairs in the attic, Andrzej Sulecki stroked his stubble and sipped steaming coffee as he sat wrapped in an eiderdown on the edge of a camp bed. After the frenzy of the last few days Sulecki valued the opportunity to take his time and restore his energies within the relative protection of the church.

'You are Andrzej Sulecki!' It was a statement, not a question from the man on the camp bed beside him. Sulecki was taken aback and did not reply. The voice was self-assured, the accent sharp and guttural, the pronunciation clipped and Teutonic.

'I heard Janusz, one of our comrades, talking to you when you arrived in the early hours. There are plenty of secrets in this room, but we try not to share them. It's too risky. Silence is our protection.'

Sulecki took another gulp of coffee. 'Thanks for your advice,' he said. 'We're going to be together for some time. You know my name. May I know yours?'

'Just call me Mirek.'

Sulecki stirred his coffee dregs, the spoon tinkling gently on the side of the glass beaker. 'You come from the north-west, from the German border region, somewhere near the Oder river ... I can tell by your voice ... I'll guess ... How about Pomorskie?'

Mirek nodded. 'You're right. I come from Szczecin, to be precise.'

Sulecki pushed the conversation forward as much as he dared. 'So what are you doing here in Warsaw, Mirek? Under martial law regulations you're meant to have returned to the Voivodship where you're registered.'

'I am a Solidarity courier. Last week union leaders in Szczecin knew something was about to happen. They didn't dare risk communicating by telex, so they sent me down with their plans for underground operations. I was meant to return after Saturday's National Commission meeting in Gdansk. But you know the rest, and I was trapped here in Warsaw. I sought refuge in the St Stanislaw Kostka church out in the Zoliborz district. The priest, Father Popieluszko, said it was too dangerous for me to stay, so he sent me here. He said there was more protection in the centre of Warsaw near the Cathedral and the Primate's palace. Now I'm waiting for a chance to leave. Until then I'm stuck ... And how about you, Andrzej? By your voice I can tell you come from the east. Maybe from near the Russian border?'

Sulecki knew he needed the confidence of underground activists like Mirek in order to perfect his cover as a committed union activist who harboured a deadly grudge against Poland's military leadership. So once again the KGB Lieutenant Colonel spun the long story of his fake background on a farm near Trczianka, his job at Ursus, his telex duties at Solidarity headquarters, then his internment and escape, his journey to Warsaw and his arrival at St Martin's.

As Sulecki talked he began to weigh up Mirek and formulate a strategy. '*Suspend operation temporarily,*' Moscow Centre had ordered him in its radio message. '*Take precautionary measures to protect existing cover. You have full authority for any self-generated contingency plans ... re-activate operation within twelve weeks.*'

'Szczecin,' thought Sulecki, 'Szczecin could be a first step towards fulfilling what Moscow has ordered. A first step to the West.'

37

It was Friday morning and Bogdan refused to die. Somehow he had survived the night in the freezing cell and now he lay curled up in the driest corner he could find. No SB officer had visited cell 3/65 since four o'clock on Thursday afternoon when the two thugs had returned drunk for a second session of torture. They had whipped his hands, arms and feet with truncheons; tried to suffocate him with a ZOMO gas mask which still reeked of tear gas; pummelled his weakening body with a sand bag; then left him unconscious slumped against the chair.

Now, thirteen hours later, at five o'clock in the dead of that early morning, the bitter cold woke Bogdan. His clothes were still damp, and pain shot without mercy through every corner of the steelworker's frame. As physical sensation returned, Bogdan felt as if his body had been crushed. He feared paralysis or semi-paralysis and thought his bones and organs had disintegrated. As the night became dawn he examined his body and was appalled by the extent of the bruises and subcutaneous blood clots scattered around his face, arms, legs and stomach. Without water or medical aid of any kind he was forced to pick the crusts of dried blood from his face and lick clean the open cuts and sores.

Concern about Jola, Miatek or Jurek faded, forced out by the pain. Only the hourly bleep of his quartz watch kept Bogdan in touch with reality. His emotions and needs were selfish. His ambitions were for the most basic: a drink of water and for relief. He no longer had the mental and physical resources to concern himself with matters of principle.

The SB captain arrived at nine o'clock sharp, and for the first time he was unaccompanied. It seemed he too had been up all night. His hair was straggly, his suit creased, and the knot of his tie was already loosened. Once again the captain brought with him the sheaf of files marked, 'Miskiewicz, B'. As he entered he had to step over Bogdan's legs which were sprawled across the floor. He strode towards the desk in a straight line of small, neat paces, and the staring whites of Bogdan's eyes followed his path as if locked on by radar.

'I hope you are well, Citizen Miskiewicz and had a comfortable night. Now, where were we?'

Instead of a 24-hour break it was as if the captain had merely been away for a brief moment to relieve himself.

'Citizen Miskiewicz. Let us continue our little discussion. I really don't think there are too many differences between us now. I can't help feeling we are now most certainly on the same wavelength.' The captain turned from examining the files to gaze out of the filthy windows. 'Since we spoke yesterday we have completed our enquiries. We know *all* about you: your illegal activities, the printing press and your incitement to people to protest in the streets.'

The captain paused to inhale on an imported Dunhill cigarette and Bogdan savoured the sweet, refined taste of the western tobacco.

'By the way, two colleagues of mine visited your wife yesterday. They tell me she is under a lot of strain and spent the whole ten-minute visit hiding behind the kitchen curtain. They say the apartment has suffered extensive damage but mysteriously your wife cannot tell us how it happened. She's obviously too frightened to tell us anything. And by the way, my comrades report that Miatek's health is getting worse and he screams continuously.'

Bogdan shivered with rage, fear and powerlessness at the thought of what Jola had gone through. But it still did not alter his defiance.

'So you can see there is only one way out. Cooperation. A signature now and you can minimise the suffering for you and your whole family.'

The captain turned and sat at the desk. For the first

time that morning he looked at Bogdan. 'Now ... these recent activities hardly fit with your excellent earlier work as a police informer, do they, Citizen Miskiewicz?'

Bogdan struggled to understand this new tack the captain was taking. What police informer? The SB captain had to be referring to someone else.

'Your job has always been to help us, not to organise opposition against us,' the captain continued. 'Why the change of heart, comrade? Why the deviation from your well established history of cooperation with the Polish security forces?'

The captain stared at Bogdan's blank face which in turn stared vacantly back at him. Bogdan began to work out what was happening, but still he felt too weak to speak and challenge the captain. This was the final ignominy: the SB frame-up from which he knew there would be no escape.

'I have the records here, comrade.' The captain fingered the papers in the file. 'Your police name is Piotr Glowacki. Here's the first receipt – for 1,000 zlotys in January 1980 for information you gave to Captain Warian.'

The captain held up a copy of the 'receipt' and Bogdan could see the signature which was a perfect forgery. The captain held up a second photocopy.

'How about this payment? 1,800 zlotys, for what's called here invaluable information about the establishment of the Solidarity branch at the Warsaw Steelworks: date September 1980.'

The captain held up his file and flicked through what were apparently twenty photocopies of receipts.

Bogdan slowly shook his head. 'No,' he groaned. 'It's a lie.' Each syllable exacted its toll in agony. Bogdan wanted to say so much, but he could formulate no words.

The captain ignored him. 'Imagine what would happen now,' he threatened, 'if at some time we were to show your friends these receipts? That would be the end of you Citizen Miskiewicz – the end of the Solidarity rat who betrayed his friends to the SB; the end of a man with a police pseudonym who had regularly told the SB everything his union colleagues had been planning.'

The captain stood over the desk and flicked through the pages with the tips of his fingers. 'Comrade, if this little lot is made public life would have no meaning to you in Poland. You might as well jump to your death from the Palace of Culture. . . . Or, of course, if you don't jump then we can always arrange it for you.' The captain drew arrogantly on another cigarette and shrugged.

Bogdan formulated his reply carefully. 'I deny it. I maintain my innocence.' The words stumbled painfully from his swollen mouth and lips.

The captain got up and walked to the door where he beckoned in a large, buxom woman carrying a tray loaded with bread, jam, butter, hot coffee and medicines. Because of Poland's shortages it was months since Bogdan had seen such luxuries, and what he saw must have come straight from the militia's privilege commissary. The captain fetched a second chair from the corridor, put it by the desk and gestured for Bogdan to sit on it. 'Now I am sure we can come to an agreement, can't we Citizen Miskiewicz?'

The big woman carefully lifted Bogdan onto the chair. 'I'm sure you'd like some coffee, but take it slowly . . . There are painkillers and antiseptic cream too. Take what you need, and take your time.'

Bogdan cursed such bribery. But he clutched the steaming beaker of coffee, stirred the thick black liquid and winced as the heat touched the sores in his mouth. Then with great concentration he steered the shaking fingers of his right hand towards the wedges of rye bread which were neatly laid on the plate in a fan-shape. After two days without food, the bread, butter, jam and coffee were like nectar.

The captain waited until the woman had left the cell, then he spoke. 'So! I think it's time to conclude our discussion. Let me sum up . . . There are two sides to any deal. This morning I've argued with my superiors on your behalf.' The captain lied. Bogdan knew it was an

189

old SB trick but he did not dare challenge him. 'I have saved you from a particularly unpleasant fate. But I expect something in return. In return for your freedom and return to good health I expect you to continue your work for Solidarity.'

The captain said *work* with a sneer and particular emphasis.

'From time to time you'll report to me. You will tell me what is happening, what is planned, and who in the underground has which responsibilities – just for our files, of course. I cannot honestly see that you'll have any objection, as I'm sure you're now anxious to return to your wife and child...'

The captain knew how to press every emotional button.

'Think of the awful persecution they have endured in the last couple of days. You should not expect Jola to go through all that again, should you? And, of course, if your cooperation is excellent we might be able to help you both with food supplies. Here in the State Security service we don't have the supply problems experienced by you riff-raff.'

Bogdan sank into the chair emotionally crushed. To reject the proposal meant more torture, and, despite his great resilience, Bogdan knew he no longer had the energy to resist. Slowly he realised that Poland's vast security apparatus had won, for the moment anyway. Bogdan swallowed two painkillers and rubbed ointment into those cuts and bruises he could reach without removing his clothes.

'Your cooperation will be gauged on results, Miskiewicz. The sooner you are able to deliver, the more sympathetic we will be ...' the captain continued.

Things were moving too fast for Bogdan. He could not muster arguments or resistance as the captain continued his torrent of 'agreements'. The captain had won, and like a chameleon he changed his image to suit the new situation. Once again he reverted to an officious and business-like manner. He did up his top button, slid the tie knot up and under the collar, then tucked the file neatly under his left arm.

'You can go home to your wife and son. We will be in contact very soon, to confirm your agreement, then there will be no doubt in both our minds and no ambiguity.' He pushed the chair squarely under the desk and looked into Bogdan's bloodshot eyes. 'I will arrange for a car to take you back to Dzika Street. Thank you for your cooperation.'

The captain started to walk out, and Bogdan swung round painfully. 'At least,' he pleaded, 'allow me the dignity of returning home by public transport, instead of being delivered in one of your stinking 'bitch' wagons or *Volgas*.'

'Suit yourself, Miskiewicz,' the captain replied arrogantly. 'If you consider yourself fit enough to face winter and the city transport system after your accidents, then go ahead.' He strode out leaving the door open. A thin, ugly militia stalwart peered round the door. 'Out!' he yelled at Bogdan. 'We need the room urgently for a new customer.'

Bogdan raised himself stiffly from the chair then shuffled slowly forward. In the doorway he rocked precariously with both arms clutching the frame for support. Ahead was the straight, wide expanse of the Mostowski Palace's stone corridor. He tried to calculate the distance: sixty metres to the corner, another sixty to the staircase, two flights of stairs down, then another forty metre walk past the guard post under the long archway and out through the gates.

The Warsaw steelworker flinched but did not waver. Bogdan would show the SB they had not broken him.

38

The rich, ruby, mid-morning sun poured powerfully through the brown-tinted glass of the office occupied by General Martynov, head of the KGB's 'S' Directorate in Moscow. During major operations Martynov always became a reclusive workaholic. This Friday he had sacrificed his backgammon and bear hunting with senior Kremlin aides to concentrate his energies on *Amber Monkey*. He clutched the telephone tightly, spoke into the mouthpiece in his usual low, confidential manner, then drew nervously on a Bulgarian cigarette as he steeled himself to speak to General Semenov.

'I request you delay the Friday morning conference for ninety minutes, Dimitri Fedorovich,' asked Martynov.

Martynov's manner towards the KGB first deputy chairman was ingratiating. Outwardly he exuded confidence but privately the veteran spymaster was a little terrified. He stood next to the office windows waiting for the response from his superior which came after a long, reflective pause. '... Very well, Vasili Pavlovich ... Eleven o'clock then, instead of half past nine.' Martynov was relieved because the delay bought him valuable time after an uneasy forty-eight hours.

Where the hell was Major Petrovsky? There had been fierce winter blizzards on the Polish border in Byelorussia, but Soviet Television had shown the arrival of the food convoys in Warsaw three days ago and Petrovsky should have been among them. Surely he must have made contact with Sulecki and be on his way back to Moscow by now? If so, why had he not made contact the moment he crossed the border?

Apart from the cable from General Klimanov, KGB liaison officer at the Polish Interior Ministry, there had been an ominous silence on all operational fronts since

Wednesday's confirmation that Radio Free Europe had broadcast the fake Solidarity bulletin. Martynov had filibustered successfully for two days by convincing Semenov and the other generals that the operation was on course. But Comrade Chairman Andropov's office was now applying unrelenting pressure for results and Martynov knew that Semenov's patience was wearing thin. He also knew that his own reputation was on the line, despite his distinguished thirty-two year record.

Precedents at the KGB were well established. Success with this clandestine operation would bring personal congratulations from Chairman Andropov and national honour, maybe a second Order of Lenin. Failure would bring the KGB humiliation abroad and Martynov a personal disgrace with banishment to a lowly post in outer Kazakhstan.

It was another anxious hour before a direct-dial telephone rang next to Martynov's desk. He grabbed it instinctively.

'It's Petrovsky!'

The gruff, distinctive tone rang sharp and clear, and from the clarity of the line Martynov guessed Petrovsky was back in Moscow.

'Don't talk now. Where are you?' Martynov instinctively assumed his phone was bugged by 'K' Directorate.

'I'll be with you in ten minutes,' said Petrovsky.

'Don't come to my office. Make it the first floor conference room,' ordered Martynov.

Petrovsky was in the marble lobby of the First Chief Directorate's headquarters standing at the line of internal telephones. His yellow-brown ID card had already been checked twice by the well-drilled, armed sentries from the KGB Guards Division, crisply dressed in their white gloves, grey overcoats and distinctive hats of Persian lambswool. In his dirty, stained driving pullover and jeans the KGB major felt uncomfortably obtrusive as he strode up the sweeping staircase to the first floor.

He found the head of his directorate standing alone at the end of the long, gently curving corridor. Petrovsky tried to shake hands but Martynov refused. Time was limited. The postponed meeting with deputy chairman Semenov would begin in less than twenty minutes.

'Forget the conference room and let's walk.' Martynov stared ahead, his podgy, stumpy frame pacing along the corridor with both hands clasped behind his back. It took Petrovsky two lengths of the corridor to report what Sulecki had told him in Warsaw.

Nervously General Martynov consulted his watch. 'Thank you, Comrade Major. Now I suggest you have a bath and remove those unpleasant clothes. I want a written report in my office by 13.00 hours, then you should await my call.'

General Semenov's delayed conference began punctually at eleven. The head of the First Chief Directorate perched on the edge of his black leather chair signing urgent cables and operational orders as he spoke in short bursts into one of his eight hotline telephones. Without disturbing him, the other three generals quietly sat themselves in the Scandinavian-style chairs and opened their files. Semenov slammed down the phone and pushed his paperwork aside.

'You won't need those this morning, gentlemen,' he said, gesturing towards their leatherbound memo folios. 'This meeting's off the record with no minutes.' He removed his glasses and squinted penetratingly at General Martynov. 'What news then?'

'Good news, Comrade General. Within the last half hour Petrovsky has returned with a full report. Lieutenant Colonel Sulecki is in good shape. He had received the activation order which Comrade Agent Rybicki planted at Radio Free Europe in Munich. He also received our updated message on the repeater wavelength. Sulecki realises both the new timescale and the new expectations of him.'

'We now have two priority decisions to make then, comrade Generals. First, Vasili Pavlovich, the "active measures" – the weapon to be used by Comrade Sulecki. The Laboratory of Special Weapons in Department 14

194

of your directorate must draw up a list of suitable options. For the overt option I'm thinking of a weapon from somewhere in the West, and the priority must be the United States so we can point fingers of blame at Washington directly. For the second option – the clandestine method – I suggest something like a gas gun where the effect is lethal but no traces are left in the body . . .'

Semenov slowly revolved his black leather chair on its pedestal. He faced General Anatoli Zuyenko, the 49-year-old KGB whizz-kid, who was responsible for Service A, the Active Measures Service, the *Sluzhba Aktinvykh Meropriyatiyi*. Zuyenko had a young, egg-shaped face like Al Capone with the same large curving lips and plaintive eyes but without the Chicago 'Big Shot's' famous knife slash on the chin.

'Your task, Anatoli Georgevich, is for Service 'A' to organise a disinformation campaign. World opinion must be manipulated to expect a terrorist act by Solidarity extremists against the Polish leadership. Those extremists must be shown to be operating with full CIA support to get rid of Jaruzelski. Our disinformation must reveal how the CIA have infiltrated Solidarity and supplied money, weapons and logistics support.'

General Zuyenko nodded. He could call on the full resources of Service 'A': forgery, blackmail, manipulation, bugging, rumour and Western 'front' organisations representing covert Soviet interests. Under his command Zuyenko boasted thousands of the most gifted and imaginative KGB agents – academics, journalists, intelligence officers and scientists all dedicated to furthering the interests of Soviet propaganda.

'How long do we have to make these preparations, Comrade General?' Zuyenko asked.

Semenov took a few moments to work through his answer. 'Chairman Andropov has given us two weeks to prepare an outline plan for approval then eight weeks for completion of preparations.'

Semenov did not expect any discussion or disagreement. Whatever their doubts the four could not alter a decision by the Comrade Chairman himself. The die was cast. But a deadline of eight weeks presented an awesome schedule for the KGB's lumbering, bureaucratic machine.

39

The knock which roused Jola Miskiewicz from her broken sleep was weak and empty. She inched towards the door, clutched the handle, then slowly turned it. After the visit by the two drunken SB thugs the previous day she was petrified. Hesitating, she pulled back the door and the dark void of the freezing corridor opened out in front of her.

With a gasp of terror she recoiled into the room clutching her mouth. Bogdan stood before her: an emaciated and battered shadow of the young steelworker she knew as her husband. His eyes stared from dark recesses, three days' growth of beard masked his pale skin, his hair hung straggly and matted together by frozen snow. Jola was too frightened to hug Bogdan as he shuffled towards her.

'I've come from the Mostowski Palace ... It took me two hours to walk two kilometres ... But I did it myself ... I wouldn't let the bastards break me...'

Bogdan spoke in a feeble voice through lips ripped open by the bitter cold. Jola knew what the Mostowski Palace meant. She encouraged him to make faltering steps as he headed towards the cot to see Miatek.

'I want to hold him,' said Bogdan, his arms hanging rigid by his side, his hands clenched. 'But in my present state I might drop him. Just lift him so I can see my son and he can see me.'

Jola reached into the cradle and picked up Miatek's tiny body. Tears ran freely down both their faces as together they clutched their baby.

'I hope he grows up to live in a better Poland than Moscow has imposed on us,' said Bogdan in a choking voice.

Jola willingly let Bogdan talk as she began removing his stinking clothes.

'I told them nothing, darling. You would have been proud of me. I told them nothing.'

She gasped as slowly she revealed the bruises and blood clots, then began bathing them with tepid water. 'Not a limb or organ in my body is untouched by those bastards,' coughed Bogdan. His face tensed and he winced with pain. Then he told her about his ordeal. The detail matched exactly what Jola had feared during her long, empty hours in the apartment.

'They've got me by the balls,' said Bogdan as he ended his two-hour narrative. 'I have two choices. Either I go underground, or I submit to their pressure which will never go away.' Bogdan clenched his fist weakly and pummelled it defiantly onto his kneecap. 'I'll make them sweat, but I need a few days. I've got to try to see Jurek. I must warn the underground what's happened. I must tell them what the militia want and what they know. But at the same time I've got to play along with that bastard SB captain – at least until I've done my duty by the union.'

There were suddenly two heavy knocks at the door. Their hearts pounded. Then two more knocks, heavier this time. Jola helped Bogdan raise himself stiffly from the bed. Slowly he straightened, then shuffled to the door and cautiously opened it. 'Yes?'

An SB officer pushed his ID card under Bogdan's nose. 'I'm just here to check, Comrade Miskiewicz. Have you made your decision yet . . . ?'

Bogdan shook his head slowly. 'No . . . I spent three days in your stinking Mostowski Palace and I've only been home four hours.'

'Just be warned, comrade. The captain is an impatient man. Remember, functionary Miskiewicz, like us you have a job to do!'

Bogdan was determined to show his disgust. He slammed the door in the SB officer's face. The SB had lit a fire of hate in Bogdan which would never be extinguished.

40

By Sunday the 20th, strength had begun returning to Bogdan's frail and battered body. After two days in the apartment he realised that, however strong his character, the psychological scars were deep. He was ravaged by guilt, and each day he sat perched on the edge of the sofa-bed huddled in a tartan blanket staring for hours across the snow-covered Warsaw rooftops. When it grew dark he dozed or slept, and tossed violently with nightmares.

Should he submit to the SB to protect himself and his family, or should be defend his ideals and protect Solidarity? The terrible dilemma tore his mind apart.

Jola was sure her husband was suffering from shock but she did not know how to treat it. She could not leave the apartment because of his condition, and with all phone lines cut she could not call her family or her doctor either. Alone and forgotten they had to ride out their crisis in silence, Jola chain-smoking and Bogdan in a trance.

It was after dusk that Sunday evening, as Jola went into the tiny kitchen, that her eye caught sight of a slip of paper half under the front door. She unfolded it, her cold fingers struggling excitedly to discover the contents. The paper measured just four centimetres square – the recommended size for underground messages because it was small enough to be screwed up and hidden in a person's clothing. Jola stepped forward into the dim light above the dining table, then began to decipher the neat, closely-packed handwriting.

Jola
Must talk urgently re Bogdan.
Am desperate.
Need news and clarification.

Suggest Gong Cafe tomorrow, Monday, at 1100 hours.
Will wait till 1130 only.
Best wishes.
J.

'J', Who was J? Jola was uncertain whether to excite or worry Bogdan by showing him the note. In the end she decided to show it, and it proved to be the best course. His eyes lit up and immediately he recognised the scrawl as belonging to Jurek.

'Where did this come from? When did it arrive?' he enthused. Jola had no idea, but for the first time in over two days Bogdan had spoken with a hint of his old passion. Jola looked at the note again. It reminded her of how her brother Woytek had double-crossed them to secure Bogdan's arrest four days earlier. This time they had to be doubly cautious.

'Darling. Are you absolutely sure that the SB aren't leading us into another trap?'

Bogdan re-examined the writing. He shook his head

'I'm certain. I've worked with Jurek for too long. If it's a fake it's the best possible. I don't think the SB are that well organised.' Bogdan straightened his back and winced with pain, but his face was filled with a new spark and vitality.

'Jurek's message is addressed to you, darling. But it's me who has to take the risk. I've got to do it. I owe it to Jurek to tell him face to face what happened to me.'

Bogdan gripped Jola's arm affectionately and peered out of the window towards the ice-blown car park below. '... It gives me an excuse to go into the City with you and do some shopping for Christmas. We'll buy the biggest Christmas tree we can find. I promise.'

41

Sulecki stood on his toes squinting down through the skylight of the dormitory in the roof of St Martin's Church. In the pre-dawn gloom of this second week of martial law he watched the silent, nervous progress of a seven-man army patrol. At last the KGB Lieutenant Colonel felt refreshed. He had enjoyed the sanctuary of St Martin's for three days, his injuries were mended and his tired limbs were revitalised by rest and food. But his mind was still in turmoil about what to do next. He knew it was inconceivable for him to remain at St Martin's for twelve more weeks.

For much of Sunday night Sulecki had lain fully clothed on his camp bed in the freezing attic assessing the options and dredging his mind for names and addresses of contacts in Warsaw. Then just before 6 a.m. on Monday he checked the sleeping bodies around him, silently pushed back the bedclothes and padded across the stone floor in his socks. Sulecki hoped no one would hear or notice him, but he was wrong. Across the attic Mirek, the union courier from Szczecin, watched his silhouette moving through the gloom.

Sulecki opened the door and squeezed through onto the narrow staircase. Outside in the pitch black he sat on a step and wrenched on his boots, the leather stiffened by the cold, and within ten minutes he was walking out of the alley from the church onto the dimly-lit cobbles of Piwna Street.

Curfew had ended a few minutes earlier and Warsaw's Old Town was deserted apart from a handful of figures making their way to work. Sulecki walked a kilometre west, past the Primate's Palace on Miodowa Street, through Dzierzynski Square, down Elektoralna Street and then past the complaining voices of the day's first queues for Christmas food. The half dozen passengers rattling south on the No. 12 tram were engaged in heated debate about the episcopal letter from Archbishop Glemp which had been read in churches throughout Poland the previous day. The Archbishop had said the Roman Catholic Church was 'powerless in the face of evil', that 'there should be no bloodshed' and that Poles should 'not raise up arms in hatred against one another'. It was an empty appeal and the passengers accused the Archbishop of being weak-willed and of conceding to Jaruzelski.

The whining, bone-shaking, four-kilometre tram ride to Raclawicka Street in the southern district of Mokotov took fifteen minutes and by seven o'clock, as the first streaks of purple brightened the dapple-grey sky, Sulecki stood in the snow under the winter skeleton of a tree on Gimnastyczna Street.

At No. 68, three lights already blazed. From the movement behind the curtains Sulecki assumed that Jeb Theobold was up and about. The villa was typical of the type of Warsaw house rented to Westerners by rich Poles for a mixture of hard dollars and soft zlotys. By Polish standards it was large and lavish – detached with two storeys, a basement, and a built-in garage.

Across the street Sulecki quietly stamped his feet and moved his limbs to keep warm, his priority to make sure he could not be seen from the militia sentry boxes two hundred metres down the street.

It was 7.55 when Jeb Theobold emerged from the front door, stepping carefully down the ice-covered steps. He was forty and single, a dapper, thin faced Californian with steel-rimmed glasses. From their many contacts during Sulecki's time at Solidarity headquarters, the KGB Lieutenant Colonel was sure that Theobold was not a middle ranking 'political counsellor' at the United States embassy as described on the Warsaw diplomatic list. Instead, Theobold's personality closely fitted Moscow Centre's classic profile for a typical CIA agent. His politics were those of a hardline anti-Soviet hawk instinctively at home with the right-wing views of the

President. He was a wheeler-dealer who attracted the attention of the SB and militia because of his late-night drinking, naked jacuzzi parties and his passion for icons bought illegally for dollars on the black market.

Theobold swung open the flimsy double gates and unlocked the door to his blue BMW 520, the standard purchase among higher-ranking Warsaw diplomats.

'Jeb!'

Sulecki's voice from across the street was firm but deadened by the snow. Theobold threw his briefcase onto the back seat and looked up. 'Andrzej,' he called out in surprise as Sulecki stepped out from under his tree. '... Hey ... How are you? ... Say, what are *you* doing here?'

Theobold's voice boomed embarrassingly loudly around the neighbouring villas as he smiled patronisingly in his well-worn diplomatic manner. 'Great to see you, Andrzej. What's the problem? Why the early hour?' They smiled and shook hands.

'I haven't long – just a minute or two,' said Sulecki. 'I musn't be seen with you. The militia are still everywhere. I'm in trouble, Jeb. I need your help. I'd like something from you in return for all the information I've given you from Solidarity headquarters over the months ...'

Sulecki spoke fast in a low, anxious voice. He paused and waited for the diplomat's response. Even in his lowly job in the telex room, Sulecki knew of Theobold's efforts to push the union in a more radical, anti-Soviet direction. He was sure they were part of an overall American strategy to undermine communism.

'Go ahead. I'm listening. But I can make no promises.' said Theobold.

Sulecki had rehearsed his story during the long hours at St Martin's.'My life in Poland is over, Jeb. I've gone underground, but I don't want to be there for ever. Nowhere's safe. If they catch me it'll mean fifteen years in jail. I need to get out. I'm more useful to Solidarity outside Poland than inside. I need a false identity, a passport and passage to somewhere in the West. Sweden will do fine as a first stop ... It's the least you and your country can do for me after all I've done for you and your interests within Solidarity...'

Theobold was trained in crisis management. He smiled genially to defuse Sulecki's anxiety and slapped his ski glove patronisingly across Sulecki's shoulders. But it was an empty gesture of encouragement because in reality Theobold could give Sulecki nothing. If the US Embassy felt duty-bound to help every Solidarity activist who had knowingly helped US intelligence in the last year then Washington would have had to approve ten million sets of false documents for Poles wanting to defect, and Sulecki was not important enough to be an exception.

'We always try to help people who help us ...' said Theobold. Like Sulecki, he was trained to lie convincingly. '... You are no exception, Andrzej, and I'll work on it.'

'Thanks, Jeb.'

'But you should know one thing, Andrzej my friend ... you are more use to us as an undercover agent inside internment camps and prisons here than as an exile in Sweden. And we pay people much better for taking those kind of risks and dangers.'

It was Theobold's way to warn Sulecki that he could expect no privileges or help, and the message had sunk in. The KGB Lieutenant Colonel tried the second stage of his strategy. 'What if I were to assassinate Jaruzelski? Could you supply me with a weapon, then smuggle me out of Poland and give me political asylum in the States?'

Theobold shook his head but Sulecki pressed his point. 'Surely, Jeb, supporting the assassination of Jaruzelski would be in line with Washington's disgust at martial law and events in Poland?'

The American diplomat was taken aback by such an extraordinary suggestion, but he had an instant answer. 'Assassination is ruled out by Executive Order of the President of the United States ... No can do, Andrzej!'

'Hypocrites. That's what you Americans are. Hypocrites!' The KGB officer feigned fury, even though he had always known that the American embassy would not

204

be a willing accomplice either to spiriting Sulecki out of Poland or to supporting the assassination of Jaruzelski.

Theobold smiled his ingratiating, diplomatic smile. 'I'll do my best to help you get out, my friend. But don't expect too much – if anything. How do I contact you?'

'I'm staying at St Martin's Church in the Old Town, but don't approach me there. If an American diplomat were to be seen among the aid workers it would threaten the church's neutrality and jeopardise my security. I'll contact you, same time, same place, two days from now on Wednesday ...' Sulecki's tone was curt. 'And if I don't come it means I've been picked up again.'

Sulecki turned abruptly and disappeared in the direction of the tram stop. It did not matter whether or not Theobold eventually helped him. What the KGB Colonel wanted most was to create in Theobold's mind, and thereby CIA files, a vivid portrait of Sulecki, the fervent Solidarity activist-cum-terrorist.

42

Bogdan spent the first part of Monday morning soaking in the bath to relieve the pain of his bruised body before he ventured out to meet Jurek. And when he left the apartment just before ten o'clock he walked less stiffly, determined to give any watching SB agents the message that he was recovering and enjoying a Christmas shopping expedition with his family.

He and Jola walked arm in arm with Miatek asleep in a sling on Jola's back. Periodically they stopped to gaze in the shop windows so that Bogdan could study the reflections to see if SB agents were hovering behind them. After stopping nine times he believed he was safe and by 10.45 Bogdan, Jola and Miatek were outside the Palace of Culture where they joined the snaking, baying crowd queueing for scraggy Christmas trees.

'I'll return here in one hour to help you and take the tree home,' Bogdan promised. 'There's no reason for them to pick me up this time. I should be safe.' Bogdan clutched Jola's shoulders to reassure her, then he peeled off, merging into the greys, browns and blacks of the crowd.

The Gong was a run-down cafe half a kilometre away across the windswept expanse of Defilad Square on Aleja Jerozolimskie. To either side were empty shop windows and above were rambling floors of offices and private apartments. As he approached, Bogdan slackened his pace and swore. A brown *Fiat* 125 was parked alone on the pavement outside the cafe. The two long, floppy aerials betrayed it as an SB car. What the hell were the SB doing there?

Bogdan controlled his alarm and walked on past the two SB men dozing in the front seats. He walked on to the traffic lights, crossed the wide dual-carriageway and tram tracks, then doubled back up the street. It was 11 o'clock. Two minutes later he saw Jurek arrive. Apparently alerted by Jurek's appearance, the SB men sat up but made no signs of making a following move as Bogdan kept watching from an alleyway alongside the Aeroflot office. He could not warn Jurek by crossing the road to meet him. Instead Jurek would have to sit alone patiently in the cafe until the end of the half hour limit he himself had set.

By 11.30 there was still no move from the SB, and none from Jurek. Then at 11.32 Jurek emerged, and Bogdan watched the outlines of the two SB heads in the car revolve as Jurek passed their *Fiat*. Again there was no move. Jurek walked rapidly west on the north side, and on the south side Bogdan walked at the same pace. They reached the junction opposite the Forum Hotel simultaneously, and Bogdan watched Jurek's orange ski cap disappear down the steps into the subway. On his side of the street Bogdan did the same. After the biting cold at street level the underground passageways were oppressively warm, the dripping water from the melting snow in the road above generating a dank, toilet-like smell. Peasant women in moth-eaten fur coats chewed tobacco as they sold anything from crumpled plastic bags and flowers to firelighters and stalks of garlic.

The subway was laid out as a square of four underground passages with ten staircase entrances. It gave Bogdan no more than a fifty-fifty chance of meeting Jurek. But he struck lucky, and they converged through the ill-lit tunnel. Only when the two men were ten metres apart did Jurek spot Bogdan approaching him. Instinctively they both slowed and sidestepped into an area of shadow between two fluorescent lights, but still they kept moving. There could be no attempt at conversation. Instead their eyes exchanged glances in a visual shorthand before Bogdan spoke briefly: nine words, which were clear and concise in a low voice. 'Make contact through Jola ... they know about the hideout.'

Behind him Bogdan heard the heavy boots of an army patrol, but the meeting had already terminated, leaving them to go their separate ways, Jurek south through the snow drifts towards the allotments, Bogdan north across Defilad Square to rejoin Jola near the Christmas trees.

It was a journey Bogdan would never complete. A stern voice bellowed after him as he limped across the ice. 'Citizen Miskiewicz! This way please!'

Bogdan stopped, frozen rigid in his steps more out of astonishment than fear. He glanced left. Fifteen metres away sat a pea-green *Polonez* estate car with a freshly-shaven face staring out of the open driver's window. 'Can we give you a lift?'

The tone was polite but the meaning clear: it was the SB and Bogdan had no option. After the Mostowski Palace he knew that fighting or running was pointless. He walked towards the car, head up with an illusory self-confidence. But in reality Bogdan was scared.

'Sorry to interrupt your Christmas shopping, Comrade Miskiewicz. The captain would like to see you.'

The *Polonez* picked up speed, the engine over-revving and screeching as the bald tyres struggled for grip. Sandwiched between two SB men on the back seat Bogdan caught a brief glimpse of the Christmas tree compound and Jola standing alongside awaiting his return.

The SB never failed to humiliate.

43

In Monday's bright, warming midday sun Sulecki
tramped through fresh snow, systematically attempting
to open each of the five entrances to Warsaw's prestige
hotel, the Victoria. But each had been firmly locked to
minimise contact between Poles and the diminishing
number of Western guests inside.

Following his dawn meeting at Jeb Theobold's house,
Sulecki was now trying to find Dick Werner, Eastern
Europe correspondent for the *Washington Post*. Werner
had some of the best Solidarity and government contacts
at all levels, and Sulecki had spent several months cul-
tivating him.

During the Solidarity crisis the Swedish-designed
hotel had become the unofficial Western press centre
where SB agents, prostitutes and illegal money changers
had taken advantage of the new liberalisation to do a
roaring trade. But eight days into martial law the free
enterprise bonanza was over. Most pressmen and TV
crews had been expelled from the country and only the
handful of journalists permanently credited to Poland
remained.

Sulecki hovered, freezing and uncomfortable under the
canopy at the front entrance. One o'clock ... two o'clock
... three o'clock ... He counted the hours as the sun
arched across the sky and lengthened the winter shadows.

Sulecki eventually heard Dick Werner before he saw
him. First the boots crunching through the frozen crust
of snow, then a sheepskin anorak emerging from the grey
dusky gloom across Victory Square. Closer now, and
Sulecki could see Dick's gaunt face with its familiar black
moustache and rimless glasses. Sulecki stood at the corner
of the hotel block, the fading light of dusk helping him
to merge with the stonework.

'Dick . . . !'

Werner slowed and strained to find the source of the voice among the hotel shadows. As they shook hands, Sulecki's arms skilfully guided the *Washington Post* Correspondent round the corner into Malachowski Square and out of sight of the hotel doors. For Werner this was just one more clandestine contact with an underground activist whom he knew well.

'Andrzej! . . . Good to see you.'

'Let's take a quick walk, Dick . . .'

They headed west past the State Bank and down Kredytowa Street towards Dabrowski Square. They talked in a mixture of broken English and Polish as Sulecki catalogued his experiences since martial law.

'Dick, I need help . . . I'm here with the authority of an underground cell of the Warsaw branch of Solidarity. For obvious reasons I cannot give you the names of my colleagues. We already have lots of printing material and equipment as well as food. But we need other help. We need money: hard currency, as much as possible and as fast as possible, so we can keep our cell operating and buy what we need on the black market . . . And we need arms. Pistols. Grenades. Explosives. This is a war, and we have instructions from the union leadership to fight. It's the only way to show those bastards in government they must take notice of us. . . . You'll have heard the communique from the Solidarity leaders in Gdansk broadcast by Radio Free Europe last Tuesday . . .'

Sulecki thumped his left arm amicably round Werner's shoulders. 'Dick, my friend, I've helped you in many ways. I leaked documents, tips and information, and you've made your name on the Polish story. Now you Americans must repay us. We need that equipment, Dick, and we need it fast. Fighting is the only answer: a guerilla war.'

Werner was appalled. He knew the strength of anti-government feeling in Poland, but no union member had ever discussed armed action seriously in his presence. Everyone knew such actions would play right into the hands of the Polish hardliners and the Soviet government.

Werner dug further. '... And what will you do with the arms?'

'Don't ask too much. We need the arms for action early next year. We have targets in the government.'

'Assassination?'

Sulecki nodded and Werner pushed him further.

'Jaruzelski?'

'The prime target. It will take time to get ourselves ready but we're planning ahead, Dick.'

Werner whistled his astonishment as they walked east between the towering stone facades of apartment blocks.

'Andrzej, you say the union leadership is right behind you? But armed resistance was never discussed publicly by them. So how do you claim to have their "full backing"?'

Sulecki stared at Werner.

'Don't be stupid, Dick. If word had leaked out it would have warned the SB and the Interior Ministry and played into the hands of their propaganda in the build-up to martial law. That's why no one knew – even well-connected reporters like you.'

'But the leaders always warned me that if I ever heard of a plan for armed resistance I should consider it an action by undercover SB agents who had infiltrated the Solidarity structure. So how can I know this is genuine? How do you know you're not being manipulated by some agent provocateur?'

Sulecki was unperturbed. 'I don't know, Dick. I can only say that I know my colleagues well. None of them are provocateurs. We're committed. What more can I say? If every time we planned something we worried about a "plant" then we'd never organise any resistance.'

Werner had to concede that Sulecki had a point, but a nagging doubt remained in his mind. Why would Sulecki think that he, a journalist, could organise weapons for the Solidarity underground?

'Andrzej, I'm pleased we met. But it's not my business

to help you with arms or money. I'm just a journalist.'

Sulecki narrowed his eyes and cursed. 'So now we know the real limit to Western support for our revolution.'

Werner snapped back. 'You must know one thing, my friend. I don't draw up US foreign policy. I report it. If you have a gripe with Washington then take it to the embassy and the diplomats. Get one thing straight, Andrzej. I'm not an undercover agent of the State Department or the CIA. OK? What I will do, though, is write a story on your internment and escape, then smuggle it out by train to West Berlin.'

'Seems like you get the best part of the deal, Dick. Something for nothing.'

Sulecki and Werner halted by the Diplomatic Meat Shop in Baczynskiego Street.

'I was glad to see you again, but you do understand, don't you, Andrzej?' said the *Washington Post* correspondent.

Sulecki did not need to understand. He had left the impression he wanted in the American journalist's mind.

44

By five o'clock that evening Bogdan was back at the Mostowski Palace, exactly where he had been on Friday. Same room, same spindly table, same chair, same freezing temperatures. It was as if he had never hobbled out in agony three days earlier.

Dusk had been and gone, and for five hours Bogdan sat on the concrete floor propped against the wall. There was no food, no drink and no interest from the SB men pacing the corridor outside.

Then at ten o'clock from beyond the door and down the corridor, Bogdan heard the clomping of the captain's footsteps. The door creaked open.

'Good evening, Comrade Functionary Miskiewicz.' The captain strode arrogantly across the room and tossed his files once more onto the table. He sat down to the piercing screech of a chair leg as it was dragged across the floor. 'Thank you for agreeing to come to this meeting ... Now let us discuss our strategy.'

After a long silence Bogdan braced himself. 'I was not aware we had even agreed to have a strategy, Captain. You should not make assumptions. I haven't agreed to cooperate.'

The captain slammed both his fists violently onto the table and stood up. 'Comrade Miskiewicz, this is a state of war,' he shouted. 'In war there are no rules or timescale. In war we fight an enemy like Solidarity and scum like you. In war there's no room for a leisurely reflection on what's right and what's wrong. You, Comrade Miskiewicz, are making a big mistake if you think you can play for time! We want access to the underground, and if you don't help us we won't waste any more time on you. We'll dispose of you and you'll just disappear.'

The captain's lips, chin and hands shook with the rage of failing to break Bogdan, but the steelworker remained silent and unmoved by the threats. This was no longer just Solidarity against the SB but a personal trial of strength between Bogdan and the captain. Despite his threats, the captain could never torture Bogdan to death. He had assured his senior officers that his prisoner was 'turning'. He had to deliver a live intelligence asset and not a corpse.

'I will give you a few more hours,' the captain said between clenched teeth, trying not to betray the weakness of his own position. 'Then if you don't volunteer a "yes" I warn you I will spare no effort to force it out of you.'

The captain stormed out of the cell and slammed the door, the echo lingering menacingly in the corridor for several seconds.

Bogdan felt a flush of elation. Had he won this round? If so, he feared his victory would be short-lived.

45

Jola's nerve broke as Monday's grey, snow-laden dusk sky turned to black. Last time she had seen the SB seize her husband. This time it was worse. She could only speculate that the SB had seized him again. Alone and frightened, she could no longer take the bleak isolation of the apartment. She desperately needed help to save her from collapse.

During one of her shopping expeditions she had heard that an aid centre had been set up at St Martin's Church in the Old Town. That evening she arrived there with baby Miatek just as preparation of the aid parcels for internees was winding down for the night.

'Can I help you my child?' The female voice was soft and sympathetic. It came from a middle-aged nun with a pale complexion and rings of fatigue around her eyes.

'I need help,' Jola whispered. 'The SB have taken my husband ... I'm at my wits end.'

'Come this way, my dear.'

The nun turned and led Jola under the arched stone ceiling of the library and between the piles of aid packages. They sat down at a table in a back room amidst vast uncoordinated piles of clothing, food and gifts which still had to be sorted. 'My name is Sister Janina,' said the nun as she prepared some sheets of paper.

'Mine is Jola Miskiewicz ... and this is my baby, Miatek.' Jola spoke softly and shyly but the ice of formality was broken. Someone was taking an interest. Tears of relief welled up as Sister Janina wrote onto a card the details of their plight.

'Jola, I'll just go to Father Bardecki. He always likes to meet personally everyone who comes here for help ... but he's already working more than twenty hours a day.'

Jola's reception here was in heartening contrast to her

visit to the militia depot the previous Thursday. Within five minutes, Sister Janina had returned.

'Father Bardecki sends his personal greetings and heartfelt sympathy, Mrs Miskiewicz ... He suggests you come back tomorrow to see if we have any news from the authorities about your husband. We'll start making enquiries first thing.'

The door behind Jola swung open and a man asked the nun if he could take a bar of soap so he could wash. 'Why don't you come in?' asked Sister Janina. Jola swung round to see a man in his mid-thirties with two day's growth of beard.

'Jola, you might like to meet some of the people staying with us. For security reasons we'll stick to first names ... Let me introduce you to Andrzej ...'

The KGB Colonel showed little interest. He merely smiled a polite acknowledgement.

46

Jeb Theobold rubbed his sore eyes then leaned back wearily into the revolving chair in his brightly-decorated office at the US Embassy. He had spent eleven hours closeted in conferences, monitoring incoming signals traffic and preparing cables for urgent dispatch back to CIA headquarters in Langley, Virginia. Washington had a voracious appetite for all available detail from Poland, and the cables which passed across Theobold's desk were one of the principal channels through which the West was able to bypass Polish travel and censorship restrictions to receive whatever new information was available on martial law.

It was 8.15 p.m. As the two military newsreaders on the evening television news ended their nightly litany of new martial law regulations, Theobold filed his hand-written notes, switched off the television set then stretched his arms and body. From the volume of work still on his desk he knew he would not finish until well past midnight. With curfew beginning at ten o'clock the CIA agent knew he would have to spend the night on a camp bed at the embassy.

It was time to eat and Theobold decided to take a break at the American Club located inside the embassy compound. He locked all his documents in the safe, told the duty marine where he would be, then walked through the embassy's plate glass front doors onto the deserted Aleja Ujazdowskie. He could have reached the club in a matter of seconds by going out through a back door and crossing the compound, but he wanted a few minutes relief from the dry, centrally-heated atmosphere of his office so he took the longer route around the embassy-perimeter.

As he entered the modern two-storey club building,

he surveyed the ragged collection of Westerners seeking refuge from the inconveniences of martial law and the twenty degree below temperatures. Most were younger diplomats, but there were half a dozen Western journalists eating chilli-con-carne and drinking canned American beer as they loudly swapped hardship stories and complaints about the inconsistent censorship policy of the Jaruzelski regime.

'Hi Jeb, how you doing?'

Dick Werner, correspondent for the *Washington Post*, walked into the club behind Theobold and slapped him playfully on the back. 'You eating?'

'Sure am,' said Theobold. 'But I don't plan on taking a long time about it. I need to be back at my desk in a half hour.'

Werner pointed towards an empty corner table. They ordered hamburgers, french fries, crispy salads and two Budweiser beers: all of it like nectar to foreigners living with the chronic shortages of Polish life beyond the embassy walls.

For once Theobold was in a bad mood. He complained about the long hours and the endless demands from his desk officers in Washington. Werner reciprocated about the demands from his newspaper's foreign desk.

'Washington wants more of everything,' he complained. 'No matter how many stories I smuggle out through East Germany to West Berlin, they always want more. But they ignore the new realities of working in this goddam place.'

Theobold nodded sympathetically. Within a few minutes Werner leaned forward. He sensed that Theobold's diplomatic guard was dropping a little.

'Jeb, d'you know a guy from Solidarity called Andrzej Sulecki? ... He's an ex-telex operator at the headquarters in Mokotowska Street ... Always seemed well plugged in to what was going on?'

Alarm bells rang immediately with Theobold. Although he knew Dick Werner well, he used the well-tried diplomat's ploy of not making his move until he had a much clearer idea of how much his dinner partner knew.

Werner spent ten minutes giving Theobold details of his afternoon meeting with Sulecki outside the Victoria Hotel. In the light of Werner's information, Theobold began to view differently his own meeting with Sulecki twelve hours earlier. That morning, Sulecki's pressing request for CIA help to leave Poland had barely stirred Theobold's interest. The American diplomat had treated it in the same way that he had treated several similar emigration requests from long established Solidarity contacts. He had written a short memo to the embassy's consular and security sections for processing, and their eventual recommendations would come many weeks later.

Dick Werner's meeting now added new fragments to what might soon turn into an intriguing mosaic. Was Sulecki who he claimed to be? Or did he, perhaps, work for someone else? If so who? From what Werner said, Theobold realised that the journalist was probing to discover whether Sulecki had a connection to the CIA. Tactically, Theobold knew he would have to reciprocate with a little information in order to get more from Werner.

'I seem to know Sulecki about as well as you do,' the diplomat began cautiously, 'though I can't go into detail about why I know him well ... Before we go on, can we agree one thing? Technically I'm breaching regulations by divulging anything at all. This discussion must be off-the-record. Don't even quote a "Western diplomat". And as a friend I can tell you there could be security matters involved. So for the moment, don't quote anything. You agree?'

Dick Werner nodded a discreet, gentlemanly gesture which Theobold knew meant 'yes, sort of.'

'You're right, Dick. Something stinks,' said Theobold, and he began outlining a few of the details of what had happened at his dawn meeting with Sulecki on Gimnastyczna Street, including the offer to assassinate Jaruzelski in return for political asylum in the United States.

'But Jeb,' Werner responded with a hint of impatience, 'Sulecki offered me the same deal: assassination for asylum ... Are you going to help him and do business?'

Theobold had to raise his voice a notch above the noise from Werner's journalist colleagues across the room.

'Don't be half-brained, Dick! The US government doesn't do those kind of deals, and even if we did we wouldn't tell you. As for murdering the Polish leader ... for us to support that kind of terrorist act is strictly forbidden by order of the President, no less.'

Werner knew as well as anyone the history of American involvement in covert actions designed to destabilise leaders. President Ford's Executive Order in 1976 specifically forbade covert assassination operations.

The *Washington Post* correspondent did not challenge Theobold. Instead he began examining what they had both heard from Sulecki.

'It doesn't match up, does it, Jeb? He tells us he wants money and guns to blow the whole regime out of the water, but it bears no relation to Solidarity policy. So what's the guy up to?'

'I've no idea,' confessed Theobold. 'But there again, Dick, perhaps it's not so ominous. Maybe Sulecki's just a shrewd Solidarity operator using his contacts. Perhaps he really is part of an underground plan to organise violent resistance which they hope will get Poles onto the streets to rise up against Jaruzelski. That would explain why they want arms and money. ... Secondly, Sulecki thinks he'll need an escape route out of Poland one day, and that's why he came to me asking for the US to smuggle him out.'

Werner tapped his empty beer can on the stained table-cloth. 'You have a point, Jeb. But I say it again – a strategy of armed resistance goes against every policy statement Solidarity has ever made. They know armed attacks will discredit the union, and worse still that they'll be used as a pretext for a more ruthless crackdown. What's to say, then, that Sulecki is not a provocateur?'

'You may be right,' said Theobold pushing his empty plate to the side of the table. He looked at his watch. Having planned to spend thirty minutes in the club he had stayed almost an hour. 'Sulecki told me he's hiding at the aid sanctuary in St Martin's Church,' said Theobold getting up from the table. 'I think we should find out more: who he is and what he's up to.'

The two Americans briskly donned their heavy-duty anoraks and shook hands. Outside on Piekna Street, Werner pushed his Ford Granada out of a snow drift and headed home to the Hotel Victoria to beat the ten o'clock curfew.

Theobold, meanwhile, returned to his desk in the main embassy block to draft a cable to CIA headquarters. Within hours, CIA director William Casey would have on his desk at Langley the first details of the new and violent tactics to be adopted by a hardcore of Solidarity's more extreme underground activists.

47

'Brother Andrzej . . .!'

It was seven o'clock on Monday evening and Father Bardecki spoke urgently in a low voice through the ornately carved screen of the confessional box. 'Please come to my study at half past ten tonight . . . after curfew . . . when the church doors are closed.'

Three hours later as the bell of St John's Cathedral tolled ten o'clock, Sulecki stood silently in his attic hideaway watching from the tiny skylight. Below, Piwna Street lay silent with the hard-packed ice shining under the streetlamps. As he gazed across the white, jagged angles of Warsaw's rooftops he took time to reflect on Jola – her surname unknown – the woman he had met briefly earlier that evening.

'Jola' had revealed little about her troubles even under his polite but probing questions. Yet during those few minutes she had divulged enough for him to sense that she was under intense pressure. At the same time, 'Jola' had tantalised him. Her eyes and mouth had seemed to talk in a beguiling, seductive rhythm. For the first time since he and Magda had been separated at the Wilcza Street militia depot eight days earlier Sulecki had pushed his professional feelings to one side and felt himself aroused.

The cathedral bell struck the half hour and Sulecki slipped out of the attic into the gloom of the spiral staircase. In the rectory lobby he pushed through the heavy felt curtain and quietly tapped on the door to Father Bardecki's study. The priest sat inside the dark, claustrophobic room in his soiled black cassock, the dogcollar slightly stained, his bloodshot eyes betraying the pressure of work.

'Brother Andrzej! I have a warning.' The priest's voice

was unusually stiff with anxiety as he laid his fountain pen on the green-leather top of an oak desk. 'I must tell you something I have learned today in confidence. It confirms what the Episcopacy and Curia have long feared, and we must take precautions accordingly.'

Father Bardecki hunched forward across his desk, his head supported on the splayed fingers of both hands. 'You are no longer safe here, even in the House of God. You must find a sanctuary elsewhere. A sympathiser in the militia told me that Department Four of the Interior Ministry – that terrible section responsible for church surveillance – is about to start a campaign called Operation Raven designed to divide and discredit the Church. They will sink to any depths to discredit us with their dirty tricks. Priests like me will be categorised as members of a "dangerous, extremist, insignificant minority" which dares to challenge the authorities. The submissive priests who don't challenge the regulations will be publicly classified as the "moderate majority". Our Church will become just like the Church in Czechoslovakia, where the only legal priests are those quislings who've been bought out by State privileges like petrol coupons, passports to go abroad and food.'

Sulecki was amazed – not at the SB operation itself but at the fact that Father Bardecki had confided so much to a new arrival who was hardly known by anyone. But Father Bardecki hadn't finished.

'My information is that they'll try to isolate priests like me from our bishops. They'll use every kind of dirty trick – planted evidence, alleged caches of weapons and explosives in our churches, accusations that we abuse alcohol or break our vows of celibacy ... Nothing will be safe, and nothing too dirty. St Martin's will be crawling with informers and agents. The SB will even use altar boys or student priests. Then within a few weeks they'll have what they will call their "evidence" and they'll move in to compromise me – the "extremist" priest from St Martin's.'

Father Bardecki sat motionless, hunched over the piles

of paperwork on his desk. Sulecki spoke only when it was clear the priest had nothing more to add. 'You're sure of your information, Father?'

'I'm sure, Brother Andrzej ... For the moment we must both seek to preserve what we believe in. In your case Solidarity and your freedom to challenge the system, in mine the Church and my pastoral duty to support those in my care. My love for Poland and our people is not illegal. I give humanitarian and spiritual support not what the Interior Ministry calls "political support".'

Father Bardecki leant further forward and lowered his right hand onto Sulecki's shoulder.

'Brother Andrzej! Never fear! Our faith will survive these terrible times even if we have to pay a price, like the three years imprisonment paid by our dear Cardinal Wyszynski under Stalin in the Fifties. At our seminaries we read Marx and Lenin so we can find the ways to coexist with the authorities. What they can't understand is that we are not against them.'

Father Bardecki sat back having unloaded his giant burden. Sulecki stood up. He spoke in colloquial Polish which did not match the elegant college language of the priest. 'Father I understand you. And I must thank you for your kindness and hospitality. But I need a day or two to arrange things. I have to consider what to do and where to go. And what about the others here? May I tell everyone else up in the attic?'

'Tell no one. I'll talk to your colleagues one by one this evening. I decided to disclose this to you first and alone because your experiences make you the biggest security risk here ... Please tell me your plans when you know them. May God be with you.'

The priest wished Sulecki goodnight, his index finger cutting the cold air in front of the KGB officer's face in the shape of a cross.

A bitter north wind screamed down from the Baltic all night, and by the first light of Tuesday it blew a leaden sky and fresh snow flurries across the Polish capital. In the attic Sulecki tried to formulate his next moves. Across the room Mirek, the shipyard worker from Szczecin, lay on his camp bed gazing at the slanting oak beams supporting the roof. Sulecki threw Mirek a cigarette and box of matches.

'Mirek! Tell me about Szczecin!'

The KGB officer's words sliced through the icy winter air. 'I've never been there. I'm just a peasant farmer's son from the east. If I wanted to escape from Poland through Szczecin how would I do it?'

Mirek sniggered at Sulecki's stupidity. He blew bursts of cigarette smoke upwards from the camp bed. 'Over the years, many have tried, my friend, and almost everyone has failed. What are the possibilities? ... First by train through East Germany to Berlin? Forget that. The border is closed to Poles. You'll never get a legal passport and if they catch you with a forgery they'll execute you as a spy. They'll be tearing that train apart – every compartment and panel will be searched. I know, I've seen it.'

Sulecki sat with his legs dangling over the edge of the camp bed. 'What about by sea?'

Mirek was just as dismissive. 'There's the ferry to Sweden from Swinoujscie – that's the port sixty kilometres north of Szczecin at the mouth of the river Oder. But I'll bet you that border will be sealed. The BBC said tonight that journalists trying to get into Poland at Swinoujscie had been turned back ... In any case, Andrzej, how do you get a passport? The only chance is to smuggle yourself onto one of the ferries. That's almost impossible unless you swim to the ship. In these conditions you'd die in minutes from hypothermia. Impossible! Then, how do you avoid the Polish and East German naval vessels moored at the big base there? And there's always at least one Soviet ship in the harbour. We call it "Big Eyes", because it's Moscow's way of keeping a watch on the Polish Navy.'

Stoically Sulecki took in Mirek's advice. 'How do you bypass all that then?'

Mirek lay almost invisible in the dark across the room.

'You can't, Andrzej. Not even by stealing a boat from the yacht club. It's a border area. Even in the good times every civilian sailor has to be "verified" and their loyalty checked. And civilians need a special pass to sail in those waters. Polish or East German radar would pick you up, or one of the border patrols would find you before you'd got into the neutral part of the Baltic ... If there *was* a way, then half of Poland would be streaming there to get out. No! Jaruzelski's put the iron noose round us.'

Sulecki had to respect Mirek's local knowledge, but there also had to be a way out: not legally as a KGB agent in an embassy car and on a diplomatic passport but illegally as a convincing Solidarity activist taking exceptional risks to seek asylum in the West.

Mirek was astonished by Sulecki's interest. 'There's one thing I don't understand, Andrzej', he continued. 'Why d'you want to go? As a member of Solidarity your place is here in Poland helping our struggle.'

Sulecki was caught off guard.

There was no way he would tell Mirek the truth: that he saw escaping from Poland as a vital part of his cover for *Amber Monkey*. Sulecki had come round to the view that escape would reinforce his image as a Polish activist in exile who had been specially trained by America to be sent home to Poland for the express purpose of assassinating General Jaruzelski. The KBG Illegal feigned despair about life in Poland and the future of Solidarity.

'I'm a broken man,' he lied. 'I have been interned and you haven't ... Anyone who protests here will be arrested and neutralised for years. They did it under Stalin. They did it in Hungary in '56. They did it in Czechoslovakia in '68. They tried to do it here in '70. And now they're doing the same under Jaruzelski. There's no future now. I'll be more use fighting for Solidarity outside Poland than here. That's why I want to leave.'

Sulecki tried to watch Mirek's face. He was still unsure whether he had convinced him.

In silence Mirek threw back his blankets, tied the laces of his boots and walked to the attic door. 'You should be

226

ashamed of yourself!' he hissed at Sulecki. 'While you take advantage of church hospitality, thousands of others are suffering in jails and internment camps. While they make a stand, you want to leave ... like a rat!'

Mirek's fury was stoked up. 'But what's more evil than all of that is what you're up to. You know this church is watched by the SB, yet you selfishly slip out of the church at dawn, openly walk the streets of Warsaw, then hold a doorstep meeting at the home of a CIA agent. And don't tell me you thought it was safe. The SB are everywhere. And they're watching the Americans in particular, so they can accuse Reagan of orchestrating any disturbances!'

Mirek slammed the door and stomped down the stairs.

Sulecki raged silently. How the hell had Mirek known so much about his movements? Was it because Jeb Theobold had come to the church asking questions? Or had it been Dick Werner or an informer? Or was he being watched?

The KGB Lieutenant Colonel knew he must disappear.

Fast.

48

Sister Janina sat opposite Jola, who tightly clutched Miatek to her chest. 'The central militia office claim to have no record of Bogdan,' said the nun. 'They say they have not detained him.'

Sister Janina saw Jola's knuckles turn white and her fingers clench angrily around the straps of the baby's sling.

'Rubbish! It's the old lies and tricks. It means that if Bogdan's body is found floating in the Vistula the SB can call his death an "unexplained mystery".'

'You're right,' said Sister Janina sadly. 'We know of many similar cases.'

She fingered her card index and pulled out one of the personal records. 'Leszek Witkowski, aged twenty-eight. Fitter at the FSO car factory. We heard this morning that he was picked up by the SB two days after martial law. Three days later he was seen being thrown from a *Fiat* car on the bridge construction site next to the Zeran power station. A worker there heard them shout, "Get rid of him! Let the bastard's body be blessed by a priest!" Witkowski's now in hospital partially paralysed and with terrible injuries. But the militia and SB say they know nothing about him.'

Sister Janina replaced the card. 'I have another twenty cases like Witkowski's, and that's only in Warsaw ...'

Jola was too depressed to speak. She got up and shuffled aimlessly into a neighbouring room which was stuffed high with secondhand gifts being prepared for the next shipment of aid packages for internees.

Sulecki stood at a table with three other men assembling the gifts into individual boxes: a vest, a shirt, underwear, trousers, a jacket or anorak, first aid kit, toothbrush and toothpaste, tobacco, soap and shampoo.

It was Sulecki who took the initiative. 'Sit down and join us. Have they got any news of your husband?' he asked Jola.

Jola shook her head but was too depressed to elaborate. She recalled how the previous afternoon she had opened her heart to this stranger who like her was enjoying the relative safety and sanctuary of St Martin's. She just about remembered the face, the lean frame and the black, swept-back hair from their brief conversation the day before.

'What brought you here?' Jola enquired as she hugged Miatek.

Sulecki told Jola about his Solidarity job and what he had been through since the SB hauled him out of bed in the early hours of Sunday the 13th. But he did not mention Magda. The KGB Lieutenant Colonel no longer thought about his mistress and never talked of her. Their love affair had outlived its usefulness.

'We're both facing the same kind of difficulties, Jola. Perhaps we can help each other,' the KGB officer ventured.

'Perhaps . . .' Jola replied non-committally and somewhat perplexed.

Sulecki inched his face nearer so he could speak confidentially in a near whisper.

'Father Bardecki says the church is no longer safe. I have to leave St Martin's urgently . . . But I can't go back to my apartment. The SB are waiting for me. I hope to leave the country, but in the meantime I need somewhere to stay without worrying about the next SB threat to my freedom . . . Could I – perhaps – beg space at your apartment? It'll be safe because they know your husband's in custody, so they won't be watching you . . . It would only be for a few days. When they relax the curfew over Christmas I'll move on . . .'

Jola was stunned by such a brash request from a man she barely knew. Where would Sulecki sleep in the tiny apartment? But then she began to see advantages. Sulecki would be a new face – a distraction during the long hours

229

marooned high above Warsaw with a screaming baby. He would help take her mind off Bogdan's predicament. And there was also the tradition of mutual hospitality among Solidarity activists.

'Of course,' she replied after long and careful thought.

'You don't know how grateful I am,' Sulecki responded. 'This has to be a private arrangement just between you and me. The SB's eyes and ears are everywhere, and if I'm discovered you'd be charged with harbouring an escaped internee. I'll tell Father Bardecki that I'm moving out, but I won't say where. I'll just tell him that I'll keep in touch.'

'Of course,' Jola readily understood his fears. 'When will you come?' she whispered.

'As soon as I can. Is tonight possible?'

Jola nodded agreement and gave him her address.

'And perhaps I should know your name,' said Sulecki with a smile.

'Jola ... Jola Miskiewicz. And yours?'

'Andrzej ... Andrzej Sulecki.'

49

The SB captain still hoped to break Bogdan. During Tuesday the only contact he allowed his prisoner was with the heavily-built woman orderly who three times brought him weak coffee, bread and lard. Otherwise the steelworker sat against the wall or paced the floor trying to resist the disorientating effects of isolation.

Bogdan recognised the two junior SB officers the moment they walked in that evening. They were the same big bruisers as last time, and they wore the same leather jackets and neatly pressed corduroy trousers which stank of long days of heavy drinking and torture. The senior officer was the larger, and Bogdan christened him Big Brute. The second was younger and trimmer, so Bogdan christened him Young Brute.

The twin Brutes said nothing. Instead they prodded Bogdan to accompany them along dank corridors which reverberated with eerie, uncoordinated sounds; then down into the courtyard, where he was thrown flat onto the rear seat of a white *Fiat* 125. Big Brute sat on Bogdan's chest as the driver sped south-east along the wide boulevard of Marshalkowska Street and across the modern concrete spans of the Poniatowski Bridge. Big Brute showed his special 'W' pass at the roadblock on the Otwock road, then the *Fiat* roared southwards again among the snow covered dunes on the east bank of the frozen Vistula.

Before the village of Skrzypki the car slowed to a crawl as the driver searched for a familiar landmark. Rychnowska Street was blocked by snow as deep and soft as icing sugar, and the *Fiat* could not negotiate it. Big Brute and Young Brute dragged Bogdan out before the car had scarcely halted. The SB men half-hauled and half-dragged him away from the *Fiat* towards the Vistula,

Bogdan's feet gouging two ruts as his toes dragged limply through the snow.

They never reached the river. They stopped at a beauty spot where in summer Poles threw off their city inhibitions to sunbathe naked or make love among the birch trees. As the last light of the headlamps faded in the distance they threw Bogdan into the snow. He disappeared under the wet, clammy top snow which penetrated every stitch of his clothing and began burning the brittle skin of his uncovered head and hands. He floundered to regain his balance. Big Brute pulled out a pistol. 'We'll shoot you if you try to escape.' They were the first words the SB officer had spoken. From his knapsack he pulled the gasmask which he had used to almost suffocate Bogdan a week earlier. He forced it over Bogdan's head and as the steelworker inhaled the lingering stench of gas he was overcome by a terrible need to vomit.

'Get up you vermin!' yelled Big Brute. Disorientated by the mask, Bogdan swayed and struggled to hold himself upright. In the blackness there was no horizon on which to focus and no reference point against which to calibrate his balance. Young Brute blocked the air intake. 'Run, you bastard, run!' he screamed.

Bogdan tried to run towards the one thing he could see in the pitch dark – the two distant specks of the *Fiat*'s headlamps. But his legs moved like slabs, and his arms rotated like mad windmills as he struggled for balance, the gas burned his windpipe and the oxygen locked in the mask ran out. Bogdan buckled, but the SB men picked him up. 'Run, you bastard, run!' Big Brute and Young Brute yelled alternately, one in his left ear, the other in his right.

Finally Bogdan collapsed, his energy spent. But the brutes would not let him rest. The SB men rolled him out of the snow just before he lost consciousness, then they propped him between Big Brute's legs, the whites of his eyes staring, his mouth open, his body feeble and limp.

Bogdan was already underdressed. Now Young Brute

tried to remove his captive's trousers, but Bogdan kicked and wriggled and his trousers didn't budge. Such was Young Brute's fury that he lunged towards Bogdan, kicking him savagely in the stomach. Bogdan could only pray for survival. He crumpled like a rag doll into the deep snow as the narrow beams of the car lights picked out the ghostly silhouettes of the SB men heaving breathlessly and brushing the snow from their jackets. The torture had ended as abruptly as it had begun.

'And next time we'll bury you alive in an unmarked grave!' taunted Big Brute.

He turned to Young Brute. 'Let's go back before this sweat freezes and we get pneumonia.' He cared only for their own welfare, not Bogdan's.

They lifted their prisoner like a carcass of horsemeat and returned the frail wreck of a body to the *Fiat*. 'Now perhaps you'd like to talk to the captain,' said Big Brute.

The return drive to the Mostowski Palace took just twenty minutes. But there was no hurry. The SB captain planned to leave Bogdan alone in the bleakness of the interrogation room for the rest of that night.

50

Sulecki told no one about his departure except Father Bardecki. At 6.30 he tapped quietly on the door of the study where the priest sat alone in silent contemplation before evening Mass, his balding head propped in his hands.

'My brother ... !'

He welcomed Sulecki by raising his right arm.

'My apologies for disturbing you, Father. I'm leaving now. But I promise to stay in touch ... I just wanted to thank you again for your help and hospitality.' The atheist KGB officer had to force himself to speak like a loyal Catholic churchgoer.

The priest clasped his hands across his chest as the traditional mark of respect. 'Where are you going now?'

'It's better I don't tell you,' said the Russian. Sulecki wanted Father Bardecki to interpret this as meaning he was joining an underground Solidarity cell.

'Good luck, my friend. God is with you.'

Sulecki made an uncharacteristic but dignified bow of the head. 'Thank you, Father and goodbye.'

He turned and left, and within a minute he was in the dark alleyway leading from the cloisters onto the cobbled pavement of Piwna Street.

It took forty-five minutes for Sulecki to reach Dzika Street. He was greeted at Jola's apartment by the faint sound of a short-wave radio crackling with the jammed signal of Radio Free Europe. In a corner, a black-and-white picture flickered from the old Polish television which Bogdan and Jola had recently bought for an exorbitant price at the Sunday flea market. The nightly 'puppet show' by the military newsreaders was underway and Jola greeted Sulecki with grim news.

'It's bad. The trouble in the south is getting worse ...

twelve hundred miners are underground at Ziemowit ...
The shaft's blocked, and another twelve hundred are
refusing to leave the new Piast mine nearby ...' Jola drew
heavily and regularly on a cigarette. 'They claim the
strikers are not letting doctors, priests or Solidarity
advisers underground. And now even the Soviets are
reporting armed resistance at Huta Katowice where steel-
workers are threatening to blow up the furnaces.'

Sulecki raised his eyebrows in order to give the
impression of concern, although in his mind he wanted
the ZOMO to crush every counter-revolutionary Solidarity thug.

'Were you followed?' asked Jola.

'Don't think so,' said the Russian. 'No one showed any
interest when I left the church. On the way I kept checking and doubling back but I saw no one.'

'Good.' Jola was noticeably relieved.

'Still no news,' she shrugged. 'But it's not surprising.
Poland's now a country of no news.'

They sat at either end of the sofa and conversation was
difficult.

'I'm fascinated by your accent,' said Sulecki, trying to
break the chill. 'It's not from Warsaw is it? Where do
you come from?'

'Szczecin.'

'And Bogdan?'

'Szczecin too ... And what about your accent Andrzej?
That's not from Warsaw either.'

'No! ... From the east. I was brought up on a farm
near Bialystok on the Soviet border ...'

Conversation faded as Jola kept her eyes on the television. Sulecki, though, used the time to begin piecing
together a possible future strategy. Here in this high-
rise apartment at 6 Dzika Street, the KGB Lieutenant
Colonel believed he had found the ideal underground
'nest' from which to launch the next phase of *Amber
Monkey*.

51

Bogdan sat propped against the cell wall like a homeless vagrant. He was wrapped in two thin blankets which smelt of terror and burnt cooking fat, but which had separated life from death during that long night. As he sat shivering, Bogdan wondered how much strength remained inside his emaciated frame, and how much longer he could endure the SB's tortuous games.

The captain arrived unannounced at nine o'clock. He spoke immediately, picking up from yesterday's interrogation as if there had only been a momentary pause.

'Now ... Your name is Piotr Glowacki. We have records of your past cooperation with the police and we expect your renewed cooperation ... Please sign here.'

The captain once again returned to the idea of Bogdan's new identity as a police informer. Bogdan fought to overcome his fears. 'I will not sign. We have agreed nothing,' he said defiantly.

The captain's stare lingered, revealing his fury at Bogdan's continued stubbornness. But then his manner changed.

'Citizen Miskiewicz ...' As suddenly as the captain had introduced the pseudonym 'Glowacki' a few minutes earlier, he dropped the name. 'You and your family have a small apartment on Dzika Street. Your screaming baby has to sleep in the same room as both of you, and that room is where you live and eat. I have authority to promise you a new apartment with better heating and more rooms ... If you cooperate, you will receive privilege coupons. I guarantee you unlimited, good-quality meat. You can live as well as functionaries like me. It's an offer you can't refuse.'

Bogdan sat assessing the captain's attempt at bribery.

It was what in Soviet labour camps they called the 'Menu 9A syndrome' – the method camp officials used to tempt prisoners into cooperating by offering them the improved 'Menu 9A' which was diabolical, but still better than the worse food of Menu 9B.

Bogdan sensed that the captain's switch of tactics might mean that he was getting desperate.

'Captain, I wish to remind you that under Polish law you cannot keep me for more than forty-eight hours without formally arresting me. I am a trade unionist and a member of Solidarity. I do not sell my ideals and principles for a privileged ration ticket. Do not demean me and what I stand for . . .'

The captain jumped up, thrusting his juddering face and skewed, evil eyes directly at Bogdan. 'Comrade, don't you dare demean me either! I am a security officer of the Polish People's Republic. I know the law, but we are above it. If you don't cooperate, then in forty-eight hours we can arrange things . . . And don't assume we'll give you one of our quick, easy deaths – the "Unexplained car accident" or throwing you from a train. We can make you suffer indignity indefinitely – for years if necessary. We'll start sending political criminals like you to special camps. I've already seen the plans for "civil defence units" where people like you will sleep in tents or railway carriages in the middle of nowhere, and do twelve hours a day of heavy manual work, just as Soviet criminals do in Siberia.'

The captain lowered himself back into his chair, adding in a lighter tone of voice: 'You see, comrade, those are the options. Signing this agreement is the solution.'

Bogdan stared vacantly and there was silence . . . One minute . . . Two minutes . . . Five minutes . . . Ten minutes . . . Neither adversary could break the other.

'Fuck you, you bastard!'

The captain stormed out of the interrogation room knowing the appalling consequences for Bogdan. Over the next hour, fifteen junior and middle-ranking SB officers came to cell 3/65 to thrash gratuitous hell out of

237

him. At eleven o'clock the captain returned to confront Bogdan's crumpled body.

'Now! What is your response, Citizen Miskiewicz. You will sign, I hope.'

Bogdan was barely conscious. He could scarcely understand the question, let alone reply. After a minute the captain's words sank in. Bogdan could not speak, but he strained his torn body to make a faint nod.

It was day eleven of martial law and two days before Christmas. At last the captain believed he had broken Bogdan Miskiewicz.

The captain left Bogdan for four hours until the afternoon, during which time aches and pains matured into bruises, and the steelworker's head spun with a chaotic mix of hallucinations and thoughts for Jola. He lay groaning in a blanket on the bitterly cold floor. Mercifully, however, he had been spared the most obscene SB techniques – hammers to hit the body, pliers to tear tendons and muscles from limbs, and gadgets like a potato peeler to plough through skin and disfigure him.

The captain returned at three o'clock. He brought a second chair and was accompanied by the fat woman orderly who carried a chipped vacuum flask of fresh steaming tea plus a bowl of hot water and medical dressings. The captain lifted Bogdan onto the chair then resumed his own dominating pose behind the files on the table as the woman bathed and dressed Bogdan's injuries.

'Cigarette?' The captain made his offer from a new packet of western cigarettes. Bogdan took one gratefully. 'Take the rest!' the captain added patronisingly. 'We can get many more where they came from, Comrade.'

Bogdan had decided to pre-empt any further efforts by the captain to destroy him.

'I want to leave Poland. I want to apply for a passport and passage to the West.'

Bogdan believed the emigration request was the way to avoid compromising his underground colleagues. The captain responded with a sly and malicious laugh as he shook his head slowly and complacently.

'No!' he snapped. 'You can't get out of your commitments that easily, Comrade. In fact you can't get out of them at all. You'll be staying in Poland ... and when we tell you to dance, you'll dance. You have work to do here, and you're no use to us in the West.' The captain paused and flicked dust off the table. 'I refuse your request. I will not even record it in the files.'

'No passport indefinitely?' asked Bogdan incredulously.

'Nothing is ever final. Long term I don't rule out the possibility of your getting one .. but not until after you have fulfilled your commitments to the security services. Maybe in six months or a year? Not before.'

Bogdan was trapped. 'Oh dear God,' he thought, stiffening as a wave of shame swept through his body. He had finally given in. But what had happened to Bogdan Miskiewicz, the robust Warsaw steelworker and young lion who had risked everything to help create Solidarity? Even Bogdan didn't know.

The captain re-opened the top file and read it like a military order. 'You will be classified as what we call a *'wire'*. You will continue your activities in the Solidarity underground but you will not tell colleagues any details of your arrest, detention and interrogation. You will report regularly on your underground cell to me. I will be the only functionary aware of your identity. I will want from you full details of all counter-revolutionaries who you know to be involved in anti-state activities. I need the locations of meeting points, underground caches and clandestine printing presses. I expect to be informed of the locations and times of all planned meetings and demonstrations ... Any questions?'

Bogdan winced as the pain tightened every injured muscle in his body. 'Yes ... And what about your promises?' he ventured, his voice weak with fear. 'What about the new apartment, the new washing machine, the new cooker, the new furniture, the regular supply of good quality meat: when will my wife and I start receiving them?' Bogdan's dry empty voice rang with cynicism.

'You receive them when you deliver your side of the deal,' the captain lied. Suddenly the SB officer had become abrasive and dismissive.

'And how do I know whether to trust you?'

'Comrade Functionary Miskiewicz, you have no alternative.'

'You mean the promises were lies?'

The captain gave a non-committal shrug of the shoulders. 'Just piss off. Get out of here!'

The captain had won, but Bogdan still had the defiance to know that he would not let the SB crush him. For the second time in a week he hobbled the length of the Mostowski Palace corridor, then hauled his bruised body onto the tram which rumbled north towards Dzika Street.

When Jola opened the apartment door she froze in horror for the second time in a week. Facing her was a gaunt, battered, skeletal figure with swollen cheeks, weeping blisters and cakes of dried blood in his hair. Bogdan was in an even worse condition than after the previous interrogation so Jola did not dare embrace him for fear of worsening his injuries and inflicting more pain. 'Dar-l-ing!', she screeched as she gently took his hand and guided him into the apartment.

Bogdan was transfixed by the black-and-white images of the uniformed newsreaders unemotionally announcing the end of the Katowice steelworks occupation. For a full minute he stood mesmerised by the television pictures, his lower arms outstretched, his fingers crooked and splayed painfully like the delicate ivory ribs of a Japanese fan.

'They almost killed me ... They mashed me like a potato and taunted me with death ... They wanted me to betray everything I stand for ... The SB have no respect for human dignity ...'

Only now did Bogdan register the unknown face staring at him from the kitchen. He turned slowly towards

240

Jola, his eyes silently posing the questions he did not dare ask. Jola clutched his arm and stroked his neck.

'Darling, this is Andrzej Sulecki ..,' Jola began hesitantly, uncertain how Bogdan would react. He merely stared at Sulecki as Jola continued, 'Andrzej's from Solidarity and he's in trouble. I went to the Aid Committee at St Martin's Church two days ago. I needed help – any help – to find you. That's where I met Andrzej. He's on the run. The SB are watching his apartment and he needs somewhere to stay for a few nights. The priest said it was getting too dangerous at St Martin's – too many spooks and informers. So I said he could stay with us for a few days.'

Stiffly, Bogdan half-raised his arm to shake hands but it was a cold, suspicious greeting. The stranger's response was ingratiating as he tried to break the ice and reassure Bogdan. 'I'm deeply grateful to your wife. Perhaps we could help each other ... make plans together?'

Bogdan turned stiffly towards Jola. He wanted to tell her about the horror of the Mostowski Palace but now it would have to wait. Was Sulecki a genuine Solidarity member on the run, or an undercover SB agent? 'You're taking a bloody big risk aren't you, darling?' he whispered.

Jola's response was nervous but razor sharp. 'But .. Andrzej was desperate. It's only a stopgap. If he had stayed at St Martin's he'd have been rearrested.'

Again Bogdan gave no sign one way or the other. Perhaps Jola was right after all. He lowered himself slowly onto the sofa-bed, his face contorting as pain shot through his body. Jola bathed his wounds and began to remove his filthy clothes while Sulecki began telling his story.

Bogdan watched Sulecki's face for clues. Slowly he recalled the guttural tones, the sunken features and the distant – oh so distant – manner. Bogdan faintly recalled Sulecki at the Mokotowska Street headquarters – a man with a routine job at a telex machine, but a radical mind. He remembered too how Sulecki cruised the corridors picking arguments with union activists at all levels. And he recalled how Sulecki had provoked furious discussions and urged leaders like Zbigniew Bujak to pursue the most radical policies – kicking out the Communist Party, then a workers' takeover of power with more strikes and total defiance of the authorities. And Bogdan began to remember how some people had asked why a person with such strong convictions never got beyond a job in the telex room. But in the turmoil of Solidarity's constant battles with the government, no one had had time to care.

Whatever Bogdan's first suspicions about Sulecki, slowly they warmed to each other, talking for hours and swapping dramatic details of their experiences in the eleven days of martial law. The conversation comforted Bogdan and helped mask the pain, but he still had to find a way to talk to Jola alone.

As he could not bath himself he asked Jola to help him, and once inside the tiny bathroom with its stained, unpainted walls he kicked the door firmly shut. Bogdan and Jola sat on the flaking enamel rim of the old steel bath hugging each other just as they had done eight years earlier when they were two young lovers perched on the pier at Gdynia on the Baltic. Bogdan turned on the tap and tepid water dribbled slowly out, drowning their whispers. For the first time Jola saw a tear roll down her husband's cheek.

'They broke me ... The bastards broke me and I couldn't take any more, darling.' Bogdan spoke slowly. 'But you mustn't be ashamed ... I kept my honour to the end ... It was too horrible. You know enough of the SB's tactics without me having to spell them out ... They pushed me to the point where if I'd resisted any longer they'd have killed me, and then I would have been dead ... a forgotten martyr.'

Jola gasped as she peeled the bloodied clothes from her husband's body. Bogdan shuddered. 'Remember our conversation last week? The time for that decision has now come. I'm useless to the underground now because I threaten the security of the whole structure.' He paused

242

and steeled himself. 'Darling, there's only one option. We must leave Poland immediately ... Legally? Illegally? ... I don't care how, but we must leave.'

The silence was broken only by the noise of the tap slowly filling the bath. Bogdan saw that Jola did not want to speak. 'I know it'll take time to organise things: a few days if we're lucky, several weeks if things don't work out. But my thoughts now are to feed the SB captain enough bullshit to keep him off our backs. By the time he discovers I've deceived him I want to be out of Warsaw – and hopefully Poland too.'

Jola's whispered reply was immediate. 'You're right, darling.' Uppermost in her mind was the future for Miatek. 'I want us to live as a family, and if we can only do that outside our mother country then that's a fate we have to accept.'

The bath had filled to the brim, the water lapping against the lip of the bath under their overhanging buttocks. They leant against each other – forehead to forehead, nose touching nose.

'And what about Andrzej?' asked Jola.

'What about him?' Bogdan asked indifferently.

'Before you returned, he told me he was planning to escape to Sweden ... He wants to leave Poland like us.'

'What's his idea?' asked Bogdan.

'He's given me no details,' shrugged Jola.

Bogdan was sceptical. 'Can we really take the risk of him joining us? Isn't it a bit odd that he turned up while I was in the Mostowski Palace? Was that a coincidence? How do we know he's not an SB agent planted by the captain to check on me? We only have his word about the story of his capture and his escape.'

Jola was more sympathetic. 'But you said you remembered him from Mokotowska Street ... Surely that's good enough? And he could even be an asset. Three minds are better than two. Then there's more chance of spotting traps and dangers.'

Bogdan brooded.

'An extra person is an extra liability,' he snorted. 'But

don't let's waste valuable time making a judgment on
Andrzej. We've got more pressing things to do. We need
to make full use of the relaxations in curfew and travel
restrictions over Christmas. We must use every minute
of every day before the captain rumbles my deception.'

'So what do we do next?' asked Jola in a fraught voice.

'Tomorrow's Christmas Eve, darling. We start by
deceiving your brother Woytek, that bastard who
betrayed me to the SB. You must go and see him. Play
it straight and don't give any hint that we know it was
him who trapped me. Take him a small Christmas
present. Tell him a string of white lies. Tell him how
worried you are about me. How I was hauled in by the
SB, interrogated and tortured. Tell him that I'm now a
broken man, and that my interest in Solidarity's underground has gone. Tell him about the deal with the
captain, and how I plan to cooperate with the SB to
guarantee our freedom. But don't stay too long, don't let
him ply you with too much vodka to get the better of
you.'

'And then . . .?'

'Then tomorrow you take the train home to Szczecin.'

'Szczecin?' said Jola incredulously. 'But no one can get
out of Poland through East Germany, and no one can get
on a ferry to Sweden except foreigners. So for God's
sake, why Szczecin?'

'Martial law regulations say all Poles must return to
the place where they're officially registered,' said Bogdan.
'The Polish bureaucracy is inefficient, so we'll take
advantage of it. You've lived in Warsaw for five years but
the Ministry has never caught up with the fact. They still
think you live in Szczecin. I know it will be Christmas
Eve, but when you get to Szczecin celebrations will have
to take second place to finding your cousin Romek.'

'Why drag Romek into this?' snapped Jola who by now
was increasingly confused.

'Think of his job . . .'

Jola stalled, frantically trying to remember what
Romek did.

'He's an aircraft mechanic,' said Bogdan. 'He maintains crop sprayer aircraft for the State Foreign Trade Enterprise. My plan is for Romek to fly us out of Poland.'

Jola was stunned. 'But he's not a proper pilot, just an engineer.'

'But he must know how to fly. Tell Romek that if he agrees, and if he can arrange the plane, then he can bring his family too.'

Stress lines on Jola's young face tightened as she clenched her hands. 'You're mad! Has the Mostowski Palace damaged your brain, Bogusz? The Baltic coast and Oder estuary are bristling with the Warsaw Pact's most advanced early warning systems and radar stations. Even if we get off the ground, the Polish military will shoot us down. And if they don't, the East Germans will do the job for them and we'll be blown out of the sky.'

Bogdan cut Jola dead, holding her firmly by each shoulder. 'Not if I'm right. I have a hunch, and if it works we can make it...' Bogdan spoke in a warm tone of confidence and self-assurance. 'But we need to know from Romek what possibilities he has for stealing a plane.'

'Stealing a plane?'

Bogdan ignored his wife's look of amazement. 'If Romek says it's possible then we'll all uproot and take the train to Szczecin. Tell him we'll discuss details when I get there.'

'What about the roadblocks and ID checks? How do we get you and Andrzej there?' squealed Jola.

'We'll find a way. You always can in Poland.' Bogdan's grip on Jola was firmer now. 'Darling, your journey tomorrow will be a test run. Your job is not just to find a plane, but to check security between here and Szczecin too.'

'And once I get to Szczecin, how do I justify to the militia and army why I'm returning to Warsaw?' Jola was still shaken by the suddenness of developments.

'You'll be returning to visit your sick husband and family. In the circumstances it's not far from the truth.'

Jola's hands began to shake with fear, and she bit her

nails. 'When do you want me back?'

'It can't be until the 27th at the earliest. Probably later. That'll give you at least two clear days – Christmas Day and the 26th. Meanwhile I'll make preparations this end. There are plenty of Baltic herrings to plant with the SB.'

'And what about Andrzej?' asked Jola.

Bogdan had yet to calculate how to accommodate Sulecki in the plan, but his instinctive answer was positive. 'Andrzej comes too. It's the least risky option ... We can't dump a fellow union activist out on the street. That would not be the solidarity our union preaches.'

'Do we tell him tonight?' asked Jola.

'No,' said Bogdan firmly. 'I'll tell him when you're away. Leave me to choose the right moment.'

Jola sighed, closing her eyes in despair. 'It will be a grim Christmas ... You here. Me on a train to Szczecin and cooped like a chicken in my parents' overcrowded apartment...'

'... but preferable to internment or prison,' added Bogdan pragmatically. 'And soon it will be even better: we'll be in the West and away from this socialist shit-hole.'

In the main room Jola and Bogdan found Sulecki slumped uncomfortably against the dirty wall behind the sofa-bed. He appeared to be asleep. But unknown to them throughout their hour in the bathroom the KGB Lieutenant Colonel had tuned his ears to listen through the thin plasterboard. The Russian agent had not heard everything, but he had gathered the gist of Bogdan's plan. It was masterful and he liked it. The method was perfect and the cover ideal.

Sweden! ... Perhaps in a few days, perhaps in a month or two. Wrapped in a couple of old blankets and feigning sleep, the KGB Lieutenant Colonel was enthused by what he had just discovered.

52

It was not the ideal way to spend Christmas Eve. Immediately curfew ended at 6 a.m., Jola kissed Bogdan farewell and travelled across Warsaw by tram to leave baby Miatek with a friend before visiting her brother Woytek to deceive him as planned.

By late morning, Jola was at Warsaw's central station for the lunchtime train to Szczecin. She felt vulnerable and exposed as she pushed through the dense crowd of grim-faced Christmas travellers shoving past each other with over-stuffed bags and flimsy cases. The atmosphere was thick with stale air and diesel fumes; the mood was sullen and depressed. As she queued for her ticket Jola scanned the giant concrete and marble concourse, watching the conspicuous SB men loitering ill-at-ease as they surveyed the crowd. Nearby, jumpy, spotty-faced ZOMO conscripts clutching sub-machine guns hovered alongside the ticket queues watching eagle-eyed for signs of 'counter-revolutionary' opposition and 'terrorists'.

Jola feared for the future. Was her journey really worth the risk? Would it not be more realistic for Bogdan to abandon his defiance and retreat into a shell of domestic seclusion somewhere in Poland? As she sat crammed for nine hours on a plastic seat in the corner of the unlit and unheated second-class compartment, her overwrought mind helter-skeltered through the viability of the escape plan. But whatever her doubts, for Bogdan's sake she could not back down.

At dusk, while Jola's train was snaking into the city of Poznan three hundred kilometres west of Warsaw, Bogdan was trudging home to Dzika Street. For Bogdan, Jola and most of Poland, Christmas Eve 1981 under General Jaruzelski was a shadow of Poland's euphoric Christmas of 1980. This was a Christmas to forget and the worst since the horrors of the Second World War.

Instead of sitting down to the traditional seasonal feast with his family on Christmas Eve, Bogdan was alone with Andrzej Sulecki in a cold apartment. There were no lights, no Christmas gifts and no tree. There were no friends with whom to celebrate and share the traditional fun of telling fortunes by sticking hay under the table-cloth. No family with whom to eat the customary seven-course meal of borsch and *uszka*, ravioli, *babas* and poppyseed cake, then carp in grey sauce followed by prune compote and gingerbread. All Bogdan could find in the refrigerator was a scraggy lump of pork, some milk, a knob of rationed butter and a few vegetables.

That evening the military censors made an effort to lift the nation's depressed mood by replacing news broadcasts with Christmas carols and a seasonal play. And sandwiched between them, General Jaruzelski broadcast what was for him an uncharacteristically emotional Christmas message. The deaths of seven miners at the Wujek colliery were what he called 'my own personal tragedy,' but he denied there had been hundreds more deaths under martial law. The Polish leader said that reports of mass arrests and of people being held in freezing conditions and being tortured were lies, and he concluded: 'I cannot wish you a merry and prosperous Christmas. This year's holiday is a modest but safe one ... May the festive season promote wise, patriotic reflections.'

Only later that evening did Polish Radio announce that the twelve hundred miners at the Ziemovit colliery in Silesia had ended their occupation and that the militia had found 'ten and a half tonnes of explosives' inside the pit.

'They're systematically crushing and outmanoeuvring us, Andrzej. We haven't got a chance,' Bogdan said despairingly to Sulecki as the broadcast ended.

Such was the authorities' control after eleven days of martial law that they felt confident enough to suspend the curfew for Christmas and permit the broadcasting of midnight mass. Bogdan was determined to go in person.

248

At eleven o'clock he left Sulecki in the apartment and crossed the railway bridge to the church of St Stanislaw Kostka's in Zoliborz district. it was an uplifting experience. This year, the celebration of Christ's birth was a spontaneous and emotional rallying point for defiance, with open calls among the congregation to mobilise resistance to military rule. 'Every action of protest, even the most insignificant, strikes a blow and hastens the returning of the army to barracks,' urged an underground Solidarity bulletin circulating at the mass.

As Bogdan hurried home through the snow flurries, across the Atlantic in Washington the American President, Ronald Reagan, was appearing on television to denounce the 'outrages' of martial law. 'Free men cannot and will not stand idly by in the face of brutal repression,' Mr Reagan said before announcing economic sanctions 'to underscore our fundamental opposition to the repressive actions against the Polish people.'

The words of the American president were loud and passionate, but Bogdan, Sulecki and all sides in Poland knew such furious condemnations from the leader of the Western world would make no difference in the new militarised Poland of General Jaruzelski.

53

Warsaw Radio was announcing that Tuesday 29 December had been Poland's first strike-free day for fifteen months when Bogdan heard the loud metallic clunk of the lift outside the apartment. It was followed by the distinctive clopping of boot heels in the corridor, the familiar routine of a rattling key ring, and finally a shove to open the front door. Jola burst in and collapsed. It was 9 a.m.

There was no need to speak. They hugged each other in silence for several minutes, half-watched by Sulecki who stood brewing tea in the tiny kitchen. Jola was so drained that she burst into tears. Bogdan waited. Then he asked gently, 'How long was the journey?'

'Eleven hours,' sighed Jola. 'Timetables no longer mean anything. The train stopped everywhere and we stopped for hours in the middle of nowhere ... I didn't have a seat and I had to stand the whole way back from Szczecin ... There was no heat or food on board either...'

Sulecki volunteered a beaker of tea which Jola grabbed gratefully and pressed against her chilled hands and face. 'How's Miatek?' she enquired anxiously.

'He's fine. Your student friend brought him over for an hour or so yesterday. The dear little boy slept the whole time.'

'What about the SB – did they visit you again?'

'No! Haven't seen them. I'll volunteer nothing to them until they come for me.' Bogdan chuckled and Jola began to look brighter.

Bogdan sensed the atmosphere was right to switch the conversation. 'How was Szczecin?' he asked blandly.

'As bad as here ... freezing, empty, depressed and at a standstill. The word is that hundreds have been arrested.

The shipyard's officially working but little work's being done because of a go-slow. Managers and workers who are politically suspect are being kicked out and the canal outside the docks is jammed with ships waiting to be unloaded. A friend told me the stevedores are just moving goods around the docks to give the impression of work.'

'What about factories?'

'The same story ... some workers are pushing their machines to the limit so they break down. Others are secretly sabotaging equipment, which stops production because there aren't any spare parts.'

Sulecki plied Jola with more tea as Bogdan began pressing the important questions. 'Who did you see?'

'On the 24th I went straight to Romek's home. I spent Christmas there with his youngest brother and his sister. His middle brother's in hiding and hasn't been seen since the 13th.'

'Are they well?'

'Surviving ... just! Danuta – Romek's wife – has been sacked from her teaching job. A military panel found her views too radical. She'd done too much work for Solidarity.'

'And Romek ...?'

'He's been going to work at the airfield every day as if nothing has happened. He's doing what he says he does every winter – getting *Pezetel's* Antonov biplanes ready for crop-spraying to start in the spring.'

Bogdan interrupted her. 'And what about my proposal?'

Jola clutched the beaker hard and bit nervously on the rim. 'When I first put up the idea, Romek said you must be mad. So I had to work on him. For two days he thought about little else. He turned over in his mind all his future prospects – for work, and for life in general. Then on Monday, the news that the nine hundred miners at Piast had ended their sit-in seemed to clinch it. He suddenly swung round in his chair and said: "I'll do it". And that was it, without a second thought.'

'How does he rate our chances?'

'He said he wouldn't have agreed to try if he didn't think there was at least a better than even chance of succeeding. But he wants to be sure we appreciate the risks – and not just of being shot down either. Romek's only a mechanic. He knows how the Antonov works and the theory of how to fly it, but he's never actually flown the biplane himself . . .'

'Does he think he can do it?'

'Yes, but with reservations. He says he'll need another pair of hands and eyes in the cockpit in case things go wrong.'

'Who?' asked Bogdan jumpily.

'Another mechanic called Stefan Glabinski. He's from the *Pezetel* base in Poznan . . . Romek says he's reliable and they've known each other for years. One day in the hangar he said he'd even overheard Stefan joking about leaving Poland.'

Bogdan was reluctant to bring in yet another person and his family. The greater the number of people involved, the greater the risk of making a mistake and being discovered. But he realised that for practical reasons there was no option and he would have to agree. 'How many in Stefan's family?'

'Four! . . . Himself, his wife and two boys aged twelve and eight.'

'And four in Romek's too. It's a lot of people. With Andrzej and us that makes eleven plus baby Miatek. Can the Antonov take that many? With fuel so difficult to come by, the extra weight could make all the difference.'

'Romek didn't think it would matter.'

Bogdan was still unhappy, but he moved his attention on to other problems. 'What about getting hold of the plane? How easy would that be?'

'Romek has no idea, but he's working on how to do it.'

'He must have given you some idea of how long it might take to get one? After all he knows the security set-up because he works with the planes all day,' said Bogdan in a tone of exasperation.

'Maybe a week, maybe three months. He said at least

one Antonov in his care is fully maintained and fit to fly. But first he has to steal five to six hundred litres of fuel from bowsers which are now under military supervision ... And that's not all. The planes are based not up at the coast but fifty kilometres inland on the Aeroclub field in Szczecin itself. That means he's got to fly north over land and the Oder estuary before even reaching the Baltic. Romek says the first stage is for him to find a way to fly an Antonov up to the coast with military approval.'

Bogdan huffed impatiently. He had always known there would be problems, but until now he had no idea of their exact nature.

'Romek says the uncertainty means we must be ready for anything at a moment's notice,' said Jola. 'If we're serious about the escape we must not sit it out in Warsaw. We must use the curfew relaxations to get to Szczecin while we can, then lie low so that we are ready to move the moment the first opportunity arises.'

Bogdan had already reached the same conclusion. He turned to Sulecki, who had already been told of Bogdan's plan that morning. 'What do you think, Andrzej?'

The KGB Colonel was in no hurry to respond.

'I'm as desperate to leave as both of you,' he finally ventured thoughtfully. 'I like the idea ... but the risks appal me.' In his mind he pondered the options again. Did he really have to go to the extreme of escaping to the West in order to confirm his identity as a disaffected Solidarity extremist?

'Yes, I'll go with you,' he said eventually. 'But how do we get to Szczecin?'

Bogdan swung back towards Jola. 'What was security like on the train, darling?'

'In the end not as tight as it was on the way up there. There were a lot of militia, SB and the army at the stations, but no actual checks on the train at either end. I didn't have to show my ID once.'

'Even to get the ticket?'

'No, not even then!'

'Right,' said Bogdan determinedly. 'We've got two

days. We must pack, collect Miatek, and leave by train on New Year's Eve. We have to take full advantage of the curfew relaxation over New Year before Jaruzelski clamps down again ... Are we agreed?'

Agreement was unanimous.

'I'd go tomorrow if I could,' said Bogdan, 'but first I must try to contact Jurek again. I can't leave a loyal mate like him in the lurch. Jola! First thing in the morning you'll have to go round to Sergiusz Marwinski's...'

It was Sergiusz who had carried the trick message from Jola's brother Woytek which had led to Bogdan's capture by the SB. Despite his fury when Sergiusz turned up at the hideaway, Bogdan had to risk using him. Sergiusz was the only union colleague who knew the location of the allotment shed and the only person Bogdan could trust to find Jurek.

'Tell Sergiusz to go to the hideout. I know I told him never to show his face there again but now it's different. He should tell Jurek to meet me at the Gong cafe at four o'clock tomorrow afternoon.'

For the first time in many days Bogdan had forgotten the lingering pain of torture. He was fired with a renewed determination. For the first time he realised that the captain at the Mostowski Palace had not crushed him.

54

A murky, ochre-coloured dusk enveloped the Stalinesque blocks of central Warsaw as Bogdan threaded his way through the late afternoon crowds towards the Gong cafe on Aleja Jarozolimskie. This time, he carefully circled the block three times to check the SB were not following. Then at four o'clock precisely he pushed open the cafe's rusty metal door, stamped the clogged snow from his boots and swept back the scabby velvet draught curtain. Without speaking he handed his anorak, scarf and woollen hat to the unshaven attendant who sat behind the cloakroom counter chewing tobacco and collecting two zlotys from each customer. Bogdan pushed cautiously through a second set of doors into the smoky, interior where dirty lace swags hung over the windows and the walls were painted black.

The cafe was not full, but like each customer Bogdan had to wait for the blonde-rinsed head waitress to seat him. He hovered nervously, his eyes scanning the two dozen tiny food-stained tables. Jurek had not arrived but there was still time. He also took the opportunity to search for the SB agent normally on duty in the cafe. His eyes eventually found him in the far corner: a young red-faced man in his early thirties with greasy hair, a black jersey and new denim jeans from the west. An empty beer bottle and the tell-tale ashtray piled high with cigarette stubs stood on the table, and under his chair lay the usual white plastic bag containing his radio microphone and recording device.

The waitress smiled a mouthful of stained, black teeth at Bogdan and guided him away from the *U-Bek* to a table along the wall, half-hidden by other customers. Martial law had crushed the usual high spirits of cafe life. As he tried to relax at the table, all Bogdan could hear was the gentle babble of low voices inside and the growling of trams on the street outside. In one corner an officious *apparatchik* sat stern and upright in a grey suit sipping Bulgarian brandy and reading the Communist Party newspaper *Trybuna Ludu* from behind tinted glasses. In another sat a scruffy middle-aged couple gazing incongruously into each other's eyes.

'Coffee, please! Milk and sugar!'

'*Nie ma!* No milk or sugar!' the waitress replied.

'But I thought martial law had normalised life?' retorted Bogdan sarcastically. He and the waitress grinned at each other. Nothing was ever normal in Poland.

It was ten past four. Where was Jurek? To kill time Bogdan sauntered across to the ageing German juke box and inserted twenty zlotys. Ringo Starr? Neil Sedaka? Johnny Halliday? Elton John? All the ageing western artists were carefully selected to be non-political and non-controversial. He chose what had become the cult song of the Solidarity era: Boney M and 'Gotta go home'. Across the cafe, the SB man showed no interest and Bogdan returned to his table. As he sat down, the cafe door clunked open and Jurek brushed breathlessly through the draught curtain. When he spotted Bogdan he was visibly shaken by how much his colleague had deteriorated since they met briefly in the subway ten days earlier. Bogdan clutched Jurek's hand, and Jurek leaned forward to speak in a low, voice. 'You look terrible! Where have you been?'

'Mostowski Palace. Twice . . . We shouldn't spend too long here. The SB goon is sitting behind you in the corner but doesn't seem interested for the moment.'

Both men fell conspiratorially silent as the waitress brought Jurek's coffee. They sipped the tepid black liquid and Bogdan began relating what he had been through.

'I was a terrified wreck and in the end I had no choice but to submit – for me, for Jola, for Miatek, and for Solidarity. The ZOMO have already created seven martyrs at the Wujek mine. I didn't want to become another. But they didn't just break me, they forced me to collaborate and become a *'wire'* – an informer.'

Bogdan shook his head slowly from side to side with shame. 'But whatever the SB thinks I've promised them, the reality is that I'm not going to help them, Jurek. So don't worry – I won't jeopardise the printing operation ... I've thought of a way out.'

'I shouldn't concern yourself anyway,' said Jurek. 'I've had to close it down. It was becoming too risky. The SB are burrowing deep into Solidarity cells. Their wires are identifying the printers, the communications, supply lines for ink, paper and information – the lot. Then when the SB decide the time's right, the heavies move in for the mass arrest – what they call the "clean-up" ...' Jurek snapped his fingers '... then puff! The wire disappears to another cell to protect his cover and the cell is busted. And so it goes on, the SB worm burrowing deeper and deeper and systematically destroying our union's underground structure.'

Bogdan sighed dejectedly. The SB's dirty tricks had always been a fact of life in Poland. From the first days of the Gdansk shipyard occupation in August 1980 Solidarity leaders like Bogdan had always had to be vigilant to protect themselves from the wires.

'Listen,' he said looking straight at Jurek. 'I've thought of a way to deal with the SB. I'm getting out, Jurek ... Jola and I are secretly leaving Poland.'

Jurek did not try to conceal his amazement. 'When d'you intend going?' he asked.

Bogdan eyed his colleague. He did not want to give away too much. 'When we're ready, Jurek. Maybe a week or two. There's no frantic urgency ...'

'How?' Jurek persisted. 'Train? Car? Boat? Smuggling yourselves somehow?'

'Secret means secret!' said Bogdan stubbornly. 'Even to a good colleague like you.'

Jurek chuckled. 'You're a brave man. And you think you can survive escape routes that have killed others tougher than you in the past?'

257

Bogdan nodded humbly. 'I just can't stay, Jurek. If I can't work in the underground then my principles won't allow me to stay in Poland. I won't become a neutered stooge. But you and Solidarity haven't lost me yet. I'll be a decoy. While I'm planning our escape I'll feed false information to my new SB godfather – the captain. I'll direct his efforts *away* from clandestine operations instead of towards them. My misleading intelligence will keep them occupied in the wrong areas for a few days.'

Jurek appeared shaken by Bogdan's news. 'You're brave and I admire you, my friend,' he said finally.

'The feeling's mutual, Jurek,' said Bogdan. 'You must reopen the printing press as soon as you think it's safe again.' He flicked a 100 zloty bill onto the glass tabletop to pay for the coffees.

Outside, under the street lights, Bogdan and Jurek clutched each other firmly and emotionally as they said farewell. Neither knew when – or if – they would ever meet again. Then a gust of freezing wind vacuumed up a blast of ice particles which peppered their faces like flint chippings.

Inside the cafe, meanwhile, the middle-aged couple in the corner ended their kissing. Within an hour the report on their afternoon's undercover surveillance duty would be on the desk of their divisional SB commander at the Wilcza Street depot.

The train journey to Szczecin on New Year's Eve was as grim, cold and uncomfortable as Jola's lone reconnaissance trip eight days earlier on Christmas Eve. But this time Miatek's screaming and regular baby needs made the journey even more unbearable. To minimise the risk of all four of them being picked up by a random security swoop during the ten-hour journey, Sulecki sat two compartments down the corridor from Bogdan and Jola. The authorities had announced a last-minute suspension of curfew for New Year's Eve; it meant that when the four reached Szczecin two hours late at ten o'clock that evening they did not have to spend an uncomfortable night at the station.

With telephones disconnected by martial law there had been no way for Jola to warn of their arrival, so the Toczeks were taken by surprise when they arrived at the tiny house on Golienowska Street. But surprise turned quickly to delight, and the five adults talked, drank, ate and swapped tales of martial law long into the night.

By the first dawn of 1982 the vodka, moonshine and smuggled whisky bought from a Polish seaman had spun their deadly charms and left all of them struggling to make coherent conversation. But the unexpected New Year celebration had sealed a vital new bond of trust between the Miskiewiczes, the Toczeks and Sulecki for the immense dangers which lay ahead.

As the last snow of 1981 fell in Warsaw, a sergeant and lieutenant from the Mostowski Palace parked their grimy, mud-splattered *Polonez* outside No. 6 Dzika Street, paddled through the slush of a slight temporary thaw and took the lift to the fifteenth floor.

It was the ninth SB visit in as many hours. Once again they thumped persistently on the door of apartment 80, and once again there was no reply. To be absolutely sure that the Miskiewiczes were not secretly hiding inside the apartment, the two officers ostentatiously walked away from the front door and pressed the lift button as if they were leaving. As the lift clunked down to the ground they tiptoed back towards the apartment, where once again the SB sergeant put his ear to the door. Still there was no sound, so this time the two officers forced open the door. In a matter of moments it became clear from the tidy apartment and the absence of belongings that Bogdan Miskiewicz and his family had gone.

The SB captain at the Mostowski Palace had been outmanoeuvered. Now he knew for certain that the intelligence received from his agent at the Gong cafe the previous evening had been significant. The captain would never forgive Miskiewicz. And the SB would never forget.

PART 2

'Freedom?'

1

January became a test of endurance for Bogdan, Jola and Sulecki. As the days turned to weeks they were forced to leave Romek's crowded little house on Golienowska Street. They moved to Krzekoszow, a modern, featureless concrete sprawl in the southern suburbs of Szczecin where they camped in a run-down, two-room apartment which had been rented several years earlier by Romek's mother but which was no longer occupied. In the spartan, semi-squalor they awaited the outcome of Romek's efforts to secure an aircraft.

Romek's employer, *Pezetel*, was a state-owned organisation which chartered small aircraft to industrial and farming enterprises. It ran a score of regional airfields across Poland and operated a large fleet of lumbering Antonov biplanes bought from the Soviet Union. The AN-2's were rugged workhorse aircraft mass-produced in Kiev to serve the most inhospitable Soviet terrain – whether the remote mineral and fur trapping communities of the Arctic north or the near-desert settlements of the south. *Pezetel* gave each mechanic like Romek personal responsibility for servicing and maintaining a single aircraft, and Romek was expected to care for the biplane with the kind of loving attention given to his own children. Wherever Romek's Antonov went he went too. Whether on a crop spraying contract from a state farm in Poland or on a cargo shuttle operating from a remote airstrip abroad, Romek always had to stay for as long as his Antonov stayed. Such professional attachment to one plane ensured each mechanic had great pride in keeping his plane flying, even if it meant improvising repairs or scrounging hard-to-come-by parts.

In the snowbound depths of January there was, of course, no crop-spraying work. But Romek spent the long, dark weeks of winter in the small hangar at the end of the airstrip at Szczecin Aeroclub overhauling the engine and repairing damaged or faulty equipment. Only in mid-February did the first bookings for crop-spraying usually begin arriving from the directors of the state farms. It was this annual routine which created a possible opportunity for Romek to secure access to an AN-2.

Romek focused his hopes on Edward Urbanski, director of the Kamien Pomorski Cooperative outside the small fishing town of Dziwnow seventy kilometres north of Szczecin and just one kilometre from the Baltic coast. Romek knew that each year Urbanski always tried to be one of the first farm managers to charter a plane. At *Pezetel*, Urbanski had the reputation for refusing to be beaten by other cooperatives or defeated by the permanent shortages of fertilisers supplied by the inefficient state system. Romek therefore decided that his prime objective was to ensure that Dziwnow was at the top again this year. Because phone lines were still cut he could not phone Urbanski to check his requirements. So he exhausted his petrol ration to drive north and plant personally in Urbanski's mind the idea that martial law meant it was vital to reserve his crop-spraying Antonov as soon as possible.

By the end of January Romek had completed the overhaul of the thirteen-year-old Antonov in his care. Then, earlier than expected, on 8 February, his patient persuasion bore fruit. As he sat in *Pezetel*'s smoky mess room, the door swung open to reveal the craggy weatherbeaten face of the organisation's Senior Pilot, Zenon Nowak.

'We fly first thing tomorrow!' said the veteran pilot.

'Where are we going?' asked Romek. As an engineer Romek knew he should never upstage his pilot, not least because Nowak was a hardline *apparatchik* of the Communist Party.

'To Dziwnow. We leave at 08.00 hours.' Nowak slammed the door and stamped off down the corridor.

'Jammy bastard,' said one of Romek's mechanic colleagues jealously when Nowak had gone. 'How did you fix that, you bugger?'

Romek smiled and shrugged the question off.

He was thrilled as he examined the authorisation document which was approved, stamped and countersigned by four different authorities: the militia, the Military Border Security Office, *Pezetel*'s regional office, and the headquarters of cooperative farms in Szczecin.

> *Approval: effective one month 8 February, until 8 March.*
> *Renewable: monthly.*
> Location: Kamien Pomorski – Dziwnow
> Approved senior pilot: S. NOWAK
> Approved co-pilot: P. ZAREMBRA
> Approved mechanic: R. TOCZEK

Romek bounded through the snow towards the hangar with a new energy. He had to make full use of the remaining twenty hours in Szczecin before the Antonov was billeted to the remote airstrip on the Baltic where experience reminded him that there would be only the bare minimum of spares and back-up. Romek had every confidence in the biplane's serviceability, but with the ageing AN-2 there were always good grounds for doubt. Officially no Polish Antonovs had ever crashed. But through the grapevine Romek knew of seventy colleagues who had died during the last ten years after their Antonovs fell out of the sky. Sometimes the reason had been the antiquated, badly-maintained equipment, but often the planes had simply run out of fuel.

Tuesday 9 February dawned bright and crisp with a sky criss-crossed by long thin fingers of low-level cloud. Outside the hangar a rusting thermometer read minus ten degrees. It was bitterly cold but a good day for flying.

'Fucking Zarembra. Where is the bastard?'

Nowak never tried to hide his anger. It was already nine o'clock, an hour after they should have left. Still there was no sign of his co-pilot. 'Never did trust the bugger. I'll give him another fifteen minutes.'

The buccaneering veteran of *Pezetel* contracts in Libya, Ethiopia and the Sudan chewed on his cigarette and pointed at Romek.

'If Zarembra doesn't turn up you'll be my co-pilot. Sod the regulations! With your experience you must have some idea how to fly this crate. You're as good as a pilot. As long as the commissar in the control tower sees someone sitting there with headphones on, that'll be enough.'

Romek walked briskly around the Antonov to make his final inspection and made a flamboyant thumbs-up sign towards the cockpit with the padded fingers of his winter gloves. Nowak acknowledged, then slowly the four propeller blades rotated as the ignition strained and they began to tick over. Finally, the single, 1,000-horsepower *Shvetsov* engine positioned on the nose of the Antonov roared into life, enveloping the rear half of the fuselage in black exhaust fumes from the low-grade Soviet aviation fuel. Noise abatement was no priority of Soviet technology. To Romek the nine cylinders of the newly tuned ASH-62 hummed sweetly and smoothly.

By a quarter past nine Zarembra had not appeared, so Romek strapped himself into the co-pilot's seat while Nowak defied safety regulations and lit a cigarette in preparation for take-off. Romek knew that Zarembra's absence was an incredibly lucky break and more than he could have hoped for. He realised that the one-hour flight north to Dziwnow might be his only chance to learn about the plane in which he hoped to fly himself and the others to the West.

As they waited on the frozen airfield Nowak made radio contact with the militarised air traffic control centre at Goleniow airport twenty kilometres to the north. Final clearance took several minutes and Nowak sat grumpily silent. Then without warning he released the brakes. Oozing the machismo and complacency which came from thirty-two years of flying experience, Nowak taxied the biplane forward at speed, then violently swung the tail wheel so the plane turned right.

A light sprinkling of snow blanketed the giant airstrip, but not enough to cover the icy tufts of grass. The rattling fuselage bumped noisily past the hangars and between the two lines of empty AN-2s awaiting their first flying instructions for 1982. At the end Nowak glanced left, pinpointed his take-off track to the west, and swung the plane hard to port. He was an unorthodox, seat-of-the-pants pilot who never concerned himself with technical niceties like wind direction. Instead he just plunged the throttle forward and relied on instinct as the plane kangarooed across the airstrip throwing up a swirling plume of loose snow in its wake. Within seconds the four tons of steel, timber and the most basic Soviet avionics were airborne, climbing slowly above the acres of allotments at the end of the airfield.

At an altitude of 400 feet Nowak banked the plane hard to starboard and headed due north. With its low airspeed the crop-sprayer seemed to hang above the wide expanse of Lake Dabie. Nowak took her up to 1200 feet and levelled-off below the cloud base so he could navigate visually. He held the throttle at 200 kph and headed along the normal route to Dziwnow down the Oder estuary towards the Baltic and parallel to the East German border. For a senior pilot like Nowak the flight was routine, but for Romek it offered what he hoped would be the last aerial view of his home city: a dirty, incongruous, mishmash of old, grey tenement buildings and new apartment blocks in a grimy haze of industrial pollution which hid Szczecin's usual skyline of shipyard cranes and factories. Slowly the city gave way to country, as the frozen marshes and sandbanks of the Szczecin basin were followed by the vast, black expanses of pine and birch trees in the Goleniow forest.

In his mind Romek had already half-finalised his escape plan, but there were still locations to be examined and details to be checked. As the Antonov approached Dziwnow, he took advantage of the altitude to scan the flat open countryside for possible emergency landing sites. After severe flooding the low land was frozen, so the only way to land an Antonov would be on the long straight roads.

Eventually the Baltic lay ahead, a thin strip of grey-blue beyond the sand-dunes. Across a road and alongside the cooperative buildings Romek could just see the airstrip which was marked only by a tattered windsock hanging from a pole. Nowak banked to starboard over the frozen reedbeds in the Kamienski river basin, then lowered the Antonov onto the field and steered the biplane to a halt. Before he opened the door to face the biting wind Nowak grabbed the usual vodka bottle from his plastic briefcase, took three giant swigs then offered it to Romek. 'Welcome to Dziwnow, centre of the world ...' Nowak said sarcastically. 'Gay night life, fine food, unlimited hooch, a good screw any time you want it ... what more could we ask for?'

Romek laughed dutifully. 'Where are you staying?'

The senior pilot brusquely removed his headphones and clambered out of the cockpit. 'I'm not,' he said. 'I'll get the cooperative to drive me to the station at Kamien Pomorski and then take the train back to Szczecin. I'll bring my car up next time. There'll be no trouble with petrol. I'll get round the rationing: the farm can fix it ... Urgent – official business, you know the kind of thing!' Nowak smiled a broad grin which revealed his five silver-capped teeth. 'And you?'

Romek needed time to make checks on escape arrangements. 'I'll do the same. But if you don't mind I won't travel with you. This charter booking took me by surprise and I still have some maintenance to do on the spraying equipment,' Romek lied effectively. 'Any instructions for me, Comrade Nowak?'

'Just the normal checks ... We'll be flying on Friday – probably a day's spraying somewhere inland. We only have enough fuel left in the tanks for a minute's flying, so don't bother to drain them. It's quite safe. No one will get far with less than five litres of fuel.'

Romek stiffened with shock when he realised how close they must have come to running out of fuel. He unclipped the aircraft's giant batteries to recharge them in the make-shift hangar. Both men walked at a spritely pace carrying the heavy batteries between them.

'You must make sure she's as secure as possible,' Nowak ordered arrogantly. 'Remember the new martial law regulations. Don't assume she's safe because there are army and militia patrols and a dozy watchman around. For the sake of our own skins we can't afford to take risks. I don't have to tell you that up here on the coast there's the biggest danger of hijack.'

'Don't worry,' Romek assured Nowak, 'I'll install an alarm and extra lighting. But I'd feel happier if you looked after the two keys for the gasoline and ignition. I know it's normally my duty to keep them, but I don't want the responsibility if anything were to go wrong.'

A plan began to crystallise in Romek's mind. Nowak snorted agreement and pocketed both keys. 'Anything to stop some counter revolutionary getting us into trouble,' the senior pilot chuckled.

In the distance a tractor and covered trailer appeared and puttered across the airstrip to collect them. 'Don't wait for me, I have to set up the security,' said Romek.

'Because of the curfew don't expect me much before eight o'clock on Friday,' sniffed Nowak. He clambered onto the trailer, and the tractor chugged away. Romek removed his gloves, unzipped a pocket inside his anorak and pushed his hand through the cold nylon lining. His fingers searched for two small tongues of steel. The duplicate keys for the biplane were safe. Escape to the West was one vital step closer.

2

Streaks of red filled Friday's dawn sky as Romek arrived at the airstrip. It was 7.40, and he was twenty minutes ahead of Nowak. Alongside the hangar stood six pallets loaded with the long-awaited shipment of fertilizer which must have arrived by lorry the previous night. Now Romek was sure they would fly today. He walked slowly around the aircraft checking the propeller blades, the engine casing, the metal skin of the box-like fuselage and the fabric cover of the control surfaces. Then he scraped frozen snow from the flaps and ailerons, kicked away blocks of ice jamming the wheels and checked the free movement of the rudder.

An army jeep halted alongside.

'Morning!' Romek volunteered cheerfully.

'Hi. Where are you from?' asked the army captain sitting in the passenger seat.

'Szczecin,' said Romek as he busied himself with the checks and scarcely looked at the officer.

'How long are you going to be here at Dziwnow?'

'Maybe two or three months.'

'What are you doing?'

'We begin spraying those potash granules today. It's the first day of the season. Why do you want to know?'

'Just checking.' The captain consulted his notebook. 'I have the official notification here. Who are you? Pilot Nowak? Co-pilot Zarembra? Or mechanic Toczek?'

'I'm Toczek!'

'Been here before?'

'Yes! Many times. You should know me. I was here at the same time last year.'

'But conditions aren't the same as they were last year, are they Comrade Toczek? Just a little warning: security's much tighter, so tell Comrade Nowak to stay well away from the coastline, and the border defences.'

'Don't worry about Nowak. No one's a more loyal member of the party,' Romek assured the officer.

'It's a good day to fly,' said the captain, as he gestured for the jeep to drive on. His driver crunched the gears and the vehicle rumbled back across the snow towards the farm buildings.

'Shit!' On the far side of the airstrip Nowak slammed the door of his *Polonez* car, and began stomping towards the biplane in one of his routine bursts of bad temper. 'Seen fucking Zarembra?' the pilot shouted accusingly at Romek.

'No!' said Romek somewhat mystified.

'Without telephones you can't do anything in this goddam country! That arsehole Zarembra told me to pick him up at 6.15 at his apartment this morning. When I got there, there wasn't a sight or sound, and that's why I'm late. What the hell's he up to? First, he doesn't turn up on Tuesday, now the same again today. I'll have him on the carpet for this.'

Nowak reached the plane and bellowed. 'How are we doing on fuel, Toczek? Is the fertilizer loaded?'

'No,' said Romek. 'I need the keys to open up.'

'Hell! Of course! . . . I forgot.' Nowak rummaged in his pockets and handed Romek the keys.

'How much fuel do you want me to load?' asked Romek.

'We'll be flying all day. Fill her up. 1200 litres. All tanks.'

Romek unwound the rubber pipe from the rusting bowser next to the shed and two farm workers began loading potash into the hopper fixed inside the Antonov's cramped cabin.

It was nine o'clock before they completed the work. Nowak was behind schedule and furious. 'Still no Zarembra,' he complained. 'I'll string the bastard up when I get back to Szczecin tonight. Romek, you'd better stand in as co-pilot again.'

It was Romek's second lucky break. The Antonov finally took off at 9.30, the flight giving him a golden opportunity to familiarise himself with the coastline as the AN-2 flew parallel to the Baltic at an altitude of less than 1,000 feet. Four times during the morning the crop-sprayer returned to Dziwnow to replenish the hopper and by midday Nowak and Romek had blasted six tons of potash from the dusting gear slung under the belly of the fuselage. When they returned for the last time a tractor driver was waiting on the airstrip. He handed Nowak a note from Urbanski, the manager of the farm cooperative. After reading Urbanski's scrawl, Nowak screwed the note into a ball and trampled it contemptuously into the snow.

'Well, Comrade Romek ... martial law still has a lot of arses to kick. There's no more flying for us today. That other six tons of potash we were expecting has disappeared on its way from the railway yard at Szczecin.'

'Disappeared?' queried Romek

'It's the same old story. Urbanski says the lorry left the yard with it yesterday and somewhere between Szczecin and here the bloody stuff got lost. Hardly seems credible, does it? Maybe the driver sold it to peasants on the black market. Who knows? All we know is that it won't be here today.... Let's pack up and go home for the weekend.'

'So no more flying till Monday?'

'No,' Nowak shook his head.

'There's still 400 litres of fuel on board. I'll syphon it out,' said Romek.

'No! Don't bother,' snapped Nowak. 'It's not worth it. Just take the batteries out. Lock them in the shed so no one can fly the bugger away.'

Had Ramek heard correctly? Had Nowak really told him to leave the fuel on board the Antonov? Romek could not believe his luck.

As he drove back to Szczecin that evening, Romek's mind turned somersaults. This was the opportunity which he, Bogdan and Sulecki had spent weeks waiting for. He drove straight to their tiny hideout in the jungle of apartment blocks on the southern outskirts of Szczecin

272

where he made the agreed three long and two short knocks at the front door. Inside he found Bogdan, Jola and Sulecki angry and irritable, their faces gaunt, their nerves in tatters after five weeks of self-imposed isolation.

'At last I think I have good news,' Romek told them excitedly. He sat on a wooden box in the middle of the bare, damp room and explained his optimism. Their response was unanimous. 'Let's go for it,' they agreed.

Romek had already calculated that they could have no more than twenty-four hours to organise their belongings. First thing on Saturday he drove south to Poznan to collect his fellow mechanic Stefan Glabinski, his wife and two children. There were no long family goodbyes. Stefan and Isabela calmly collected two overnight bags then told their parents they were going to an all-night party in Szczecin and might not return until Monday.

In Szczecin that night, the seven adults in the escape group gathered at Romek's tiny house where they sat in the sparsely-furnished living room at a table loaded with vodka bought on the black market and what by Polish standards was a sumptuous buffet of food which Danuta had scrounged from shops during the week.

Romek's welcoming words were unambiguous.

'My plan is for us all to fly out on Monday. Everything's in our favour. We have to take this chance because there may not be another for months, especially if the authorities are forced to tighten flying regulations even further.'

'Why are you so confident?' asked Bogdan, his tired eyes gazing blankly.

Romek counted the reasons on his fingers. 'First and most important, the Antonov is ready and waiting. It's sitting on the Baltic coast and there's 400 litres of fuel in the tanks – just enough to get us to Sweden. With every litre now controlled by the military, how long might we have to wait for another guarantee of so much fuel?'

Romek rubbed his sore eyes. 'Second, on Monday morning the military are expecting the Antonov to take off from Dziwnow. I know that the army captain has the paperwork for an authorised spraying trip using my plane. Nowak has also filed the flight plan for an early morning take-off. Because they're expecting my Antonov to fly, it's unlikely the military air-traffic control will scramble fighters or helicopters. That'll give us a few critical minutes to get across the coast. It will make the difference between us being shot down and our survival. . . .'

Romek watched the reaction of his fellow mechanic who nodded slowly and reassuringly in agreement. 'What about Nowak?' Stefan asked.

'We'll fix his car so he can't drive to Dziwnow,' said Romek, before continuing his justification for flying on Monday. '. . . My third reason is that today is Saturday 13 February. It's a Name Day – not just one Name Day but two Name Days!' he emphasised. 'When have you known a Pole not celebrate a Name Day, especially two popular names like Gregory and Katherine? It means that even with martial law everyone will be having a good time and getting drunk tonight, and that'll include the army and the militia in their barracks. Stefan, you know what it's like after a big party. There's a definite feeling of slackness in air traffic control for the next day or two. Two months of martial law won't have changed a thing. Instead of reporting for duty at seven o'clock, the junior ranks probably won't roll in until eight. And for the officers it's more likely to be nine. So I calculate that we must aim for that clear hour on Monday between seven and eight when there'll be just enough daylight to take off.'

Romek broke off to chew some smoked sausage. The living room was blue with cigarette smoke as the seven adults privately worked through the risks and alternatives. They all had to respect Romek's professional judgement because apart from Stefan none of them knew anything about flying or the way the border guards worked. Sulecki, the KGB Illegal, had listened intently with a grudging admiration for Romek's detailed reasoning. 'It's tight, damn tight,' he said clenching his teeth.

'What's the margin for error?'

'Zero,' said Romek in a matter-of-fact tone. 'One mistake, and we're dead.'

'We'll be shot down. I know it,' said Romek's wife Danuta frantically. 'If the Polish Airforce don't get us then the Russians will. They'll make damn sure of it, I know.' She hinged forward on her chair, throwing her face into her open hands. 'Oh God! Our children – Wlodek and Bozena. They're too young to die . . .'

Romek put his arm reassuringly around his wife and kissed her. 'You must have confidence in me,' he whispered. 'I'm not going to fly that damn plane to kill myself. I want to live, just like you, and we want to live in the West.'

Romek's eyes scanned the faces. 'Are we agreed then? Do we go to Sweden?'

By midnight the escape plan was agreed. The following night at eight o'clock, the seven adults and five children would assemble for the last time at Romek's summer *dacha* on the Baltic coast seventy kilometres north of Szczecin.

That night before they retired to their beds and sleeping bags they drank a toast. 'To our dear and absent friends on their Name Day. To Gregory and Katherine.'

3

Romek spent most of Sunday alone on the shores of the Baltic in and around Dziwnow. He needed to calm his own nerves and triple-check the plans. He surveyed the village and the coast, and watched the army and ZOMO patrolling the roads. Then he drove to the family *dacha*, a modest wooden cabin set back several hundred metres among the sand dunes which had not been occupied since the holidays of the previous summer.

To kill the dank and lingering cold, Romek lit a paraffin stove using tractor fuel stolen from the Dziwnow cooperative. Then he drove to the airstrip where he crouched low in the winter shadows of a pine copse and double-checked his memory against what he could see. Were there any vital danger signs he had missed? This was his last chance to check.

After an hour, Romek retraced his steps and drove for two more hours through the flat, open countryside. By mid-afternoon his reconaissance was complete and his doubts dispelled. The mechanic had finally convinced himself that his judgements were correct and the escape would work. He was now as sure as he could be that by tomorrow night they would be in Scandinavia.

At dusk Romek returned to Szczecin to collect his family with a new confidence. But the moment he stepped through the front door the voice of his wife Danuta greeted him ominously from the other end of the hallway.

'My brother Zenon's here, darling,' she called excitedly. 'I told him what we are doing.'

Romek stopped in his tracks. Danuta stepped forward to grab his shoulders. 'I had to tell him. I couldn't just leave my home and my two brothers without saying anything,' she stuttered.

'How much did you tell him?'

Danuta pleaded with her husband. 'I only told Zenon the minimum – that we'd found a way out across the Baltic, but I didn't say how or when. . . !'

Romek slammed the kitchen door. 'You idiot,' he yelled. 'We make an agreement and you break it. Twelve lives are now in danger. I love your brother and your family, but I wish I had as much faith in his discretion as you do.'

Danuta stood her ground. 'Zenon is as trustworthy as I am. He knows the risks . . . I trust him . . . He asks only one thing. How will he and the rest of my family know we're safe in the West.'

'He must listen to the BBC or Radio Free Europe,' said Romek irritably. 'If he hears news that we've arrived then we're safe. If there's no news, then he should put flowers on the family graves in our memory.'

Danuta's face drained at the thought, but Romek was in no mood to be sympathetic. 'Are Wlodek and Bozena ready?' he snapped. 'Time's short. We've got to reach the *dacha* well before curfew.'

Eventually Romek and Danuta emerged from the kitchen. Romek held Zenon hard on the shoulder. 'You're lucky that you know our plans. Danuta should not have told you. All I ask is that you don't follow us and that you tell no one. Our lives depend on it. You must promise.'

Together the five of them clasped hands – Romek, Zenon, Danuta and both the Toczek children. As they parted, Romek pressed the house key into the hands of his brother-in-law.

'I promise you,' Zenon assured Romek firmly. He plucked a drooping pink rose from the vase on the bookcase and gave it to Danuta in the traditional Polish token of love and respect.

The slow drive north to the Baltic in the overloaded *Polonez* took the Toczeks an hour and a half. Their excited six-year-old son Wlodek and three-year-old daugher Bozena both believed they were going on holiday. To them it was a fantastic mystery adventure. Meanwhile in the southern suburbs of Szczecin, Bogdan,

Jola, Sulecki and baby Miatek were sneaking out of their apartment hideaway having commandeered a tiny *Fiat* 126 from Jola's sick grandmother without her permission.

For Jola the arrival at the *dacha* was a return to the simple life she remembered with affection from her childhood holidays spent with Romek on what Poles called their 'sea coast'. The wooden cabin was set back from the coast road beyond a dense screen of silver birch trees and had not changed in the twelve years since her last visit.

Sulecki hid the *Fiat* behind a sand-dune and hurried inside out of the howling wind. Romek had instructed them not to light the oil lamp, so they had to grope around by the light of the paraffin stove. A light burning in the depths of winter among the shuttered holiday chalets and deserted hostels in this border area would raise the suspicions of any army or militia patrols passing on the coast road. Already a saucepan of Danuta's soup sat steaming on the paraffin stove: the heat and tart smells of the soured rye and peasant sausage warming both the hut and their spirits.

As Romek passed around wedges of bread, his mechanic colleague Stefan interrupted the slurping. 'I can assure you all that Nowak won't make it to the airstrip tomorrow morning. I slashed all four tyres on his car this afternoon.'

The adults chuckled. Sulecki nodded quiet approval and dipped his mug into the pan for more soup as the blue-yellow tint of the paraffin flames danced across the pale faces around him. The *dacha* was designed to sleep only four people not twelve. As Romek and Stefan were the pilots it was agreed they would enjoy the relative comfort of the camp beds while the women and children slept in blankets on the floor.

As soon as the children were bedded down, Bogdan proposed a short prayer and the seven adults knelt in a circle. Romek clutched the St Christopher medallion hanging around his neck, and Bogdan and Jola fingered their cherished Solidarity badges which they still carried secretly in the linings of their boots.

'Oh heavenly Father! May you guide us across the Baltic to safety tomorrow, just as St Christopher guided Jesus to safety through the water. And let us remember our vow ... to live in Sweden or to die as patriots in Poland.' Bogdan whispered slowly but precisely, his words spontaneous and unscripted. 'Let us pray too for our colleagues in Solidarity. Those arrested. Those interned. Those tortured. Those who may not see their families for months. May God give them guidance. May he give them strength to endure the indignity and uncertainty. Dear Father! We leave our homeland not as deserters of a cause, but as seekers of justice for what we believe in. Amen.'

They remained kneeling with their heads bowed for several minutes before Bogdan passed a mug to each of the women and poured generous shots of vodka. 'This is partly to help you sleep tonight, and partly for courage tomorrow,' Bogdan said with a broad, confident smile to help calm their nerves. 'But vodka is not a good idea for us men. Your lives are in our hands.'

'What time do we leave tomorrow?' asked Sulecki, his KGB mind working through his obligations to *Amber Monkey* and what lay ahead.

'We leave at one minute past six – the end of curfew,' said Romek decisively.

Outside, the Baltic wind cracked through the birch trees as inside the nervous adults tried to sleep.

4

It was five o'clock on Monday morning. No one spoke, not even the children. They breakfasted in the pitch black on tea, untidy stumps of sausage, dry crusts of rye bread with lard, and cheese. Romek checked the exact time from the radio. The pips signalling six o'clock cut through the silence. Curfew was over – they hoped it would be their last curfew in Poland.

Romek and Stefan zipped up their anoraks, pulled on their gloves and donned leather caps. For the last time Romek confirmed the details for those staying behind.

'You will leave in the *Polonez* half an hour from now. Bogdan will be in charge. We will see you all at the airfield in an hour and a quarter. That will be at 7.15 ... It is now four minutes past six. Good luck!'

Outside, the Baltic storm had subsided and there was a pre-dawn calm. But the stinging Siberian cold still seemed to cut through their clothing like a drill as way above the birch trees a cloudless sky arched overhead containing the tiny glows of its winter constellations.

'We're on time. It's started well.' said Romek as he and Stefan crunched through the ridges of frozen snow on the dunes. 'Clear sky; good visibility; minimal wind. They're good flying conditions.'

'But they're also ideal conditions for the border guards to see us and shoot us down,' Stefan cautioned solemnly.

To avoid drawing attention to their departure, Romek and Stefan pushed the tiny *Fiat* quietly onto the coast road, rolled it down a gentle incline, then jumped in. The road snaked through the dunes, past empty holiday homes, an army firing range and on through trees as high as schooner masts. There was no sign of pre-dawn activity, and ten minutes later the *Fiat* chugged onto the deserted Lukecin airstrip.

The Antonov stood bathed in the light of Romek's specially installed anti-theft floodlamps. Immediately, Romek spotted the five tonnes of fertilizer which should have been delivered on Friday and which must have turned up the previous afternoon after he returned to Szczecin.

Romek parked the car close to the hangar, then he and Stefan put on their usual mechanics overalls as if starting their routine work. Romek had calculated that if the army or militia challenged them, he could get away with describing the unusually early take-off as a test flight to iron out engine problems before pilot Nowak arrived for the day's spraying operation.

'Damn!' squealed Romek. 'Someone's locked the workshop. See that padlock? It wasn't there on Friday. The Antonov's batteries are inside but I haven't got a key. I've only got duplicates for the gasoline tanks and the plane itself.'

'We've got tools,' said Stefan. 'We'll just saw through the lock.'

'That's not exactly routine *Pezetel* practice at 6.40 on a dark Monday morning a kilometre from the Polish border, is it?' Romek retorted sarcastically. But the padlock was small and made of soft Polish steel, so it took Stefan just five minutes to release it using the metal saw and wire cutters from his tool kit.

Already a breeze had begun to stir, and the first wispy grey light of dawn filled the eastern sky beyond the low apartment buildings of the farm. Romek and Stefan knew they had to have the Antonov airborne within forty-five minutes.

'*Dzien dobry!*'

Romek and Stefan stopped dead.

It was a woman's voice, which was deep and rustic. Romek and Stefan turned slowly and nervously to see a middle-aged lady security guard wearing a skewed peak cap, black anorak and trousers, and quilted boots. They watched her dumpy body sway. Stefan turned to Romek and tapped his neck with two fingers in the traditional gesture to indicate that someone had been drinking. 'She's out of her mind,' whispered Stefan with a degree of relief. 'Leave this to me!'

He remembered he had one unopened bottle of vodka which they had not consumed at Saturday night's goodbye party. He pulled it from the leg-pocket of his greasy overalls and stood up as Romek tried to hide the severed padlock under his anorak.

'Good morning, my dear!' said Stefan cheerfully. 'Lady! Bring me a glass so we can drink vodka together. And bring one for yourself. I am still suffering from the Gregory's Name Day party I went to on Saturday so I need a top up.'

'But I have no glasses,' she replied, her slurred speech barely understandable.

'Well, go to the farm and get some. It'll make a welcome end to your night's guard duties. They can't have been very pleasant in this weather.'

The guard swayed awkwardly as she tried to keep her balance on the ice. Within a short time she disappeared round the corner of the hangar.

'Where the hell did that bitch come from,' hissed Romek, clearly ruffled by the shock. 'I thought I knew everyone here, but she's a stranger. She must have replaced someone who's been sacked under martial law. She obviously didn't know what she was doing because it's against regulations to leave her post on duty.'

'But at seven o'clock in the morning who the hell's going to know anyway?' asked Stefan.

'She'll be in big trouble after we've gone. Let's ignore her and work as if nothing's happened.'

The noise of the creaking hangar door echoed across the airstrip as Romek and Stefan lifted the heavy lead battery into the *Fiat* 126, then drove it over to the Antonov. Romek unlocked the plane and the gasoline taps. In a matter of minutes the battery was installed in place.

'So here you are!' This time the drunken guard stood at the plane door peering into the gloom and screaming like a schoolmistress. 'I have the glasses!' She propped herself against the wooden ribs of the fuselage and waved four vodka glasses wildly. 'Let's drink to a new week of martial law,' she burped.

Romek and Stefan knelt inside the freezing tail section screwing down the battery hatch. Stefan reluctantly clambered forward to talk, crouching in the doorway behind the port wing.

'Look, darling. My boss in there has just told me to work a bit harder,' he whispered conspiratorially. 'There's some urgent work to do on the engine. We've got to make a quick test-flight before the pilot arrives at eight this morning. We'll have a good time later, my dear ... Yes?' Stefan winked. He gave her the vodka bottle and she wandered away.

Romek and Stefan walked round the Antonov making their visual check, then they clambered inside the cockpit. 'What about the spraying gear?' asked Romek. 'Shouldn't we dump it? It's extra weight. It'll slow us down and take up extra fuel.'

Stefan disagreed. 'Too late. It'll have to stay bolted into the cabin. It would take hours to remove it. The wives and kids will just have to squeeze around it. I know it means they won't be able to use the tip-up seats down the side, but that's just tough. All we can do is remove the dusting gear from under the fuselage and the propeller-drive from the roof. I know we're meant to be flying a spraying mission today, but when that old girl out there looks at the plane she won't know the difference.'

The dusting nozzle was slung longitudinally under the fuselage. Romek and Stefan crouched in the shadows under the biplane's belly and began removing it. They released the security bolts then manhandled it into the hangar. Romek looked at his watch. It was ten to seven and farm workers were beginning to arrive for work.

'Let's go for it!' said Romek with a sudden sense of impatience.

The two mechanics hurriedly clambered back into the cabin where an unpleasantly sour chemical smell still lingered overpoweringly after the potash spraying of the previous Friday. Stefan slammed the flimsy door behind them and they strapped themselves into the cockpit, Romek to the left in the pilot's seat and Stefan to the right.

Romek had more experience and would fly the plane. Stefan would monitor the instruments and navigate. For six months Romek had tried unsuccessfully to find parts to repair the compass but it still didn't work. As a substitute Stefan had brought with him an infantry compass from the Second World War which was too small to be accurate but reliable enough to give them a rough heading for the Antonov. In Poland there were no maps of either the Baltic or Europe for sale, so across Stefan's knees lay a torn forty-year-old German map of the Polish coast borrowed from a historian friend in Poznan. A near vertical pencil line already marked the escape route – due north to Rønne, capital of the Danish island of Bornholm, then north-north-west to Sturup airport twenty-five kilometres east of the southern Swedish city of Malmo. Stefan estimated that the total distance for the dog-leg journey was 230 kilometres direct over the sea with no allowance for headwinds or course corrections.

'What do you reckon on the wind speed?' asked Stefan looking out of the cockpit canopy towards the fluorescent windsock.

'It's starting to blow much harder. Maybe sixty-five kilometres an hour now,' said Romek, surveying the swaying skeletons of the trees on the perimeter of the airstrip.

'Direction?' asked Stefan.

'North-north-easterly. From between twenty and thirty degrees.'

'I'll assume twenty-five degrees with an average cruising speed for the plane of 200 kph. Fair?'

'Fair,' agreed Romek.

Stefan scribbled rapid calculations in a corner of the tatty map. Using a protractor and ruler he drew vector lines between Poland, Bornholm and Sweden to assess the heading needed to compensate for the stiffening wind blowing in from Finland.

'Mary, Mother of Jesus! It's going to be tight. I estimate actual flying distance to Malmo will now be 285 kilometres. At 200 kph that means a total airborne time of one hour thirty-five minutes. With 400 litres of fuel that will give us no more than five minutes flying time at the end ... There really is no margin for error.'

Romek grabbed a pencil to cross-check Stefan's calculations.

'We make for Denmark not Sweden ... It's 120 kilometres due north to Rønne. From the airstrip here you should make a heading of 07 degrees ... With estimated wind speed at 65 kph we will fly 160 air kilometres. First landfall on Bornholm should be the giant lighthouse at Dueodde. Rønne is a few miles northwest up the coast. Flying time to Bornholm should be fifty minutes, then we turn to port on heading 317. Actual distance to Malmo is 110 kilometres. Estimated air distance: 130 kilometres. Flying time on this leg should be forty-five minutes, with first landfall at the Sandhammaren lighthouse. I agree with you, it'll take one hour thirty-five minutes.'

Stefan was impressed. 'One day you'll make a pilot, Romek ... Maybe in the US airforce!'

Time pressed as the February dawn sky began to brighten into a rosy hue. The trees blew wildly now along the fringes of the airstrip.

'It's three minutes past seven. We have twelve minutes before the others arrive,' advised Stefan.

'Let's get this crate in the air, then,' said Romek, his voice suddenly loaded with bravado. Stefan flicked on the aircraft's VHF radio and tuned it to the military frequency of the border guards. For the moment the airwaves were silent. Romek turned the key to open the fuel cocks then activated the ignition. As the thousand horse-power engine spluttered awkwardly, the four scimitar-shaped blades in front of the cockpit canopy made their first hesitant revolutions.

'Go, you bastard, go!' The engine wheezed uncertainly.

Starting the engine was always rather like seducing the peasant girls he always met on the long summer crop-spraying trips. One minute; two minutes – the dashboard lights and instrument gauges flickered in a regular rhythm. How long would the batteries last?

Romek bit his lip. It was ten past seven. Suddenly the *Shvetsov* roared with an enormous billowing cloud of exhaust fumes. The aluminium fuselage shook and rattled. This was the agricultural version of the Antonov – a no-frills, stripped-down aircraft with minimal sound insulation.

'Trouble approaching us on the right side!' Stefan screamed over the intercom as he pointed to starboard. 'Over there! An army jeep.'

'Make things look routine!' ordered Romek. 'We'll acknowledge them when they get nearer.'

Romek and Stefan busied themselves in the cockpit and the ploy worked. The army captain recognised Romek from their brief meeting the day before and the jeep just rolled past and off the airfield.

Romek slowly released the handle for the pneumatic brakes, but not slowly enough. The biplane jumped forward. Romek taxied it along the verge to the far end of the airstrip while Stefan watched for signs of second thoughts from the army or militia. 'There they are! ... Andrzej and Danuta are right by the airfield gate!'

As planned, Sulecki and Romek's wife had walked the last kilometre to the airstrip arm-in-arm masquerading as a courting couple who were returning home after curfew from an all-night party. Romek eased back the throttle, halted the plane, and swung the ageing machine hard to starboard ready for take-off. Ahead lay the straight line of the coast road airstrip, the tarmac barely visible beneath the wind-blown hummocks of snow and ice. Romek idled the engine then wiggled the ailerons and flaps as if continuing the usual checks before a test-flight.

'Give me the all clear as soon as you can.' Romek bit his lips then anxiously chewed his tongue. 'Tell me when there's no sign of any goons and when you can see the car with Bogdan and the kids.'

Stefan strained through the half-light of dawn to see the car and the 'lovers'. 'Go!' he screamed excitedly above the roaring engine. 'Go for it now.'

Romek raised his anorak hood twice as agreed. Through the scuffed cockpit glass both mechanics watched the two matchstick figures seventy metres away break into a run, their legs kicking high through the snow and their bodies bent forward. Stefan flicked off his headphones and went aft, squeezing through the gloomy cabin past the fertilizer hopper to throw open the door. First he pulled in Danuta, then Sulecki, who both fell panting into the grime and potash granules next to the hopper.

In the cockpit Romek checked the sky and the weather. There was almost full daylight as Stefan returned breathless to the co-pilot's seat. 'Where the hell's the car with our wives and children? What's Bogdan up to?'

For a third time Romek flicked his hood and raised it. 'Come on!' he urged impatiently, the adrenalin pumping, his knuckles white on the control stick. His eyes and head swivelled frantically to left and right as the first hint of sun began strobing in the revolving propeller blades. Romek would not take off without his wife and two children. Why had they still not seen the signal?

'Why don't they get out and run?' he screamed through his clenched teeth.

But Romek's words went unheard – drowned by the revving engine of the Antonov.

5

One hundred metres from the plane, Bogdan, Jola, Isabela and the five children were still packed uncomfortably into the *Polonez* parked behind a row of trees. They did not dare move as they waited listening to the roar of the Antonov behind the hedge.

Bogdan hunched in his driver's seat, shivering from the cold sweat running slowly down his back. He was sure he had positioned the car as agreed, but now it was obvious they were too far from the plane to see Romek's signal: there was no clear line of sight and the early morning sun glinted on the cockpit canopy.

'Mama!'

The innocent voice of Isabela Glabinska's younger son Adam broke the muggy silence. Adam's head poked above the parcel shelf, his young alert eyes staring. 'Mama, there's a militia wagon behind us!'

'Down!' snapped Bogdan.

The two mothers ducked and pulled the five children hard down on to the seats and floor. Bogdan had no more than an instant in which to work out what to do. He turned the ignition and eased the car forward, his right foot rapidly pumping the accelerator so that the car kangarooed and gave the impression of having broken down.

'Stay right down. Squeeze into every corner.' Bogdan flung open his door and leaped out. He raised the bonnet and tinkered deep in the engine's bowels before thumping the car's wing in mock exasperation.

'Fucking Polish cars.' It was a regular complaint in Poland. Bogdan raised his voice angrily on purpose so that the militia would see and hear, but he knew they would never stop to help. As he appeared to pull frantically at wires and rubber hoses, the *Nysa* swung past,

288

the four militia officers staring out apparently noticing nothing inside the car.

Bogdan slammed the bonnet down. It was 7.20, five minutes later than the agreed time. Where the hell was Romek's signal? He could wait no longer. He knew the Antonov could not sit roaring indefinitely. Even if there was a danger which he could not see, they had no option but to rush for the plane without waiting for Romek's signal. He drove the *Polonez* forward, bumping at speed onto the airfield as the thin crust of icy snow cracked under the spinning wheels. He braked abruptly next to the door halfway down the port side of the fuselage. Sulecki, who had been monitoring the approach of the *Polonez* through a porthole window, kicked open the door.

'Out! Out! Fast!' shouted Bogdan.

The women and children sprang from their hiding places and fell from the car clutching bags of belongings and mementoes. Bogdan grabbed packages and hurled them deep into the cabin. Then he pushed each woman and child to be hauled in by Sulecki.

'Get as far forward as you can,' Sulecki shouted. It'll make take-off easier. We need weight at the front. Don't use the fold-down seats: lie flat on the floor.'

Sulecki's voice strained above the roar of the engine as he guided each of them past the hopper's giant inverted cone which blocked the centre of the cabin.

Outside, Bogdan left the car engine running, and the doors and tailgate open as he ran towards Sulecki who was crouching in the bi-plane's open door.

'Pull me in,' he yelled.

The Antonov jerked forward and Bogdan grabbed Sulecki's arms. The plane picked up speed with Bogdan hanging precariously onto Sulecki, his body dangling from the open door, his legs and winter boots dragging limp below the fuselage through the snow. Inside Jola anchored herself to the hopper and clung to Sulecki's waist. As Romek taxied the plane for take off, the slip-stream swung Bogdan's torso and legs half horizontal outside the fuselage.

'Everyone on board?' Romek asked Stefan through the cockpit headset.

Stefan nodded. Unaware of the drama in the cabin behind, Romek zigzagged the plane across the snow and pressed the button in the throttle to lower the wing slats. Then he checked that the trim-tabs were flush with the four wings to ensure a level take-off. Finally he locked the tail wheel.

'Let's go!'

Romek wanted fast, maximum lift from the AN-2. Stefan pushed the throttle lever forward to its full, ear-splitting limit and the medium-pitched hum became a roar. Ears popped and teeth rattled, and the women braced themselves against the floorboards as they huddled to protect their children. Romek's eyes strained to pick out the take-off path which would be in an easterly direction along the coast road through the sparkling carpet of thin snow. The Antonov rumbled forward, the fuselage jolting as Romek steered across the bumps and tufts of frozen grass.

'2,500 revs,' yelled Stefan. It was the maximum permitted for the *Shvetsov* and beyond the preferred safe limit. The tail tried to rise, but Romek fought to keep it on the ground because a tail-up made lift less efficient.

Still Bogdan hung petrified as the airfield rolled by below his dangling feet. Sulecki crouched in the door, his teeth bared as both arms fought to pull Bogdan in. After 170 metres – the textbook distance – the Antonov was airborne, a strong gust of wind kicking the plane violently to port as the wheels stopped spinning. Another gust jerked the tail down. Children screeched with fear and the women gasped as Romek wrenched the column hard to starboard to regain control and trim.

In the cabin Sulecki made one last wrenching effort. He hauled Bogdan onto the fuselage floor and slammed the door shut.

The AN-2 was an anachronism of the Fifties, not a jet of the Eighties. It climbed slowly and laboriously into the Arctic wind and the clear, red morning sky. The rate of climb should have been 210 metres a minute but seemed much faster. Romek sat in the pilot's seat too frightened to look at the gauges. He closed his eyes and colour drained from his face as his taut knuckles gripped the column and the plane seemed to fly itself, climbing slowly over the grimy villages of Gostyn and Pobierowo, their farmyards and dingy houses higgledy-piggledy among the birch trees.

Romek and Stefan had always known that from the moment they lifted off they would be flying into the restricted military airspace 'EP(D)-19' which straddled the coast for five kilometres inland and eighteen kilometres out into the Baltic. They knew that the classified aircharts carried a warning in bold purple print. '*Aircraft infringing on non-free flying territory may be fired on without warning*.' Poland's Baltic coast was a frontline military region and the Warsaw Pact's first line of defence against a NATO attack. But the defences had been designed to halt the capitalist enemy getting *in* across the Baltic, not to stop escapees getting *out* from Poland.

Stefan tweaked the VHF radio and squeezed the headphones hard against his temples with both hands, listening to the military radio frequency. There was an uncanny silence. 'Where are the military?' he asked. 'There's nothing – not even on the air force wavelength.'

'Maybe the Russians have switched to a secret frequency?' yelled Romek.

Stefan tried the civilian frequencies which Romek had stolen from Nowak. First 118.1 MHz for regional air traffic control. Then 124.75 MHz and 134.875 MHz for Poznan Radar. 'Not a squeak from Poznan,' he shouted.

'Try Warsaw,' yelled Romek.

Stefan retuned – 134.575 MHz and 134.175 MHz for Warsaw Control, then 129.25 MHz and 133.475 MHz for Warsaw Radar. 'Nothing! Not even civilian!'

Romek and Stefan knew that Soviet Commanders had ultimate control of Poland's regional security. The Baltic border zone through which they were flying spilled over into East Germany and the Soviet Union, running from the giant Soviet base at Sassnitz in East Germany to Kaliningrad inside the Soviet Union east of Gdansk. It was a three-tier air defence system with Polish MIGs and reconnaissance planes at the lowest command levels, then Soviet fighters and helicopters in overall command.

'Airspeed?' asked Romek.

'280 kph . . . 22 kph faster than the maximum allowed.'

'Engine temperature?'

'Far too high, but not yet over the top.'

'We need every gram of speed to clear the coast. Keep the engine at 280. Warn me when we hit real danger levels.'

At 600 feet Romek levelled off, retracted the flaps, then banked the plane to port on the planned heading of 07 degrees. As the plane cut an arc northwards Romek could see Dziwnow below: the yellow, state-owned trawlers tugging their moorings in the tiny harbour; the reed stalks tossing to and fro in the frozen marches at the mouth of Lake Kamienski; and finally the familiar wooden draw-bridge on the coast road west to Miedzywodzie. Among the sand dunes, Romek could also see the square block-house and smoked glass of the military radar tower and early-warning station on the Dziwnow headland.

'Arena One! Arena One!'

The crisp voice on the military wavelength was Polish, its air force call sign distinct and clear. 'Arena One. They are crossing the coast. Suspected escape. Suspected escape.'

The radio message sounded like an observation and not an order for action. The unnerving radio silence returned once more. Bogdan stood in the cockpit doorway, clutching the bulkhead to steady himself. Stefan swung around, half removing his headset.

'They've seen us. You and Andrzej take positions either side. Watch for MIGs, *Sukhois* and choppers.'

The Antonov crossed the sandy Baltic shoreline. Below them Romek could see about four hundred army conscripts exercising next to a tented camp, and ahead lay a vast, uninterrupted expanse of choppy, ice-grey waters.

The sharp early morning sun burned through the cockpit canopy and tingled the right side of Stefan's face. There was no conversation. Romek pointed his right index finger downwards as a clear message to descend to minimum altitude. Stefan nodded agreement and eased back the throttle. The plane rapidly lost altitude. Thirty seconds later Romek halted the descent at six feet above the Baltic.

The brilliant Soviet aviator Oleg Konstantinovich Antonov had designed his biplane to fly at altitudes of thirty metres with speeds as low as 90 kph. Now Romek and Stefan would test the AN-2's much-praised low-flying capabilities to their limit. Below them, the bitter north-north-easterly wind whipped up the hostile waters as the white-crested waves chopped and turned, throwing up an intermittent wall of freezing spray which over-worked the plane's wipers and basic de-icing unit. At this altitude the sea rushed below them at a frightening speed, and 270 kph seemed more like 500 kph as the plane wallowed and yawed, buffetted by the turbulence thrown up by wind and waves. Romek had no navigational luxuries like autopilot. It was manual flying, so his hands had to constantly work the electric elevator trim as his cold feet seesawed between the rudder pedals.

'Four kilometres off the coast!'

The anonymous radio voice returned as clear as before, but this time the accent sounded Russian. Still, however, there were no instructions or orders. Was it military inefficiency and incompetence, or were they probing for a reaction? How many planes had the commander scrambled?

With no on-board radar, Stefan's eyes had to strain to scan the sky ahead. He tuned his reactions to spot the tiny black dot of an *Iskra* – the advanced Polish-built patrol plane which Romek knew was stationed near Dziwnow. The *Iskra* was a deadly aircraft as thin as a pencil with high-velocity 23mm nose cannons, 7.62mm air-to-air guns and a phenomenally powerful jet engine which enabled it to chase and destroy intruders or unidentified aircraft.

Bogdan returned breathless to the cockpit, leaned forward and yelled into Romek's ear. 'The seaspray's freezing on the wing surfaces!'

Romek swung his head to port and looked back down the fuselage. He could just make out the ominous grey tails of ice on the biplane's upper wing which whipped violently with the strain.

'We can't get out to chip it off,' he replied sarcastically. 'What else do you suggest?'

Stefan estimated they were ten kilometres offshore. Still there were no signs of planes or a chase.

Suddenly Stefan yelled. 'Ahead!' A vertical bank of cloud swirled a couple of kilometres ahead at sea level. At this time of year it often continued for long distances. It might hide the plane and guarantee their safety, or by cutting visibility it might send all twelve of them to their deaths.

'If we go on and I can't see then we have no way of knowing our position,' Stefan warned over the headset. 'I only have this tiny compass and my watch. When the fuel runs out I won't know where we are. We might even be heading back to Poland.'

Each air pocket punched at their stomachs and sapped endurance. 'We fly on,' Romek said determinedly.

Sulecki appeared, having clambered forward through the tossing fuselage. The undercover Russian had been on watch in the tail section where conditions were least stable. For the first time his instinct for survival had overtaken his professional KGB duties.

'Did you hear it?' he yelled.

'Hear what?'

'An almighty cracking sound . . . It came from the back of the fuselage.'

'Must be ice breaking off and hitting the fuselage,' Romek replied confidently. 'Could be the plane breaking up, I suppose, but we're going on.'

Sulecki was not amused by Romek's buccaneering spirit. He recalled his basic aeronautics training at KGB college. 'You're giving us a goddam terrible ride at the back. You're running her at full revs, but with ice on the

294

wings the stress is going to break her up. Can't you slow her down? Surely once we're clear of the twenty-kilometre limit there's less risk?'

Romek remained unimpressed. 'Comrade Antonov won a 10,000 rouble prize from Stalin for designing this crate. He may be Soviet but nothing can beat it.' Romek was almost hoarse by the time he had finished putting down Sulecki's fears. In the crisis no one had noticed how the former Solidarity telex operator had suddenly seemed to know a lot about flying.

As the AN-2 hit the mist, the bright fingers of sunlight in the cabin suddenly disappeared and the portholes darkened. There was a terrifying closing of the shutters as they flew through a complete void, the only colour now a varying shade of grey broken by the white horses of the winter seas below.

Stefan flicked through the civilian VHF band. Warsaw control, Warsaw radar, Warsaw approach, Poznan tower and Poznan radar. He even checked the frequencies for East German radar at East Berlin's Schoenefeld airport. But still nothing. Romek and Stefan flew on blindly, convinced the Polish and Soviet border command must be monitoring the plane as a clear dot moving northwards on their radar screens.

Stefan glanced at the oil and temperature gauges. 'The engine's overheating,' he yelled. 'Ease it back or we'll never make it to Sweden.'

This time Romek had to relent. 'Hold at 200 kph,' he ordered. The plane's momentum slowed, bringing a small but welcome drop in the noise and vibration. But the Antonov shook violently, losing height and bouncing like a skimming stone across the wavetops as the spray kicked hard against the wings and fuselage then froze instantly on the struts and fabric skin. First one wheel crashed into the wave-tops, then the other. The Antonov's nose jerked to port, then to starboard. Romek fought for control. He pulled back the stick. Such was the physical efford needed that Stefan had to help Romek's struggle to hold the column steady.

After flying for thirty minutes, the revolving propeller blades in front of the cockpit began to play games with Romek's and Stefan's eyes.

'Pull up! Pull up!' screamed Bogdan from behind as from out of the cloud red and green navigation lights came racing towards them, followed by the wooden mast of a fishing schooner. Romek jerked back the control column and the Antonov vaulted over the vessel.

'We must be in international waters,' Bogdan told them.

They could see the black hulls of first one, then two, now six fishing boats looming out of the grey below them.

'You see, Stefan,' said Romek as he gave his first smile of the flight, 'we're on course for the West.'

Stefan was not convinced. 'How can you be so sure? How do we know they're not Polish or Soviet or East German fishing boats?'

'I just know . . .' Romek grinned arrogantly.

Stefan persisted. 'If you're so sure . . . if they really *are* western fishing boats then let's ditch now. Let's hitch a ride on one of them. That'll guarantee we reach the West somehow instead of flying in circles around the Baltic, getting lost then crashing back behind the Iron Curtain.'

'Don't be crazy! If we ditch we're dead.' Romek's tone was know-all and insistent. 'The water temperature down there's no more than plus two degrees at best – just above freezing. If we ditch we'll die from hypothermia within minutes. And it's not just us. Think of our wives and children. In any case there's no guarantee the fishing crews will see us ditch in this mist, and if they don't see us they can't rescue us.'

Stefan gave in. He examined his watch. 'We've been in the air for fifty minutes. We should be at Rønne on Bornholm island now.'

None of those on board had ever visited the West so no one knew what Bornholm looked like. In his mind Bogdan had the image of an elongated windblown hump lying strategically placed in the Baltic. Friends who had visited the island years ago told him of the wind-crushed trees, the tiny farms and villages, the red roofs and weatherboarding, and the chessboard of small fields and lanes. Above all he had been told of the jungle of NATO monitoring aerials and masts installed at the southern end of the island which permanently swept the Soviet Bloc airwaves for military and civilian air traffic and intelligence.

'Shall I risk the radio again?' asked Stefan.

Romek shook his head. 'No! Don't transmit – see what we can receive.' Stefan criss-crossed the busy early morning radio traffic on several dozen frequencies. But if Copenhagen or Malmo air traffic control centres had detected their flight they were not discussing it publicly over the air waves.

'NATO radar must have us. We must be sitting on top of that listening station on Bornholm. Surely we have to be in the West by now,' said Romek in a tone of exasperation.

'Let's call Rønne ... Let me at least tell them who we are and where we're going,' Stefan insisted. He threw the switch to transmit, but got nothing. He tried again. Still no response. 'Fucking radio's dead!' he cursed. 'It must have been working intermittently ... That's probably why we only picked up two military messages. It means the Soviets may have been chasing us through the cloud with MIGs and helicopters for the last hour and we never realised!'

'So where the hell are we then?' asked Bogdan.

'We don't know and we can't find out,' said Romek. 'We've been flying for an hour; we're still on heading 07; but we can't find Bornholm and we're lost.'

'Surely the Danish or Swedish Air Force will scramble a plane to have a look at us?' asked Stefan.

'Doubt it in this weather,' replied Romek. 'Cloud base zero. Visibility zero. Would you fly a fighter or a chopper in this? The Soviets and Poles might have risked it in an effort to stop us leaving. But the Swedes and Danes won't. They wouldn't risk a twenty million dollar aircraft for us.'

297

'So what now?' yelled Stefan. 'Maybe we just missed the island? Let's turn to port on heading 317. We're bound to hit some part of Sweden, even if we don't make it to Malmo.'

Romek listened attentively but preferred his own judgement. 'We fly on. Heading 07,' he insisted.

For several minutes conversation ceased. Then suddenly red danger lights lit up the oil and fuel gauges. 'We have fuel for thirty minutes flying time,' yelled Stefan. 'Oil in the engine's running low.'

'More boats to starboard,' Bogdan called excitedly from behind in the doorway.

'I told you,' bellowed Stefan in panic. 'We're flying round in circles. They're the ones we saw earlier. We're burning fuel to kill ourselves!' he screamed.

'Let's check again!' said Romek calmly. He banked the plane to starboard and flew a tight circle over the boats. 'They're different boats,' he yelled. 'I don't recognise any of them.' He circled a second time, and fishermen in red fluorescent oilskins looked up from among the wooden fish boxes stacked on the pitching decks.

'They're Swedish,' confirmed Bogdan. 'I can see the name of the port – Skillinge. We must be moving in something like the right direction.'

'Then we stay on 07,' said Romek. 'It's all we can do.' He stared into the cloud ahead then suddenly shouted. 'Two o'clock,' he yelled, jamming the throttle forward and roaring the AN-2 into a steep climb as a dark black shadow emerged from starboard. It was a large cargo ship with rows of containers clearly visible stacked six high along the decks.

Romek eased back the throttle, banked to the right, circled and flew along its length. Now it was the turn of Bogdan to weaken. 'Let's ditch here. The ship's crew will take us to Sweden if we ask them. Ditch, Romek!'

'You're crazy, Bogusz. Look at the name on the hull. "*Gorzow Wlkp, Szczecin*"'

'Polish! ... Dammit! ... A Polish container ship.'

Romek hit the throttle forward again, banking hard

and high to port in order to disappear into the clouds and try to regain the northwards heading. Now they began to imagine that every vessel was a potentially hostile Soviet battleship or Polish freighter.

'Fifteen minutes fuel remaining!'

Stefan sat mesmerised by the blinking red lights on the gauges. He began to hallucinate. Among the ever-changing hues of grey cloud around him he imagined things which did not exist. Squares. Oblongs. Odd shapes. A thin, dark streak. To the left. To the right. Straight ahead. Were they islands? Was it land? Or was it just a break in the cloud?

'Five minutes fuel remaining. Altitude one hundred and fifty feet.' Stefan's voice was now matter-of-fact, but there was no reaction from any of the faces around him in the cockpit.

Suddenly wild yells broke out from the rear of the cabin.

'Rocks below ... there are rocks below!'

The normally unemotional Romek could not control his joy. He cheered as Stefan grinned and Bogdan strained behind him to peer down from the biplane's bulging cockpit canopy. Through occasional wispy gaps in the cloud there were grey, neatly-rounded rocks, their windward sides white with the crusted ice of frozen spray.

'Which country do you think this is?' asked Bogdan impatiently. Was it Sweden or had the Antonov flown in a giant arc and returned to Poland?

No one answered because no one knew.

6

At last the cloud opened up.

The Antonov flew perilously close to the breaking waves and the water, the picture below the fuselage clear and exhilarating. First the biplane skimmed over an expanse of rocks, then a denser band of stone, the wild winter waves crashing and periodically submerging them. The AN-2 crossed the welcoming lines of the foreshore at a right angle, the open ground beyond covered with the faded green turf of a tired winter pasture. The land rose gently ahead, so Romek enthusiastically jerked back the column and pushed open the throttle to gain more height.

For the first time in half an hour Romek ignored the pressing fuel and oil problems. Instead he concentrated on keeping the plane in the air while Bogdan scanned the ground on the port side and Sulecki the ground to starboard. What lay beyond the shoreline and who would be there to receive them? A Polish or Soviet militia patrol armed with AK-47s and live ammunition or a Western police force carrying asylum papers for them? The crop sprayer flew up the pasture so low that the escapees felt they could almost lean from the door to pick the trim blades of grass. Now there were patches of snow, then a clump of brushwood. Onwards over two trees warped by the prevailing wind, then a low stone wall, a neat rack of a dozen letter boxes, and nearby a car park with four cars.

'W-w-western cars!' stuttered Bogdan euphorically as he peered from a port window.

'Let's crash-land,' screamed Stefan in a voice of desperation.

'Land where you can,' urged Sulecki.

'Land where?' asked Romek irritably. 'Tell me where!'

'Let me take control then,' threatened Stefan, grabbing

his back-up control column. But Romek ignored him and focused his eyes dead ahead.

The Antonov skimmed dangerously low over a modern housing estate. Then it roared over a small crowded harbour with a modern factory building on the quay, refrigerated lorries loading fish outside and a dock filled with the white hulls of trawlers and fishing boats.

From the air the town and harbour seemed clean, smart and well-kept. These were not the signs of dilapidated, decaying, under-capitalised Polish or Soviet industry. Romek flew so low that Bogdan could read the registered names on the trawlers' hulls. 'It's the West,' he yelled.

'We made it,' shouted Stefan joyously as he punched the air and grinned.

They were over the small fishing town of Skillinge on the southern coast of Skåne in Sweden. But Romek remained stoical and unmoved. He still faced the final terrifying duty of landing the Antonov and delivering the families safely to Sweden. The euphoria had yet to register in the dank cold cabin which reeked of vomit, stale sweat and fertilizer. The three women and five children were so ill that nothing could excite them, not even the sight of Sweden.

It was a long two minutes before Romek caught a glimpse of a straight asphalt road on his left, but the line of telegraph poles made it unsafe to consider a landing.

Then the escapees' borrowed time finally ran out, and the engine began to splutter.

'Brace yourselves,' screamed Romek.

Bogdan passed the word back, then joined Sulecki and the three mothers to comfort the ailing children in preparation for an emergency landing. Outside, a narrow hole opened in the clouds, and ahead through the swirling mist lay a patchwork of ploughed fields, the ridges and furrows carved to perfection.

Romek had to size up instantly the mixture of muddy-green turf and brown corrugations. In many ways what he saw reminded him of the part of north-west Poland they had just left – the dead corn stubble from last summer, the frozen pools, the dirt roads criss-crossing the fields, the straight lines of silver birches forming windbreaks and the last intermittent patches of dirty snow.

The landing would be rough but there would be no luxury of a choice. Romek knew he had to make fullest possible use of the Antonov's greatest asset: its ability to glide then land within one hundred metres. He noted the Antonov's air speed which was 130 kph and perfect for a landing. All he could do now was balance the flaps and trim the aircraft for the glide path. 'We're going in!' he shouted calmly through clenched teeth, his knuckles white from the tension.

Suddenly, starved of fuel, the engine stuttered for the last time and the propeller blades freewheeled. The six wing tanks were empty and the *Shvetsov* was dead.

'The engine's gone!' screamed Stefan.

Romek targeted his landing site amongst the mud then steered for it, the biplane yawing and swinging silently in the wind as the wings kicked and the tail dropped.

'Tell me the height!' Romek did not dare take his eyes off the field ahead. Stefan obeyed as the Antonov glided across the mud and slush. 'Twenty-five metres ... twenty metres ... fifteen metres ... ten metres ...'

A sudden powerful gust of wind blew them hard to starboard, and Romek compensated, praying that the aircraft still had enought momentum to keep itself airborne. The undercarriage wheels narrowly missed a billowing tarpaulin protecting a haystack.

'Eight metres ... six metres ... five metres ... three metres.'

The Antonov hit the mud hard, crunching the shock absorbers as the wheels sank into the ruts. Romek struggled to hold the aircraft straight. He applied the brakes and the Antonov slowed. The starboard wheel turned, and the fuselage juddered to the left. Then the port wheel clogged with mud and swerved the plane hard to port like a cripple dragging a broken leg. Within seconds the biplane finally jerked to a halt.

It was ten past nine: one hour and forty-five minutes after they had taken off from Dziwnow. The plane sat immobile, buffeted by wind against a backdrop of low, racing storm clouds. On board there was a nervous silence. No one dared move. The twelve men, women and children sat frozen in disbelief. They were all too stunned and exhausted to know what to do. In the cockpit Romek kissed his St Christopher medallion, flung down his headphones and slumped forward over the column control, his head deep in his folded arms. He and Stefan were both too emotionally drained to embrace. Instead, they unclipped their safety harness, smiled and shook hands. Stefan's praise for his fellow mechanic was heart-felt. 'Well done, you bastard,' he said, just managing a half-smile.

Bogdan and Sulecki slapped the two pilots hard on the shoulders then turned to help the women and children.

'Yah-hoo!' shrieked Bogdan as his reserve collapsed. 'We made it!' All around him the numbness and tension broke. Those who had the energy hugged each other in a passionate round of high emotion and tears which lasted unashamedly for many minutes.

Eventually Bogdan opened the aircraft door to take his first look at Sweden. As he crouched in the doorway, the vicious, biting wind cut through his face and clothes like a chainsaw. Romek joined him and together they traced the two short wheel ruts which curved away from the Antonov in a long arc that cut diagonally across the stubble lines. They could see the landing points at the far end which were marked by two wider, deeper scars.

Romek shook his head in disbelief at what he had done. '120 metres,' he estimated aloud. 'No pilot would ever dare try to land on mud in that short a distance.'

But the Antonov mechanic had, and he grinned proudly.

7

'... *Hej!* ...' It was a man's voice outside the Antonov – deep and gruff with a hint of anger. Bogdan peered through the porthole. The biplane was not ringed by armed troops or militia and there were no armoured personnel carriers. Instead, standing in the corn stubble was a thin, elderly man wearing a red baseball hat, a duvet jacket and rubber boots. He was waving a wooden stick aggressively and alongside him stood an elderly woman, her face craggy and weatherbeaten.

Bogdan tentatively re-opened the Antonov door. '*Dzien dobry!*' he said waving and smiling heartily. '*Jestem Polski!*' he added pointing to himself and the others inside in an effort to convince the man they were Polish.

The man nodded and smiled a sort of understanding. '*Svensk!*' he said, pointing at himself and his wife.

Bogdan turned reassuringly to everyone inside the aircraft. 'It's Sweden,' he grinned. 'It really is.' But the response from inside the cabin was flat. All the women and children wanted was warmth, food and sleep.

Outside, more people began to gather, bumping over the ploughed fields in a Volvo estate car, a red Toyota van and a tractor. Bogdan jumped from the plane, followed by Romek. They could not communicate with the Swedes but wanted to express their feelings somehow. So enthusiastically they embraced the farmer and his wife, who then guided them towards their farmhouse at the edge of the field. It was a long, low, whitewashed building with large windows and a second floor under the low-slung, brown-tiled roof. The sweet-scented smoke of pine logs greeted the Poles. As they washed the grime from their hands and faces, the farmer telephoned the police while his wife prepared soup and tea.

It was an hour before two police Volvos arrived,

carrying two plain clothes officers, four uniformed constables, and a translator from the Swedish immigration office in Ystad. The memory of Poland's ZOMO and secret police lingered fresh and painful in the refugees' minds, so their instinctive reaction was fear as the officers walked in. The Poles stood up out of respect, but their fear was dispelled instantly.

'Welcome to Sweden,' grinned the ruddy-faced translator. In turn the six police officers shook hands with the adults and two elder children. It was a million miles from the misery and ignominy of the Wilcza Street Police Depot or the Mostowski Palace in Warsaw.

The inspector removed his fur hat, snow gloves and anorak, then sat at the farmhouse table opposite the Poles who were sipping tea and grinning warmly. Meanwhile, outside, young constables cordoned-off the Antonov. Its emergency landing had already been reported on Swedish radio and the police had to control a growing crowd of sightseers, cameramen and journalists.

Inside the farmhouse, the atmosphere was cordial as the middle-aged inspector made his first attempts at conversation.

'You are in Sweden, which is a neutral country ... This is the West and there is no need to hurry ... We have plenty of time,' he said encouragingly.

'Where are we, please?' asked Sulecki.

'You are one kilometre from the eastern coast of Skåne and four kilometres from the southern tip of Sweden, near the village of Mälarhusen in the administrative county of Malmöhus Län.'

The Poles nodded gratefully and Bogdan spoke for all of them when he said proudly: 'We request asylum.'

The inspector nodded, looked at his watch and made a short note. Bogdan had been well briefed by underground contacts on the asylum procedure to be followed. He knew that the request had to be made to the authorities of the host nation immediately on arrival.

'We'd been tracking your aircraft for some time,' said the inspector. He unfolded a large-scale map of the Skåne peninsula and traced their route with a pencil.

'... The air force first spotted you on their radar when you were fifty kilometres south of Bornholm and still in Polish airspace ... They saw four Warsaw Pact aircraft chasing you – probably fighters and helicopters ... The East Germans scrambled two helicopters from their amphibious base at Peenemünde. Our air force scrambled two fighters to escort you to Malmo airport as soon as you reached Swedish airspace. But in this low cloud the planes couldn't get a visual fix on you ... They tried to radio you. So did the coastguard. But you did not reply ...'

As he followed the inspector's explanation on the map, Romek realised why they had never seen Bornholm island during their escape. The north-east wind had been stronger than they had calculated. It had blown the Antonov off course and well to the west of their planned track. Not only had they missed Bornholm, they had also missed the southern coast of Sweden and flown for twenty kilometres parallel to the eastern coast of Skåne without realising it.

'You almost hit a Danish patrol boat south of Bornholm. The coastguard tracked you crossing our coast. You were so low over the land that you disappeared. We thought you had crashed somewhere on the road from Borrby to Simrishamn. We got several phone calls that a plane was flying dangerously low, then you vanished again and we thought you'd ditched in the sea. You'd never have survived more than two minutes in the freezing water. We ordered boats and a helicopter to scramble for a search. Then came the phone call from farmer Nilsson.'

The inspector's finger pointed to a green area on the map. 'You are now here, well south of where you first crossed the coast. It shows how lost you were.'

'So we confounded the sophisticated tracking systems of both East and West,' chuckled Bogdan.

There was a knock on the farmhouse door and a sergeant stepped in to relay a message from the journalists outside who urgently needed pictures and details of the escape for the evening newspapers.

'They'll have to wait,' snapped the inspector, his tone more official now. 'The refugees are too tired to face journalists.' He turned back to Bogdan. 'We'll have to escort you to the police station at Ystad. There are formalities and paperwork to be completed. We need to ask questions and establish your long-term plans and intentions ... The journey will take forty-five minutes and then we'll provide accommodation for you.'

It was two o'clock. The seven adults and four elder children each clutched their pathetic bundles of personal belongings and lined up in the farmhouse scullery to bid farewell to Ulf and Inga Nilsson. As the twelve filed out they were confronted by an intimidating wall of impatient pressmen, television lights, camera motor drives and questions in Swedish which they did not understand.

The harassed Poles were bewildered and frightened by the undignified scrimmage. On the inspector's orders, half a dozen police officers cleared a narrow path through the scrum and the Poles threaded their way to the police cars. Even inside, the Poles could not avoid cameramen who craftily poked their cameras through the windows for clearer, closer and more candid shots. The women sat stoically, their faces pale and strained. None of the Poles had ever witnessed such behaviour in their homeland. Across the Baltic in Poland news wasn't made, it was engineered. But whatever their feelings, the Poles knew they must accept the openness and freedoms of the country they had chosen. Who were they to protest or express resentment?

But the refugees also knew the price of such freedom. That night the film would be on Sweden's television news and their pictures would be splashed across the Swedish newspapers. The West would watch. And so too would the Swedish-based agents of the Polish SB and Soviet KGB.

Sweden was a country of democracy and freedom. But that also meant freedom for the Soviet Bloc's security services to exact their revenge.

8

In Moscow it was half past three in the afternoon when the decoded signal detailing the Polish escape dropped on the desk of General Semenov. It was an hour and a half after Swedish Radio had anounced the arrival of the Antonov in Skåna.

Only the head of the KGB's First Chief Directorate understood the possible significance of the brief, six-line message. Had he been in Sulecki's position he would have strongly considered defecting to the West as the way to lie low and reinforce his cover. For three weeks now Semenov had ordered the directorates and departments under his command to provide full reports on every defection from Poland, however skimpy the details. But no defection report had yet produced Sulecki's name or one of the Polish aliases allocated to him by 'S' Directorate.

Semenov dialled General Martynov, head of the Illegals directorate, on their private telephone line: two long buzzes, then one short one. Semenov let it ring once, then put down the receiver. In his neighbouring office Martynov recognised the signal agreed with Semenov to indicate that the general wanted to bypass his chef-de-cabinet and usual office procedures to talk confidentially without fear of being bugged by Department 'K'. Both generals stepped through their personal office doors into the wood-panelled corridor. The balding Deputy Chairman wiped the sweat from his face with a perfectly ironed handkerchief.

'See this, Vasili Pavlovich ...' Semenov grinned his usual lop-sided grin and pushed the flimsy telex paper under the nose of the head of 'S' Directorate. 'I want to know who was on this escape ... I want full names ... Full details ... Normal conditions – no one else must know ... Just you and me!'

Martynov's eyes rapidly scanned the decoded signal. He nodded, and within thirty seconds both directors had returned to their offices.

Martynov's coded cable to the Soviet Embassy in Stockholm arrived at 17.00 hrs Swedish time, two hours behind Moscow. A breathless cipher clerk immediately delivered the cable to Aleksandr Nikolaevich Striganov, First Secretary (Cultural), in his second floor office of the modern embassy building on King's Island overlooking the ice-flows of Riddar Fjord.

Striganov had been about to leave the office. He cursed. The tall and dapper Line agent for the First Directorate broke the seal, ripped open the envelope and unfolded the cable. Then he took the decoding manual from the wall safe and began to unscramble the signal from KGB Centre.

URGENT
CLASSIFICATION 'A' PRIORITY
PRO COMRADE STRIGANOV, STOCKHOLM
EX COMRADE DIRECTOR MARTYNOV
   'S' DIRECTORATE
17.30H 15 FEBRUARY 1982
REF: ESCAPE ANTONOV AN-2 POLAND-SWEDEN TODAY
REQUEST URGENT FULLEST DETAILS RE NAMES AND
IDENTITIES OF CREW AND PASSENGERS. NO DELAY.
ACTION URGENT. REPEAT MOST URGENT.

Striganov irritably tossed his fur hat at a hook on his office door and missed. That night he and his wife had planned to celebrate her birthday at the Stockholm Opera. But whatever the promises he had made he knew he could never ignore urgent orders from Moscow Centre. Still, with luck he would need to make only one call, and if his contact was there he should have an answer for General Martynov within an hour.

Striganov picked up the internal phone and dialled his wife in the Soviet diplomatic compound alongside the embassy. 'Tanya? ... I'm going to be late.'

His wife moaned as usual.

'It's urgent business. I'll call you when I'm about to finish. I think we'll still make it to the Opera.'

He slammed down the phone, scooped up his duvet coat and hat, then hurried down the two flights of stairs. Standing First Directorate orders meant he could never use the normal embassy telephone lines for sensitive business. KGB communications officers had recently discovered conclusive evidence that Swedish intelligence were bugging all incoming and outgoing phone lines.

Striganov set off down the long embassy drive through Mariebergs Park, then out through the black, floodlit gates. At a taxi rank on Västerbroplan he picked up a cab which dropped him ten minutes later at the main railway station in the centre of Stockholm. The station hall was the size of two ice-hockey pitches and covered by a vast curving steel roof. Striganov wandered among the mêlée of evening commuters until he was sure he had not been followed. Then he found a free telephone kiosk and dialled the direct number of an office at Swedish Police Headquarters in Ystad.

'*Hej*!' The Swedish reply was sharp and business-like. It was the voice Striganov had hoped to hear. He and his contact had never met in person and it was always understood that they would never identify each other on the phone, but after three years of regular telephone contact neither needed to introduce himself.

'It's Stockholm calling. I need names!'

Striganov's voice was confidential. He spoke perfect Swedish with an air of impatience. 'I know you're there ... Names! I need them immediately. All of them.'

The call was the latest of many such clandestine requests from Striganov to Ystad since the Polish government had declared martial law two months earlier. But this time the First Secretary's tone was more urgent than his last call following the Polish defections from the Swinoujscie train ferry.

'You must give me two minutes!'

Striganov heard the police officer put down the receiver

and shuffle papers. The KGB officer pumped more coins into the payphone and waited.

'Glabinski, Stefan and Isabela; children Zygmunt and Adam ... Miskiewicz, Bogdan and Jola, with baby whose Christian name is Miatek ... Sulecki, Andrzej, alone. No accompanying family ... Toczek, Romek and Danuta. Children named as Wlodek and Bozena.'

'Registered places of residence?'

'Szczecin, Warsaw, Warsaw, Szczecin,' said the officer.

'Where are they now?'

'Can't tell you,' replied the Swedish officer. 'You know procedures here ... Their location's a secret to ensure their safety ... No officer outside the enquiry knows.'

Striganov pushed the officer harder. 'You know the price if you don't cooperate, Inspector. I'll make sure your involvement in that pornographic empire is rein-vestigated. I don't have to spell out what that might mean for your police career.'

There was silence down the phone line from Ystad. The inspector coughed then rattled out the answer he had known all along. 'They're at the Frostavallen Hotel in Skåna.'

Striganov replaced the receiver without offering either an acknowledgement or a word of thanks. He folded the tiny piece of paper on which he had written the names and pushed it into the lining of his fur hat. Fifty minutes after leaving the embassy, Striganov had returned to his office. He drafted an urgent reply to Martynov, then had ample time to go home to the residential compound and bath before taking his wife to the Opera.

By midnight the full list of names would be in Moscow. By tomorrow the headquarters of the First Chief Direc-torate in south-west Moscow would have the evidence to confirm Sulecki's arrival in Sweden as a 'Polish refugee'. It would signal the go-ahead for Semenov to move to the next stage of *Amber Monkey*: shipment of the assassin-ation weapon to Sulecki.

9

As the police convoy left the Nilsson's farmhouse and turned onto the narrow coast road, large yellow posters in the windows of the Mälarhusen village store trumpeted the day's 'special offers' on groceries. The Polish eyes stood on stalks. There were no queues, no empty windows, and inside they could see shelves piled high with tins and fresh produce.

In these first kilometres, comparisons with Poland were stark and unsettling. That morning the refugees had left behind a decaying nation struggling in conditions which Sweden had last experienced thirty years ago. Here there were no peasants and horse-drawn farm carts, the cars did not belch on low-grade Soviet fuel and there was not the itchy sensation of polluted air which lingered permanently in Poland. In Sweden, everything looked so plush and well-maintained: here there was money and no black market.

As they approached the suburbs of Ystad, a handful of hardy Swedes stood among patches of snow, playing with a tiny white ball and steel sticks.

'What are they doing?' asked Romek.

'It's golf,' said the police translator.

Golf? It meant nothing to the Poles.

Even Ystad police headquarters was a shock. It did not resemble Poland's fortified militia compounds, guarded by armed conscripts in camouflage fatigues. This was a long, modern building with free access from the street. And instead of rusting 'bitch' wagons, there was a fleet of newly washed Volvos.

The refugees were led through a small green door at the rear, along a well-lit corridor and into a waiting room. Instinctively the adults stiffened. Any police station brought back evil memories, especially for Bogdan.

For four hours, police and immigration officials interviewed the Poles family by family. Only Sulecki was questioned alone. The processing was frustratingly bureaucratic. Each of the adults had to explain why they sought political asylum in Sweden and the pressing reasons why they had left Poland.

Romek and Stefan knew that air piracy and theft of an aircraft were international crimes, but they would not deny their escape nor would they hide the facts. They had to trust the Swedish authorities not to return them to Poland.

Immigration officials asked each of them the same question, 'What will happen if we send you back to Poland?' And each replied that they would be jailed and would prefer to die than return to Poland. It was a sentiment even repeated by the three children who were old enough to speak for themselves.

The policy of the Swedish government was to make sure that the world's refugees did not consider this neutral country a 'soft touch'. The daring wave-hopping escape would obviously add important weight to the refugees' claim for political asylum. But final approval would take at least eight weeks: Sweden needed to make extensive checks to ensure it did not become a clearing house for undercover Eastern Bloc agents ordered to infiltrate exile communities in the West. However heart-rending the story, however mitigating the circumstances, Swedish officials had to check every detail thoroughly and there could be no exceptions.

'Perhaps you will not understand, but I can only describe this as like God's place,' said Bogdan, emotionally grabbing both hands of the oldest immigration officer.

'It's not always like this ...' joked the inspector. 'In Sweden we have organisations called civil rights groups who are always protesting about conditions in our police stations and prisons..'

By now Radio Free Europe had broadcast news of the arrival of a 'group of twelve refugees' in Sweden by small plane. It meant that in Szczecin, Danuta's brother might be spared the grim duty of laying flowers at the family grave.

'All we ask,' croaked Jola, 'is that you don't give our names to the press or the public. We appreciate your regulations, but our families and relations are still in Poland ...'

The inspector nodded. It was better to say nothing than to lie. Those who wanted to know – like the press and the Polish authorities – always had a way to get hold of the details. He knew the police could not preserve the group's anonymity. And as if to prove the inspector right, a young constable handed him a note. The inspector read it then addressed the Poles through the interpreter.

'It is my duty to formally pass on two messages to you,' said the inspector solemnly. 'The first is from the Polish consul in Malmo, the second from the Polish ambassador in Stockholm. Both invite you to meet them – the note says it would be "to discuss the errors of your actions and your immediate return to Poland without retaliation by the competent Polish authorities".'

The seven adults broke into bitter laughter. They knew such a request could never realistically expect the answer 'yes'. The true intention must be to remind the refugees that Warsaw had traced them within hours of their arrival. It was a chilling warning.

In a sombre mood the Poles gathered their few possessions and boarded a van of the Malmöhus Län social services department. It was eight o'clock and the freezing wind still whipped in from the Baltic as the van headed north in the pitch dark. Without police protection the refugees were now on their own, and even here in Sweden the SB could still exact the highest price for breaking Polish law – death. The Polish government would want such reprisals to be a terrifying example to any Pole tempted to flee to the West.

The van climbed slowly through snowy pine forests towards the winter sports resort of Frostavallen. The refugees would stay in a hotel among the beautiful rolling

314

hills and valleys of central Skåne, but they now realised they must live with the same fear they believed they had left behind that morning in Poland.

The fear of the Polish SB.

10

'Comrade Generals!'

Semenov sat at the head of his large, T-shaped mahogany desk facing the inner circle of four generals summoned at short notice to an urgent planning meeting. Each member of this close-knit Andropov coterie was an example of the successful *apparatchik* who had worked his way ruthlessly up the KGB and Communist Party ladder to the top.

General Martynov, head of the Illegals 'S' Directorate, sat nearest the smoked-glass windows overlooking the birch forest. Next to him were General Zuyenko, head of Service 'A', the Active Measures Service, General Mironenko, head of the Eleventh Department which was responsible for liaising with and penetrating the security forces of Soviet satellite nations, and General Kulagin, head of the Fourteenth Department which was responsible for developing clandestine assassination devices and techniques.

'Comrade Generals!' repeated Semenov as he fingered a single sheet of paper filled with hand-written notes. 'We are now in a position to proceed to the next stage. We now have incontrovertible evidence that Lieutenant Colonel Sulecki has arrived in Sweden seeking asylum as a Polish exile. These Swedish press pictures arrived this morning. They are the proof we have been waiting for – you can see Sulecki at the back of the group of Polish refugees leaving the farmhouse.' Semenov flicked the half dozen facsimilied photographs across his desk.

'Sulecki escaped from northern Poland yesterday on board an Antonov-2 crop-spraying plane. It was a most admirable piece of undercover work, given the security curtain along the Polish border. Sulecki is now a refugee. Our information is that he and his eleven Polish "friends" will stay at the winter holiday resort in Frostavallen at government expense until their asylum applications have been processed. So now is the moment to make direct contact but with the utmost care ...'

Semenov swung to his left, his owl-like eyes now facing General Kulagin.

Kulagin was fifty-eight and as dumpy as Semenov, but with skin freshened daily in his private sauna. The head of Department Fourteen wore spectacles and, like a ventriloquist's dummy, only his lower lip moved when he spoke. But Kulagin was renowned as the most brilliant and fluent master of KGB assassination techniques.

Semenov fingered Kulagin's thick sheath of documents.

'Vladimir Ivanovich! I have your report on the firearms which Department Fourteen recommends and which the Technical Services Directorate has available in its laboratory. Once again you have shown great ingenuity.'

He flicked through the pages. 'Let's first examine your second option – clandestine assassination equipment. You have listed a gas gun, a pen which sprays a deadly shower of chemicals, poison darts fired from a highly accurate rifle, and a machine pistol housed in a brief-case which Sulecki could aim at close range. All of them are most ingenious, Vladimir Ivanovich. But I must remind you that our Comrade Chairman insists the operation must be devised so that blame is seen to rest squarely with the CIA. In other words there must not be the slightest chance of repeating the near catastrophe of last year when Western agencies accused KGB Centre of using Bulgaria to supply the weapon used to shoot Pope John Paul. That necessity therefore rules out any Soviet weapons and technology, Vladimir Ivanovich.'

Kulagin dutifully acknowledged Andropov's orders as conveyed through Semenov.

'So we turn to option one, the *overt* method. I think we are agreed that the assassination must not be construed as the action of a madman or terrorist acting alone. It must appear to be the action of someone trained by American agents. The Polish Interior Ministry must come to that same conclusion when they make their own independent analysis of the forensic and pathological evidence after the event . . . So, comrades, the Comrade Chairman wishes to continue on the basis of method (1c): the stripped-down, high velocity Ruger AC-556F selective fire weapon made in the United States.'

Semenov waggled his cigarette at Kulagin. 'Vladimir Ivanovich. Tell us about this Ruger!'

'It's a short-barrel weapon with a folding stock known to be favoured by the United States security forces because of its high rate of fire and compact construction. We have one here in Moscow, Comrade General,' said Kulagin. 'Ours is a rare, specially adapted model captured during a secret training raid by one of our *Osnaz* commando groups on a US Special Forces base in West Germany last autumn. We've gone to the trouble of changing the weapon's serial numbers so it can't be traced to the raid.'

'And how do you propose we get it to Sulecki in Sweden?'

'We shouldn't use the diplomatic bag to Stockholm. The arrival of a Ruger would come to the immediate attention of senior embassy functionaries and certainly the KGB "resident": they would all demand the fullest details from Moscow about where the rifle was going and the assignment it was being used for. That would alert the whole hierarchy of senior officers here at The Centre, and *Amber Monkey* would no longer be confidential.'

Kulagin sneezed and wiped his nose. 'I recommend the Ruger is included in one of our regular arms shipments by way of the secure undercover route through Bulgaria, Czechoslovakia and Austria . . . We shouldn't risk our resident agents in Vienna. Instead, a German-speaking Moscow-based agent must be specially assigned to receive and handle the weapon there. He will then make use of the slack border controls within the European community to travel from the Austrian border to Sweden, transporting the weapon overland through Germany and

318

Denmark then taking the hovercraft from Copenhagen to Malmo where Scandinavian customs controls are negligible.'

The other generals did not question Kulagin. After thirty-five highly decorated years in the service his judgement was renowed for its reliability.

General Martynov, head of the Illegals Directorate, had been waiting patiently to intervene. 'Comrade Generals, one vital factor influencing our final decision must be the current assessment of Sulecki's movements by the Polish Interior Ministry. The fact that our comrade agent has turned up in Sweden means the Polish authorities have failed to catch him as they promised General Klimanov in Warsaw that they would. We therefore need to discover urgently what Poland's Deputy Interior Minister Siwinski knows and whether he'll still try to track down Sulecki. Also does Siwinski still have a character profile which confirms Sulecki as a CIA agent? Or – and this has been our growing worry – do the Polish SB still have suspicions that Sulecki is somehow connected to us?'

Before replying, Mironenko leafed through his bulky file of Department Eleven's communications with Warsaw. 'Our liaison officer at the Polish Interior Ministry has reported nothing on this matter for weeks. The Polish trail on Sulecki went dead as soon as he escaped from the internment wagon on 14 December. From Klimanov's reporting you could say that as far as Warsaw is concerned the problem has gone away, although Sulecki remains a suspected CIA agent high on the SB's "Most Wanted" list. You know the efficiency of these damn Poles, even those of them like Siwinski who were trained by us . . .'

Two of the generals snorted agreement with Mironenko's assessment, but Semenov impatiently nudged on the discussion.

'That's all useful history, Sergei Aleksandrovich, but what about the future? The Poles have undercover agents everywhere in Western Europe monitoring the actions of their refugees. Surely they'll follow up this escape to Sweden, and in due course names and details will be reported back to Warsaw through the usual channels? Put yourself in their position, Comrades. If you had all these suspicions about Sulecki's CIA backing, and if you received the first confirmation of his whereabouts in two months – what would you do? I know what I'd do. I'd get to him in Sweden bloody fast, and I'd either have him neutralised or try to haul him back to Warsaw to unravel the extent of the CIA threat.'

As usual Semenov's assessment cut with surgical precision to the heart of the operational problems. 'So, we must obviously get Sulecki safely out of Sweden and back to Poland before the SB get to him.'

Semenov did not conceal his unease. He turned to Mironenko who as head of Department Eleven was responsible for liaison with the Polish Interior Ministry. 'Sergei Aleksandrovich, we must know exactly what the Polish Interior Ministry knows.'

'That's understood, Comrade General,' replied Mironenko. 'I will make sure that Klimanov keeps us fully informed.'

Semenov shifted his gaze to the man on his right, the head of the recently expanded Service 'A' responsible for KGB disinformation around the world.

'Let's move on to you, Comrade General Zuyenko. Let's hear your proposals for Active Measures.'

Anatoli Georgevich Zuyenko was dressed in a western-style three-piece suit, a two-tone shirt and red silk tie. He was the KGB's youngest director, ran one of the most powerful departments and enjoyed an apparently limitless budget. Zuyenko was part of the vanguard of Andropov's new mould of KGB officer – a top-grade graduate from Moscow University and an intellectual wizard with encyclopaedic knowledge who had outshone his colleagues in KGB training schools at every level.

'Anatoli Georgevich, I have read the options from your report,' said Semenov. 'Indeed I think we have all read them. All I want to hear now is your conclusion.'

'Comrade General, the elements of our plan are as follows,' said Zuyenko referring briefly to the summary of his notes. 'First, we will increase warnings in our Soviet official commentaries and broadcasts about "armed counter-revolutionaries" stepping up their plot to overthrow the socialist system in Poland. The Polish press will publish details of newly-discovered Solidarity arms caches – of course these will have been planted by the Polish SB, but for our purposes that won't matter. For us the important thing will be the propaganda value of evidence that Solidarity plans to launch armed attacks against Poland's legitimate government.'

Zuyenko spoke efficiently with no hint of self-doubt.

'Secondly, we will increase our reports of American and Western support for the counter-revolutionaries in Poland. This will include evidence of America's financial and logistical support for underground Solidarity extremists. This, we will say, underlines how Washington is determined to destabilize a fraternal member of the Socialist Bloc, and how Washington wants to provoke fratricidal and bloody confrontation with the Polish security forces in the streets of Poland.

'Third, and perhaps most important Comrade General, I propose we undermine Washington's position. At a critical moment before the assassination we'll authorize a limited number of our senior Agents of Influence to break cover in the West and to warn Western governments that Moscow has uncovered evidence of a CIA-backed plot to assassinate Jaruzelski. We won't make the same mistake as we did after the kidnapping of Aldo Moro in Italy in 1978. Then we failed to convince world opinion because we left it till *after* Moro's murder to claim that there had been CIA complicity in the kidnapping. We also failed because we didn't back our claims with hard evidence. This time our agents will produce evidence of US complicity *before* the assassination attempt. This time we will even go as far as to reveal that our detailed information came from an unnamed KGB agent at a high level in the CIA, and that our information

321

shows the US plot to be devised by a three-man group of the most senior CIA directors at Langley headquarters under Director of Central Intelligence Casey without the knowledge or approval of President Reagan. Our agents will also reveal that our information shows the CIA's plot is designed to cover up any connection to them. They will say that the CIA operation has the hallmarks of an operation planned by the KGB using double agents planted within Solidarity. It sounds complicated, but it is vital to our cover for *Amber Monkey*, and I'm sure it'll work.'

General Zuyenko opened another KGB file and ran a finger through the numbered sections.

'We already have evidence of CIA complicity in assassination attempts. In Afghanistan: General Fateh Mohammad Fermaershi; in Bangladesh: President Rahman; in Chile: President Allende; in Cuba: Comrade Castro; in Grenada: Comrade Bishop; in Iran: Ayatollah Madani; in Panama: President Torrijos; in Zaire: Comrade Prime Minister Lumumba ... You see, it's a list into which the one planned for Poland will fit neatly and comfortably.'

Zuyenko now reached for a thick wallet of indexed press cuttings and skimmed through the pages.

'These newspaper articles show how the political ground for this anti-CIA theme has been well prepared following Solidarity's regrettable emergence. Since last year our brief to our Tass news agency regularly resulted in President Reagan and the United States being publicly accused of complicity in destabilising Poland. Just a month ago, Tass reported that a recent reorganisation of the CIA had led to what we termed "a dramatic increase in America's terroristic elements: murders, conspiracies, subversion and all the things which have now become for the American people themselves a repellent burden in practical as well as moral terms." ... So you see, our new warnings to Washington will be consistent with our clear propaganda line of the last few months.'

General Semenov's secretary brought a vacuum flask and poured fresh coffee into delicate bone china cups.

322

'So what happens after we've alerted the West, Anatoli Georgevich?' enquired Semenov.

Zuyenko answered without a second thought. 'Our agents will apply political pressure in Washington, at NATO Headquarters in Brussels and among the European governments to take urgent action to halt the assassination. They will say this warning must be taken most seriously at the highest level, and that it is not part of the normal East-West propaganda war. Our envoys will underline how the unofficial approaches are an act of faith – a last-minute attempt by the Kremlin to head-off a plot which will have the gravest repercussions for world peace if the CIA authorises a final go-ahead ... In this way, Comrade General, we will prepare world governments for *Amber Monkey*. Our warnings and appeals will decisively shift any possible blame from the Soviet Union to the right-wing hawks in the CIA who are taking advantage of the President's divided administration.'

Zuyenko took his eyes off the general to address the other directors.

'We expect Washington to deny any knowledge of the plot, of course. So then we will make public our warnings to Washington, and the Reagan administration will be thrown into turmoil, just as Nixon was with Watergate. Reagan will either be accused of covering up or of having no control over the CIA and its covert operations – just as he has been accused of lying over secret operations in Central America and Cuba. I expect the political recriminations to dominate American press coverage and this in turn will distract world attention from *Amber Monkey*. ... By the time the political dust settles in Washington our target will be dead, the apparent victim of a sharpshooting Polish counter-revolutionary backed by the CIA. Hopefully it will be years before anyone traces the threads of our plot through the fake signals and forged documents the KGB has planted around the world. But by that time, of course, it'll be too late. Poland will be a footnote in history and be firmly back under Soviet control.'

323

Zuyenko closed his files with a self-satisfied thud.

'Comments or questions?' asked General Semenov. Silence signified unanimous acceptance. In four years none of Zuyenko's recommendations had ever been questioned.

'Then you have my authorisation for stage two,' said the first Deputy Chairman.

Semenov stood up, flexed his hunched shoulders and arms, then thrust both hands deep into his pockets. The generals stubbed out their cigarettes and filed out of the wood-panelled room.

'Anatoli Georgevich! One minute please ...'

Semenov held back Zuyenko. 'You do not seem as satisfied as you should be, Anatoli Georgevich. Why the doubts?'

Zuyenko signalled they should leave Semenov's office on the grounds of security, so they ambled down the corridor away from the guards stationed next to the lift.

'May I give you my private opinion, Dimitri Fedorovich? My considered view is that our Comrade Chairman is going too far. The KGB has no reliable history of assassinating heads of government. So why now? And why Jaruzelski, of all people?'

'Quite so, Anatoli Georgevich,' the head of the First Chief Directorate replied thoughtfully. Like Zuyenko, he was an Andropov protégé so he had to choose his words with great care.

'The Old Guard – Brezhnev's *Dnepropetrovsk* Mafia – is on the way out. First, as we all know, his ideologist crony Suslov died in January. Then General Grushevoi, political commander of the Moscow Military District and Brezhnev's war-time comrade, died last week and we all saw Leonid Ilyich on television wearing a fruit salad of war medals as he wept over the coffin.'

None of this was news to Zuyenko but he listened patiently as Semenov continued.

'Things have deteriorated since December when the Comrade Chairman first authorised the operation. Brezhnev is now senile and dying. He's only kept alive by medical ingenuity and the Party's propaganda. Leonid Ilyich passes his days in and out of a semi-coma at the special hospital in Stalin's *dacha* at Kuntsevo. His tongue and legs are paralysed. He has a pacemaker for his heart. He can hardly talk and can scarcely read – and this is the man who leads a superpower of two hundred and seventy million people, while he leaves his loyal coachman Chernenko to sign documents in the old man's name. Can you believe it? A former chauffeur like Chernenko running the Soviet Union? Meanwhile, fifteen years of economic mess gets worse, the pressures mount and the Kremlin tucks the nation's problems under the carpet as its leaders get pissed on Western booze and become bloated on caviar and salmon. No more, though! Comrade Andropov wants to act decisively, and as a loyal Andropov protégé you have to be right behind him.'

Semenov clutched Zuyenko's arm tightly and moved closer to talk in a confidential whisper. 'There is now good reason to say that our country needs a new *Vozhd* like Stalin – some*thing* and some*one* to believe in. They want a strong leader and a vision for the future. Since Christmas Yuri Vladimirovich has begun undermining Brezhnev's control, and soon he will win ... I can assure you.'

General Semenov stared at Zuyenko and clenched his teeth determinedly. 'And I can tell you, Yuri Vladimirovich believes we are reaching the point of victory. Brezhnev and his Mafia are losing power, but some of his cronies are still trying to hang on.'

'Isn't there a danger that you're overstating your successes?' questioned Zuyenko.

Semenov sneered disapprovingly. 'No! We know Brezhnev's almost broken. The racket of the circus diamonds has finally cemented his downfall ... Brezhnev's attempted cover-up of the scandal failed, thanks to the determination of Comrade Andropov. For once, by order of our Chairman, the KGB did not rush to hush-up stories of corruption and graft in the Kremlin involving Brezhnev's family. Instead the Comrade Chairman leaked and publicised the stories to the full – against Brezhnev's express wishes.'

'There's been only one problem,' Semenov continued. 'The Comrade Chairman's plan hit an enormous obstacle when Brezhnev installed his brother-in-law – General Tsvigun – as KGB Deputy Chairman in an effort to keep Yuri Vladimirovich under control. Tsvigun demanded that Comrade Andropov hush up Brezhnev's family connection with the diamond scandal. He pulled his weight and insisted there must be no publicity, no arrests and no interrogation. Yuri Vladimirovich was so incensed by this that he secretly made sure the scandal and the Brezhnev connection were exposed as an example to others. Our Comrade Chairman first asked for Tsvigun's resignation, but the bugger refused. Even Chief Ideologist Suslov could not get rid of him. So in the end Tsvigun had to be disposed of forcibly.'

The general shuffled across to the smoked-glass windows as he worked out how best to describe the next part of the story.

'Of course in official circles the story is that Tsvigun committed suicide using a gun he kept in his office. But he ... hm ... there are ways people can be helped to commit suicide with a little persuasion from their comrade colleagues. And that's the way that Brezhnev's brother-in-law died.'

Zuyenko took the point. 'So that's why only Comrade Andropov and a few colleagues signed Tsvigun's obituary and why Brezhnev didn't? Leonid Ilyich couldn't sign all that obsequious crap about his brother-in-law because he knew the painful truth about how and why he died?'

General Semenov just stood nodding slowly with a complacent smile, then moved even closer to Zuyenko, revealing the nicotine-stained teeth behind his mean smile.

'You wait, Anatoli Georgevich! Of course dear bumbling Leonid Ilyich will still be wheeled out at ceremonies. But Comrade Andropov's plan is to let the old man gradually destroy himself in public by his own ineptitude.

Gone are the days when the KGB automatically covered up the General Secretary's incompetence. Now Comrade Andropov will spare nothing to compromise Brezhnev. Nothing!'

Semenov and Zuyenko had been walking for twenty minutes through the gently-curving corridors of the First Chief Directorate, and now they stood by the guard post at the lift shaft. Zuyenko decided he should end a conversation concerning such delicate matters with a polite greeting for Semenov's wife.

'My warm wishes to Eugenia and your new grand-daughter,' said the KGB's master of disinformation.

'I am most grateful,' said Semenov, 'and I'll pass them on'.

Zuyenko knew that *Amber Monkey* was now irreversible and non-negotiable.

11

It was 11.15 on the morning of Wednesday 17 February, and Deputy Polish Interior Minister Wladek Siwinski sat behind the cluttered desk of his third floor office on Rakowiecka Street. The SB General beamed a quiet satisfaction as he checked the text of a new communique on the latest security crackdown.

'3,500 people arrested in a major operation against martial law offenders during the last two days ... 51,000 factories and 30,000 private cars checked ... 99,000 people asked to present their identity cards ... 3,500 known "haunts" of political "criminals" checked ... as a result 29,000 people reminded of their duties under martial law, 7,000 people fined and 4,000 people referred to courts handling minor offences. In total, 145,000 people found to be infringing martial law regulations.'

Siwinski approved the draft with his personal rubber stamp and a flamboyant signature, then summoned his duty captain from the outer office to deliver it to the Interior Minister, General Kiszczak. As the captain's heavy boots echoed down the tiled corridor, a telephone buzzed on the general's desk.

'Ah! ... Comrade Wladek!'

It was the distinctive Russian growl of General Klimanov. 'Are you busy? May I drop by to see you?'

What did Moscow's eyes and ears want? The Deputy Interior Minister had no wish to meet the KGB's spy inside Poland's security headquarters, but as usual Siwinski knew he could only refuse for the most exceptional reasons.

Four minutes later, the dumpy Moldavian was sitting in Siwinski's office wearing his usual shapeless polyester suit and garish Moscow tie. General Siwinski spun the draft of the new communique across his desk towards the

KGB general, who absorbed its details and nodded a gesture of satisfaction. 'Impressive,' he muttered, 'but not good enough.'

'So what the hell do you expect?' said Siwinski in a tone of exasperation. 'I also have other important good news for you to report to Moscow Centre, Yevgenni Viktorovich. Remember our conversations in December about a CIA-backed terrorist called Sulecki? Well he turned up two days ago in Sweden ...'

Siwinski waited and watched Klimanov's reaction.

'How the hell did he manage to breach Polish border security?' snapped the astonished KGB officer, his high-pitched expression of surprise echoing round the tall ceilings and flaking plaster walls of the ministry office.

'He was one of twelve people on an Antonov-2 which escaped from Szczecin on Monday. I concede it is a major embarrassment for the Polish security forces, but not, I hasten to add, for the SB. It was the Army and Air Force who failed to halt the plane, and I am informed by the Military Council that disciplinary measures are being taken against those in the military district who failed to carry out their duties.'

'You are correct, Wladek. It's a terrible security lapse!' snorted Klimanov officiously. 'But tell me,' he added, 'How did you discover this information about Sulecki?'

'You know very well that we've had undercover agents and informers in southern Sweden for years. On Monday one of them, a journalist, got a look at the escapers when their plane crash-landed in a field near Ystad. Our agent didn't know we were looking for Sulecki: it was just the routine he carries out whenever any Poles arrive in Sweden. From his contacts, my agent was also able to learn the personal details which Sulecki gave the Swedish police in Ystad, and they match those held in the Gdynia computer on Sulecki.'

But Siwinski refrained from going further. He did not tell Klimanov that following his own enquiries he believed most of Sulecki's record on the SB's computer had somehow been faked.

'So Sulecki's no threat to Poland any more and you can forget about him. You must be relieved, Wladek?' Klimanov suggested reassuringly.

'Far from it, Yevgenni Viktorovich. Once a threat, always a threat. This bastard is an evil terrorist. Gunmen are all a special breed: they never change.'

Siwinski picked up a buff file from his desk.

'This is an intelligence report dated 10 January from our resident in Washington,' said Siwinski. 'Our shit-faced Polish ambassador Spasowski may have defected from the embassy there in December, but this report proves that the Polish People's Republic still enjoys the services of loyal and honourable functionaries who are willing to risk their lives for our socialist cause. It details a leak from one of the SB's undercover operatives who has worked for many years inside CIA headquarters at Langley ...'

The Russian general sat silently enthralled by the prospect of what Siwinski might soon reveal to him.

'The CIA have a file on Andrzej Sulecki and my source tells me that the CIA's station chief at the US embassy here updated it with some intriguing details of two meetings Sulecki had in Warsaw with a couple of American citizens two months ago on Monday 21 December. The first was between Sulecki and a CIA agent called Jeb Theobold; the second was with an unnamed journalist. According to this report, at both meetings Sulecki asked the Americans to supply him with weapons with which to assassinate a senior figure in the Polish government who he eventually named as our Comrade General Wojciech Jaruzelski. In other words, it seems that Sulecki was urgently trying to get hold of a weapon to replace the one my officers seized from his apartment on 15 December.'

Siwinski leant across to pick up a second file. 'And another CIA cable we intercepted recently reports Langley's success in channelling weapons into Poland. It mentions CIA operatives and sympathisers working inside underground Solidarity cells – activists who hope

330

an assassination will spark-off destabilisation of the Socialist order here. You see, Yevgenni Viktorovich, the evidence all points one way – to threats to our peace and security backed by the CIA using agents like Sulecki. They are threats we must not and cannot fail to eliminate.'

Siwinski refreshed himself with a glass of mineral water. Again he declined to voice his real fear that Sulecki was connected to the KGB. 'I now believe Sulecki is a CIA agent, and I believe that sometime in the future he'll try to get back to Poland to resume his mission. For that reason he must be eliminated while we know who he is and where he is.'

Siwinski's exposition unnerved Klimanov. 'Wladek, you broke the rules! Why the hell didn't you pass such vital intelligence to us in the normal way?'

'Well, Yevgenni Viktorovich, it was overlooked. You know how it is: with all the other pressures of martial law I'm afraid I forgot,' shrugged Siwinski.

But the SB general had lied on purpose. He had held back the Washington file because of his continuing suspicion of KGB involvement in the Sulecki case. From a drawer in his desk Siwinski produced a bottle of vodka and two glasses, one of which he pushed towards Klimanov.

'To the State of War!' toasted the SB general as both policemen raised their glasses and threw back their heads. Only as Klimanov lowered his glass did Siwinski note the unusual coolness of his long-standing KGB colleague.

Klimanov did not acknowledge the toast. Instead the KGB general drained his glass, then in silence stood up and stormed out leaving Siwinski alone, pacing the floor. The Polish general had spent much of his professional life studying CIA tactics and strategy against the Soviet Bloc, yet he had never heard of such a CIA assassination plot which would so blatantly contravene American law. Why had Sulecki gone all that way to Sweden when his alleged target Jaruzelski was here in Warsaw? Why would Sulecki risk his life in an escape across the freezing Baltic, only to return in a short time to attempt the assassination?

But whatever his doubts, Siwinski knew that his most urgent task was to find Sulecki.

Ten minutes later he sat down opposite Poland's Interior Minister, General Czeslaw Kiszczak, a slender, well-maintained military figure with a slowly receding line of black hair who wore a neatly-pressed officer's uniform.

Kiszczak was visibly stunned by what Siwinski revealed. 'Incredible! ...' he repeated several times. 'I find the scenario impossible to believe, even from the CIA. We know CIA chief Casey and President Reagan have raised the level of undercover actions against Poland. Last weekend Walewski, that traitor from our Foreign Ministry, was sentenced to twenty-five years for spying for them. But there's never been any hint that Casey's dirty tricks would go as far as high-level assassinations here. Comrade Wladek, your story's so incredible that I cannot take the risk of informing General Jaruzelski. That's not to say we mustn't take the plot seriously, though. On the contrary!'

It took half an hour for Kiszczak and Siwinski to agree a strategy under which Siwinski would dispatch an undercover SB agent to eliminate Sulecki.

As soon as Siwinski returned to his office he re-examined Sulecki's file. And he wondered once again if he had become snared in a KGB trap designed to implicate Moscow's friends in Warsaw in a CIA assassination plot.

Who the hell was Sulecki? Siwinski's need for an answer was now more pressing than ever.

12

Jola was torn between a childlike ecstasy and stunned bewilderment as she stood clutching a tray in the queue for breakfast at the Frostavallen Hotel. In front of her lay a bountiful counter of fresh fruit and orange juice, smoked meats and cheeses, eggs, yoghurt, butter, jam and fresh milk.

'Just think, darling,' she said to Bogdan. 'In Poland, we'd throw a party if we got hold of as many bananas as this!'

Jola couldn't adjust her mind to the new western skill of making an instant choice as the blonde cafeteria assistant impatiently waved her on and a queue of Swedish skiers in snappy ski-suits built up rapidly behind them.

The Poles sat together on benches at a long table next to a giant log fire surrounded by reindeer skins, stuffed elk heads and old skis hanging from the timber wall. To them this middle-of-the-range sports hotel seemed like utopia with its saunas, games rooms, well-stocked shops and restaurants. The refugees knew only the shabbiness of state-owned hotels in Poland – beds with patched linen, the dirty bathrooms crawling with cockroaches and the long menus of traditional Polish dishes with no more than a quarter available.

After just twenty-four hours in Sweden, Poland already began to seem like a foreign country across the Baltic. There remained only the grinding personal agony of being separated from the country they loved.

Sixty kilometres to the south it was noon at the Polish consulate in the Baltic port of Malmo. Inside the two-storey, yellow-brick building in the fashionable suburb of Fridhem, Assistant Consul Zygmunt Lebkowski listened to Radio Warsaw broadcasting the daily trumpet call from Krakow marking midday. The dapper Polish *apparatchik* ignored the two dozen people queueing for visas in the outer office –the lorry drivers and aid workers, and the western journalists trying to smuggle themselves across the Baltic into Poland. Instead he sat in the back office preening his moustache and reading the weekly telex summary of Polish news prepared by the Foreign Ministry in Warsaw.

As assistant consul, Lebkowski's official responsibility was to issue visas. But in reality, from this smart house on Adolf Fredriksgaten, SB Major Lebkowski coordinated all the Polish Interior Ministry's activities in southern Sweden. Over two years Lebkowski had built up a network of ten agents and thirty-five informers and had already broken up one major operation by Polish exiles to smuggle printing paper and ink to Poland disguised as aid parcels.

Lebkowski himself was a hardline SB purist. And like most of his colleagues, he despised General Jaruzelski's moderation, viewing the Polish leader as an Army man who had chosen the soft option as opposed to the definitive option preferred by the SB.

It was one o'clock. As Lebkowski locked the black gates and closed the main consulate door, the antiquated deciphering machine chattered into life under the stairs. Lebkowski guided the flimsy white telex paper through his fingers. De-coded, the message read:

PRO LEBKOWSKI, MALMO
02.19.82
URGENT
ASSIGN OPERATIVE TO LOCATE AND LIQUIDATE SUSPECT
NAME: ANDRZEJ SULECKI, REFUGEE LOCATED
FROSTAVALLEN HOTEL 60 KILOMETRES EX MALMO
EFFECT IMMEDIATELY.
REF: ACT 699878. POLINTMIN

Within minutes Lebkowski had drawn a Polish WZ-63 machine pistol from the consulate's safe, locked his office and driven five blocks east along the coast road where he parked in a pile of slush outside one of the four sand-coloured apartment blocks known as Vittsjöborg.

The SB major took the lift to the seventh floor and knocked five times. Eventually the door creaked open and Lebkowski stepped into the sparsely furnished single-room council flat. The scruffy occupant was only half-awake having clearly been asleep among the pile of dirty bed-linen on the sofa. Neither man spoke. Each SB officer automatically assumed that Swedish intelligence would have bugged the apartment before assigning it to this recently arrived refugee.

Lebkowski took the telex from a hidden pocket in the lining of his suit. Across the top he had scrawled 'Surveillance. Get to know Sulecki. Report back before taking action'. He tore off the names and Warsaw's official references before handing the message to the dishevelled figure who sat unshaven and shivering wearing just trousers and a T-shirt.

The agent absorbed the details and the names, nodded to Lebkowski then pointed to his watch enquiring when he should leave. Major Lebkowski pointed decisively down to the floor, indicating that Captain Zurawski should leave now. The captain and the major shook hands and the major departed. For Lebkowski, Zurawski had been the only option. The SB captain was still untried in Sweden but Lebkowski's other agents were occupied with other operations so there was no alternative.

Piotr Zurawski enjoyed an ideal cover. He had arrived four weeks earlier with new Swedish residence papers after spending six months in a Berlin refugee camp where he had convinced both German and Swedish investigators of his *bona fides*. Now, in accordance with Sweden's sympathetic policy towards asylum, Malmo City council had given him an apartment plus a weekly allowance and Swedish lessons.

Zurawski destroyed the dog-eared telex. The SB captain was as ruthless and unemotional as an abattoir attendant. He was a professional with a gun and a dirty

335

job, but no feelings towards his victim.

Within the hour he had hired a Renault 5 and driven north to the town of Höör where he checked in at a cheap motel. The next morning he drove the last five kilometres through the pine forests to Frostavallen where he passed the time chainsmoking and loitering in the hotel lobby. Zurawski expected the Polish refugees would return for lunch. His assumption was right. They appeared at half-past-twelve stamping and shaking the snow from their boots and shabby clothing after a first hesitant morning on skis. As Zurawski ate stew and blueberry flan in the cafeteria he watched them having lunch. He had no interest in the three women. He was only interested in the four men and he had to work out which of them was Sulecki. Systematically he concentrated on each of them in turn but could identify none. He realised there was no way to shortcircuit basic detective work.

It was one-thirty. Through the frozen condensation on the cafeteria window Zurawski watched the refugees disperse – the three men, three wives and four children crossing to the nursery slopes beyond the main road with their skis and plastic toboggans; the fourth man carrying fishing tackle and heading towards the meadow which sloped gently down to the frozen lake.

For Zurawski, the murder of Sulecki had to be a silent 'wet' job which left no clues. There must be no margin for error.

13

It was mid-afternoon in Warsaw when the Dodge truck
of the United States Diplomatic Service swung into the
embassy compound. For the first time since the declaration of martial law eleven weeks earlier, the regular
Tuesday delivery of diplomatic bags, embassy mail and
bonded goods from West Berlin was on time.

It was well after five o'clock before Jeb Theobold
received his mail and newspapers. The CIA officer had
no time to look at them because he was under immense
pressure to file a cable analysing this week's expected
meeting of the Polish Communist Party's Central Committee, the first since martial law. Theobold's analysis
centred on the continuing failure of the demoralised Party
to resolve the split between hardliners. It concluded that
General Jaruzelski had neither reversed the party's slump
in credibility nor healed the wounds. 'The Polish Communist party remains divided and unfit to regain its
supreme role from the Military Council for National
Salvation,' Theobold wrote. 'There is, therefore, no likelihood of Jaruzelski ceding power to a civilian administration in the near future.'

Theobold struggled with this final wording. To divert
his attention he glanced through the sizeable bundle of
European and American newspapers. As he scanned the
Herald Tribune of Tuesday 16 February, exactly a week
earlier, his attention was caught by the picture of an
escaped Polish Antonov across four columns on page
three, then by a second picture of twelve refugees after
their arrival in Sweden. Theobold studied the smudged
photographs more closely. There were no names identifying the passengers but he was convinced he recognised
at least one face. Such was his astonishment that he
ignored the pressing deadline to finish his cable. Instead,

he grabbed his anorak, locked his office and rushed out of the embassy.

After a brisk fifteen minute walk westwards down Piekna Street and across Constitution Square he arrived at Dick Werner's tiny rented apartment on Hoza Street which doubled as both his home and office for the *Washington Post*. Theobold found Werner hunched over the antiquated telex machine drafting his own analysis of the Central Committee plenum.

'Forget that crap for a moment, Dick. This is far more interesting.' Theobold slid the *Herald Tribune* across the keys of the telex machine. 'Dick! Have a close look at that picture of the Antonov! Look at the faces, especially the one on the extreme right. Remember our conversation at the embassy club three or four days before Christmas?'

Werner raised his spectacles to his forehead and examined the page closely. 'Jeez! ... Well I'll be damned! It's Sulecki ... Andrzej Sulecki!'

Jeb Theobold nodded. He took a can of Coca-cola from the Soviet-made refrigerator and tossed another to Werner.

'It answers one question,' said the correspondent. 'Now we know where Sulecki is. But it doesn't answer the other questions. Andrzej will never need arms and ammunition in Sweden, so why did he want them here in Poland? What the hell's this guy up to?'

Neither Theobold nor Werner had an obvious answer, and it worried them.

14

The euphoria of the Antonov escape was short-lived. Frostavallen was not the freedom the twelve Polish refugees had expected to find in the West.

By the end of their second week, the Poles felt a creeping depression because of the way they had become institutionalised. They could do nothing and spend nothing without the help of the Swedish state. It would be weeks before the immigration centre at Norrköping had crosschecked their credentials and background. Then it would probably be months before they were granted asylum and their residency permits.

During these first two weeks the Poles had rattled aimlessly around the half-empty hotel. No longer did they gawp in amazement at the tanned and well-to-do Swedes who drove smart cars and wore the latest in fashionable clothes. Instead, as they gazed at the smart luggage, flashy shoes and racks of gleaming skis, they felt second-class and humiliated.

'Christ!' Sulecki roared at supper that Friday, pushing back his overloaded plate of herrings, smoked pork and salad until it slid off the table. The crash of crockery silenced the packed cafeteria. 'I don't know how much longer I can put up with this! This place is slowly destroying me. It's destroying us all . . .'

Romek intervened to calm Sulecki as Bogdan picked up the food and broken plate splattered across the floor. The refugees all shared Sulecki's frustrations but none of them felt moved to announce it quite so brazenly.

But no one at the table knew the truth. The KGB Lieutenant Colonel's 'cry from the heart' had been contrived to justify his early return to Poland. And it had been watched by Captain Zurawski of the SB.

15

KGB Generals Semenov and Martynov sat behind grey curtains in the rear of an enormous *Zil* limousine gliding at high speed away from the centre of Moscow down the priority lane in the middle of Lenin Prospekt. Having finished a private meeting with Chairman Andropov at Dzerzhinsky Square headquarters, Semenov had invited Martynov to join him for the twenty-minute journey to the headquarters of the First Chief Directorate.

It was Martynov who opened the conversation as the sleek, armour-plated *Zil* swept past the end of Gorky Street and along Manege Square in the shadow of the Kremlin walls.

'Has Jaruzelski's address to the plenum of the Polish Party changed our chairman's view of the Polish crisis?' he asked.

The *Zil* sped through traffic lights set at green by traffic police on KGB orders, then on across the Moscow River past the towering monument to cosmonaut Yuri Gagarin and west towards the Olympic village.

'Jaruzelski's plenum was two days of hogwash,' said Semenov. 'The credibility of the Polish United Workers Party is so thin that you can't even see it! Examine the figures and you'll see why. A total of 2,400 party officials dismissed or resigned from the Polish Party since December. Instead of being the only organisation in Poland with total power, the Polish Party's an empty body with no power. Comrade Jaruzelski's words to the meeting were written by a clever committee of speechwriters who were under orders to convince us that all is well and under control. But Jaruzelski must think we're dumb – that we can't see what's happening in Poland – that we haven't got hundreds of our own agents there. He's still trying to walk the tightrope between what we want and what the bloody Poles want. With his brains Jaruzelski should know better – that there's only one way and that's the Soviet revolutionary way. But he still doesn't seem to realise...'

The *Zil* slowed as it hit driving spring snow in the south-western suburbs, but neither of the generals could see anything through the mud-splattered windows.

'So what will happen when Jaruzelski arrives here on Monday to visit Brezhnev?' asked the head of the Illegals 'S' Directorate. 'Who'll be brave enough to lay the cards on the table?'

'Nothing will happen. No one will say anything,' Semenov replied in a mood of resignation. 'It'll be business as usual, courtesy of Brezhnev and his bloody mafia. There'll be the same old self-adulatory claptrap: the same old Brezhnev platitudes drafted by Chernenko about the "lasting and inviolable relationship" and "full understanding", about how the "Socialist system in Poland is defending itself". It'll be the usual rent-a-phrase stuff straight out of the propaganda manuals.'

The *Zil* swished beneath the arches of the bridge which carried Moscow's six-lane outer ring-road, then turned down a heavily-guarded road through a dense birch forest to approach the curving concrete and smoked-glass of the First Chief Directorate headquarters.

'What about our reaction to the Warsaw Party's meeting?' asked Martynov.

'All we've sent is a telegram of congratulation to Interior Minister Kiszczak on his appointment as a candidate member of the Politburo...' said Semenov with a smirk.

'Is that all? Nothing else?' asked Martynov somewhat astonished.

'Nothing else!' confirmed Semenov. 'If that's our only reaction to the two days of discussion then those dumbheads in Warsaw may realise how furious we are!'

The *Zil* swept past the armed guards in their sentry boxes at the Priority access to the KGB compound, and Semenov switched the conversation.

'Now, Vasili Pavlovich, before we arrive, tell me what progress you've made getting the new weapon and radio receiver-transmitter to Sulecki in Sweden.'

'They're still held up, Dimitri Fedorovich.'

'But we've known for weeks that Sulecki needed a new weapon and radio,' barked Semenov. 'And for ten days we've known where he is in Sweden. You mean to say that they still haven't been sent? What the hell's going on?'

Martynov did not raise his voice in response. His reply was measured and calm. 'Comrade General Kulagin told me one of the ballistics experts in Department Ten found an aiming fault during pre-despatch checks. He assured me it will be ready by late tonight.'

Semenov put on his gloves and Astrakhan coat in preparation for their arrival at the headquarters. 'Vasili Pavlovich, you'd better move your arse. Let me remind you it was you and 'S' Directorate who were most worried about Sulecki being marooned in Sweden while the Polish security forces hunted him down. So it is you, more than any of us, who should have an interest in getting the weapon and radio to him as speedily as possible. And what about the latest on Sulecki? What do you know?'

'Well, I understand our comrade Colonel is taking things easy. In fact he's taken up winter fishing,' said Martynov in an all-knowing manner.

'Winter fishing?' choked Semenov. The KGB deputy chairman raised his wispy eyebrows and picked up his Fedora hat. As a keen fisherman himself, the head of the KGB's First Chief Directorate could not conceal his wry smile of jealousy.

16

Saturday 27 February marked the tenth day since Interior Minister Kiszczak had approved General Siwinski's plan to eliminate Sulecki in Sweden.

In Warsaw, Poland's Deputy Interior Minister still struggled hard to find evidence to corroborate his suspicions of a KGB hand somewhere in Sulecki's story. Such was Siwinski's paranoia that he barely left his office during the day and slept there at night. Militia officers in the outer office worked twelve-hour shifts, a captain brought food and beer, and the general's wife sent in clean clothes by official SB *Volga*.

Yet, despite such persistence, Siwinski could still only speculate. On the intelligence grapevine he had heard that Moscow Centre was furious at Jaruzelski's failure to crush counter-revolution. Had Andropov decided to remove the Polish leader by force? If so, Siwinski knew the KGB would enjoy considerable support from the disillusioned senior officers of the SB, in the same way that the Czech secret police, the STB, had sided with the KGB after the Soviet invasion of Czechoslovakia in 1968.

As the duty captain brought a tray of tepid soup and veal cutlets that evening, Siwinski re-examined what the hardliners saw as the definitive evidence of Jaruzelski's failures – the full text of the speeches to this week's Central Committee meeting. In a rambling sixty-eight-page address, Jaruzelski had tried to convince the hardliners that all organised opposition was 'terrorism' which was now being stamped out. The general had gone on to blame the United States for trying to break up the Communist Bloc and redraw the map of Europe, and he claimed Washington wanted the turning back of European history to begin in Poland. For that reason, the

General said, martial law must remain in force.

But was the hand of the United States really behind everything as Jaruzelski claimed – especially behind Sulecki? Siwinski feared the facts suggested otherwise. In the stale, smoky air of the third floor office he stood by the window gazing towards Plywacka Street and the black silhouette of the Moskwa cinema which remained closed by martial law.

Like Jeb Theobold at the United States embassy, Siwinski too had received his copy of the *International Herald Tribune* for Tuesday 16 February and now the General had a grainy black-and-white blow-up of Sulecki to add to his SB computer record. He examined the enlargement. So this was the face of the 'assassin' identified by the KGB? Siwinski concluded that the slim unshaven figure must either be a dumb and willing Polish front man or a meticulous and cunning hired killer brought in from abroad. But what was the web which linked him to CIA headquarters? And more important, why had the extensive network of undercover SB agents inside Solidarity never unearthed even a whiff of Sulecki's CIA connection before his escape to Sweden?

Siwinski spent this last weekend of February making a score of discreet telephone calls to the senior KGB officers in Moscow he knew well from his many years associated with Soviet-Bloc intelligence and security. His conversations were designed to probe for the merest hint of even circumstantial evidence to confirm Siwinski's doubts. They produced nothing. Either KGB lips were sealed and feigned ignorance, or security was watertight among a small handpicked team at the highest level in Dzerzhinsky Square.

By Monday 1 March, Siwinski still faced a blank wall of silence. And there still remained one more vital question to be answered. If Siwinski eventually discovered there was KGB complicity, where would his loyalties lie? With the SB, or with the overriding demands of the Socialist Bloc's ultimate security masters, the KGB?

It was a terrible recurring dilemma. During his training

in Moscow in 1962 the Polish SB general had sworn his allegiance to the KGB. But he knew that his ultimate loyalty would always be to Warsaw.

17

The frail stooping figure of Yuri Vladimirovich Andropov, chairman of the KGB, towered above the rest of the six-man Politburo welcoming party as the ramrod-stiff figure of General Jaruzelski marched down the steps of the Polish airliner. It was Monday 1 March. The full-dress, red-carpet welcome in the diplomatic area on the southern fringe of Moscow's Vnukovo airport had been designed to be the first clear public expression of President Brezhnev's approval for Jaruzelski's imposition of martial law eleven weeks earlier.

At the foot of the steps the general, wearing dark glasses and khaki great-coat, made his traditional rigid salute before clutching both shoulders of the doddering President Brezhnev. The Soviet Leader had been brought here from his hospital bed on the orders of his Kremlin cronies. He breathed with difficulty in the bitter Siberian wind as he leaned forward to give Jaruzelski his usual three comradely bear hugs. Then each was rounded off by a comradely kiss: two on alternate cheeks, the third almost on the General's lips. Watched by an obedient bevy of Soviet TV cameras and photographers each leader managed a smile – the grin on Brezhnev's lined face significantly more effusive than that of the reserved and unemotional Polish General.

Andropov diplomatically kept his distance, however, reflecting on whether Brezhnev really knew who he was greeting and why. He stepped forward only when protocol demanded, coldly shaking the Polish leader's hand before fading away as Jaruzelski inspected the military honour guard with Brezhnev tottering alongside giving a strained and geriatric salute. For his part Andropov was unimpressed. He stood with the rest of the Politburo, talking heatedly to Foreign Minister Gromyko as the

Brezhnev roadshow rolled past and the Soviet Communist Party's rent-a-crowd dutifully waved their flags and shivered.

The KGB Chairman wanted no part in Brezhnev's circus. He had come to the airport only to prevent any speculation of a division between himself and Brezhnev's mafia which might threaten his own secret moves to seize power. 'When I finally replace Brezhnev, these time-wasting ceremonies and protocol will be kept to the minimum,' the KGB Chairman had quietly told his close confidant, General Semenov, the previous Friday. 'I haven't time to spend a morning freezing on an airport tarmac or station platform. Instead, officials like you will go to represent me.'

That Monday evening Andropov attended the Kremlin banquet where he listened to rambling, sycophantic speeches by both the Soviet and Polish leaders. Brezhnev mumbled about martial law 'cooling passions' with 'timely measures' and pulling Poland out of an 'excruciating crisis'. Jaruzelski, on the other hand, praised the 'lasting and inviolable' Soviet-Polish alliance and claimed that 'Poland has never yielded to foreign pressure and would not yield now.'

Throughout, Andropov remained politely silent behind his thick pebble glasses. In public the inscrutable KGB Chairman betrayed none of his most private thoughts. He had calculated it would take him six weeks to build the power base he needed to eclipse Brezhnev and his cronies for good.

18

The anger of the Polish exiles echoed around the tiled lobby of the Frostavallen hotel as they congregated in front of the television for the Swedish evening news and watched Jaruzelski descending the steps of the Illyushin-62 aircraft in Moscow.

'You traitor, Jaruzelski!' yelled Romek jumping up from his chair. 'How dare you call yourself a patriot and a Pole? You've not saved Poland, you've destroyed our country and everything it stands for ... You say you saved us from the abyss. You pushed us even closer.'

The Swedish beer had taken hold. Bogdan shouted at the television set. 'Go on! Mend your fences with that senile bugger Brezhnev! Grovel to the Kremlin and get your Order of Lenin at the end of it all ... Then come back with more Soviet oil and worthless roubles!' The Warsaw steelworker kicked over a clutch of beer and cola cans. Now Stefan and the women joined in too. 'Your day will come Comrade Wojciech!'

Only one refugee said nothing. Andrzej Sulecki, who sat restrained throughout. But to one person, Sulecki was conspicuous by his silence. Across the hotel lobby sat Zurawski, apparently writing a postcard but listening and watching attentively. After a week of surveillance the SB captain was now certain of Sulecki's identity.

A dark melancholy descended over the Poles. For a while they slumped in the chairs fingering Swedish magazines they could not read and staring blankly at the log fire which dominated the centre of the lobby. Eventually they hauled themselves to their feet and drifted to their hotel rooms. By 9.30 the refugees had gone.

Zurawski sauntered out past the receptionist, climbed into his hired Renault then drove the five kilometres back to Höör. The narrow secondary road had been polished smooth by a snow plough, and snowflakes swirled wildly in the freshening wind. By the main crossroads on the road from Växjö to Lund, Zurawski stopped at a petrol station. From a telephone box he dialled a number in Malmo which he had been ordered to memorise. He immediately recognised Major Lebkowski's voice at the other end and Zurawski responded in Polish: 'Contact with target positive. I confirm intention to proceed as instructed. Expect conclusion within forty-eight hours...'

Zurawski waited a few seconds in case the major wanted to modify his orders. He didn't and Zurawski heard the line go dead. He returned to the idling Renault in a ferocious, stiffening wind. It was perfect weather for murder.

19

At the Bratislava border crossing between Czechoslovakia and Austria, two Czech customs officers sat playing cards and half watching the television report of Jaruzelski's Moscow visit. Outside, a new Mercedes pickup truck with Viennese number plates crawled slowly towards the customs hut from the Czech police and passport control fifty metres away. The senior customs officer steeled himself against the sharp night air and walked briskly across to the truck which was now parked in the floodlights.

In the passenger seat sat Klaus Boenisch, a wealthy Viennese arms dealer. He and his driver were both fresh-faced Austrians in their mid-thirties, dressed in anoraks and jeans. Czechoslovakia's state arms company was among Boenisch's best customers and he frequently used this frontier crossing to travel to Prague.

Before presenting his customs documents and export licence, Boenisch – a bubbling extrovert – greeted the Czech officer loudly in German with his usual jokes and a hearty slap on the back. Stacked behind the cab in the rear of the van was a legal shipment of thirty-six wooden boxes containing 18,000 rounds of Czech-made ammunition. But hidden underneath was also a 5.56 mm AC-556 Ruger selective-fire weapon made by Sturm, Ruger and Co. Inc. of Southport, Connecticut in the United States.

Boenisch had known the export deal was irregular from the moment he agreed to it. But two factors had persuaded him to smuggle the Ruger to Vienna. First was a $10,000 cash payment from a front organisation of the Czech secret police, the STB, and second was the promise of a large Czech arms and ammunition contract to West Africa the following month. Boenisch was a tough and calculating hustler, and he knew it was a deal he could not refuse. As to why the Czech secret police would pay him such a ludicrous sum of money to smuggle just one weapon to the West, Boenisch knew it was better he did not ask.

The Czech customs officer propped himself against the Mercedes and cursorily examined the paperwork. The open van door gave Boenisch cover to pass on the usual bottle of Scotch and half-carton of Marlboro cigarettes which the officer slipped into an inside pocket of his greatcoat. He went through the motions of a thorough search, then after twenty minutes initialled Boenisch's freight documents and ordered the red-and-white traffic barrier to be raised.

Boenisch's driver eased the Mercedes over the frozen stream marking the east-west divide and halted a hundred metres further on in the no-man's-land between Czechoslovakia and Austria where he waited behind a convoy of Czech freight trucks. For the previous half hour a customs officer on the Austrian side had been carefully watching the Mercedes because Austrian officials knew that Soviet Bloc countries viewed this frontier crossing into a neutral western country as a soft touch for smuggling operations. For that reason, Austrian officials always studied with great care the way in which their Czech counterparts handled traffic coming to the West. Cursory formalities on the Czech side usually raised suspicions and led to a detailed rummage and police examination on the Austrian side of the border. As a frequent traveller to Czechoslovakia Klaus Boenisch was well versed in this game of east-west bluff. If the Czechs did not make a long and thorough search then Boenisch knew it was vital that he contrive a delay somehow.

Inside the cramped customs office on the Austrian side the arms dealer waited for clearance. After another half-hour a bald, bespectacled clerk stamped the import documents without examining them, then Boenisch stepped outside and showed the papers to the officer in the glass cabin who raised the barrier and waved the Mercedes through.

Moscow Centre's Ruger AC-556 had arrived in the West for onward shipment to Sulecki.

The Mercedes gathered speed past the score of rusty cars abandoned over the years along the road at the border, then headed west along the Danube valley. It took seventy-five minutes for Boenisch to reach his small office in a back street of the Margareten district of Vienna just south of the city centre. His driver reversed into the high-security warehouse to unload the cases of ammunition while Boenisch switched to his Audi and drove to a public telephone box under the bridge near the railway station on Matzleinsdorfer Platz. He dialled a Vienna number given to him before leaving Prague which he had hidden in jumbled numbers scattered about his clothing to reduce the risk of detection at the border.

'It's Klaus!' said Boenisch in a conspiratorial voice. The arms dealer had no idea who he was talking to but the contact recognised both his name and voice immediately. He responded with precise instructions.

'Go to the underground car park at the Opera House. Be there half an hour from now at ten-thirty. We'll meet in Bay 68. I know your car.'

The call took just ten seconds and Boenisch drove back to his office immediately. The Ruger measured sixty centimetres with the stock folded, so he was able to squeeze it into one of his battered attache cases. Then he changed his anorak and jeans for a blue suit and red silk tie, before driving the three kilometres north into the centre of Vienna.

Boenisch reached Bay 68 on parking level 2E four minutes early at 10.26 having driven in past the glittering chandeliers of the Opera House and the fashionable boutiques next door. The bay next to 68 was occupied by a dark blue BMW and Boenisch could see a shadowy figure in the driver's seat. They were not alone. The evening performance at the Opera had just finished and opera-goers in evening dress were already streaming into the dimly-lit underground parking area. Boenisch realised it was ideal cover in which to meet.

The arms dealer switched off his engine and waited. A man emerged from the BMW. Tall and slim, he wore tweed trousers and a dark blue sports jacket with brass buttons. He tapped on the Audi's window and Boenisch lowered it electronically. The clammy, subterranean atmosphere of the car park wafted in thick with petrol and diesel fumes.

'Klaus?' the man enquired. Boenisch nodded. 'You have something for me?'

Boenisch beckoned him round to the near side and unlocked the door. The contact lowered himself into the passenger seat and shut the door.

'I want no talk and no questions. When we finish you will leave the car park last. You will not be able to follow me so don't bother to try. To leave the car park you must first visit the cash desk and pay, so you will be stuck here for at least five minutes.'

Boenisch realised he was dealing with a professional who had meticulously planned and checked every detail. He unlocked the brown attache case and handed over the Ruger. The contact unclipped the catches, opened the lid, examined the weapon and smiled. Within twenty seconds he had checked the make and serial number, deposited the $5,000 balance in an envelope in the glove compartment, shaken Boenisch by the hand and returned to his BMW.

Outside, the low ceilings already echoed to the sound of vehicles manœuvring, so the contact was able to make an inconspicuous getaway having paid his parking fee before Boenisch arrived. As the Austrian queued at the kiosk to pay, he speculated about the identity of his anonymous contact. He could tell that the contact was not Austrian and that German was not his native tongue. Rumanian? Bulgarian? Maybe even Russian? In the end Boenisch didn't really care. He had his $10,000 dollars in cash and the contact had his weapon, and that was the way he liked to do business.

Meanwhile, five streets away on Vienna's inner ring road KGB Major Petrovsky was already abandoning the hired BMW and carefully locking both doors before walking off briskly through the pedestrian subways clutching the attache case.

It was 10.40. Petrovsky knew the overnight train to Frankfurt left in fifty-five minutes. He planned to be on it.

20

It was seven o'clock on Tuesday 2 March. Captain Zurawski sipped coffee patiently for several minutes as he watched the cafeteria empty of tired skiers and saw the Poles dispersing to spend another evening killing time on the pinball machines, pool tables and juke box.

Sulecki was the last to leave. Zurawski watched him deposit his tray of dirty crockery on the conveyor belt, then weave his way between the empty pine tables, before putting on his anorak. As Sulecki approached, Zurawski stubbed out his cigarette and stood up.

'*Dobry Wieczor!*'

Sulecki stopped abruptly, taken aback by the sudden 'Good evening' in Polish. For several seconds both men eyed each other with suspicion.

'*Dobry Wieczor,*' Sulecki eventually replied with a blank stare which revealed genuine shock.

Again they stood watching each other. Zurawski spoke in a broad Silesian accent.

'I heard you speaking Polish over there ... I didn't like to interrupt. Cigarette?'

Sulecki accepted, and both men used the business of lighting cigarettes as useful seconds in which to try to discover more about the other.

'Your accent? ... From Silesia?' asked Sulecki.

Zurawski nodded. 'Katowice. I usd to be a faceworker in a pit.'

Sulecki was equally forthcoming. 'I used to work at the Ursus tractor plant in Warsaw ... I'm from Bialystok; my family had a farm there ...'

Both secret policemen played the roles learned at their respective training schools in Moscow and Warsaw. Zurawski pursued his ploy of getting to know Sulecki.

'I could see you were all refugees like me. I wanted to

meet you, but I wasn't sure how to. I couldn't face all of you together. Do you have a moment?'

Sulecki made a sweeping, vacant gesture with his cigarette. 'I've got all the time in the world. We'll be cooped up here for months.'

Zurawski realised he had found a common point for conversation. 'I know. I've just been through it myself ... I arrived in Sweden a month ago. Spent six months before that at a refugee camp in Berlin. Now I've got Swedish residence papers ...'

The SB captain produced his Polish passport and flicked through the pages to show Sulecki the Swedish residency stamp. He had to establish his bona fides as a Polish exile in Sweden as fast as possble.

'I live in Malmo now ... in a small, grubby, two-room apartment like the one I used to have in Silesia. It often makes me wonder why I bothered to take all the risks of escaping from Poland in the first place ... How about you. How did you get here?'

Sulecki related the story of the Antonov escape. The undercover Polish SB officer listened but did not give any clue that he had already been at Frostavallen for days and had seen the refugees' fury at Jaruzelski the previous night.

The cafeteria manager worked his way through the hall turning out the lights and locking up. Both Poles left the table and walked out to the frozen car park.

'What do all of you do with yourselves during the day?' asked Zurawski.

'Same as the Swedes. Ski. Toboggan. Walk. Look at the animals across the lake in the animal park. Then when we've done that we have a change – we ski, toboggan, walk and look at the animals in the animal park.' Sulecki grinned sarcastically. 'But I've taken up ice fishing. It gives me time to think and forget – time to map out some kind of future.'

'Ever catch anything?'

'Not a lot. A pike or two but nothing special.'

Zurawski realised the possibilities immediately. 'Ice

fishing is something I've wanted to do for years. Could I join you one day?'

Sulecki nodded. Zurawski hesitated. He did not want to appear too pushy. 'When?'

'Tomorrow's as good a day as any.'

'I'd be glad to come. What time?'

'After breakfast. Half-past eight.'

Zurawski shook Sulecki's hand and they parted. After a few paces Zurawski stopped and shouted back, his voice echoing around the frozen trees.

'By the way, my name's Piotr – Piotr Zurawski ... And yours?'

'Andrzej – Andrzej Sulecki.'

21

General Siwinski returned refreshed after a long cold walk down the gloomy corridor from the third floor washroom. It was seven o'clock. Wednesday's dawn on Rakowiecka Street was beginning to stir. With his braces hanging round his waist the general rummaged through the latest overnight bag sent in by his wife, then he stood in a corner of the office shivering as he slipped on a clean shirt over his pale and flabby body.

The Deputy Interior Minister's bloodshot eyes betrayed the strain and exhaustion of the first twelve weeks of martial law. He perched on the edge of his desk sipping jet-black Bulgarian coffee, the single light above him reflecting on his shiny bald head as he tried to take in yet another report of the interrogation of an active member of the Solidarity underground.

'How many more do we have to kill before these bastards learn?' cursed the SB general as he spun the report disparagingly onto the growing pile of documents scattered across one corner of his office.

The feeble buzz of his internal telephone seemed as tired as the general.

'Hm?' Siwinski grunted. 'Comrade General Klimanov! Good morning, how are you, Yevgenni Viktorovich?'

'Strained and hungover but in the circumstances very well,' replied the KGB General in a throaty voice which revealed he had been thrashing the vodka the previous night. 'What news of Sulecki? What progress?' demanded the Russian.

Siwinski had not expected a call from the KGB liaison officer at such an early hour, but he was able to think fast enough to toss Klimanov some bait, in the hope that the Russian might reveal even the faintest hint of KGB complicity in the Sulecki conspiracy.

'It's going well!' said Siwinski. He chose his words carefully. 'We've traced Sulecki successfully but we've found no more evidence of a CIA connection.'

'How much more evidence do you want, Wladek? You seem to have enough already!'

'Agent Zurawski has reported from Sweden that he will conclude the elimination of Sulecki today or tomorrow.'

'Zurawski must be withdrawn immediately,' Klimanov interjected sharply. 'I have new instructions for you from Moscow Centre. The Polish security services must suspend the elimination of Sulecki. Because the threat comes from a sovereign territory outside the Polish People's Republic, I am instructed to inform you that as from this moment the matter will be handled by Moscow Centre.'

'Yevgenni Viktorovich, those new instructions from Moscow Centre have come far too late. There's no way I can recall Zurawski now. He's incommunicado. Our operation in Sweden will proceed as planned.'

There was an awful silence, then the line went dead. There was now no way Moscow Centre could stop a bloodbath at Frostavallen.

22

In the hills of Skåne the early morning was grey and vicious as a freezing wind blew off the lake.

Sulecki was already twenty minutes late. Zurawski stamped from one foot to the other as he waited in the snow alongside a giant plastic polar bear advertising Frostavallen's zoo park. The SB captain's regulation-issue machine pistol lay holstered against the warmth of his chest under his anorak and three jerseys.

It was just before nine o'clock when Sulecki arrived as part of a babbling gaggle of six refugees and their children.

'*Czesc!* Piotr,' Sulecki bellowed across the car park.

Zurawski waved an acknowledgement. Sulecki insisted on introducing his new acquaintance to the other refugees as 'our friend from Malmo'.

'We must go,' Sulecki went on as he collected together his fishing tackle.

'It's so good to meet fellow Poles in the same situation as me,' Zurawski beamed warmly.

The two men strode off, leaving the sweet smell of burning pine logs behind them as they headed across the snow-covered meadow towards the lake. Soon the whoops of the skiers were deadened by the snow, and Sulecki and Zurawski walked alone with the giant white crescent of the frozen lake curving away in front of them. Next to the boating shed and the upturned dinghies they stopped.

'We'll go to the other side by that island,' said Sulecki. 'The warden told me the pike love it over there. They sit deep in the water around the reedbeds during the winter ... This week I caught quite a few in that area.'

Zurawski's eyes strained through the whisping corkscrews of snowflakes. Six hundred metres away across

360

the perfectly horizontal surface he could just see a tangle of light brown reed stalks in front of a black swathe of tree trunks on the far bank. 'Looks fine to me,' Zurawski agreed ignorantly.

Both men set off across the lake, their rubber boots slipping on the highly polished ice beneath the snow cover.

'How thick is the ice?' asked Zurawski trying to make conversation.

'Changes from day to day and place to place ... Spring's coming, so it's begun to melt. It's probably about thirty centimetres at the moment,' said Sulecki.

'How d'you make a hole large enough to fish in?'

Sulecki sorted through his tackle and produced a steel rod a metre-and-a-half long which resembled an enormous corkscrew. 'I use this auger. The screw at the sharp end's enough to pierce the ice, but it takes a bit of time.'

Both men lowered their heads against the snow which blew horizontally at them.

'You'll find it bloody cold sitting out there but I've brought a flask of coffee and some bread and meat from the cafeteria. Also the remains of the bottle of vodka we brought with us on the Antonov.'

When they reached the clumps of swaying reed heads Sulecki examined the ice to choose his spot. He walked ten paces towards the middle of the lake then dropped the rod and auger on to the snow. 'You'd never know I'd fished here five times in the last seven days ... The hole freezes over in a couple of hours, and the next day there's no trace, especially after a fresh fall of snow.'

The explanation gave Zurawski ideas of how he could dispose of Sulecki's body.

'Do you need a fishing permit?' he asked as the other half of his mind weighed his tactics.

Sulecki lit a cigarette and nodded. 'Normally yes. Twenty krone a day or thirty krone a week. But I got permission for nothing because I'm a refugee. The Swedish authorities give us hardly any money so it's just as well.'

Sulecki kicked away a patch of fresh snow, positioned the auger, then applied his full weight to the T-shaped handle. He began turning the shank, the thread slowly biting into the ice as it inscribed a circle eight centimetres across.

'You try!' Sulecki insisted as sweat began to freeze on his forehead. It had taken him a minute to drill ten centimetres into the ice. It took the inexperienced Zurawski double that time to drill a further ten centimetres.

'We need to widen the hole,' urged Sulecki. 'Use the tip of the auger to chip away the ice until the hole's at least twenty centimetres across.'

As Zurawski drilled, Sulecki opened an umbrella and laid it on its side to protect them both from the wind. Then he emptied out the contents of the black plastic sack in which he had brought a dozen frozen minnows for bait as well as the nylon line, lead weights, vodka, food and several old newspapers.

For Zurawski, standing on a bitterly cold Swedish lake kindled no interest in ice fishing but he had to make an effort.

'What's the principle then, Andrzej?' The SB captain tried to keep talking while he worked out his plan of attack. 'Why do the fish bite now? Surely they're hibernating at this time of the year?'

Sulecki picked up the short, whippy rod and prepared the tackle.

'When the lake freezes, the pike hibernate on the bottom. With a complete ice cover there's no air or light so they have to stay on the lake bed to survive. The hole attracts them because it lets in oxygen and light which makes them think its Spring.'

Sulecki sat hunched behind the umbrella with his legs astride the hole. He inserted a lead weight into the mouth of a dead minnow, hooked it to the line, steadied the rod and lowered it into the hole.

'You don't need a long line – two metres is enough . . . You don't need a reel either because it freezes up. Usually you can feel the pike bite, but in case you don't you can see there's a little piece of paper on the line which shudders when you've caught something.'

Zurawski crouched alongside, silently calculating his options as Sulecki continued his impromptu guide to ice fishing. 'All over Scandinavia you see lakes dotted with scores of ice fishermen. And you'll find that they all face the same way against the wind. It's so popular here that they hold national and regional competitions...'

But Zurawski's mind was elsewhere. He no longer listened as the umbrella's canopy cracked violently in the gusting wind. There was silence, apart from the roar of jet aircraft flying the busy Malmo to Stockholm air lane high overhead. It was the moment for Zurawski to attack – before the Arctic freeze numbed his mind and muscles. He felt inside his anorak for the machine pistol which Major Lebkowski had given him in Malmo. He also produced a packet of cigarettes.

'Want a bit of warmth?' he asked as he crouched next to Sulecki. But the Russian's eyes remained fixed on the fishing line. Sulecki nodded but did not turn. Instead he stretched out his right hand in which he expected Zurawski to place the lighted cigarette. Zurawski, though, did not respond. Instead he moved back half a pace on his haunches and steadied his rocking body in the wind. There would be no second chance if he screwed it up. Slow! Precise! Take no risks, Piotr, he told himself as his right hand slowly pulled the WZ-63 from its holster and aimed at Sulecki's upper body a metre away.

But the Polish secret policeman had been charmed into a false sense of security by Sulecki's apparent trance. Instead of concentrating on the finer points of ice fishing as Zurawski assumed, Sulecki had been trawling his memory. He had remembered Zurawski's face and voice from somewhere. But where? And when? The Soviet Illegal had still not found the answer when his finely honed KGB instincts sensed a sudden rush of movement to his right just beyond the fringe of the umbrella. He had no time to think or weigh his options. He swung his body a quarter turn to the right and thrashed the fishing rod like a horse whip across Zurawski's face. The Pole froze with the stinging pain, his flesh screaming, his finger temporarily unable to pull the pistol trigger. Sulecki sprung onto his haunches, grabbed the umbrella and stabbed it straight at Zurawski's head.

The Polish SB captain had the gun and the Russian had nothing. Sulecki spun round and lunged for the auger, but Zurawski regained his balance and steadied himself to try to fire the pistol a second time. Sulecki fell to his left and Zurawski's shot went wide. Sulecki rolled his body towards Zurawski across the snow, the rolling motion building up momentum which enabled him to launch the auger like a javelin. The pointed end of the drill crashed into Zurawski's shoulder, breaking a shoulder blade and spinning him violently onto the frozen lake. Sulecki heard Zurawski's head crack against the ice which was as hard as concrete.

There was silence apart from the wind and Sulecki's rapid breathing. The KGB Lieutenant Colonel crawled towards Zurawski whose eyes were open with his teeth bared in pain. Sulecki looked around. He could see no sign of the pistol which must have spun off and been buried under the snow.

Sulecki lunged violently for Zurawski's collar.

'Who the fuck are you?' the Russian yelled. 'Who the hell sent you? Why did you try to kill me, you bastard?'

Had either agent known the real identity of the other then Zurawski might have been saved. But the disciplined ranks of the SB and KGB were trained never to break the rule of secrecy, however high the price. Zurawski did not respond.

Sulecki tried again. He grabbed Zurawski and shook him. 'How did you know about me? You're not here by chance.'

There was no outward sign of Zurawski's injuries but Sulecki knew from the Pole's sudden pallor that they must be internal and serious.

'American CIA? German BND? Now I know why you were so keen to join me on this fishing trip. But as an

364

agent or hired killer you're a miserable failure.'

Zurawski lay crumpled in the snow. Excruciating pain racked his body, yet he was conscious enough to honour his vow of silence, and he made no attempt to plead mercy. Under the pressure Sulecki forgot to speak Polish, and he slipped back into Russian.

'Who the hell are you?' he persisted, his teeth gritted, the saliva freezing before it hit the frozen lake surface.

Zurawski's eyes were half-closed and his cheeks colourless. The Pole was too weak to move or struggle, but he mustered four words of Russian which spluttered painfully and slowly from his parched, scabbed lips.

'Remember Balashikha . . . in 1976 . . .'

Having forced the answer from his victim Sulecki then pretended he had not heard, just as the KGB had trained him. Instead his fingers closed around Zurawski's neck and in a few seconds the Polish agent's body sank limply into the snow.

Only now in the calm of death did Zurawski's face yield up the secret of its past. Only now did Sulecki remember the face of a young Polish SB agent he had trained during his teaching assignment to the KGB's Balashikha School outside Moscow in the mid-seventies.

Sulecki rummaged in Zurawski's pocket and removed his passport. Yes, Zurawski had stayed at a refugee camp in Berlin as he claimed. And yes, he had been given asylum. But, of course, there was no record of any allegiance to the KGB. Sulecki unclipped Zurawski's pistol holster. It was the standard Polish issue with Polish names imprinted in the leather.

'Comrade Zurawski, you served your masters courageously, whoever they were.'

The Lieutenant Colonel's priority was to dispose of the body. He scanned the lake shore and the forest beyond where he could just see cross-country skiers swishing along the marked trails. Somewhere beyond the lake shore he could also hear sporadic volleys from a hunter's rifle. But no one seemed to show any interest in the aftermath of his deadly struggle.

Sulecki had to move fast. First he straightened his victim's limbs, then he took the ice chisel and began widening the fishing hole to at least sixty centimetres. Finally he pushed Zurawski's body into the black plastic bag and tied the opening with fishing line before sliding him into the hole and under the ice. As the displaced water sploshed onto the ice, the body kept bobbing up to the surface, forcing Sulecki to use the auger to push it back under. But within a few minutes nature had begun to do Sulecki's job for him as the slush of frozen water began to freeze, thus sealing Zurawski under the ice.

The struggle had soaked Sulecki. Now the wet and sub-zero temperatures began to penetrate his clothes. But he could not yet leave the hole untended because a bubble of air might still return the body to the surface. Calmly Sulecki sprinkled chunks of ice into the hole to encourage the surface to bind faster, then he reassembled his rod, hooked a new minnow, repositioned the umbrella and sat himself on a thick wedge of newspapers as if beginning to fish again. As he waited for the hole to freeze over completely, Sulecki sipped coffee and devoured the bread and meat he had pilfered from the cafeteria. To keep his mind alert he tried to assess the dreadful implications of Zurawski's attempt to kill him. Who had the Pole taken orders from? Was it the Polish SB? And if so, had Rakowiecka Street infiltrated *Amber Monkey*?

It took an hour for the cold to weld the ice hole shut and entomb Zurawski's body under the lake. By one o'clock Sulecki had cleared up his fishing tackle and begun trudging back across the lake towards the warming smell of lunch coming from the cafeteria. It was during the fifteen minute walk that he turned over a new and nagging question. Had the security of *Amber Monkey* been blown for good?

23

Dusk fell gloomy and heavy in the hills of Skåne that Wednesday evening. To break the grinding monotony of hotel life Bogdan and Jola walked the hiking trail around the lake to the Animal Park where the ticket hut was boarded up, the turnstiles creaked in the wind and the summer pedalloes and crazy golf lay hidden under the snow.

As Bogdan spoke the howls of a snow-wolf echoed around the deserted animal pens. 'Darling did you notice Andrzej last night? While we were all ranting at Jaruzelski on television he was silent.'

Jola shrugged. She hadn't noticed.

There was no logical drift to Bogdan's ideas: he just tried to find an explanation for the change in Sulecki's behaviour.

'I never knew Andrzej well at Solidarity headquarters. He was just another face in the office. But over the weeks I've begun to remember little things. Like the day he stood up at a commission meeting and demanded a new strike when the consensus was for restraint. Then when he had a stand up row with Walesa. It was over a minor matter but it split the delegates and polarised the meeting. I know he was radical, but now I sometimes wonder if ... well ... I wonder if he wasn't some kind of agent provocateur.'

Bogdan and Jola leaned against a fence and watched an elk scratch in the snow for food.

'And that chap we met this morning: Piotr Zurawski,' Bogdan continued. 'I don't trust him either. He gave me the creeps.'

Jola remained silent. Were Bogdan's fears justified? Or was it paranoia?

*

A nervous and uncomfortable silence dominated Thursday evening's dinner in the Frostavallen cafeteria. Sulecki and Bogdan had positioned themselves at opposite ends of the table to avoid making eye contact. It was Stefan who looked up from his fruit salad and broke the chill.

'Heard the news?' said Stefan, forcing a smile. 'We're all in good company now. Wanda Wilkomirska, the violinist and former wife of our "faithful" Deputy Prime Minister Rakowski has defected. She's asked for asylum in Germany.' A murmur of delight went round the table. 'It proves there are what Jaruzelski calls unpatriotic vermin even right at the top of the tree in Poland.'

Bogdan broke his silence. 'And she's not the first Rakowski to defect either. One of his sons, Artur's already in Germany with his wife and child. And another son disappeared in Spain. It shows how desperate many people are to get out of our beloved country. Sports stars, musicians, ship's crews, lorry drivers, students – only fools or traitors would go back once they've got to the west!'

Bogdan's eyes lifted towards Sulecki. 'Andrzej!' he called, projecting his voice the length of the table. 'You've cut yourself off from all of us. We are your friends, yet you don't ski or walk with us, and you barely talk to us. You just sit out on that bloody lake fishing all day.'

Sulecki pushed his plate to one side. The six adults and three children stared at him but he would not let them interrupt his dinner.

'Just remember it was Jola and me who looked after you when you were on the run from the militia,' Bogdan continued. 'It was Romek who risked everything to hijack the plane, and it was Romek and Stefan who flew you here. Don't you owe us all something, not least an answer?'

Sulecki calmly finished his yoghurt, wiped his lips, kicked back the chair and got up. 'I don't care what you've got against me, Bogusz,' he replied coldly. 'I don't have to listen to your crap. My thoughts are none of your bloody business ... Now I'm going to my room. I've got a fishing rod to repair, and I'll see you all tomorrow.'

Sulecki's manner startled the refugees and no one dared to question him further. Upstairs the KGB Illegal left his fishing rod untouched. He lay on the couch in his room chainsmoking and weighing up his two problems – how much Bogdan suspected and the death of Zurawski.

His train of thought was suddenly broken by the sound of Jola's voice in the corridor, then her footsteps padding rapidly towards his end of the floor. He swung himself from the couch, crashed open the bedroom door and stood in the corridor blocking Jola's path. 'My dear Jola,' he grinned as he put an arm around her and began guiding her towards his room. 'May I have a word?'

Jola panicked. The fears Bogdan had expressed about Sulecki during the walk in the animal park the previous evening flashed through her mind. Where was Bogdan? He was playing table tennis in the basement five floors below. Sulecki slammed the door behind them. They were alone as he clutched her shoulders.

'I need to know why Bogdan is so angry with me. What's he worried about? What have I done to upset him? That scene at dinner is not the way to treat a friend, is it Jola?'

Jola tried to pull herself away. 'You heard what Bogdan said. That's what we all feel. You're not one of us any-more . . .'

'But that's not all, is it Jola? There's something else worrying Bogdan, I know there is.'

Jola shook her head. 'He told you everything, Andrzej.'

She stiffened as Sulecki persuaded her to sit alongside him on the couch. She tried to wriggle out of his grip.

'Dear Jola. Remember that day before Christmas when I first came to your apartment from St Martin's Church? It was kind of you to help me. Remember, too, that we were alone together until Bogdan returned bruised and battered from interrogation at the Mostowski Palace? . . . How do you think your husband would react if he discovered evidence that you and I made love together

369

several times at the very moment he was being beaten up by the SB?'

Jola was too petrified to look Sulecki in the face. The suggestion was outrageous. She and Sulecki had never even touched each other during their day together before Bogdan's return, let alone made love. Jola realised now that Bogdan's fears about Sulecki's duplicity might be justified.

'You bastard, Andrzej! How dare you even think of such an evil idea? Bogdan will never believe it because it's not true ...'

'But I could make him believe it. A few juicy facts would be enough to shock him, and without any evidence to the contrary he would never know if it was true or not. The damage will have been done. Married life will become unbearable for you both.'

'No-o-o,' Jola cried out in terror and shook her head violently from side to side.

'And what if he sees you coming out of my room in a few minutes?' Sulecki persisted. 'And what if he sees you with your clothes ruffled and me with my shirt and trousers undone. What will Bogdan think then ...?'

Jola recoiled up the couch in shock. 'What do you want?' she stuttered.

Sulecki tried to embrace her again. His manner reeked of evil. 'I have to know what Bogdan thinks of me. That's all. What could be simpler, my dear?'

'And if I don't tell you?'

'Then I'll make sure he knows about our "affair" ...'

Jola longed to hear a familiar voice in the corridor to whom she could safely scream for help. But there was no sound of any kind. Oh Christ! How could she extricate herself? Sheer panic overcame her.

'B-b-b-Bogdan thinks you're an undercover SB agent,' she admitted hesitantly. 'He thinks you've been sent to infiltrate the Polish exile community ...'

Now Sulecki understood the barbed reference by Bogdan to 'fools and traitors' at dinner earlier that evening.

Jola rushed for the door, expecting that Sulecki would try to stop her. But as she tried to straighten her clothes the Russian calmly let her go.

'Good night, my dear,' he said arrogantly. 'If I were you I'd take Bogdan to the doctor. He must be suffering from delayed shock after his torture in Warsaw.'

Jola didn't linger to argue. She disappeared hurriedly into the corridor and Sulecki kicked the door shut behind her. Now the KGB Lieutenant Colonel knew his days in Frostavallen were numbered. For some time he had been readying himself to return to Poland. The only thing which had stopped him so far was the failure of Moscow Centre to deliver his new weapon and radio.

The next morning, the first heavy mist of early spring hung at ground level, enveloping the frozen lakes and hills of Skåna all day as the forests echoed to the plip-plop of melting snow. The poor visibility made skiing impossible for all but experts, so throughout that Friday the Poles were confined to the hotel's games room. And with them was Sulecki, who spent his time alone, silently hunched over a pinball machine.

'I thought that Piotr, the new refugee we met yesterday, told us he'd be joining us here this morning. Anyone seen him?' asked Romek as he leaned on the pool table.

Bogdan pulled himself up from cueing a shot, walked around the table and lined up the next. 'No! Last time I saw him he was going off fishing yesterday with Andrzej.'

'Andrzej!' Romek shouted across the room. 'What happened to your fishing friend?'

Sulecki did not look up from the pinball machine. 'Went back to Malmo last night. Said he didn't enjoy fishing.'

'But his car's still in the car park.'

Sulecki, the KGB perfectionist, had not been quite so perfect.

'It must have broken down ... maybe he hitched to get help,' the Russian added indifferently.

Bogdan was not convinced.

24

Brezhnev was on the point of death.

The message reached the KGB Chairman by radio-phone from the blustery tarmac of Vnukovo airport twenty kilometres south-west of Moscow. Suddenly fortunes were swinging Andropov's way, but he still did not allow himself a smile. Officially, the condition of the Soviet leader was a closely-guarded secret, but as head of the KGB, Andropov knew every detail.

A few days earlier Brezhnev had cancelled his usual March holiday and insisted on flying 3,000 kilometres to Tashkent in Soviet Central Asia for a surprise trip designed to improve his image and outmanoeuvre Andropov. Brezhnev's aides had ordered full television coverage of his speech offering reconciliation with China. They also ordered coverage of his personal presentation of the Order of Lenin to the Republic of Uzbekistan.

'Tactical madness and political stupidity,' Andropov had confided to Deputy KGB Chairman Semenov. 'We'll make the old fool pay. We'll cram his programme with so many engagements that he'll be exhausted. He'll be on his knees, and the television cameras will be there to record it.'

Andropov's strategy was paying dividends. On his desk lay his midday briefing for Friday 5 March. It described in detail how there had been panic that morning when scaffolding collapsed killing workers and managers during Brezhnev's visit to an aircraft factory in Tashkent. KGB bodyguards had hurled themselves onto the President to protect him, but the shock for the old man had been such that Brezhnev's aides ordered that he be air-lifted back to Moscow immediately.

Soviet television had shown live pictures of the Soviet leader's departure from Tashkent and had planned live pictures of his arrival back at Vnukovo. But at the last moment the coverage had been cancelled. Now Andropov eavesdropped on the radio traffic to and from the commander of the KGB's Ninth Directorate who was supervising security at the airport.

'Comrade Brezhnev suffered a stroke just before the aircraft landed,' said the highly-charged voice. 'We cleared away the reception party and the photographers and journalists in time ... The Comrade President was taken off the plane unconscious on a stretcher surrounded by his family. Physician Chazov says his patient was clinically dead on the plane for several minutes. He had to be revived with resuscitation machines ... Chazov says Leonid Ilyich is in a coma ... He may be paralysed permanently ... He may not survive ...'

'And now?' said a voice at KGB headquarters.

'The patient's in the Politburo ambulance car heading north-east towards Mocow along Leninskii Prospekt ... All traffic has been cleared ... Our destination is the Kremlin clinic at Kuntsevo ... I am in my car following.'

The KGB chairman turned down the radio volume. The news from Vnukovo was the break he had long awaited. He picked up one of his battery of desk telephones and buzzed General Zuyenko, head of the Active Measures Service 'A'.

'Anatoli Georgevich! ... Brezhnev has suffered a stroke but he's not dead yet. I want you to undermine his position and question his suitability to govern. You must spread contradictory rumours to the Western community, first of a permanent paralysis and then of his death ... Quietly circulate the idea of the KGB under my command being the guarantor of national stability both during this time of crisis and in the future.'

The news of Brezhnev's condition was scarcely five minutes old. Yet the wily KGB fox had already made his move to grasp ultimate power in the Soviet Union, and thereby to draw the noose tighter around General Jaruzelski.

25

On Saturday morning Deputy Interior Minister Siwinski sat collapsed at his desk in Warsaw, his tie askew and his hair greasy and unkempt. The all-night vigil in his office had not produced a single phone call on any matter, let alone confirmation that Zurawski had successfully concluded his operation in Sweden.

The General tried to distract himself by reading the latest communiqués from the morning's newspapers. There was the first reported evidence of Solidarity extremists and church officials taking up arms. A priest had been arrested the previous night after the pistol used to murder a police sergeant on a Warsaw tram in February had been found bricked into the wall of his rectory. Then Siwinski turned to the hardline newspaper *Zolnierz Wolnosci*, the voice of the military, which reported evidence of party and government officials receiving death threats, and of anti-state slogans being painted on front doors and walls. 'The seeds of terror sown by anti-socialist elements begin to bear fruit,' warned the paper. 'These are attempts at mass terrorism to overpower the whole of society.'

Siwinski began to believe Poland's own propaganda. Now the kind of terrorist attack which Sulecki was thought to be planning with CIA backing did not seem such a far-fetched idea.

'Captain! Get me Lebkowski in Malmo on the short wave radio,' Siwinski shouted to his aide.

The connection took eight minutes on a circuit protected by encoded electronic scrambling units at either end. Siwinski had to shout as if Lebkowski was on the moon. 'Major, have you heard from Zurawski?' he yelled.

'Negative, Comrade General. I've heard nothing. I repeat, negative,' Lebkowski replied.

'But I expected news two days ago. Why is there nothing?' Siwinski was not pleased.

'I have received no message and I did not want to break radio silence,' said the Major.

'You must find Zurawski and report back. I don't care about Zurawski himself. All that matters is confirmation that Sulecki has been disposed of.'

Lebkowski simply obeyed orders. He only had his telexed instructions from the previous week and did not know the full reasoning behind Siwinski's operation. 'Understood, General.'

In Malmo, Lebkowski disconnected the radio then phoned the motel at Höör where he believed Captain Zurawski had been staying. The receptionist confirmed that a Polish national with Zurawski's name had been registered for one week and the bill had been settled in advance with cash. Had the motel staff seen him? No, not for two days. The receptionist said his room still contained a small holdall of clothes, but his bed had not been slept in since Thursday.

Lebkowski slammed down the phone. Was Zurawski still somewhere pursuing Sulecki, or was he now dead? There was no alternative but to go to Höör himself to examine Zurawski's possessions. Only then could he confirm the position personally to Warsaw.

Late that morning the SB Major drove the consulate's rusting *Fiat* through the slushy snow north-east out of Malmo along the E66, past the university city of Lund and beyond to Höör. At the motel, Room 16 was exactly as the receptionist had described it on the phone. Lebkowski had not expected to find a notebook or any written material but he rummaged through the un-ironed clothing all the same and found nothing.

26

KGB Major Petrovsky arrived in Malmo from Copenhagen by hydrofoil at nine o'clock that Saturday morning. His roundabout journey across Europe carrying the Ruger overland from Vienna had taken three days longer than planned.

Four days earlier on Monday night's midnight train from Vienna to Frankfurt, the KGB Major had struck up a conversation with the guard. Over an illegal schnapps in the baggage car, the guard had mentioned that West German customs had begun a major campaign against a gang of drugs traffickers who were paying tourists to smuggle cannabis from Turkey. The clampdown meant that the bags of every passenger would be thoroughly searched at the West German border.

The guard's information had forced Petrovsky to change his plans. He had left the train hurriedly at Salzburg, but tight airline security had made it too risky to take a plane. So there had been no alternative but to skirt Germany by train, travelling west via Innsbruck to Switzerland, then into France, and north down the Rhine valley through Luxembourg and Belgium into the Netherlands. Only at Groningen, on the most northerly part of the Dutch North Sea coast and furthest from Turkey, had Petrovsky been prepared to take the calculated risk of crossing the West German border. In all, Petrovsky had taken thirteen trains, missed four connections and spent one night camped in the waiting room at Luxembourg station. But the fact that he had now reached Sweden safely with Sulecki's Ruger testified to his well-honed KGB skills of evasion and good judgement.

In Malmo, Petrovsky hired a small Volvo and drove north into the hills of Skåne. He still wore the crumpled dark blazer he had used to impress the Austrian arms dealer in Vienna on Monday, and he felt incongruous among the crowds of weekend skiers cramming the car park outside the Frostavallen hotel.

Petrovsky had no idea where he might find Sulecki. After eating herrings and sausage in the cafeteria, he sat down in an unobtrusive chair in the hotel lobby and waited among the pot plants and ivy just as Captain Zurawski had done a week earlier.

It was not until four that afternoon that Sulecki appeared as a bedraggled red-faced figure submerged under an enormous anorak and clutching a fishing rod. He spoke to no one and seemed to be alone. Petrovsky calmly folded his newspaper, picked up the attache case and walked briskly across the stone tiles. He caught up with Sulecki on the first floor landing.

'Andrzej ... !' he whispered.

Sulecki turned and immediately recognised the face he remembered from Warsaw. He beckoned Petrovsky to follow, the KGB Major holding himself back a few yards in case they met Sulecki's Polish colleagues on the stairs. Sulecki had already checked his room for bugging devices two weeks earlier, but for additional security he buried the telephone receiver in a pillow to prevent anyone listening on the hotel switchboard. Sulecki did not fear SB or KGB surveillance as much as Swedish intelligence or even the CIA. Inside the room he and Petrovsky finally shook hands and spoke colloquial Russian in low voices.

'Comrade Major, welcome to Sweden ... I hope you had a good journey. The location is better appointed than where we last met on that freezing lorry in Warsaw, but I'm afraid we have little time.' Sulecki removed layers of cold weather clothing and used a towel to wipe sweat from his body. 'I came to Sweden to lie low and reinforce my identity as an underground activist, but I'm now in great danger. This week I was traced here by a Polish agent presumably planted by Warsaw in the exile community. His name was Piotr Zurawski. He came here trying to liquidate me and I killed him. His body is in a sack under the ice in the lake.'

Sulecki dried his hands and brushed his windblown hair. 'I have no idea how the Polish Interior Ministry on Rakowiecka Street knew about the plot and where to find me. Department Eleven at Moscow Centre will have to discover all that. But the fact is that the SB did find me and I only just survived. Major, I believe there has been a serious breach of KGB security. I believe the Polish SB know about *Amber Monkey*. Also, my Polish refugee colleagues have begun to be suspicious about me. I don't believe I can spin out this charade much longer. I can't risk being trapped here. So within twenty-four hours I plan to make my excuses here and head back to Poland.... Now, Comrade Major, show me what you've brought.'

Petrovsky laid the battered attache case on his knees, unlocked the catches and opened the lid.

'Ah - a Ruger AC-556.' Sulecki recognised the weapon instantly. He took it from the case, unfolded the stock, held it to his shoulder and stood testing its balance as Petrovsky began detailing the main features.

'It is, in fact, a US Special Forces refinement of the AC-556,' the Major said in a clipped military voice. 'The standard model would not have broken down to fit unobtrusively into your baggage. This is the AC-556 'F' – a selective fire weapon like the 556. But this model has a short barrel and folding stock for both portability and easier storage in your shoulder bag or knapsack. It's 5.56 mm and has a flash suppressor. Its weight is 3.15 kilos. It has a three position selector lever for either semiautomatic fire, three-shot bursts or fully automatic operation. Muzzle velocity is 1058 metres per second; rate of fire is 750 rounds a minute. The front sight is fixed, the rear sight adjustable. One click equals one minute of angle, and one minute is equivalent to a displacement of three centimetres at a range of one hundred metres ...'

As he handled the weapon Sulecki memorised the facts. Petrovsky handed him a typed specification from the manual, but the Lieutenant Colonel put it to one side for burning later.

'Department Fourteen has authenticated every part as American, from the bullets down to replacement components,' added Petrovsky. 'The lubrication oil used in Moscow is American high-grade ballistics oil and even the screws have been turned from American steel so that forensic analysis in Poland will trace them back to the United States.'

Sulecki was impressed by the thoroughness of his colleagues in Moscow.

'The Ruger takes 20- or 30-round magazines. We've given you one 20-round magazine,' said Petrovsky. 'You have sixty standard rounds for target practice in advance, then another nine rounds for use on the operation.'

Sulecki was not happy. 'Only nine rounds?'

'Only nine,' Petrovsky confirmed. 'Your orders are not to spray the target with one visible and audible burst of concentrated automatic fire. The Ruger has been silenced and you must devise a way to fire just one rapid but silent burst of three rounds at the most. The other six rounds are for back-up if the first attempt fails.'

After two years undercover in Poland and two weeks in Sweden, Sulecki began to sense the adrenalin now that *Amber Monkey* was moving into higher gear. He stood for several moments fingering the Ruger, checking the barrel and the bolt mechanism, and wondering what else he needed to know.

Then as he laid the weapon on the couch, Petrovsky produced a micro radio receiver-transmitter built into the body of a Japanese Seiko quartz wristwatch by General Kulagin's engineers at Department Fourteen. The hands revolved normally but the digital functions were doctored to indicate radio wavelengths and frequencies, and there was a microphone built into the underside of the body. For the aerial there was a long coil of fine cable which Sulecki would be able to carry secretly in his trouser belt. Petrovsky slung the wire in a giant swag across the bedroom then tested the radio to make sure Sulecki knew how it worked.

Suddenly Sulecki cut short the meeting. 'You must

leave!' he snapped without explanation, as he slipped out of the room to check if the other refugees had returned from the ski slopes.

'Good luck, Comrade!' said Petrovsky, his Russian voice booming through the half-opened door into the corridor. 'Until Moscow, Comrade!'

The KGB officers raised imaginary glasses of vodka in a mock toast as Petrovsky hovered briefly in the doorway.

'I forgot to ask. What about your target date?'

'It's May Day,' Sulecki told him.

27

Major Lebkowski returned from Höör to the Polish consulate in Malmo at 2 a.m. on Sunday morning. Should he dare phone General Siwinski in Warsaw at such a late hour? He decided not. He would wait until eight o'clock that morning before he radioed Rakowiecka Street.

In the end the Major's call to the Deputy Interior Minister was connected through the electronic voice encoding system at 08.05 hours.

'Comrade General ... it's Major Lebkowski in Malmo.'

'I expected news last night!' the General growled.

'I'm afraid I did not return until the early hours, Comrade General,' Lebkowski replied. 'I've checked the motel at Höör and the hotel in Frostavallen. There's no trace of Captain Zurawski at either location.'

'And Sulecki?'

'I thought an approach might be unwise in case I interfered with Zurawski's plans. In accordance with standing orders, I decided to contact you first.'

'An acceptable decision, Comrade Major. So is it fair to assume that after three days without trace Zurawski did not eliminate Sulecki?'

'Yes, affirmative, Comrade General.'

Siwinski's manner was brusque. 'So that means it's up to you, Comrade Major. It is you who must go to Frostavallen and take Sulecki out.'

'I understand, Comrade General.'

'Advise me when you return. You have a maximum of one day.'

So by midday Major Lebkowski had driven back through the hills of Skåa to Frostavallen armed with his Czech CZ-75 pistol.

The KGB's liaison officer in Warsaw, General Klimanov,

telephoned Deputy Interior Minister Siwinski exactly an hour after the Polish general issued his new order to Lebkowski.

'What news?' he asked insistently.

'The operation's continuing according to plan,' blustered Siwinski in the hope that this reply would be enough.

'But Wladek, I need to know. Is that CIA agent dead or alive?' Klimanov persisted.

'We have no confirmation either way. We must assume he's still alive.'

'And your agent, Captain Zurawski?'

Siwinski drew his own conclusion from the scrappy and unsatisfactory information which Lebkowski had given him from Sweden. 'I think Zurawski's dead. I fear he's been murdered by Sulecki. Now a second SB agent is preparing to liquidate the terrorist ...'

'Wladek! Call the second agent off. It's an order! Moscow Centre is firm,' said Klimanov.

Siwinski prevaricated. 'What I don't understand, Yevgenni, is why this matters so much to Moscow Centre? Sulecki is a Polish matter because he's a threat to Polish national interests. He's none of your business, so just get off my back. My orders come from my Interior Minister not from Moscow. General Kisczak's orders are for Sulecki to be eliminated, and to my knowledge those orders haven't changed.'

'In the spirit of fraternal cooperation, call him off, Wladek.' Klimanov slammed down the phone.

For Siwinski, the contents of Klimanov's call seemed to provide the vital confirmation of what he had long suspected. For some reason Moscow Centre was determined that Sulecki must survive untouched in Sweden. Why else would Department Eleven twice try to halt Sulecki's elimination unless they had a vested interest in keeping him alive?

The realisation of KGB complicity renewed Siwinski's determination. For the sake of Poland, Sulecki had to be stopped, whoever and wherever he was.

28

Sulecki stayed awake into the early hours of Sunday plotting his return to Poland. Within minutes of Major Petrovsky slipping out of the hotel the previous day, Sulecki had overheard his fellow refugees making plans to walk the cross-country ski trail around the lake after the end of the church service. This would be the moment to confront them with his plan.

Sunday dawned sharp, bright and windless with an arc of perfect Baltic blue across the spring sky as the Poles gathered in their tatty anoraks. For several minutes they walked down the rutted ski tracks without speaking. Then Bogdan broke the silence.

'All of this reminds me of Solzhenitzyn's words when the Kremlin kicked him out of Russia. He compared life in exile to the life of a deep-sea fish which had always lived on the bottom of the ocean under an enormous weight of water. When the fish was liberated and swam to the surface it perished because it couldn't cope with the lower pressure. It's just like that for all of us. We're so used to the pressures of living under communism that we can't get used to the freedoms and the good things in the West.'

'But here you realise how democracy can be dangerous, and how there's too much freedom,' said Stefan. 'Here you have to make choices. Back home in Poland we could always blame the government, but here there's no one to blame except ourselves.'

'And that's why I'm frightened we'll never adapt to the way of life here,' said Jola.

Such negative talk enraged Romek who had held their twelve lives in his hands during the escape. 'Why the hell do all of you hark back to a country which is twenty years behind the West? Here we can buy and sell legally. We can start a business without spending two years bribing officials. We can complain freely. We can talk back to bureaucrats. But in Poland the minute we opened our mouths we were trapped in a tangle of paperwork and bureaucratic obstacles. Only if we lied through our teeth and attended the right number of Party functions could we get enough privilege points to buy a fridge or pair of shoes. But here in Sweden, if I buy a newspaper it'll be because I want to read it, not because I have to be seen to be carrying it to the office before tearing it into strips to get round the toilet paper shortage. D'you really want to go back to all that?'

The divisions among the refugees gave Sulecki his opportunity.

'I do ...' the KGB officer said boldly. 'I want to go back to Poland. I've had enough. The West's right for many Poles. It gives us Mercedes, sports shoes, jeans, cameras, hi-fi and videos – all those things we longed for in Poland. But the West isn't Poland. And now I'm here I've decided it's better to live there and to fight the system, than to live in the West pontificating about it.'

Sulecki's raised voice ricocheted among the silver birch trees.

Romek slammed his fist into a tree trunk. 'But what on earth is there to go back to? Jaruzelski has proved there can never be freedom under communism. Poland's a long black tunnel going nowhere. All the bloody *apparatchiks* want to do is make sure the system survives – however terrible the injustices and corruption.'

The Poles were three quarters of the way round the lake. The melting snow slopped over their boots as the spring sun burned through the leafless branches and warmed their faces.

All that mattered to Sulecki now was to justify his speedy return to Poland. He had no time for any more of this moralistic claptrap.

'Well, I plan to take the risk. I'll return to Poland as a patriot and deal the military regime a blow from which it will never recover ... I've made my decision. I've agonised for days but I'm convinced I must play my part. I'll leave in my own way and in my own time and don't try to stop me.'

The six adults stood around him in the snow, envying his courage yet also despising him.

'You're mad, Andrzej,' said Bogdan. 'You're irresponsible. Don't you realise the reprisals and revenge for what you seem to be planning will hasten another national catastrophe?'

'Bogdan! Lay off! His mind's made up, can't you see?' Stefan cautioned.

Sulecki moved among the refugees, shaking their hands and giving each of them three kisses on alternate cheeks. Isabela began to sob. '*Prosze bardzo,* Andrzej. Don't do it,' she pleaded. But Sulecki took no notice. He reached the end of the line and stood facing Bogdan. Neither man trusted the other, but each knew they had to display an air of normality in front of the others. Sulecki wore his plastic smile as he touched Bogdan's cheek with a comradely kiss and shook hands.

'Remember what I told you at dinner on Thursday night, Andrzej. ... Only fools or traitors go back once they are in the West ... That means that if you're not one then you must be the other ... And after all we've done for you ...'

Sulecki did not linger to hear what Bogdan meant by his veiled warning. He wanted to leave behind the image of the committed Solidarity patriot. Instead his final words were bitter and vengeful.

'We all make mistakes, Bogdan, but some of us realise them sooner than others ...'

As he returned from the walk and entered the hotel lobby a few minutes later one of the receptionists called out to him. 'Mr Sulecki!' she shouted. 'There was a man here twenty minutes ago asking if you were still at the hotel. I told him you were ... He left no message.'

Sulecki didn't ask for a description. He knew Petrovsky had left for Moscow and that any police or immigration official would have left a message. There could only be one answer: the visitor must be a second SB agent sent to find Zurawski and discover what had happened to his intended victim.

The Lieutenant Colonel glanced quickly around the lobby but could see no suspicious faces. Upstairs in his room he allowed himself no more than fifteen minutes to pack the few belongings which he planned to take with him to Poland. With a minute to spare he threw his hiking bag over one shoulder then slipped down the rear fire escape to leave the building on the opposite side of the hotel to the main entrance.

At the same moment, Major Lebkowski returned to reception. 'Has Mr Sulecki come back yet?' the Polish SB officer asked in perfect Swedish.

'Yes, a few minutes ago. Would you like me to call his room?'

'No thank you,' the Major replied. 'That won't be necessary. I plan to meet him later.'

But already Sulecki was outside, running down a snow-covered track between the trees and heading away from the hotel. It was half past one. By three o'clock he hoped to be in Höör and hitch-hiking to the port of Ystad where he planned to take the midnight ferry to Poland.

But the crack KGB Illegal had been over optimistic. Instead, he stood for hours in the pouring rain at a crossroads in Höör as the Sunday evening line of Volvos and Saabs streamed south carrying skiers back to Lund, Malmo and Helsingborg. As a result Sulecki did not arrive among the quaint cobbled streets and half-timbered buildings of Ystad until well after ten o'clock that evening. The ferry port was deserted and eerily silent. Gone were the hordes of journalists who had crammed the town's few seedy hotels waiting for the ferries and escape boats from Poland in the first weeks of martial law. Across the main basin lay the rusting white hull of the Polish ferry *Mikolaj Kopernik* which was moored to the roll-on-roll-off terminal, her superstructure bathed in bright floodlighting and the words 'Swinoujsie-Ystad' painted in enormous blue letters on her side.

The *Mikolaj Kopernik* was not due to sail for two hours, but it gave Sulecki nothing like the time he would have liked to work out a way to smuggle himself on board. Instead he set off round the harbour basin, walking past the shuttered red-brick seamen's hostel and railway station, past the long, idle strings of empty railway wagons, then around the wide arc of dockside road to the ferry terminal.

Like Ystad itself, the ferry ticket office was virtually deserted, a shadow of former years when tens of thousands of Poles and Swedes travelled freely back and forth to Poland without visas. Inside, the familiar whiff of rough Polish tobacco and the feeling of official indifference suddenly made this a tiny oasis of Polish grimness within Sweden. As he loitered near half a dozen dozing Poles and bulging cardboard boxes crammed with Western food and electronics, Sulecki made his first important operational decision. To enter Poland as a foot or car passenger would mean him having to confront both Swedish and Polish border police as well as customs officials. Not only was Sulecki sure he was on Poland's wanted list, he also had no temporary documents or false papers. There was only one option: to smuggle himself on board inside one of the few freight lorries. It was, though, not an option he could safely rush into that night.

Instead, he spent the next hour carefully watching the freight formalities from among the shadows. The enormous, dimly-lit lorry park contained sixteen truck units and eight trailers, all of them parked along the far security fence well away from the terminal and police buildings, their engines ticking over as the drivers waited to be called forward for loading at eleven o'clock.

That Sunday night, the loading process ended ten minutes before sailing time, and it was as the *Mikolaj Kopernik* slipped its moorings at midnight that Sulecki made his second decision. He would return the next afternoon when he expected the first trucks would begin arriving for the Monday night ferry and when he hoped the dock officials would be at their least vigilant.

As Sulecki shivered and watched the ferry move slowly out of the calm harbour waters into the white-crested waves of the Baltic, he wondered where he could spend the night in a degree of comfort without being discovered. By now he could not risk a hotel or boarding house because it was possible that the Swedish police had circulated an alert for him. So he retraced his steps round the inner basin, past the lighthouse, past the station's illuminated clock showing twenty past midnight, then on past the rusting silhouette of the harbour dredger and finally the towering grain silo.

Ahead in the moonlight Sulecki's attention was drawn to the sound of tarpaulins and halyards flapping in a boatyard next to the yacht marina. From what he could see there was no security patrol, so he ambled in among the flat-bottomed cruisers, clinker dinghies, speed boats and ocean-going yachts.

Sulecki's priority was to find a boat which had not been shut-up for the winter. The sleek, ten-metre yacht *Sea Nymph* seemed ideal. He threw his hiking bag up over the gunwhale into the cockpit, stood on the wooden cradle supporting the hull, then grabbed a wooden cleat and pulled himself onto the narrow deck. For a few seconds he lay motionless in the biting wind listening for voices, but all he could hear was the lapping of the Baltic on the stone groynes behind him. He inched around the cabin canopy and forced an entry through the Venetian window blinds in the cockpit. He slipped quietly inside and closed the slats behind him. Then he cleared cooking utensils from one of the bunks, ravenously ate a bar of chocolate from his bag and stretched out.

As he lay looking up at the moon through the perspex canopy, Sulecki checked his watch. It was one fifteen. In thirty hours he expected to be back in Poland. In two days – on 9 March – he would be in Warsaw.

29

The acrid smell of new marine varnish and fresh paint awoke Sulecki at eleven. He rolled from the bunk and inched back a damp and tattered curtain. Even the grey colours of Ystad harbour seemed to gleam under a brilliant sun in the sky high above the grain silo. The boatyard buzzed with the constant clatter of halyards and straps blowing in the freshening wind coming from Soviet Estonia to the east. The only sign of life Sulecki could see was across the marina where half a dozen sailors busied themselves around two of Sweden's camouflage-grey coastguard cutters.

Sulecki knew it would be a long day but there was still plenty of time. He sat in the tiny cabin among paint-brushes, packets of wood-filler and tins of grease as he drank a carton of orange juice and finished his last two packets of potato crisps. He freshened up using tooth-paste and a razor he had found in the galley, then he spent half an hour familiarising himself with the Ruger.

It was just after midday when Sulecki raised his head out of the cockpit, checked that the boatyard was clear and jumped to the ground. He sauntered past the marina's shuttered clubhouse, crossed an unfenced railway line and walked into town. He knew he had to take his opportunity to fill himself with good food before he endured a long afternoon and evening in the lorry park and a night at sea. He took a corner table in Foffo's pizza house, where he sat surrounded by thick-set Swedes with big beards, check shirts and a great thirst for lager. The Russian agent quietly killed four hours eating spaghetti, pizza and ice cream, as well as drinking half a dozen coffees – all to the accompaniment of Dolly Parton on the restaurant's hi-fi. It would probably be his last taste of the West for many years – possibly for ever.

Dusk began at five o'clock and signalled it was time for Sulecki to return to the ferry terminal. That night's ferry, the *Wilanow*, was already moored in the dock and the first three trucks and trailers had arrived for the midnight sailing. Within minutes each driver had left his cab clutching a file of documents and headed for the customs office where Sulecki noted that formalities took at least half an hour.

Sulecki targeted the next Polish truck, which arrived at seven o'clock. From the shadows of the ferry terminal Sulecki watched it drive hesitantly through a line of bollards to park between a Swedish trailer and a mud-splattered Bulgarian truck. Through the grime and ice on the windscreen Sulecki could just see the driver in the dim light of the cab. After what must inevitably have been a long journey, the driver stretched his tired limbs, wiped his face and organised his documents across the steering wheel.

It was several minutes before Sulecki saw the middle-aged Pole jump stiffly from the cab and walk across to the customs office. Sulecki strolled slowly across the enormous expanse of tarmac just as a passenger might saunter to kill time before boarding the ferry, then he circled the trucks, apparently with no more than a passing interest. From the rear of the Polish trailer he moved towards the tractor unit at the front, past the filthy encrustations of ice on the underside and the line of hooks for lashing the tarpaulins. The only noises were the wind, the constant hum from the *Wilanow*'s engines and a cassette of gypsy music coming from the Bulgarian lorry. Sulecki merged easily into the deep shadows thrown by the floodlighting. He grabbed the door handle, flung it open, threw his hiking bag into the cab and hauled himself in. He swore under his breath. He had forgotten that the cab light would come on automatically the moment the door was opened. But he was now too committed to pull back. He dived low across the pedals in the hope he would not be seen by anyone who might be watching from the terminal building, then he pulled the door quietly shut. Once again

Sulecki waited for the sound of voices but there were none. Gingerly, he climbed onto the narrow bunk in the confined space behind the seats, then he dragged the bag containing the Ruger on top of him.

It was half-past seven, four and a half hours before the *Wilanow* was scheduled to sail. Sulecki pulled out the Ruger, clipped on the loaded magazine and returned it to the hiking bag so that its steel barrel protruded from one end.

Twenty minutes later Sulecki's attention was stirred by the sound of joking Polish voices being carried towards him on the wind. Through the windscreen he watched two drivers heading back towards their lorries, the tails of their denim jackets blowing in the stiff breeze. Sulecki sunk himself as deep as he could into the back of the bunk then pulled a musty blanket over his body. The driver opened the door, climbed into the cab and slammed the door. Before putting the documents on a shelf under the dashboard he tuned the radio to a Polish wavelength and listened to the last part of the evening news from Warsaw.

'I have a gun on you. Turn off the light.'

Sulecki's warning was softly spoken. It terrified the driver who did not dare turn round.

'I won't kill you if you do what I ask,' continued Sulecki. 'Don't worry. I don't want your cargo. I don't want your lorry. I don't want you. All I want is to get to Poland on tonight's ferry and to be smuggled safely through the customs and border police in Swinoujscie tomorrow. Then I want to disappear ... Do I make myself clear?' Sulecki prodded the driver with the gun barrel.

The driver nodded without speaking.

'My name is Karol,' Sulecki lied. 'What's yours?'

'Witkowski. Janek Witkowski.'

'Where are you from?'

'Warsaw ... the *PEKAES* transport depot in Warsaw,' Witkowski stuttered. He was petrified and astonished to be held up at gunpoint by a Pole in Sweden.

Sulecki tried to allay Witkowski's fears. 'Don't worry, Janek ... I'm not a criminal or thief. I'm a patriotic

391

Pole who wants to return to his homeland ... But the government have made it impossible through official channels ... I'm sure you understand why. So I've had to come back this way. I suggest we make friends and talk. It will be a long evening and we might as well make things as easy and comfortable as possible during our brief time together ... Cigarette?'

Witkowsi's fingers shook as they tried to grasp the cigarette. He looked straight ahead through the windscreen and had still not seen Sulecki's face. 'What do you want me to do?' he asked in a quavering voice.

'As little as possible, Janek. Just cooperate. Just get me to Poland.'

The barrel of the Ruger lay on the bunk, its muzzle ten centimetres from Witkowski's back.

30

'Andrzej's disappeared!'

Bogdan held Sulecki's key in his fingers as he confronted Jola in their hotel room.

No one had seen Sulecki all day. 'Now we know he wasn't bluffing. The bastard's gone – just as he said he would yesterday,' said Bogdan.

'How can you be so sure?' asked Jola.

'I told the chambermaid we were worried we hadn't seen him all day, so she let me into his room. The key was on his table top, his bed hadn't been slept in and his kitbag, clothes and other things are missing.'

Bogdan slumped against the wall and threw his head back in despair. 'And I've got even worse news! The maid referred to Andrzej's room as "The Russian man's room".'

'The *what*?' said Jola incredulously.

'She told me that when she was wheeling her laundry trolley past Andrzej's room on Saturday evening she heard two voices speaking Russian inside. Of course I asked her if she was sure. But she said she's seen hundreds of Polish refugees come through here in the last two months so she recognises Polish when she hears it, and she has Swedish friends who speak Russian so she knows the difference all right.'

'And you checked her description of Andrzej?'

'Yes, it was him. And she said a smart man in a suit had been in Sulecki's room for three quarters of an hour last night. It was when he left that she heard them both talking Russian. Later when she went into his room to turn back the bed she heard a Russian voice coming from somewhere but she could not see where. There was a long wire strung across the room, and when Andrzej saw her he violently pushed her out.

There was a terrible pulsing silence. Neither Jola or Bogdan immediately knew what conclusion to draw, but their own experiences of SB tactics in Poland instinctively made them fear the worst. Andrzej must either be a Russian secret policeman or a Russian-speaking Polish agent who had infiltrated their refugee group. But why, then, had he decided to go back to Poland?

Bogdan feared his hunches about Sulecki had been right. 'It's the moment we've been dreading. Do we sit here and forget about Andrzej and his threats? Or do we find some way to stop him doing whatever dreadful thing he plans to do?'

It was almost midnight. In the empty hotel lobby four floors below, the receptionist locked the till, dimmed the lights and prepared to lock the main doors. Major Lebkowski still sat next to the dying embers of the stove. He could no longer spin out his stay in the lobby so he folded Monday's dog-eared copy of *Svenske Dagblat* and bid the receptionist goodnight.

By 3 a.m. Lebkowski was back in the Malmo consulate radioing to General Siwinski in Warsaw that Sulecki's whereabouts in Sweden remained unknown.

31

The blond, clean-cut Swedish passport officer sat in his timber cabin at the Ystad ferry terminal examining Witkowski's Polish passport. The strained face of the lorry driver watched from the cab window above him as the officer overstamped the Swedish visa and entered the departure date. Witkowski chain-smoked Sulecki's cigarettes and sat hunched over the steering wheel.

In silence he and Sulecki waited another half-hour for the truck to be waved down the loading ramp and through the stern door of the *Wilanow*. At half past eleven they rolled forward into the blue haze of diesel fumes in the dimly-lit vehicle deck, then parked the lorry hard up against the rear of a Czechoslovak trailer.

'What now?' Witkowski asked irritably.

'We do what you normally do. We get out. We walk together up to the restaurant and then I buy you dinner ... But remember my gun will be aimed at you all the time.'

'I don't accept charity from crooks!' said Witkowski.

'Buying you dinner isn't charity, and I'm not a crook,' Sulecki snapped. 'You do as I say and you enjoy the meal.'

'I need to sleep. I've just driven 350 kilometres ... Tomorrow I have a ten-hour drive to Warsaw.'

'That will be no problem. After dinner we'll reserve a cabin. You'll sleep while I watch you.'

With its pretentious claims to past grandeur and its peeling plastic veneers, fug of stale air and faded posters of the Beatles, the scruffy 1960s interior of the *Wilanow* was instant Poland. Two croupiers in stained tuxedos and frayed bow ties loitered aimlessly next to the fruit machines outside the ship's empty casino, while in the hard currency shop a heavily made-up stewardess waited next to her pathetic stocks of mediocre cosmetics, clothes and Polish shoes.

Sulecki and Witkowski sat well away from the corner of the restaurant where Polish lorry drivers always gathered to chat and drink their last chilled western beers. Instead they ate smoked meats and gherkins in silence as the floodlit quayside slipped past the windows.

Watched by Sulecki, Witkowski went to the purser's office to reserve two bunks, then the two men made their way below to a fetid cabin. As the *Wilanow* steamed at a modest twelve knots through the gently rolling Baltic, Witkowski slept on the lower bunk and Sulecki lay on the top bunk dozing between the torn sheets with the Ruger still pointing down towards the door. As a last resort the Russian knew that he would be able to summon assistance from the senior members of the crew who since martial law had been under the command of two Soviet officers.

With the sound of the *Wilanow*'s engines throbbing through his head, Sulecki reminisced about his brief flirtation with Sweden and the West. He did not like what he had seen and was glad to be returning to the Marxist-Leninist system he knew and loved.

32

It was 6 a.m.

Bogdan had fidgeted all night, persecuted by what the chambermaid revealed to him about Sulecki. He still had the key to Sulecki's room, so he rolled naked out of bed, pulled on the first clothes that came to hand and slipped silently into the corridor.

Once inside Sulecki's room he perched himself on the bedside table. The possessions which Sulecki had left behind still lay exactly as Bogdan last saw them seven hours earlier. What secret did they hide? He began examining each of them one by one: a few clothes, Polish books, a picture of Andrzej and his girlfriend Magda Gajewska, and notes written during internment. Why, wondered Bogdan, had Andrzej not taken these personal mementoes back to Poland? Why was he so indifferent to the past and the people he always claimed to be so close to?

Through the windows, the red strips of dawn clouds began to cross the grey March sky above the forests of Skåne. Bogdan would not be hurried. He took each drawer from the desk and chest, then examined the bathroom and shower cabinet. It was only when he looked closely at the lavatory that he noticed small flakes of burnt paper stuck like leeches under the rim of the bowl. He used a matchstick to remove each scrap, then he laid them haphazardly on a sheet of white hotel notepaper to dry. Thirty minutes later he began to assemble the jigsaw, and bit by bit the flaky fragments began to yield up their secret – the distinctive and unmistakeable squiggles of Russian typescript.

Bogdan pursed his lips. He had only learned the obligatory basic schoolboy Russian, but it was enough for him to realise that these were technical instructions for some kind of weapon. But what? The charred words were too incomplete to make sense. Only when he looked closely at the top of one scrap did Bogdan find what he most feared: Sulecki's name written clearly in Russian script.

The discovery carried the full force of a tumbling cliff face. After his months of scheming to outsmart the SB and ZOMO he realised beyond any doubt that one of their kind had secretly been among the refugee group all along. Bogdan's fear and fury produced a cold sweat of guilt. How had he and the others been taken in? Over a two year period Sulecki must have funnelled back to the KGB all the information he had typed into Solidarity telexes and reported at Solidarity meetings. And from the moment Sulecki met Jola at St Martin's church in Warsaw in December, and throughout the planning and execution of the escape in January and February, they must have been conned by a master of manipulation and deceit who had been trained by Moscow. But what had Sulecki achieved by hiding himself in this refugee group, and why his sudden return to Poland? If Sulecki was an undercover agent there must have been a pressing reason, and Sulecki's anonymous Russian visitor on Saturday evening seemed to hold the key. Then there was the radio communication witnessed by the chambermaid a short time after the visitor left.

It was half past seven, and below the bedroom window Bogdan heard the urgent panting of a keen early morning jogger. There was no way he could avoid telling Jola what he had discovered, but first he had to make a critical decision. With all communications to Poland severely controlled and monitored, how could he warn the Polish underground of the great danger which Sulecki now posed to them?

Slowly, a single dreadful option emerged. Should he, Bogdan Miskiewicz, now throw to the wind the personal security and peace of mind which he had won by escaping to Sweden? To save Solidarity from catastrophe, should he now return to Poland to track down Sulecki himself?

33

Rusting navigation buoys clanged in the gentle swell of the Bay of Pomorski as the *Wilanow* steamed slowly through the mist into the harbour entrance at Swinoujscie.

Sulecki and Witkowski stood silently together as the ferry slipped past Soviet trawlers, crumbling coal staithes and sailors hosing down the decks of torpedo boats moored at the large Polish naval base. A kilometre up river the ferry shuddered violently, halted, twisted through a full turn in midstream, then moored with its bow door facing the car ramp.

'What now?' Witkowski demanded.

'We go down to the lorry and you drive off as normal, with me hidden behind you on the bunk. I'm sure the border guards don't regard you as a risk. You're a reliable lorry driver working for a Polish enterprise with permission to travel abroad regularly. They won't be interested in you.'

'You mean I *was* reliable and *did* have a good record before this,' Witkowski sneered.

'Don't worry, Janek,' said Sulecki in a tone of reassurance. 'All they'll want from a loyal Party member like you is your passport and freight documents.'

As they descended to the car deck past the stewards stuffing dirty linen into laundry bags, Sulecki did not let the aim of the hidden Ruger drop for one moment. A bearded deck hand waved the lorry forward and Sulecki peered from under the blanket as the lorry drove slowly up the ramp in the middle of a gaggle of Polish passengers. Ahead, he caught his first glimpse of the red-faced Polish border guards in their familiar khaki greatcoats with AK-47s slung over their shoulders.

The passport officer leaned from behind the cracked

window of his dilapidated cabin as Witkowski handed down his documents.

'Passengers?' the officer asked routinely without looking up.

'None,' lied Witkowski. Sulecki relaxed a little with relief as he heard the border guard stamp the passport. Witkowski clunked the Volvo into first gear and inched the truck forward towards the single-storey customs post.

'Don't get out: let them come to you,' ordered Sulecki.

'But that's not normal,' Witkowski complained.

'It'll be normal today,' Sulecki said emphatically.

Witkowski handed the TIR documents out of the cab. Such was the level of official paranoia under martial law that it was second nature for the customs officer to assume that each of his customers was either a black marketeer, a smuggler or potential courier for western subversive forces.

'What did you export when you left on March 3?' the officer asked Witkowski.

'Polish furniture ordered by a Swedish enterprise in Jököping.'

'And what are you importing now?'

'Food parcels and personal effects from the Polish embassy in Stockholm . . . Diplomatic bond to be opened at the customs depot in Warsaw.'

Witkowski's reply signalled Sulecki's day of good luck. Had Witkowski been transporting sensitive goods like office equipment, machine tools or electronics the truck might have been stuck for hours being searched with a fine tooth comb. But this kind of diplomatic load was likely to be waved through unchecked.

'I'll check your TIR seals.' The customs officer zipped up his olive-green anorak and walked around the lorry. 'Your personal customs declaration form, please!' Witkowski handed down yet another document.

'You have 450 Swedish Kroner and 72 dollars? Are you carrying uncensored letters or messages . . . or any more money . . . or immoral publications threatening the security of the Polish State . . . or illegal goods for anyone else?'

400

'Certainly not! I'm a loyal Party member, not a smuggler.'

'*Prosze bardzo!*'

The customs officer stamped the documents and waved the lorry through. Witkowski pushed the stick into first gear and the Volvo weaved its way forward. 'Where now, you lucky bastard?' he asked Sulecki, half turning towards the bunk.

The Russian poked his head from under the stale blanket and was relieved to taste fresher air. 'Just drive on to Warsaw and I'll tell you when to stop.'

'All the way?'

'Just keep going until I say.'

It was 8 a.m. The Volvo turned into the town of Swinoujscie itself, where the grubby streets and distinctive smell of Soviet petrol confirmed to Sulecki he was as good as home again. The truck snaked through dirty pot-holed streets and past shop queues. Then it bumped over the single railway line leading from the docks to Szczecin and Warsaw, before finally heading east through the sand dunes.

In the pine forest among the sand dunes ten kilometres east of Swinoujscie, Witkowski's 40-tonne truck picked up speed past conscript soldiers exercising in full battle kit and a gang working on a derailed freight train in the marshalling yards at Wolin. Sulecki's destination was another six hundred kilometres and twelve hours to the south-east.

Meanwhile, at the ferry terminal the militia colonel in charge of the border guards detachment arrived for duty. As usual, his staff officer brought him the clipboard updated with orders received by the dockside border post during the night. Most prominent was a cable from Deputy Interior Minister Siwinski in Warsaw timed at 05.10 that morning and transmitted via the militia's regional headquarters in Szczecin. It read:

REQUEST FULL IDENTITY CHECK AND FULL SEARCH OF ALL PASSENGERS ON FERRIES ARRIVING SWINOUJSCIE UNTIL

FURTHER NOTICE. RED ALERT FOR SUSPECT NAME ANDRZEJ
SULECKI, RPT SULECKI. ADVISE IMMEDIATELY ANY TRACE
OF DEVELOPMENTS. BY ORDER.

Siwinski's cable had arrived too late to catch Sulecki.

34

It was ten o'clock by the time Bogdan emerged from Sulecki's abandoned hotel room. He knew he could no longer delay the moment when he had to confront Jola with his discovery.

'My God! So the enemy has been among us all the time,' she sobbed. 'What have we all told him to compromise ourselves? ... He must know everything – and worse still he'll have passed it on to Moscow or the SB ...'

Bogdan sat beside her, his head cupped in his hands. 'The name and reputation of Solidarity are at stake, and Andrzej's going to try and destroy them both.'

'How do we stop him?' Jola asked passionately.

'I just don't know,' said Bogdan. 'Phones to Poland are still down, and we can't write because of censorship. Somehow we have to get a message to the Warsaw underground. The problem is *who* in the underground and *where*? Stuck here, we don't even know who's still a member, let alone who's in charge and who's been arrested. We could try to find a courier in Sweden but I'm sure a message would be confiscated at the border or the courier arrested.'

Jola was in despair. So much made sense now – even Sulecki's threat to blackmail her four days earlier, which she had convinced herself was just a cruel joke. 'Can't we warn someone else then – the Swedish police or the government here, or NATO countries, or the United States? ... *Anybody*?' she squealed.

'But darling, be sensible! What can *they* do? If any of them sent a warning to Warsaw the Polish regime would simply accuse them of interfering in the internal matters of a sovereign state. They'd say it's none of the West's business.'

Jola's suggestions became increasingly impractical.

'Then why not warn the Polish militia directly? We could earn a few points by warning them that an escaped internee is returning home?'

Bogdan was astonished that Jola could be so daft. 'But d'you really think they'd believe the word of a discredited Solidarity leader like me who tricked the SB in Warsaw?'

Of course, Jola knew Bogdan was right. 'So what's left Bogusz?'

It was the question Bogdan dreaded. He had already spent hours that morning anguishing over the answer.

'I must return to Poland to hunt down Andrzej myself. I know him, I know how he operates.'

Jola jumped to her feet. 'You have to be out of your mind, Bogusz! After all we've endured? ... After all *you've* suffered. And after all your promises to the SB which you broke?'

Bogdan steeled himself. Having made his decision he could not waver in his conviction. 'Darling Jola! I'm your husband and I'm Miatek's father. But I'm also a Polish patriot and a Solidarity leader with a loyalty to our millions of members and our cause. We mustn't give up our struggle. If we do, God will never forgive us ...'

Jola knew well the I-will-not-be-moved tone of Bogdan's voice. 'We must discuss this with Romek and the others,' she insisted.

'No we won't!' said Bogdan. 'No consultations.. No one will stop me. But once I've found Andrzej and neutralised him, I'll be back – there'll be ways.'

Jola shook her head sadly.

'But look at the effort it took the first time. You'll never come back to Sweden. Miatek and I will never see you again ...'

Jola was unable to look her husband straight in the face. She made a dignified effort to compose herself. 'When do you plan to leave then?'

'There's a bus to Ystad at a quarter past four this afternoon. The ferry to Swinoujscie leaves at midnight. That means I'll be in Warsaw tomorrow night.'

From the precision of Bogdan's answers she knew his

404

decision had been carefully thought through. 'But without your passport and Polish ID how will you get through customs and passport controls at Swinoujscie? They won't exactly wave you through.'

Bogdan had yet to work out every detail, so he fudged his answer. 'All I want you to know is that I have ideas which I'm sure will work. You must have faith...'

'So you smuggle yourself through the border – but what happens when the SB pick you up in Warsaw and discover you're the turncoat who double-crossed them at the Mostowski Palace?'

'They won't pick me up.'

It was supreme blind arrogance by Bogdan, but Jola knew she no longer had any influence.

The six adult refugees assembled in Bogdan and Jola's bedroom at midday. It was a sombre gathering. Tempers were frayed and the camaraderie of the last three months had gone. Like Jola before them, none of the others could persuade Bogdan to reconsider. After two hours of trying, all they could do was wish him luck and give him the few Swedish krona which remained from their meagre social security allowance.

It was four o'clock when Bogdan finally kissed and embraced his Polish friends at the hotel entrance then walked hand in hand with Jola to the bus stop.

The winding cross-country ride down the muddy humpback road through the Frostavallen forest towards the Baltic took an hour and a half. As soon as he reached Ystad, Bogdan went to a grocery store near the bus station and bought high carbohydrate foods and drink which he hoped would help ensure his survival on the overnight ferry journey to Poland.

Despite his brave words to Jola, Bogdan still had no firm plan of what exactly to do. Like Sulecki on Sunday, he wandered under cover of darkness around the deserted ferry terminal probing the lax security for a way to hide himself on board the *Mikolaj Kopernik*. He knew he could not just walk on board the ferry or inveigle his way into one of the few overcrowded lorries or cars. Neither could he risk buying a ticket and negotiating Swedish passport formalities. But unlike Sulecki, Bogdan had no gun and no training in clandestine tactics. His only qualifications for subterfuge were his well-tried instincts, his initiative and the courage of his convictions.

He loitered in the shadows, and a diesel locomotive slowly shunted four freight wagons past him down the rusty track towards the stern door of the ferry. As the clanking trucks inched slowly past him, Bogdan made an instant decision. He leaped onto the moving chassis of the third wagon, clinging to a handle and trying to force open the heavy steel-framed door. It would not budge, so he slid off the running board, ran back a few metres then jumped onto the second truck. Again he tried the door. This time it moved a few centimetres and just enough for Bogdan to insert his right arm to lever it open. He forced himself through the gap and heaved the door shut again, locking it from inside.

Bogdan crouched on the dirty floorboards in pitch darkness. There was no time for fear. Beneath him the wagon wheels clunked slowly over two sets of points and down the ramp on to the *Mikolaj Kopernik*. Through thin cracks in the slatted wooden sides, Bogdan could just work out that the locomotive was shunting the four wagons along the deck towards the bows. The fact that there was only a single stern door on this ship meant that the first on board tonight would be last off in Swinoujscie tomorrow morning. The wagons rolled to a halt as, outside, the car deck echoed to the raucous singing of the ferry crew and the violent crashes of steel hitting steel as deck hands secured the trucks and lorries with heavy shackles.

It was half past eight. Bogdan would have to lie low for many hours enduring the foul smells and discomfort of a wagon apparently used to ship chemical products. He sat in a corner dozing until just before midnight when he heard the hydraulic hum of the ferry's stern ramp being raised, then felt the shudders of the twin propellers revving as the *Mikolaj Kopernik* slipped out of Ystad harbour into a freshening force five wind and the rolling Baltic.

The luminous figures of Bogdan's watch glowed in the dark. It was half past midnight. Within six hours he expected to be back in Poland.

35

For Bogdan, Wednesday's dawn did not come when the
sun rose among the Soviet trawlers in the mist outside
Swinoujscie harbour. It came when the public address
system woke him playing Acker Bilk tapes from the 1960s
and with the lorry drivers returning to the car-deck to
rev their diesel engines. Bogdan felt weak and fragile after
a night spent cooped up in the swaying freight wagon.
Nursing a headache, he shuffled silently around the floor
of the wagon on his haunches. Within a few minutes the
car-deck was empty and quiet. Peering through a hole he
counted nine other railway wagons on board but the
lorries and cars had gone. He calculated it would be at
least another hour, possibly two, before a Polish locomotive arrived to haul them into Swinoujscie's dockside
sidings.

In fact it was three hours. As a tractor hauled Bogdan's
four wagons slowly up the ramp he could just see through
the slats that the vehicles from the *Mikolaj Kopernik* were
still queueing at the militia and customs posts, where
baggage and packages littered the quayside and were
being searched rigorously. Clearly the railway wagon
Bogdan had chosen by chance in Ystad the previous
evening had been the most secure place in which to hide.

The four wagons slowly freewheeled to a clunking
halt somewhere in the marshalling yard. Silently Bogdan
released the internal lock on the wagon's door and by
levering it open a couple of centimetres, he confirmed it
had not been locked outside. As he scanned the shining
railway tracks Bogdan could see that the sidings were
surrounded by a two-metre high wire fence patrolled by
at least five fresh-faced young army conscripts. The only
visible exit was a pedestrian crossing three hundred
metres behind him along the tracks. How the hell could

he get across the wide expanses of the marshalling yard without being spotted?

It was ten thirty. After a night at sea and a nerve-racking start to the morning, Bogdan's energy and stamina were fast draining. He sat in a corner eating the last of the food he had bought in Sweden, then gave himself until midday to work out his escape.

It was a quarter to twelve when he felt the first vibrations, then heard the rumbling of a slow moving freight train arriving in the marshalling yards. The approaching diesel was twenty metres down the track, and behind it snaked scores of coal wagons. Bogdan could clearly see both drivers relaxed in the cab as the diesel roared by at about ten kilometres an hour. Meanwhile, four hundred metres away in the other direction, the conscripts sauntered wearily back and forth along the fence.

It was the moment for another instant decision. He clutched his bag under his arm, wrenched back the wagon door then jumped. The moment his boots hit the mixture of snow and railway ballast he picked himself up to run at the same steady speed as the train in the hope that the bogies of the coal trucks would hide him. From now on only luck could get him to Warsaw. He ran harder than he could ever remember running, the crunching ballast underfoot drowned by the roaring diesel and the clickety-click of the coal wagons.

One hundred metres ... Two hundred metres ... He ran onto the black cinder pedestrian crossing and killed his sprint dead in three paces. Breathing heavily he turned away from the coal wagons then walked through the small gap in the fence trying to look natural and relaxed. He composed himself, using the cover of the last fifteen coal trucks as they thundered by, then he turned left heading along a narrow tarmac track into Swinoujscie. The coal trucks rattled away.

To anyone watching, Bogdan wanted to look like a dishevelled, unshaven Swinoujscie worker walking to work. But with his body heaving and the blood surging after his sprint, Bogdan scarcely felt in control of himself. He tuned his ears for the sound of running boots, a militia wagon or an alarm. Every clunk from the railway yard and every crash of a ship's cargo on the quayside kept his frayed nerves tingling with anxiety. But there was nothing.

Fifteen minutes later Bogdan stood at the railway station checking the times of trains to Warsaw. For the first time he felt less vulnerable. He pulled a wad of crumpled *zloty* notes from his pocket and bought a second-class ticket.

It was all so unreal. Was he *really* back in Poland? Had he *really* entered the country with no ID or passport?

One fact haunted him more than any. Planning the escape from Poland had taken him two months. By the time he reached Warsaw his return to Poland would have taken just two days.

Life was cruel. But Bogdan owed it to Solidarity and to his conscience.

PART THREE

Amber Monkey!

1

By Friday 9 April, Sulecki had been in his cottage hide-away in a birch forest sixty kilometres south of Warsaw for exactly a month.

Sulecki was no unwelcome squatter who had broken into the *domek* like a criminal on the run. Instead he was a familiar face to the locals. He was well-acquainted with the crumbling grey stone walls and the cavernous unfurnished rooms with their sanded wooden floors and flaking plaster because the cottage belonged to the family of Magda Gajewska, Sulecki's long-standing girlfriend.

It was Good Friday, and the KGB Lieutenant Colonel had spent much of the morning warming his fingers in front of the enticing glow of a rusting cast iron stove in the kitchen. Four weeks earlier, after Sulecki had smuggled himself into Poland through Swinoujscie docks, the ten-hour lorry journey had taken him past the industrial city of Poznan, across the undulating plains of Wielkopolska and through a score of half-hearted roadblocks. At the small town of Sochaczew, fifty-five kilometres west of Warsaw, Sulecki had made Witkowski stop the truck in a lay-by near the bridge across the river Bzura, knocked him out with the butt of the Ruger, dragged him from the cab to a nearby strawberry field, broken his neck and hidden the body under a snowdrift.

Afterwards, Sulecki had boarded a bus and two hours later got off among fields two kilometres west of the market town of Grojec south of Warsaw. Using his KGB orienteering skills, he hiked south in the night drizzle along deserted back roads and farm tracks to reach this typical Polish summer cottage which, as usual, had been shut up for the winter.

That Friday, as Sulecki sipped stale coffee and sat on a rickety stool among the sagging cobwebs, he recalled his weekends with Magda at the *domek*. He remembered how on Saturdays they would borrow a car in Warsaw and bribe a petrol station attendant for a double ration of fuel so they could drive south to spend a day or two rejuvenating their exhausted bodies alone. Often they discussed political strategies long into the night with union colleagues over bottles of wine and bootleg brandy, then made love in front of a roaring fire. The locals knew Sulecki from those many visits with Magda but no one knew his name.

When Sulecki had first arrived from Sweden he told various half-truths about Magda's fate to those neighbours who asked after her, but he was sure no one in this remote area would try to check his story. The Russian had given himself four days to recover after the gruelling trip from Sweden before embarking on a daily training programme designed to return him to the tip-top physical condition vital for the perfect execution of *Amber Monkey*. During the first three weeks, long hours of exercise had removed excess fat and freshened his complexion. The fatigue of martial law which had once been ingrained in the black and sunken recesses of his eyes had gone. The KGB Lieutenant Colonel now had the body sharpness expected by Moscow's Balashikha training school for any sabotage or assassination operation. Sweden had also changed his appearance. His beard had progressed from ragged stubble to the kind of thick bushland growth which had become the trademark of Solidarity activists and intellectuals. He had also restyled his straggly hair into the look of a peasant.

When the weather was too bad to take exercise, Sulecki passed the time planning the final stages of *Amber Monkey*, doodling with pencil and paper at the kitchen table for hours, drawing sketches and maps of locations in Warsaw and listing what he knew of the itineraries and habits of General Jaruzelski. Then, to while away the evenings, he dismantled and reassembled the Ruger by the light of a paraffin lamp.

May Day was now three weeks away and Sulecki began

to concentrate his mind on the various assassination strategies. As he worked through each option, the KGB Illegal knew the risk of capture and failure was enormous.

2

During the same four week period, Bogdan had lived the
lonely nocturnal existence of a badger – hibernating and
plotting by day in his secret burrow in Warsaw then
scavenging by night under cover of darkness. When he
had first arrived back at the family apartment in Dzika
Street on 10 March there was no sign of SB surveillance.
Bogdan assumed that by then the Mostowski Palace must
have known that he and Jola had escaped to Sweden. It
was for that reason that he calculated his safest haven
would be the apartment itself rather than the shed in the
allotments.

For a month Bogdan had survived in a permanent state
of fear, and had met no one. During daylight hours, when
the pale spring sun or the racing clouds arched across the
sky, he mulled over ideas, slept or picked at the few tins
of food which he and Jola had left behind after their
departure to Szczecin in December. Each evening he
sat himself just a metre from the old black-and-white
television with the volume low so that no sharp-eared
neighbour or informer would know the apartment was
occupied. Then, during night-time forays, he risked
journeys by tram to buy whatever fresh food he could
find.

But in four weeks Bogdan had made no progress tracing
Sulecki. He had even failed to find Jurek or the half-
dozen Solidarity colleagues he could trust. When he had
visited the allotment shed on Raclawicka Street and
peered through the grimy windows, Bogdan had detected
signs of a struggle or a sudden enforced departure.
Upturned furniture, printing equipment and papers had
lain strewn around the floor. Had Jurek been seized or had
he abandoned the shed to pool his efforts with activists
elsewhere? There were no clues, so Bogdan had made it

his aim to track down alternative contacts in underground Solidarity.

One new contact offered hope – a young car worker named Marek who claimed to be a first rung on the ladder which led to the underground leadership. After days of on-off contacts through intermediaries Bogdan met Marek on the evening before Good Friday at a tumbledown cafe in the Rozycki market area of the shabby Praga district across the Vistula. Marek was in his midtwenties – a short, stocky man with an adolescent toothbrush moustache. In the cafe's dark, whispering atmosphere they exchanged small talk for ten minutes as they each noted the faces of those around them in the cafe who might be secret policemen. Then they stepped into the sharp damp air of the April evening to walk the dimly-lit streets for almost an hour.

As they walked Bogdan detailed what he believed was Sulecki's involvement in an undercover conspiracy to discredit Solidarity. Marek listened in total silence, absorbing the facts. When they finally shook hands by the vodka shop on Zabkowska Street, Bogdan's parting words retained his old defiance. 'Tell our underground leader Bujak that we must protect what we stand for,' he told Marek. 'Tell all the underground leaders we must never let that bastard Sulecki discredit our union. Never!'

Ten minutes later, as the swaying tram clattered back across the Dabrowski bridge and into the tunnel under Castle Square in Warsaw's Old Town, Bogdan realised there was no way he could know for certain if or when the message had reached the union's fragmented leadership. He could only hope.

3

'Remember me?'

It was the evening of Good Friday. A pale, bedraggled young woman stood shivering in the drizzle at the top of the stone steps outside Jeb Theobold's residence. Magda Gajewska's walk through the dark back streets of Warsaw to Gimnastyczna had left her weak and breathless. As she stood under Theobold's porch, her skeletal hands clutched the half-shredded plastic bag of meagre possessions she had gathered during her three months of internment. Magda stared at Jeb Theobold, who stood in his bright green American jogging kit with a towel round his neck, trying to recognise the emaciated figure. The CIA officer was shocked by her pale complexion, jutting cheekbones and sunken eyes.

'You still don't remember me do you, Jeb? I'm one of Jaruzelski's proud statistics. One of the two thousand five hundred internees released since December... They let me out last night.'

It still took Theobold several minutes to recognise her. Magda Gajewska had been just one of a hundred or so contacts co-opted by him during the sixteen months of Solidarity.

'Why, of course I remember you. It's Magda, isn't it? ...Yes... Magda Gajewska,' Theobold said warmly with his instinctive veneer of American bonhomie. 'Where the hell have you been? You took a big risk coming here.'

He grabbed Magda by the elbow, ushering her in past the heavy wooden door and glancing down the street to satisfy himself there was no SB officer watching the house from the usual position under the spruce tree across the road. Magda squinted in the brightly lit hall to protect her tired eyes. Theobold handed her a towel and helped remove the top layer of her sodden clothes which stank

418

after three months cooped up in an internment cell.

'What can I offer you? Coffee? Tea? Vodka? Cognac? Or perhaps a hot bath first?'

'One of your best American coffees please. Hot with plenty of sugar. That would be a real treat.'

Magda perched herself on a stool in Theobold's smart American-style kitchen. She dried herself vigorously, the water dripping on to the cork tiled floor.

'You looked so ill that I hardly recognised you,' said Theobold as he spooned coffee into the percolator. 'Where did they keep you?'

Magda spoke in intermittent spurts of clipped phrases.

'Three camps. First Jaworze in the south, for just a few days. Then they drove us to Goldap, right up in the northern part of the Mazurian Lakes a few kilometres from the Soviet border. It was designed as a reminder to us of who was ultimately in charge.'

Theobold pivoted sharply and corrected her, ignoring any fears that the SB might be bugging the house.

'I wouldn't be so sure. Jaruzelski's in deep trouble with Moscow ... The Soviets aren't as fully in charge here as some people in the West think.'

Magda seemed uninterested in what Theobold said. Instead, as a form of therapy, she was determined to relate her gruelling experiences to him.

'Finally, because I protested too much – what the camp director amusingly called "misbehaviour" – I was transferred to Darlowo, the special camp near Slupsk three hundred kilometres west along the Baltic.'

Theobold nodded. He was familiar with the names and locations of the camps from CIA's satellite reconnaissance reports and the embassy briefing documents.

'Officially Darlowo was a worker's rest home,' she went on. 'There were only women internees, almost all of them radical women like myself ... We had a smuggled radio. So from Western reports we knew conditions were better there than in many camps. We knew it was a showcase, but it was still a pigsty.'

She gesticulated wildly with a half-lit cigarette. Theobold could see that internment had not defeated her. 'How did they treat you?' he asked.

Magda shrugged her shoulders and stared into the damp towel. 'How does any totalitarian government treat its enemies? . . . With the same dignity as they treat a rat.'

'Did they beat you?'

Magda nodded. 'Only twice . . . They beat anyone on the slimmest pretext: making too much noise, not eating enough food, or just because they wanted to remind us who was in charge.'

Before continuing her story Magda rapidly devoured three sandwiches of succulent roast beef which Theobold had bought at the US embassy commissary that morning.

'Did you get any of the church aid parcels?' he asked.

'Nothing! The guards took everything. Martial law regulations allowed us to have them, but the guards said we'd done nothing to deserve charity so they kept the stuff for themselves.'

'Didn't the camp doctor help you?'

'What could he do? He was an alcoholic – a bastard like the rest of them.' Magda ate ravenously. 'He only had a few drugs and none of them were any use to us. There weren't even basic antibiotics and painkillers. We were all suffering – decaying teeth, duodenal ulcers, stomach pains, bronchitis, stress and so on. But he was under orders to do nothing, even for pregnant women. One woman died. . . . Obviously they didn't want us to survive.'

Theobold sat three feet away, gulping Budweiser beer and listening avidly. 'Did you get any visits or letters?'

'None at all. They refused everything. Three women were even refused permission to attend the funerals of a father and a son . . . Last week I received a smuggled message saying it had taken seven weeks for my mother to extract news of my whereabouts from the militia. Today when I saw her she told me she'd been to the Wilcza Street depot and written every day, but I got none of the letters. I suppose they penalised me because I spoke my mind.'

420

'Did they make you sign anything before you left?'

Magda hammered the work surface defiantly with the side of her hand.

'No! They tried many times, but I refused. Every two or three days they put a piece of paper in front of me declaring that I admitted the charges against me and that I wouldn't engage in illegal activities in the future. They said I'd never be released unless I signed. But I always said that release was not as important as my honour ... They also wanted me to become an informer but I refused every time.'

'Did they give you any warning before they let you go?'

'No. They came for me at half past five yesterday evening and told me to pack. Then at six o'clock an armed guard took me in a "bitch" wagon to the local railway station, gave me eight hundred zlotys and just left me to get back to Warsaw by my own devices.'

Theobold's CIA instincts told him to find out Magda's reasons for visiting him. 'But why come here?' he asked. 'You don't know me that well. You must have closer friends who you need to see first. Why take the risk of being stopped by the goons in the sentry box down the street?'

'I needed to prove to myelf that internment hadn't frightened me so much that I wouldn't do things I·always did before martial law – like visiting American diplomats ... And I needed to find out what was happening ... And there's something else too. I got a secret message in Darlowo that my man – Andrzej Sulecki – had escaped, and that the SB and ZOMO were searching for him. Have you heard anything?'

It was the one question Theobold hoped he would not have to answer. He had news about Sulecki but how much should he divulge? He had always known about Magda's affair with Sulecki, and he did not want to upset her by revealing the man's suspicious appeals for money and weapons before he disappeared. He doodled the beer can around his lips then braced himself to break the news.

'Andrzej is in Sweden...' he said guardedly.

'*Sweden*?' squealed Magda in amazement.

'He escaped there in a small biplane on 15 February.'

There was a pained, disbelieving silence. After hearing on the camp grapevine about Andrzej's escape from internment, Magda had cherished a hope that after her release she would find him again through the network of underground contacts. 'How do you know?' she demanded.

'At the embassy I have a photo which shows Andrzej standing with eleven other refugees in Sweden after their escape.'

'Where is he now?' she asked.

'I don't know. Probably in a refugee camp, but I have no other details.' Theobold clumsily crushed the empty beer can and threw it into the trash bin.

'I don't believe it. It's not his way,' she insisted. 'He's too Polish and too committed to just abandon us all. And what about leaving me?'

'Maybe he never cared about your feelings?'

'Care about me? He always cared,' snapped Magda.

'You're sure?'

'Of course I'm sure. We were in love. Anyway, what business is it of yours to question our life together?'

'Let's just say it's none of my business but it's all of my business,' said Theobold trying to deflect Magda's anger. He pulled another Budweiser from the fridge and offered Magda a cola. 'You have no doubts, you're sure he meant everything he said to you?'

'Why shouldn't Andrzej be who he said he was? And why should he want to use me? Are you sick or something? If you love someone, you love someone. You can't just fake it for two years.'

Theobold kept turning the knife of his suspicions. 'You're sure he wasn't just a good actor?' Theobold spoke in riddles. He knew it was a gamble. 'Let me put it a little more clearly. Are you sure he didn't take advantage of you because of the cover you might provide? You're a radical dissident, a marked enemy of the Polish state. Are you sure Andrzej didn't manipulate himself into your arms with the idea that you would hide his real identity?'

'How dare you! You become more incredible by the minute.'

'But sometimes, Magda, the truth *is* incredible.'

He ignored her protests. 'Let me put it like this, Magda. Are you sure you weren't cleverly duped by an undercover intelligence agent seeking a perfect cover from which he could penetrate Solidarity?'

'Cover? Penetration? What the hell do you mean?'

For Magda the conversation had become unreal. She had visited Theobold for solace and information, not for a confrontation. But instead she found herself on the receiving end of the kind of humiliating tactics used by the SB at the Mostowski Palace.

'Well, Magda, I suggest you'd better think,' said Theobold. 'Maybe it's not just you. Maybe we've all been duped. Think of how you met Andrzej. Think of what he told you. Simple things like where he was born, his background, his parents. But did you ever meet his parents or go to his home?'

Slowly Theobold's persistent questions began to find a place in Magda's own jigsaw of concerns about Sulecki which had begun with his strange behaviour the night martial law was declared four months earlier.

'Andrzej always said he came from a farm near Bialystok, and that his parents were old,' she said. 'He said he'd never return to see them because of a row with his father who had wanted him to take over the farm.'

'And did you ever check his background?'

'Why should I? Do you check the background of your lovers, Jeb?'

It was a fair point but Theobold refused to let himself be distracted. 'I hope what I have to say won't upset you too much. But I know your past loyalties well enough to believe you'd want to know. There are some people in Warsaw who believe Andrzej is not who he says he is.'

Magda crushed her empty cola tin. Theobold leaned

across the kitchen unit and touched her shoulder but she pushed him away.

'We have good reason to believe Andrzej is a threat to Poland's security,' Theobold continued. 'I can say no more than that. But we have to find out exactly who he is and we need your help. We want you to tell us everything you can remember.'

'We? Who is "we"?' she whispered.

'You're a wise Pole, Magda ... You're aware of the realities of life here. I work at the United States embassy so I'm sure you know who I mean by *we* ... I don't have to spell it out.'

Magda stiffened. She sensed that her country's fate was slipping out of Polish hands into those of more distant, sinister forces.

By 'we' Theobold could only mean the CIA – America's Central Intelligence Agency.

4

It was seven o'clock on Easter Sunday and an hour after sunrise. In Grojec, a horse-drawn milk cart clopped slowly across the town square as Sulecki boarded a battered bus. The KGB Lieutenant Colonel was dressed in the typical clothes of a Polish peasant: a creased oversize black suit with a grubby white shirt and a badly-knotted, frayed tie.

The religious outing to Warsaw would give Sulecki his first opportunity to visit the capital since his return to Poland. He had delayed the trip for several days to take advantage of curfew relaxations over the three days of Easter. Playing a dangerous hunch, he had reserved a seat on this bus which had been hired by a local church to take pilgrims to Easter mass at St John's Cathedral. He gambled he would be safe because Easter excursions were unlikely to be stopped and searched at militia roadblocks.

Sulecki's gamble paid off. The bus reached the triangular expanse of cobblestones in Castle Square in the centre of Warsaw at nine o'clock that morning. Since first light tens of thousands of churchgoers had been attending Easter masses to pray for those interned and express revulsion for martial law. The Grojec men and women snaked across the shiny cobbles between the ZOMO patrols. Their loud excited babble bounced off the pink-brown walls of the castle and the stucco façades of the buildings painstakingly rebuilt after their wartime destruction. Sulecki, however, did not follow the pilgrims to St John's Cathedral. He slipped away, heading south from the Old Town.

As he approached the large roundabout at the junction with Aleja Jerozolimskie he slowed down. Across the junction stood the forbiddingly Stalinesque Communist Party headquarters with a ragged red-and-white Polish

425

flag fluttering limply from the roof.

Sulecki lingered by the shuttered newspaper kiosk on the corner opposite. During his weeks at the *domek* the KGB Illegal had planned to hide in the apartment of a Swedish diplomat who lived just above where he was now standing. At a reception for leading Solidarity activists in the apartment the previous summer he had noted how the third floor bay window offered a perfect unobstructed view across to the heavily-guarded Party headquarters. But as he surveyed the scene, Sulecki quickly realised that at least two of the entrance points were obscured or too distant for accurate aim with the Ruger. There was also no reliable line of sight into the offices because the windows on all five floors of the Party building were covered by net curtains.

Sulecki wasted no more time. Under the warming spring sun he hurried across the traffic lights, past the militia guards and headed south. A kilometre beyond the Party headquarters he reached the Council of Ministers, a sprawling triangular compound of squarish four-storey buildings which stood opposite Warsaw's famous Lazienkowski Park where in summer audiences sat among the beds of pink roses enjoying Chopin piano recitals. But not today; not on this dank Easter Sunday when the April moisture clung to the soggy ground.

In his peasant disguise, Sulecki ambled the 800-metre length of the high, black wrought-iron fence which encircled the building. Then he turned south into First Army Street on the opposite side of the road to the crack counter-intelligence guards of the Army Internal Service in their steel helmets, breeches and highly polished jackboots.

It was still early – just a few minutes after ten. As Sulecki walked slowly along the wide pavement beneath the naked plane trees he recalled the stories about Jaruzelski which he had heard during his last weeks at Solidarity headquarters on Mokotowska Street. Jaruzelski had been described as uncharismatic, a perfectionist and a disciplinarian who calculated everything to the minutest detail. He was also a shy, compulsive workaholic with a razor-sharp memory and no time for fools or slackers – a military genius trained by the Soviet Army but who nevertheless retained a defiant streak of Polish nationalism. He was a leader with the self-discipline to work tirelessly from eight in the morning until three or four the next morning; a military autocrat and brilliant tactician with few real friends but a solid bedrock of political support throughout the army and among moderate Party members. Above all Sulecki recalled how it was said in official circles that Jaruzelski always wanted to be known as the 'patriotic Pole' and *never* as the 'Soviet stooge'. And it was this streak of renegade Polish independence which had frightened Sulecki's own superiors at KGB Centre in Moscow into proceeding with *Amber Monkey*.

The walk round the Council of Ministers took Sulecki fifteen minutes and confirmed the discouraging assessment he had made during his days of brooding in the *domek* outside Grojec. Just like the Party headquarters, the Council of Ministers offered no opportunities for a foolproof assassination. It had too many entrances and there was no way Sulecki could be sure which one the general would drive through on any one day. In addition, the Soviet embassy was in the next block and all the surrounding buildings were under government control which gave Sulecki no chance to find an attic or similar hideaway nearby.

Briskly the KGB Lieutenant Colonel moved on to consider his third option – Jaruzelski's daily route to work. Sulecki caught a No. 19 tram south down Pulawska, the broad tree-lined boulevard and legacy of Stalin's days which served the suburban concrete jungles of Sluzew, Ursynow, Grabow and Imielin. The four-kilometre journey took fifteen minutes, and Sulecki alighted at the ski jump in southern Mokotow which had recently been shut down after a spate of dreadful accidents.

He briefly headed north again for two hundred metres before stopping at the entrance to Ikara Street, a narrow residential road which snaked through an exclusive villa district. It was here that General Jaruzelski lived on an escarpment overlooking the sprawling suburbs of Wilanow and Stegny. His villa was a modest building – a square brick house painted sandy-yellow, with a shrubbery of military aerials sprouting from the roof. The General occupied the house with his teenage daughter Monika and his wife Barbara who was a doctor of linguistics and renowned for her fluent command of German, Swedish and English. They lived surrounded by the villas of Polish government and Communist Party *apparatchiks* as well as the rented homes of senior western diplomats including the lavish red-brick residence of the American ambassador, a home substantially larger than that of the Polish leader.

To avoid attracting attention, Sulecki had only a few minutes in which to cull a large amount of information. At the western approach to Jaruzelski's villa there were two armoured personnel carriers and barriers patrolled by half a dozen soldiers with fixed bayonets. Beyond them, was a second roadblock manned by another four soldiers.

Sulecki turned south and skirted the security cordon. At the end of Czerniowiecka Street where it joined Ikara Street he could see an army post directly underneath the giant steel stanchions supporting the ski jump. Sulecki had seen enough to realise the chances of a successful attack against the Polish leader here were minimal.

There was only one other option. He returned to Pulawska Street and walked north along the General's daily route by car into the centre of Warsaw. On several occasions during 1981 Sulecki had seen Jaruzelski's dark blue BMW 2500 screaming up the tree-lined boulevard in the fastest of the three lanes closely followed by up to three carloads of security men, their headlights shining at full beam. Inside the BMW, Sulecki remembered seeing a driver and a senior security offficial sitting in the front with Jaruzelski sitting bolt upright in the nearside seat at the back hidden behind a copy of the Communist Party newspaper *Trybuna Ludu* or the Army daily *Zolniersz Wolnosci*.

But four months away from Warsaw had critically blurred Sulecki's memory of the finer details of the Polish capital. His favoured plan to locate himself and the Ruger in one of the few apartments or houses occupied by Americans or Westerners overlooking Pulawska Street now seemed over-optimistic. He had already passed the homes of three acquaintances from the Western diplomatic corps but it was clear that none was suitable. As he headed north past the maroon billboards and gaudy posters outside the *Teatr Nowy*, he felt a cold sweat of worry. For once his usual self-confidence seemed to be draining: his mask slipping as his memory and hunches failed him.

Only now, as the six lanes of Pulawska Street curved to the right past the giant Supersam supermarket, and the Sunday traffic slowed to negotiate the roundabout at Unii Lubelskiej Square, did a new strategy crystallise unexpectedly. As he stood in the tram queue opposite the central fire station, the crumbling edifice and flaking reddish-brown bricks of number 15 Bagatela Street towered in front of him. Sulecki smoked several cigarettes and let a dozen trams go by before the plan formed in his mind.

That evening as he sat on the church bus returning to Grojec he overheard the words of a peasant woman whispering to her neighbour in the seat behind him.

'The priest told me there's talk of a big demonstration against martial law on May Day ...' said the woman.

That single fragment of information finally established the time and the place of Sulecki's operation. At last the disparate pieces of Sulecki's jigsaw slotted neatly into place. But unknown to the KGB Lieutenant Colonel a new and unexpected factor threatened the success of *Amber Monkey*.

The CIA.

5

That evening Magda Gajewska waited frantically in the middle of Jeb Theobold's living room refusing to speak until they were alone. The CIA officer reluctantly broke off his regular Sunday evening game of backgammon, made an excuse to the off-duty sergeant from the US embassy Marine Corps, then led Magda into the kitchen.

'I saw him ... I saw Andrzej!'

Magda spoke with tears in her eyes and her lower lip quivering. She was still shaking having run the full six hundred metres from the tram stop. Theobold offered a brandy in an effort to calm her.

'What do you mean you saw him?' he asked.

'I saw Andrzej in Warsaw this evening ...'

'That's just not possible. He's in Sweden. Get that into your mind and accept it ... Right?'

He lunged across the kitchen to his briefcase, flicked open the catches and rummaged through some non-classified files. 'See! There's the proof!' Theobold showed her the *Herald Tribune* picture of Sulecki's arrival in Sweden, but she ignored it.

'It was half past five ... Just an hour ago. I was on my way to Easter mass in the Old Town ... The ZOMO's water cannon were lined up in Senatorska Street. I was walking across Castle Square when I passed some peasants being put on to a bus by a young priest ... I just glanced up at them as I passed ... and one of them was Andrzej. He was wearing a dirty suit. He had a scruffy moustache and beard, and long, straggly hair ... I've never seen Andrzej in a suit, and I've always known him as clean-shaven, with his hair much shorter. But it was Andrzej.'

Magda sipped the brandy and stared at the disappearing red glow of the April dusk through the kitchen window.

'It took a minute or two. At first the resemblance was so uncanny that I was too frightened to say anything. Then I plucked up the courage to shout his name. By then he was already inside the bus with his back to me. He seemed to half-stop – as if he'd heard me and recognised my voice. Then he moved on down the bus ... I waited, and as it drove off I saw his face again just for a few seconds. He was on an inside seat. He seemed to be trying not to look at me ... Jeb, I've known Andrzej for two years and I'm *sure* it was him.'

Theobold wondered how seriously to take Magda. He had to urgently know more details.

'What kind of bus?' he demanded.

Magda shrugged. 'There was nothing written on it.'

'What about the registration?'

Again she shrugged. 'It was a Warsaw number plate – "WAZ" – an official plate ...'

'How about the peasants. Did you overhear anything they said? Any names? Any places? What about their accents?'

'I'd say they came from this area but outside Warsaw, not too far away.'

'Can you guess where?'

'More south of Warsaw than north ... but that's only a guess.'

Magda knew Sulecki better than anyone so Theobold had to take her seriously.

'And if it *was* Andrzej on that bus and if he still loves you as deeply as you say he does, then why didn't he answer when you shouted?'

Theobold knowingly rubbed salt into Magda's emotional wounds. He wanted to force her to accept his assessment of Sulecki's ominous intentions. 'Let me tell you again, Magda. For two years he's used you, and now he no longer needs you ... Andrzej isn't who he says he is.'

'Well ... who the hell is he, then?' Magda screamed.

431

6

Alone and a thousand kilometres from his wife and child in Sweden, Bogdan was drained psychologically. In the five weeks since his return to Poland he had failed to track down Sulecki. He had also failed to find Jurek and an explanation for the ransacked allotment shed. Instead he had found only one underground Solidarity contact, Marek, but he had no idea whether his warning had filtered through to the union leaders who mattered.

Now Bogdan played his last hunch. In his head he carried a mental list of the names and addresses of five Western diplomats to whom he had provided information before martial law. In the previous few days he had met four of them: a French diplomat in a car park, a German in a city centre queue for mushroom-burgers, a Swede in a workers' bread queue, and a Briton in the armchairs of the Interpress newspaper reading room. But all the meetings had produced nothing. Not only had the diplomats been unwilling to repay his favours – none of them had believed his story.

Now only one remained – an American. The rendezvous would be at a quarter to five at the height of the evening rush hour under a bus shelter on the vast windswept expanse of Victoria Square in the heart of Warsaw.

Bogdan arrived early and stood under the bus-stop canopy. He felt vulnerable and exposed after days cooped up in his apartment. What he saw as he waited made him doubly nervous. In the Opera House car park two hundred metres away a group of workers, pensioners and intellectuals had gathered around a giant cross of flowers and pine branches lying across the paving stones. In recent weeks the impromptu shrine had become an unofficial memorial to the dead of martial law. At first

Bogdan assumed the gathering was spontaneous. But soon, to what was clearly a prearranged plan, the crowd began laying flowers in the shape of a giant 'W' on the pavement in memory of the Wujek colliery in Silesia where security forces had killed seven miners on 16 December. A hymn of defiance rose slowly above the evening wind as the crowd sank to their knees, placed candles and sang '*Poland is not yet lost, as long as we live ...*'

Then a ZOMO patrol made its first warning sweep towards the crowd and the atmosphere stiffened. An officer stood next to the flickering candles and raised his bull horn.

'This gathering contains more than four people,' he shouted. 'It therefore constitutes an illegal gathering under martial law ... I order you to disperse immediately.'

Bogdan stood at the bus-stop gripped by panic as the crowd ignored the order. He could not allow himself to become embroiled in running battles or to be netted by a ZOMO snatch squad.

Where the hell was the American?

The minutes seemed like hours as ZOMO trucks snaked in convoy onto the paving stones.

'Bogdan?'

The voice when it came was firm and definitely American. Alongside Bogdan stood a slender sharp-eyed man in his late thirties, dressed just like a Pole in casual, dowdy clothes. As agreed, he clutched half a loaf of rye bread in his left hand. 'It's too dangerous here,' said Jeb Theobold. 'Let's walk.'

As they headed into the trees of the Saski Gardens, Bogdan briefly outlined what had happened and why he had returned to Poland. Finally he described his conviction about Sulecki's role as a KGB agent who had been planted to discredit Solidarity and murder General Jaruzelski.

'Interesting!' Theobold murmured cautiously.

Bogdan had expected more than this perfunctory

response, but it was all the American diplomat said as they twice circled the drained duck lake.

'So now I need your help,' Bogdan insisted. 'I know the American embassy has contacts in the underground leadership. You have to warn them about Sulecki. Andrzej Sulecki, that's his name. He's a terrible danger to our union and to Poland. Somehow you must get a message to Bujak and his colleagues.' The diplomat still promised nothing. 'How can I contact you again?' Bogdan asked.

'Same place, same time, tomorrow.'

'And afterwards?'

'Same place, same time, the next day – if you insist.'

Jeb Theobold bade a curt farewell and strode arrogantly off towards the US Embassy a mile away leaving Bogdan enraged at the American's indifference. Now there was only one way Bogdan could hope to find Sulecki.

By himself.

At home that evening Theobold sat in his kitchen drinking beer and working through what he had heard. Not only was it dynamite, it also corroborated Magda's sighting of Sulecki on Easter Sunday and confirmed that Sulecki was a professional terrorist. As Theobold gazed across Gymnastyczna Street he remembered how Sulecki had stood under the tree opposite the house before Christmas demanding American weapons and resources with which to murder Jaruzelski.

The following morning, 13 April, Theobold faced his CIA Station Chief, Frank Jefferson, across a cluttered desk behind the plate glass in the high-security section of the US embassy. For half an hour Jefferson listened to Theobold's presentation of the new evidence from Bogdan, but he was not impressed.

'It's whisky talk, Jeb. Circumstantial crap. That sighting by Sulecki's broad on Sunday is of doubtful credibility. Magda's an emotional woman who's just got out of internment and is looking for her lover and a good screw. She's an unreliable witness.'

The crew-cut station chief spoke in a classic Louisiana drawl. Dressed immaculately, with a diamond-studded pen poking ostentatiously from his breast pocket, Jefferson always seemed better suited to the Washington cocktail party circuit than to working in Poland under martial law. He tossed his note pad disparagingly onto the desk, then peered over his half-rim glasses.

'Jeb, your outline of an assassination plot against Jaruzelski is too far-fetched. You should know better. Your information's not precise enough. And this other guy? Bogdan Miskiewicz? ... He must be out of his brain. Why would anyone risk himself and his family to escape on a crazy flight to Sweden only to come back again a few weeks later? It's what I'd call an F.F.D. – a funny fucking deal!'

Jefferson's racoon-like smile was mischievous. Theobold bristled with impatience at his boss's superficial analysis and contemptuous attitude.

'Get me reliable facts instead of questionable sightings, then we'll be in business,' said Jefferson. 'Until then I won't release either you or anyone else to investigate this matter.'

Theobold plucked his anorak from the coat stand and stood by the half-open door. 'Has something else dawned on you, Frank? ... This KGB conspiracy – if that's what it is – is not just a conspiracy against Jaruzelski and the Polish government. It's also a plot designed to implicate the United States as the most powerful supporter of Solidarity.'

Jefferson sniggered dismissively. 'Jeb, it's all bullshit. Get your imagination back under control before I whip your arse. This is the CIA not a screenplay conference for a Hollywood spy thriller.'

Theobold knew his Station Chief was wrong, and now he had to prove it.

7

After weeks of uninterrupted pressure, Deputy Interior Minister Siwinski was beginning to tire. He desperately hoped Sulecki would soon make his move and end the suspense.

At ten o'clock, the ministry's daily summary of security operations for the previous day, Monday 19 April, arrived on his desk. It detailed all significant SB and militia activity during the weekend up to midnight on Sunday. Only one death had been reported, and apparently it was unconnected to martial law protests. The body of a lorry driver named Janek Witkowski who worked for the *PEKAES* transport enterprise had been formally identified after being found on Saturday hidden under a pile of melting snow near the town of Sochaczew sixty kilometres west of Warsaw.

Militia records showed it was five weeks since Witkowski's empty lorry had been found abandoned in a lay-by seven days after passport records showed the driver had brought the truck into Poland on board the Swinoujscie ferry from Sweden

Siwinski read the report of a post mortem which detailed how the base of Witkowski's skull had been fractured by two hard blows, and his neck had been cleanly broken. The pathologist concluded that Witkowski had been murdered between four and six weeks earlier. Then Siwinski took the trouble to re-read the first intelligence reports from March which suggested Witkowski had gone into hiding after returning to Poland, even though he was a loyal Communist Party activist with an impeccable record.

The General took his notepad and mapped out a speculative chronology of Witkowski's disappearance.

9 March: 7.30   Arrives Swinoujscie on ferry. Drive to
            Warsaw takes 11 hours.
9/10 March: Witkowski murdered Sochaczew. Assume
            time of death is in evening as lorry
            approaches Warsaw. Was Witkowski
            stopped and attacked, or did he have a
            passenger on board?
            Security records from Swinoujscie show
            only Witkowski on lorry when he arrived
            in Poland. Could he have picked someone
            up afterwards?

Siwinski consulted his bulging file on the hunt for
Sulecki in Sweden. From Major Lebkowski's information Sulecki seemed to have disappeared on 8 March.
Could Sulecki have hidden himself on Witkowski's lorry
in Sweden, smuggled himself into Poland before the
special security alert came into effect, then murdered
Witkoswki to ensure his secret return to Poland was not
reported to the security forces? By this superficial analysis
all the dates dovetailed and there had been no further
sightings of Sulecki in the West since Frostavallen six
weeks earlier.

At the daily conference for the SB's commanding
officers later that morning it was reported that an SB
undercover agent from Section Five who had infiltrated
deep into Solidarity's underground structure, had just
filed details of a warning which was now being passed
through the Solidarity grapevine. Someone described as
'a security agent from the Soviet Bloc' and disguised as
a 'radical Solidarity activist' had just been smuggled into
Poland to discredit the union by undertaking acts of
terrorism against the Polish leadership. The 'activist' was
claiming to have backing and weapons from the CIA and
access to Western diplomatic locations in Warsaw.

'Name?' Siwinski eagerly asked the head of Section
Five.

'Sulecki, Andrzej Sulecki.'

The picture fully crystallised and Siwinski's worst

fears were confirmed. He leaned across his desk and buzzed his duty militia captain.

'I need a complete list of the residences of all American diplomats, embassy administrative personnel and suspected CIA agents in central Warsaw.'

Twenty minutes later the captain returned and Siwinski slowly drew the tip of his ballpoint pen down the names and locations.

'I want permanent 24-hour observation on these twenty-two American locations,' he told the commander of the SB's Department One who was responsible for the intelligence and protection of diplomatic locations. 'All arrivals and departures must be noted. There must be photographic and infra-red surveillance on the five prime locations on Pulawska Street and Aleja Niepodleglosci with particular reference to this picture.'

Siwinski produced his grainy blow-up taken from the picture of Sulecki in Sweden.

'Andrzej Sulecki is a highly dangerous counter-revolutionary. His photo must be circulated to all agents, and he must be caught.'

Siwinski then turned to the head of Department Four, responsible for SB operations against the Catholic church. 'I also want raids on six churches where radical priests are suspected of harbouring and assisting plans for armed attacks by underground activists. Your men must search for guns, weapons, explosives and ammunition. The life of Comrade Jaruzelski and the survival of the Polish government will depend on the thoroughness of your actions.'

8

Like SB General Siwinski, KGB First Deputy Chairman Semenov was also suffering from the prolonged stress of martial law in Poland and Sulecki's operation. For once he could not face eating with the usual *apparatchik* elite at the exclusive KGB restaurant in central Moscow. Nor could he face one of the private hotels run by the Central Committee near the Khimki reservoir outside the city. So that Tuesday evening his official *Zil* limousine crunched to a halt in the slush-filled gutter outside No. 6 Gorky Street which housed the famous Georgian *Aragvi* restaurant opposite Moscow's City Hall.

The KGB General's mistress, Irina, was out of Moscow at a political seminar in Leningrad so he had invited his close colleague and young protégé Anatoli Zuyenko, the high-flying head of the Active Measures Service. To gain entry to the *Aragvi*, Semenov and Zuyenko did not have to queue for hours, or press roubles into the doorman's hand like normal members of the public. As privileged figures in the Party they could always secure a table.

The three rows of tightly-packed tables in the basement were not full, despite the queue on Gorky Street. Watched by two plainclothes KGB guards, the generals settled themselves in a curtained alcove alongside gilt friezes depicting Georgian dancing and folklore which decorated the restaurant's low arched ceiling.

Semenov and Zuyenko cut their first chilled *Stolichnaya* vodka as the waiter brought a plate of steaming deep-fried Georgian cheese.

'I didn't invite you to dinner to discuss business, Anatoli Georgevich,' Semenov began. 'But for the moment I'm afraid we can't avoid it. I've just had some important news. Things are moving in Warsaw so it's time for us to move as well.'

The overweight, workaholic General devoured the *sulguni* and hot rolls as if he had not eaten all day. He took some handwritten notes from his inside pocket and spoke inelegantly between mouthfuls. 'Yesterday one of our clandestine monitoring devices permanently trained on the high security section of the United States embassy in Warsaw picked up details of a significant conversation ... This transcript details how the CIA Station Chief – a man called Jefferson – received a verbal report from one of his field agents – someone called Theobold, who's listed as a first secretary at the embassy. Theobold told his Station Chief he had information confirming that Sulecki had reappeared in Warsaw. The fact that the Americans know about Comrade Sulecki is worrying enough. More worrying though is that Theobold told Jefferson about one of Sulecki's fellow escapees who had now followed him back to Poland. His name is Bogdan Miskiewicz. Does that name mean anything to you?'

'Never heard of him,' replied Zuyenko.

'Miskiewicz is apparently trying to track down Sulecki in Warsaw,' added Semenov. 'Having returned from Sweden, Miskiewicz is determined to destroy our operation – singlehandedly if necessary.'

Semenov gulped his third vodka and wiped his lips with a starched white napkin as Zuyenko poured another shot of vodka into the tiny thimble-shaped glasses. Together, they picked at a new plate of *sevruga* caviar and smoked salmon.

'There is, however, a positive side ...' said Semenov. Zuyenko dutifully cocked his head.

'Station Chief Jefferson did not accept Theobold's story. He found the scenario too incredible, and complained that there weren't enough substantiated details.'

'So ...'

'So, the Station Chief refused to sanction a more detailed CIA investigation.'

'Is he one of ours, then?'

'No. Our detailed records show that Jefferson has no

sympathies our way at all. He's a right winger from Louisiana; a hardline Reagan type and one of CIA Director Casey's new personal placemen in Eastern Europe.'

Semenov shovelled a fillet of spiced Baltic herring into his mouth. 'But no reason to gloat, Anatoli Georgevich! We all screw up from time to time. Sometimes it's us. This time it's them.'

'But the plan should never have been discovered by them in the first place,' complained Zuyenko.

'I have to admit you're right, Anatoli Georgevich.'

Without even taking an order, the waiter reappeared and served them the Georgian dish Semenov always requested – Chicken *Zatsivi* – cold boiled chicken overlaid with a spicy walnut and coriander sauce. Semenov clutched his cutlery and raised his eyes slowly towards Zuyenko.

'We must now take advantage of that CIA failure. So I am authorised by the Comrade Chairman to tell you to proceed to Stage Four of *Amber Monkey*.'

Zuyenko understood precisely.

Suddenly the burden of professional duty had been lifted for the evening, and Semenov was able to change the mood as they toasted the Chicken *Zatsivi* with *Mukuzani* No. 4, one of the most sought-after red wines from Georgia.

'Now Anatoli Georgevich! . . . Tell me more about your daughter's success at the Academy of Sciences . . .!'

Semenov could afford to be cheerful. As he spoke he knew that beyond the Kremlin's ochre-red battlements his mentor Yuri Andropov had finally achieved his great ambition. At last the chairman of the KGB had ousted the Brezhnev dynasty in a bloodless coup. The Andropov *putsch* had been breathless and devastating. But for many days yet the people of the Soviet Union and the world would know nothing of it.

9

Jeb Theobold ignored his Station Chief's order to forget Sulecki. He was determined to contact Magda again, but by the evening of 21 April his search had achieved nothing. Once more he walked through the dark lobby on the fifteenth floor of the shabby modern block at the bottom of Gornoslaska Street. For the twelfth time in three days he rapped gingerly on Magda's front door and waited. One minute. Two minutes. Four minutes. Suddenly a sliver of light shone through a crack under the door and inside he heard footsteps. He tapped again.

'Who is it?' It was Magda's nervous voice.

'A friend,' replied Theobold in bad Polish designed to confirm his foreign identity. 'A special friend,' he added quietly, his lips hard against the door. Magda turned the key and the door opened slowly as she peered into the gloom to check his identity.

'I've been trying to find you since Sunday,' said Theobold.

Magda was not impressed. 'After our last meeting I had the impression you didn't want to see me again, Jeb.'

Theobold did not respond.

Both of them assumed the SB would be bugging Magda's apartment following her return from internment. So using one of the ritual charades of martial law Theobold pointed to the ceiling, cupped his hand round his right ear, then pointed to the front door and used the signal of two walking fingers to suggest they leave the apartment.

'Oh, fuck them!' cursed Magda. She put on her winter coat and boots, then locked the door behind them and together they strolled north along the west bank of the Vistula, where the air of the April evening was muggy with the first warm tang of real spring. For several

442

minutes Theobold talked pleasantries in order to win back Magda's confidence, then he applied the pressure.

'Have you seen Andrzej again?'

'No.'

'Do you have any doubts that you did see him on Easter Sunday?'

'I'm as convinced now as I was then.' Conversation was drowned as above them the trams rumbled across the ageing stonework of the Poniatowski bridge.

'Then try and second-guess him. What might be going through his mind? Where could he have gone?'

'But I haven't seen Andrzej for four months. So how the hell do I know what he might be thinking?'

'Don't chicken out, Magda. You know him better than anyone . . . I need answers and I need them fast,' insisted Theobold. 'The security of Poland is at stake. And so ultimately is the fragile peace between Moscow and Washington which could now depend on tracking down the bastard. Washington is sparing no effort.' Theobold had to lie in the hope of forcing an answer.

'You may be right . . .' Magda began slowly, carefully choosing each word. 'In the eleven days since my release, I've had time to think and time to remember. And now, perhaps things begin to slot into place. If I force myself to believe that you're right, and Andrzej was never a true lover but a KGB agent . . . then . . . then that helps explain something which has persecuted me since the SB dragged us away the night Jaruzelski declared martial law . . .'

Magda left the thread of thoughts suspended in midsentence. She walked in silence along the riverbank, ordering her ideas precisely before deciding what to reveal to Theobold.

'I remember it so clearly. It was gone midnight on 12 December when Andrzej returned to the apartment. He'd worked late at Solidarity headquarters handling telexes coming from the big meeting in Gdansk. I was in bed asleep and he woke me up. Andrzej told me about the National Commission's decision to call a strike for the 17th. I was thrilled. I sat up in bed and we talked. I'd been asleep. But Andrzej had been on the streets and must have seen the first signs of Jaruzelski's martial law. He must have been in the Solidarity headquarters, but he said absolutely nothing to me and I still can't believe it. . . .'

They were now walking in the dark along the river bank below the glorious floodlit spires of the Old Town and the Royal Palace.

'Let's suppose you're right, Jeb. Let's suppose Andrzej is a KGB agent,' Magda went on. 'Then it would explain why he said nothing that night. He wanted us both to be picked up by the SB to add credibility to his disguise.'

Magda tailed off, deeply depressed by the growing realisation that she had been taken in by her lover, who must have been one of the hundreds of agents who had infiltrated Solidarity and the underground. But Theobold feared this new circumstantial evidence would still not be enough to convince Jefferson to change his mind.

'So where's the bastard now? . . . A KGB agent is always well prepared. So where's he hidden himself?'

Magda shrugged fatalistically as she and Theobold turned and began the silent two kilometre walk back to her apartment.

10

Bogdan had left his meeting with Jeb Theobold on Victoria Square in despair. He realised he was on his own and could now only rely on his own instincts. Urgently, he tried to find his new underground contact, Marek. Bogdan's message was passed by word of mouth through the same intermediary as before and he gave Marek three days to make contact.

It was Wednesday 21 April, just nine days before May Day. Bogdan and Marek met as planned at half past six in the smoky gloom of the Cafe Mazovia on Ordynacka Street, a cul-de-sac in the heart of Warsaw's main shopping area. Both men arrived separately, ordered mineral water, then spent several minutes checking for plain-clothes SB men. Ten minutes later they each walked out.

Marek walked protectively a few paces behind Bogdan as they headed downhill in the dark towards the Vistula between the shop fronts on Tamka Street. As they passed the four grimy smokestacks of the city heating plant, Bogdan felt Marek catching up and brushing shoulders on his left. Both of them knew they could risk only a few seconds walking together, their whispers fighting against the heavy traffic roaring up the hill towards the city centre.

'Did Bujak and the underground leaders get my message?' asked Bogdan.

'I've got no firm news ... I fear they didn't,' said Marek. 'There's been a crisis since Monday night. The militia and SB have been making massive sweeps of the city. They're clearly looking for a big fish. They've picked up hundreds of people. I'm just the first link in a long underground chain, so I've no idea who's been picked up or how far the message went, and it's too dangerous to try again.'

'Who's the big fish?' asked Bogdan.

'No one knows,' said Marek. 'The goons haven't let on'.

The blue flashing lights of a militia wagon turned into Tamka Street and the vehicle growled uphill towards them at full revs. Instinctively Marek peeled away, turned left and without saying a word disappeared into the gloom under the trees on Topiel Street.

Bogdan walked on towards the Vistula, his heart sinking. Solidarity's underground leaders still knew nothing of the threat from Sulecki. Now, more than ever, Bogdan was on his own.

11

It was Lenin's birthday and in all fraternal socialist countries Thursday 22 April was a day for celebration.

In Moscow western diplomats awaited the annual unctuous tribute and political address made by President Brezhnev's chef-de-cabinet Konstantin Chernenko. But this year, without warning, Chernenko did not appear. Instead it was Yuri Andropov, Chairman of the KGB and sworn enemy of Brezhnev, who gave the tribute.

Andropov's unexpected appearance as head of the Politburo delegation intrigued seasoned Western observers, and was the first public clue to the Kremlin coup which had taken place a week earlier. Instead of being the focus of the celebrations, President Brezhnev sat on the dais alongside the KGB Chairman as no more than an ailing political passenger.

At his *domek* hideaway in the Grojec forest south of Warsaw, Sulecki listened to Andropov's address on a battered Polish radio. He interpreted correctly the unspoken explanation for Andropov's appearance leading the Lenin celebrations, along with its political importance for the KGB. He also knew it gave added weight and urgency to *Amber Monkey*.

12

Jeb Theobold spent three days reassessing the strength of his new evidence before risking another confrontation with his Station Chief. By Friday evening he felt suitably prepared. He ambled along the corridor to the Marine Bar in the annexe of the US embassy, as many staff did on Friday nights. Because of the crowds and the hi-fi he had to shout his order to the off-duty marine behind the bar. As he waited for his beer he could see Jefferson in the mirror sitting alone behind him at a small table next to the dart board. Theobold grasped his beer can and shouldered his way through the high-spirited drinkers. 'May I join you, Frank?' he asked.

'Yup,' said Jefferson. 'How y'a doing, Jeb? Come on across here. Sit yerself down. Haven't seen you all day. Where've you b'en?'

'Paperwork. Cables. Review meeting with the NATO embassies' group. All the routine crap,' said Theobold.

'Anything special?'

'No. Would have told you if there was, Frank.' Theobold braced himself to confront his boss again. 'But I've gotten a bit more information about Sulecki. It firms up what I told you before. I've had a second meeting with Magda Gajewska – you remember, Sulecki's girlfriend.'

'Jeez! Can't all this wait until Monday, Jeb? We shouldn't be doing company business in this bar of all places.'

'It can't wait. I've got to tell you now, Frank. Time's running out.'

Jefferson fidgeted. But for the moment Theobold thought his chief seemed prepared to listen, so he launched into the details of his meeting with Magda in which she described Sulecki's odd behaviour on the night martial law was declared.

'You see, Frank. The evidence of a KGB operation is there,' Theobold concluded. 'I know it's not complete, but we can't sit on it any longer. It has to be passed to Washington.'

'Who the hell's shooting you all this shit, Jeb? It's malicious and provocative garbage fed to you by a couple of unreliable and highly emotional Poles.' Jefferson pointed his finger at Theobold. 'You're being led by the nose. There's nothing in it, Jeb . . . *forget it*! Understand? Stop wasting your time! And, more important, stop wasting mine.' Jefferson angrily pulled the ring-cap to open his next can of beer.

Theobold was shaken. Had he really lost his sense of judgement, or was Jefferson rejecting his evidence because of some high-level power struggle inside the CIA about which he knew nothing? Either way, he had to patch up relations with his boss because, in the end, his first priority was to protect his career.

'A drink, Frank? Another beer, or perhaps a Marguerita this time?' Jefferson accepted, and the matter of Sulecki was shelved. But by even broaching it the damage had been done. By talking as openly as they had in a non-secure area Jefferson and Theobold had broken the most basic CIA security regulations. The SB bugging devices located in the Marine Bar ensured that the radio officers of the Polish Interior Ministry's Department One had heard every word.

13

> '*Strategic disinformation assists in the execution of state
> tasks and is directed at misleading the enemy concerning
> the basic questions of state policy, the military and econ-
> omic status and the scientific and technical achievements
> of the Soviet Union*'
>
> *KGB Training Manual*

General Zuyenko had activated the KGB's new disinformation campaign within hours of it being sanctioned
by Semenov at the *Aragvi* restaurant. The new pitch of
Service 'A' anti-American propaganda became clear a few
days later when Bob Haggerty, duty officer and Political
Counsellor at the US Embassy in Moscow, snipped open
the bundle of Saturday's Soviet newspapers in his office.
Light traffic splashed through the springtime slush
outside the ageing building on Tschaikowsky Street as
Haggerty clutched a mug of coffee and began preparing
the embassy's daily press review.

Few readers would ever have noticed the subtle change
in the tone of Soviet propaganda on Poland. But to experienced sovietologists like Haggerty the new twist to the
normal string of warnings about both 'United States
interference and destabilisation' in Poland and 'President
Reagan's anti-communist crusade' was immediately
clear. As he scanned *Pravda, Isvestia* and the army newspaper, *Red Star*, Haggerty read warnings which were
written in a new bellicose tone.

The news agency *Tass* complained of 'dangers of direct
US complicity in terrorist attacks in Poland', of 'worldwide state terrorism through the widespread clandestine
activities of the CIA', and of how the 'black army of the
American knights of the cloak and dagger use assassination to achieve the political ambitions of the White

House'. The Communist Party newspaper, *Pravda*, charged the United States with having 'the closest possible links with extremist terrorist groups bent on murder' to destabilise Poland. *Isvestia* accused the CIA of using 'terrorism, banditry and gruesome crimes to suppress the legitimate democratic leadership of the Soviet Union's fraternal friends', as well as listing the names of people said to have been terrorised or murdered by covert CIA operations in Afghanistan, the Middle East, Latin America and Europe. *Isvestia* concluded that 'Washington wants to provoke fratricidal and bloody confrontation with the security forces in the streets of Poland.'

The frequent connection of terrorism to the United States was new and Haggerty was taken aback by the unusually large volume of it all. The fact that the articles appeared in all three newspapers was a clear signal that they were no accident. They must be evidence of a new propaganda line from the Central Committee's Information Department or the KGB. But for what purpose? And, more important, what was the coded message of this carefully orchestrated campaign?

With his long experience of Soviet affairs, Haggerty became convinced that the articles must be a Kremlin alert to an imminent development. But what? And when?

Despite his alarm, Haggerty decided he had no need to phone the most senior embassy officials or send urgent cables to the State Department in Washington. Even on a Saturday, he was sure his ambassador would be abreast of developments having read the newspapers at his residence.

But Haggerty was wrong. For once, the Political Counsellor at the US Embassy had been caught out.

In Warsaw, SB General Siwinski also studied that morning's Soviet press as he sat overlooking the first spring colours to penetrate the winter grey on Rakowiecka Street. Like Haggerty in Moscow, Poland's Deputy Interior Minister understood the subtleties of Soviet propaganda because of his veteran experience and KGB training in Moscow. To Siwinski, the Soviet articles were a transparent Soviet front which fitted the pattern of Soviet activity which had already made him concerned. They were also the clearest endorsement yet for his longstanding suspicion about who was really behind the so-called 'terrorist' Sulecki.

And that morning's routine report from the clandestine monitoring department of the SB's Section One seemed to support Siwinski's belief. The transcript of the conversation between two CIA officers chatting in the Marine Bar at the US Embassy the previous night, confirmed his suspicions about Sulecki's Soviet connection. The only grain of consolation was that Siwinski's veteran policeman's instinct had been right all along.

Now, however, the SB general deeply resented his KGB comrades in Moscow. They had set their Polish colleague up for professional disgrace in Warsaw the moment Sulecki carried out his deadly KGB assignment.

It was a crisis of loyalty. Siwinski was determined to make sure Warsaw would win.

14

Following Semenov's dinner with Zuyenko at the *Aragvi* on Tuesday 20th, it took six days for the carefully selected 'Agents of Influence' in the KGB's Line PR sections to receive their coded briefings and orders from Service 'A'. Each agent was handpicked by Zuyenko, having painstakingly established respected credentials over the years in a prestigious position in the West. Each agent also enjoyed the unqualified confidence of leading international policy makers.

In Washington, Academician Yuri Nikolaevich Rostovsky, an eminent visiting lecturer from Moscow's prestigious US and Canada Institute, phoned his host professor at Georgetown University to excuse himself from the morning seminar on East-West relations. Then he left his modest hotel on Connecticut Avenue and walked two blocks south towards the White House. The lean, slightly stooping, 58-year-old Russian academic had to assume he was being watched as usual by the FBI, but he was not worried about being seen to use a public pay phone in a Korean delicatessen on De Sales Street. Rostovsky's only concern was to make sure the contents of the call were not recorded by the bugging device in his hotel room. Three minutes after putting down the phone, he hailed a taxi and drove to the National Gallery of Art overlooking the Mall on Madison Avenue. In the basement coffee shop he bought a bagel and an orange juice, then sat down at a table near the waterfall whose glinting water cascaded down the full length of one wall.

Fifteen minutes later Rostovsky caught sight of the towering slender figure he had come to know well during the last fifteen years. Daniel T. Robertson had served at the US Embassy in Moscow, first as a counsellor, then ambassador. Robertson was now a senior official in the

State Department where he was listed as head of a major policy-making section.

Rostovsky and Robertson greeted each other with the traditional and demonstrative bear hug they had used many times over the years. But whatever the outward smiles, neither man was under any illusions. Their personal relationship had always been one of professional convenience. Each knew about the other's undeclared role in diplomatic channels between East and West. Rostovsky knew that as a former US ambassador to Moscow, Robertson was among the highest fliers in the US intelligence community with direct access to the top. Conversely, Robertson knew that Rostovsky's academic post at the Academy of Sciences was a front. In reality he was a KGB Colonel from the First Chief (Foreign) Directorate's elite Twelfth Department, which was made up of distinguished KGB veterans.

Robertson came straight to the point, his manner workmanlike but still genial and diplomatic. 'How nice to see you again, Yuri, but I don't have much time. I have an important meeting in twenty minutes. Why the sudden urgency to see me?'

Rostovsky flicked the bagel crumbs from his fingers, then wiped his hands and mouth with the paper serviette. He spoke the perfectly constructed English of a seasoned international traveller, but with occasional hints of a Russian accent. 'First of all, Dan, we must agree this meeting never took place. It's an informal get together between two old acquaintances ... You know what I mean.'

Robertson did not give an answer and Rostovsky didn't expect one.

'There are circles in Moscow who have in their possession details of a proposed American terrorist action which, if carried out, will have the most catastrophic repercussions – not only for relations between the USSR and the United States, but also for those between East and West ...'

Former Ambassador Robertson sat rigid and silent as

Rostovsky expressed himself in the Soviet jargon familiar to any Westerner posted to Moscow.

'... My information is that the United States has sponsored an assassination operation against the Prime Minister and Chairman of the National Defence Council of Poland, Comrade General Wojciech Jaruzelski. My information is that the aim of the CIA operation is to destabilise our fraternal ally and to sow havoc in the socialist alliance in order to realise America's political ends. We understand that the CIA plan is for their involvement in this contemptible operation to be disguised as the work of one of the more extreme wings of Solidarity. The CIA will portray these extremists as KGB double agents who have adopted the cover of genuine Solidarity activists ... I am instructed to convey to you that our government views the existence of this plot in the gravest possible terms. I am asked to urge your government, through you, to halt this operation as a matter of extreme urgency. Prospects for a resumption of *detente* will be irrevocably harmed if this assassination is carried out.'

Robertson was stunned by what Rostovsky had told him, but he knew further questioning would be unproductive. He had to assume that Rostovsky was passing on what someone in Moscow had primed him to say, which meant he would not be able to expand on the detail.

'I have no information about this matter, Yuri,' Robertson told him. 'It's news to me, and I'll treat it as the gravest of matters. But why aren't you conveying this warning officially through the normal diplomatic channels of Ambassasdor Dobrynin, or through the Moscow – Washington hotline?'

In response, Rostovsky merely repeated his brief parrot-fashion. 'I am making this approach because Moscow believes the matter is such a serious and misguided aberration by the United States that it should not become a matter of record between our two countries. Our aim is to effect an immediate defusing of the potential explosion inside and outside Poland rather than to create a major superpower incident.'

'Yuri! The old days when the CIA tried to assassinate Castro in Cuba or Allende in Chile are over. What you're accusing us of is inconceivable – especially after President Reagan's Executive Order of 4 December last year which *explicitly* forbade any American involvement in assassination, or conspiracy to assassinate.'

'But Dan, our information from Soviet intercepts of US signals traffic is that the CIA is acting *without* the knowledge or consent of the President, or even the National Security Council . . .'

'Out of the question,' snapped Robertson. 'The US administration doesn't work like that, and with all your experience in this business, Yuri, you should know better.'

Rostovsky would not be deflected. 'Even with Reagan's new CIA Director, William Casey? We believe the plot has been conceived in secret by a three-man group of the most senior hardline CIA directors at Langley.'

'Again, Yuri, it's not possible,' Robertson replied with the confident authority of a senior official involved daily in the nation's most critical security decisions.

'Then I have to tell you, Dan, that you must review your procedures. Perhaps the only way to ensure the White House and National Security Council take this unofficial warning seriously is for me to reveal the kind of source we have. Our information comes from inside the CIA, from a double agent working at a high level at Langley.' Rostovsky emphasised his point by pressing his index finger hard onto the table until its tip turned white. 'It's not up to me, as a Russian, to pass judgement on US intelligence efforts. But this seems to be blatant disregard by the most senior CIA operatives, and it justifies your President's fears about the legality and propriety of covert CIA operations. It explains why Mr Reagan established the Intelligence Oversight Board last December. He did it because the White House didn't know everything it should about Langley's secret activities, eh Dan?'

Robertson realised that Rostovsky was well briefed. But while the Soviet Academician had come prepared for this conversation, Ambassador Robertson had not. After fifteen seconds of tense silence the two men parted without exchanging a further word.

As Robertson's chauffeur-driven Cadillac took him the eleven blocks back to the State Department, he jotted notes into his leather scratch pad. He tried to work out what lay behind Yuri Rostovsky's warnings. But with his years of experience in Soviet affairs Robertson knew the Soviet Union must never be taken at face value.

Never.

Nikolai Baykov, plenipotentiary at the Soviet Foreign Ministry in Moscow, smiled and leaned forward.

'Ambassador, perhaps you could spare me a few moments for a quiet word?' said the Russian.

US Ambassador Charles Jackson ended his conversation with the Swedish military attaché and nodded politely. He and Minister Baykov stepped away from the guests thronging the Swedish Embassy's reception hall and found a quiet corner in one of the panelled anterooms.

It was a rare meeting. In the frigid Cold War atmosphere which followed the Soviet invasion of Afghanistan and martial law in Poland, it was virtually unheard of for senior American and Soviet officials to hold talks. But that evening, Jackson and Baykov were conveniently in the embassy of a neutral, non-aligned nation where unofficial contacts could be made without creating a fuss. While Russian waiters served sturgeon canapes, wine and vodka, Baykov and Ambassador Jackson drank mineral water and talked diplomatic niceties. Only after the remaining guests had drifted from the room did the Soviet minister carefully turn the conversation.

'Ambassador, I don't have much time. My superiors are in possession of details of a proposed American terrorist action which, if carried out, will have the most severe repercussions ...'

Thirty minutes later, as the ambassador's American-built limousine sped north-east along Mosfilmovskaja Street through the light mid-evening traffic towards the centre of Moscow, Jackson turned over the details of his conversation. The rule of thumb for any Westerner in Moscow was that any Russian who talks doesn't know, and any Russian who knows doesn't talk. So why had Baykov talked and what did he know?'

Ambassador Jackson recalled the strident anti-American tones of the Moscow newspapers two days earlier and weighed up the likelihood of a connection. Within two hours he had dictated his '*Top Secret Eyes Only*' report, and by 1 a.m. Moscow time his deciphered cable was sitting alongside Robertson's on the Soviet desk at the State Department in Washington.

Within twenty-four hours there would be cables from a total of twelve such meetings orchestrated by the KGB's Service 'A'.

15

General Zuyenko was tightening his propaganda screw in a masterly fashion at a time when he was sure that Washington was least able to counter it.

The White House, National Security Council and State Department were already plunged into crisis by another pressing issue. Argentina had just invaded the British Falkland Islands in the South Atlantic and the Reagan administration was trying to carve out a role for itself as international mediator. Britain's dispute with Argentina had diverted world attention from Poland, and to the great relief of both KGB Chairman Andropov and the Polish leadership, the Polish crisis had slipped from Washington's mind and the world's headlines. It was the distraction of the Falklands war which had given Zuyenko the ideal cover behind which to crank up the pitch of Polish disinformation by yet another notch.

For Bob Haggerty at the US Embassy in Moscow, the Soviet newspapers on Tuesday 27 April had the same impact as Saturday's. This time *Tass* accused 'CIA spies and instigators' of supervising the activities of 'Solidarity extremists and plotters'. A signed article in *Pravda* by commentator Arkady Timoshkin described details of an elaborate CIA terrorist conspiracy codenamed 'Operation Polak' aimed at destabilising Poland and fomenting counter revolution. And there were other attacks on the CIA, all in the same vein.

Within an hour, Haggerty had produced a translation of the most inflammatory articles for Ambassador Jackson and by midday, Jackson had drafted an urgent five-paragraph cable to the State Department which supplemented his *'Top Secret Eyes Only'* message of the night before. The ambassador concluded:

459

'I consider you must treat this matter with great urgency and the utmost delicacy. By the tone of Soviet propaganda, the United States stands to be drawn into a crisis the proportions of which I am not yet in a position to predict. My considered advice is Beware!'

At the headquarters of the KGB's First Chief Directorate in the birch forests south-west of Moscow, General Zuyenko was content. It was clear that Service 'A's two-pronged disinformation campaign had begun to ring alarm bells in Washington, but they rang in secret.

In the basement of the White House, the Operations Advisory Group of the President's National Security Council assembled in the Situation Room in emergency session immediately after lunch, having been summoned at an hour's notice. The five senior members of the OAG sat at the conference table – the Secretary of State, the Defence Secretary, the National Security Adviser, the Director of Central Intelligence and the Chairman of the Joint Chiefs of Staff. Also present as observers were the Attorney General and the Director of the Office of Management and Budget. The President himself was not present: he was on his way back from California to Washington on Air Force One.

There were no pressing developments in the Falkland crisis, so the Secretary of State moved immediately to the new brief from the State Department which had precipitated the unscheduled meeting.

'What the hell's going on?' he asked his colleagues. 'Is there something happening which some of us on the National Security Council have not been told? Is there a clandestine operation being launched in Poland without our authority – an operation that blatantly defies the President's Executive Order on Intelligence Activities?'

The Secretary of State detailed the unprecedented developments of the last seventy-two hours. 'Who knows what about all these extraordinary allegations?' he concluded bluntly in a mood of clear agitation and anger. He glanced towards the Director of Central Intelligence, Bill Casey. 'Bill? Allegations of a covert CIA plot? You run the CIA. It's your baby. Tell us about it.'

William Casey, the testy, arrogant and calculating self-made millionaire and ex-banker personally appointed by the President to run the CIA, hardly stirred. In appearance he was not unlike some of his adversaries at the KGB's Moscow Centre 7,000 miles to the east, with his owl-like face, podgy skin, baggy eyes and thick-framed glasses. His gruff, mumbling New York accent barely cut through the committee-room atmosphere.

'It's news to me, Mr Secretary. To the best of my knowledge, there's nothing in it and I know nothing about it. Try me again. What else do you know?'

In his first months at CIA headquarters, Casey had already pioneered what Washington insiders had come to call *plausible deniability* – the art of evading an allegation with a plausible but inaccurate explanation. Mindful of Casey's reputation and his passion for clandestine operations dating back to World War II, several of those gathered around the table remained unconvinced.

'It's a simple question, Bill, to which there must be a simple answer. Is your agency involved in an illegal and covert assassination operation against Jaruzelski in Poland, without either the President's consent or the agreement of the National Security Council or the consent of the congressional intelligence committees, as required under United States law?'

'Not that I am aware of,' mumbled the CIA Director with a contrived air of innocence as his eyes gazed across the wooden wall panels and he doodled with a pencil. Casey's contempt and disdain for the State Department compounded his unwillingness to say any more.

None of the four other members of the Operations Advisory Group had enough detail to challenge Casey's denial, but most of them knew that the CIA Director always liked to think he was above the law. Since his appointment by the President a year earlier, Casey had injected a new spirit of aggressive pride into the once demoralised CIA. He was the first CIA Director ever to hold cabinet office, the agency's budget was up and morale was at its highest for years. Casey was also one of the President's closest and most trusted confidants: so much so that his political enemies accused him of trying to be the 'shadow Secretary of State'. Enemies also cursed the presidential immunity which seemed to allow Casey to ride unscathed through the fiercest of criticisms.

The Secretary of State then asked the other three OAG members in turn what they knew of a Polish operation. The Defence Secretary, National Security Adviser and Chairman of the Joint Chiefs of Staff all confirmed they knew no more than what the Secretary of State had told them. 'The line from the Soviets is that they believe this assassination will happen any day,' said the Secretary. 'Sitting on our intelligence and doing nothing about it won't make it go away.'

After half an hour the meeting adjourned with each member of the Operations Advisory Group under instructions to make the most searching enquiries to determine the facts.

'Remember, Bill, I want no more of that "plausible deniability",' the Secretary of State warned Casey. 'I want facts, and I want the truth.'

An hour later the President made his scheduled arrival on the White House lawn by helicopter from Andrews Air Force Base. As a matter of urgency he was briefed in the Oval Office by the National Security Adviser, Michael James. The President was still dressed in his west-coast ranch clothes as he sat next to the log fire listening to James's report on both the Soviet claims and the outcome of the OAG meeting. The President wore the agonised face of an inexperienced poker player trying to work out his opponent's hand. As he pondered what James had told him, the soft silence was broken only by the crackling of burning wood and the tick of his favourite grandfather clock.

'Are the Soviets on the right track, Michael?'

It was the President's only question. He had never

trusted Soviet intentions and had long christened the Soviet Union the 'evil empire'. His eyes swung across the Oval Office to Theodore Roosevelt's Nobel Peace Prize of 1906. Was the peace of the world threatened yet again?

'At this time, Mr President, there is no firm evidence to support Moscow's claims of a CIA conspiracy against Jaruzelski in Poland,' said James. 'Even so, the OAG has authorised immediate enquiries to determine if there are any grounds at all for the Soviet accusation of a covert CIA operation without your Presidential authorisation.'

The President was still in holiday mode and was clearly reluctant to confront the matter, even though the inscription on the glass paperweight in front of him reminded him that 'The Buckeroo Stops Here'.

'Get me Bill Casey on the phone please, Mike.'

James pressed one of the buttons on the white, ten-line telephone and passed the handset across the desk to the President. The President and Casey had been friends for twenty years, and Casey had run Mr Reagan's election campaign two years earlier. Such was Casey's admiration and loyalty that he would do almost anything for the President.

As the President gazed out over the crocuses and daffodils massed across the White House lawn, he and Casey talked like brothers.

'Bill, how yer doing? ... Mike James just brought me up to date with the OAG meeting. Is there any truth in this Soviet claim of a CIA covert operation unknown to you or me? ... None, you say! You're sure, Bill? ... But I know you'll be checking it out! ... I have every faith in you, Bill, but I want no double-dealing. I know it's part of the CIA's business to do one thing and say something else. But I want it straight. No cover up. No long term political baggage for me. Make sure that none of the right wingers, or your new tough-guy Head of the Operations Directorate, are trying to do something I wouldn't approve of. No one must be allowed to take things into their own hands. Not even at the CIA ... You know what

I want, Bill. I don't want to know everything that's going on, I just want you to make sure our back's safe and the deficit slate's clean. I want no repeat of last summer's senate investigation into who's fit to hold office at the CIA ... Above all – and I want to make this clear – just make sure you keep the lid on this one, Bill.'

Casey mumbled an inaudible response to reassure the President, and hung up. As he sat in his seventh floor office overlooking the rolling Virginia countryside, the CIA Director perspired with rage. What the hell was going on? And why did he, as the member of the President's cabinet responsible for protecting US security interests, know nothing about this alleged American assassinaton plot?

16

Casey fumed. Like the Secretary of State, he wanted to know what was happening in Poland behind his back. His coded cable from CIA Headquarters in Langley, Virginia reached the deserted US Embassy in Warsaw at midnight. Casey had classified it *'Highest priority'* and addressed it to Jefferson. The duty communications officer immediately called the CIA Station Chief at home, but because all telephone calls were bugged there was no way he could discuss the contents.

Jefferson rolled out of bed, pulled on a pair of jeans, a sweatshirt and anorak, then drove five miles across Warsaw to the American embassy compound. When he read the cable in his cold office he knew his journey had been worth the risk of being detained by the Polish militia for breaking curfew.

HQS
272245g

PRO JEFFERSON WARSAW

URGENTLY, REPEAT URGENTLY, DEMAND ANY DETAIL AND EVIDENCE OF POSSIBLE SOLIDARITY TERRORIST ACTION PLANNED AGAINST JARUZELSKI. UNVERIFIED CIRCUMSTANTIAL EVIDENCE DETECTED IN WASHINGTON OF ATTEMPT TO IMPLICATE COMPANY IN ASSASSINATION ATTEMPT IN POLAND WHICH NOT BEEN AUTHORISED BY US PRESIDENT. YOU HAVE FULL PRESIDENTIAL AUTHORITY TO USE ALL MEANS TO PREVENT ANY SUGGESTION OF 'COMPANY' INVOLVEMENT. PLEASE ADVISE.

REQUEST ACTION SOONEST.

DCI.

The rare signature 'DCI' – the Director of Central Intelligence William Casey himself – underlined the importance of the cable. It was Casey who had personally appointed Jefferson eight months earlier because of his reputation as a tough, can-do operator. As with this cable, Casey often ignored standard CIA procedures to contact his own appointees directly.

Jefferson nervously crumpled the telex paper. Dishonour and dereliction of duty confronted him. He felt a cold sweat beneath his anorak as he realised that ignoring Jeb Theobold had been a catastrophic professional miscalculation. Damage limitation suddenly became Jefferson's immediate priority: he had to cover both his own backside and the CIA's reputation. Rapidly he jotted down a brief holding reply to DCI Casey which, although less than truthful, contained the kind of half-truths and positive responses which had won Jefferson his tough, swashbuckling reputation.

WARSAW
280015g

PRO DCI

ACK YR 272245. CONFIRM ACTIONING YR REQUEST WITH FULLEST ENQUIRY MOST URGENT POSSIBLE.

REGRET NO DETAIL YET AVAILABLE RE JARUZELSKI PLOT PLS CONFIRM THAT YR REF TO 'FULL PRESIDENTIAL AUTHORITY TO USE ALL MEANS' INCLUDES SPECIAL DISPENSATION TO WAIVE PRESIDENTIAL EXECUTIVE ORDER 12333 ORDERING ASSASSINATION BAN.

Jefferson believed there was little chance such a blatant lie to Casey would be discovered. Apart from Theobold no other member of the embassy staff knew about Sulecki Jefferson was therefore certain that he could contain any risk of Theobold betraying him by using a combination of threats and promises about his colleague's career prospects.

It was half past two and the dead of night. Jefferson fidgeted and chain smoked in the embassy cipher room alongside the chattering signals equipment. The adrenalin of a deadline began to flow as it always did towards the climax of an operation. He gave up any idea of sleep and tried to dial Jeb Theobold at home, but the line was dead. Instead he heard the hypnotic female voice of the censor's scratchy audio loop at the telephone exchange: '*Rozmowa controlowana* ... *Rozmowa controlowana* – conversation controlled ... conversation controlled ...' Jefferson realised that Theobold was incommunicado until he arrived for work at 8.30.

The Station Chief tossed ideas around his mind until 5 a.m., then disappeared to grab a cat nap on the camp bed he had installed in his office during the first days of martial law. When he woke again at seven he washed and shaved in the restroom along the corridor, then replaced his overnight clothes with a suit and shirt which were still hanging in his cupboard from the last all-night security alert six weeks earlier.

Jefferson's first incoming phone call was at 8.35 and came from Theobold.

'G'morning Frank. I got the note you left on my desk. You got some news? I'll come right along.'

Thirty seconds later Theobold poked his face into Jefferson's office.

'G' morning Jeb ... Come on in.' Jefferson gave no hint of apology that he may have been wrong a week ago. 'Langley have just notified me they have evidence to support the assassination conspiracy theory involving Sulecki ...' He frowned as his phone rang with a call from the secretary of the chargé d'affaires'. 'Yes, I'm here, Diana. Put him through.' Jefferson opened his second packet of cigarettes since midnight.

The embassy's chargé d'affaires and the CIA Station Chief had the kind of turbulent relationship which had developed in foreign posts between senior CIA officials and the career diplomats of the US Foreign Service since Casey's appointment. Under the old Kennedy doctrine the ambassador had overall responsibility for all members of the US government staff in Poland. But the CIA's true liaison with diplomats depended less on a carefully documented protocol than on individual personalities. In Warsaw, Jefferson's strong personality often held sway.

'Morning, Frank,' said the chargé. 'Please would you put me in the picture. My overnight cable traffic contained an "*Eyes only*" message from the Secretary of State in Washington about a CIA terrorist assassination conspiracy involving Jaruzelski. I have to say I've heard nothing about it. Have you? And if it's true, why was I not kept informed as a matter of courtesy?'

From across the desk, Theobold watched his boss respond to the chargé with an outright lie. 'I know nothing about this matter. I too received a service from Langley overnight, and I've already begun a re-analysis of intelligence data currently available.'

'Frank, be kind enough to keep me in touch,' the chargé insisted. Jefferson put down the phone and turned back to Theobold.

'Jeb, it's all hands on deck. I want from you a revamped, up-to-date report of what we know about Sulecki. And I want it by ten o'clock. I'll free you from anything else you're committed to.'

The shift in Jefferson's attitude was remarkable. Theobold did not expect the Station Chief to eat humble pie, but he still tried for his pound of flesh.

'Bit late, isn't it Frank?' he asked smugly. 'May Day's only three days away now. You realise we're badly behind because we failed to follow up clues and leads?'

But Jefferson gave no hint of contrition. 'In that case Jeb, we just have to work that bloody bit harder,' he blasted. 'I want no shit from you. I know it's a tall order, but the President has personally ordered that Sulecki must be stopped. So what would you recommend, smart arse?'

Theobold had to think fast. He had not come prepared to give advice. 'Sulecki's former lover, Magda Gajewska, is our best chance of a lead. I'll try to find her again. We need to get her to think of a place where he could be hiding.'

If they did manage to catch Sulecki, Theobold wondered which of the two CIA officers would be commended. Would it be Jefferson, the professional snake with highly-placed friends back in Langley? Or would Theobold be rewarded for his perseverance and diligent detective work?

Having worked closely with Jefferson for eight months, Theobold feared he knew the answer only too well.

17

As Wednesday's glowing dawn burned layers of April mist from the Potomac River, the Reagan administration in Washington was gripped by uncertainty. In mid-morning, the President chaired a full session of the six-member National Security Council. Facing him in the rollback sofas and easy chairs of the Oval Office were the same five senior administration figures who had met without him as the NSC's Operations Advisory Group the previous day – the Secretary of State, Defence Secretary, Chairman of the Joint Chiefs of Staff, the Director of Central Intelligence and the National Security Adviser. Also present was the President's Chief of Staff to take notes.

'What progress on the Polish problem?' the President asked directly. 'First of all tell me straight. Is the United States or the CIA involved or not?'

The Secretary of State and the CIA Director shook their heads, but the President sensed their doubt. For the moment he did not feel inclined to push the matter.

'Give me a rundown on what we're doing now!'

The responses were not encouraging. Using their embassy diplomats and field agents, State Department and CIA intelligence field analysts were still struggling to establish the source of the coordinated Soviet leaks and the anti-American propaganda campaign. CIA Director Casey reported that his agents throughout the Soviet Bloc were trying to piece together any evidence of new terrorist cells. The State Department, meanwhile, was making frantic diplomatic efforts to allay private fears among Western leaders that the United States was orchestrating an assassination in Poland. It was not easy.

'And if the assassination cannot be halted and goes ahead, then God forbid,' said the President. 'Have we prepared our response to the monstrous allegations of US complicity?'

Both CIA Director Casey and the Secretary of State nodded. The President walked across to the glass-panelled door overlooking the Rose Garden, then he turned and addressed the group in an unflustered voice and a manner akin to that of an avuncular old-timer sheriff.

'I must make it clear, gentlemen: whether or not there is a genuine basis for this alert, I want nothing to become public.'

The President paused, pulled a jelly bean from the glass jar on the desk and shifted his eyes briefly to Michael James, his National Security Adviser. He wagged his finger in the way James knew meant that the following remarks should not be recorded in the minutes.

'If you all conclude that there are American mercenaries, double agents or renegades implicating the United States government in the assassination then you have my full authority to neutralise them before they do irreparable damage to East-West relations. And you should interpret "neutralise" as you think fit. If you conclude it's a clandestine Soviet-backed operation then you know that I'll be right behind you. Use the fullest possible measures to remind the Soviets of the enormous political price they'll pay worldwide for their folly. All I ask if that I be kept fully informed.'

The lines on the President's ageing face suddenly seemed much deeper. The next three days would be a rare period of full-time trauma for the man whom Americans called their 'part-time President'.

18

In Moscow, General Zuyenko's thirteenth and final agent of influence began spinning his part in the web of disinformation.

Arkady Timoshkin, political commentator for the Communist Party newspaper, *Pravda*, lunched with Fred Steele, Moscow correspondent of the *New York Times*, in the ornate first-floor restaurant at the National Hotel, one of Moscow's oldest and most famous, where the smell of *shlashlik* mixed with the sweat of unwashed bodies and stale cigarette smoke. Timoshkin sat at the gold-painted table opposite Steele and next to the enormous plate-glass windows which overlooked the walls of the Kremlin Palace rising like a stage set from the grubby April drizzle and swishing Volga cars on Manege Square.

For any normal Russian, political nervousness about meeting Westerners meant that such social encounters were rare. So when it came, Timoshkin's invitation was something Fred Steele knew he had to take up.

The KGB had done its groundwork admirably. The lunch had been arranged seven days earlier when Timoshkin had phoned his invitation to Steele's office an hour after receiving operational instructions from Service 'A'. Yesterday Timoshkin had published in *Pravda* his stinging attack on American-backed terrorism around the world.

Beneath the cut-glass chandeliers, Timoshkin and Steele lunched on *rassolnik* fish soup, followed by beef *angliski* as they talked and tested each other. It was an hour before Steele dared to raise the contentious matter of Timoshkin's ferocious piece in *Pravda*. By now a vodka bottle stood almost empty in the ice bucket alongside a half-empty bottle of Russian champagne.

With his tongue loosened, the American journalis

demanded to know on what grounds Timoshkin felt able to accuse America of organising a CIA conspiracy to murder 'prominent political figures' in Poland. Steele bluntly accused his Russian host of publishing outrageous inventions which were wild distortions of American policy designed to inflame East-West relations.

Timoshkin feigned shock at Steele's outburst and rejected the American's accusations.

'I wrote about such things because they are true. Of course I cannot tell you everything, Fred. But I don't think I'm breaking any confidences if I tell you that the Soviet Union has irrefutable evidence of a CIA plot to murder a senior Polish politician.'

'What evidence . . .?' Steele insisted impatiently. 'And who's the target?'

'We are off-the-record, I hope?' ventured Timoshkin. After fifteen years as a foreign correspondent Steele was experienced enough to know that Timoshkin would somehow say what he had been ordered to say whether Steele agreed to the off-the-record charade or not. The American was willing to be a player in the game of bluff, so he nodded agreement.

'The target is the most senior of all,' said Timoshkin.

This time Steele took a few moments to consider his response. A regular chinking of vodka glasses and the hushed babble of Russian voices around them filled the silence.

'Jaruzelski?' asked Steele.

Timoshkin nodded agreement and his gold teeth glinted. 'If you were to ask me officially, Fred, then of course I would have to deny it. But yes, the name you just mentioned is the CIA's target for this unpardonable plot.'

'I find it hard to believe,' sneered Steele. 'That sort of tactic was once used by the CIA in third world countries. But with new executive orders from the President it's not only lunacy, Arkady, it's illegal. Washington would never use assassination as a destabilisation technique in the Soviet Bloc.'

Timoshkin interrupted. 'That's why my information says the Soviet leadership is so surprised. It's taken weeks to assemble the evidence from our intelligence sources.'

Steele sipped black coffee and speculated on how much the man from *Pravda* was trying to use him. Reporting by western correspondents in Moscow was usually based on a mixture of official Soviet statements and unsourced rumours which always had to be carefully weighed. It was highly unusual for a Soviet source like Timoshkin to emerge from the official woodwork and pass on information at first hand, the very circumstances of the lunch itself made Steele sceptical and alert.

'Why are you telling me all this Arkady?'

'Because, my friend, we admire and trust your reporting of our country. You understand us, and you get things as right as any of your western colleagues can here.'

Steele despised such gratuitous flattery, and it made him even more suspicious. But despite such doubts Fred Steele knew he had the basis for a story, as long as the facts stood up to close examination. In Moscow, western journalists usually worked in a pack, so it was rare good fortune to secure an exclusive story. As he drove back to his office across the Moscow River, Steele resolved that his foreign desk in New York would receive a first draft of his copy by eight o'clock that evening, Moscow time.

In New York and Washington it would be midday.

19

On Capitol Hill, veteran Senator Harry Ordeleau, the doyen of Republican senators and chairman of the powerful Senate Intelligence Committee, descended from his office in the Russell Senate Office Building and stepped into his Chevrolet Impala waiting on Constitution Avenue.

The Senator's drive across town to lunch at the prestigious Four Seasons Hotel in Georgetown took ten minutes. His guest was an old friend, senior State Department official and former ambassador to Moscow, Dan Robertson. The two men sat among the tropical plants of the lower ground-floor restaurant, and were well into the main course on the *nouvelle cuisine* menu before the conversation turned to the crisis unfolding in secret at the White House.

'All hell's broken loose at State, Harry,' Robertson confided to the Senator.

'No more hell than usual, I shouldn't doubt. What d'you mean, Dan?' asked Ordeleau gruffly.

Robertson had no details of the National Security Council discussions that morning, and word of the President's order to reveal nothing about the Poland emergency had not yet reached him.

'There's strong circumstantial evidence of a CIA plot to assassinate General Jaruzelski in Poland . . .' Robertson refused to divulge his own personal involvement or his meeting with KGB Colonel Rostovsky, but he went on to elaborate on the few extra details he knew.

'*Jee-zus!*' said the Senator. Even with his many years experience of American public life and the Washington rumour machine, Ordeleau was stunned by Robertson's disclosure. He half-choked on his fillet of New England salmon, then felt the blood rush of anger to his head.

'What the hell are Casey's new le Carré lookalikes at

Langley up to? Has the Company still not learned its lesson? That arrogant poker-player Casey thinks he can subvert the world single handedly outside the law – unchallenged by the new Intelligence Oversight Board which we set up specifically to prevent such abuses.'

In disgust the Senator pushed his half-eaten salmon to one side. 'As committee chairman I should have been given a classified intelligence briefing by now, but they haven't even called me. My committee's going to nail Casey. I'll make sure we get that son-of-a-bitch, damn it! I'll phone him the moment I get back to the Hill ... What else d'you know, Dan?'

'Nothing more, Harry.'

Ordeleau let it ride, but he knew his old friend from the State Department too well to believe his claim of ignorance.

It was a quarter to three when the spry but ageing Senator marched back from lunch through the pastel-green corridors of the Russell Senate Office Building and stormed through the secretarial area of his suite of offices. He was on the point of asking to be put through to Casey when his personal assistant buzzed him.

'Could you take a call from John Boagland, Assistant Editor of the *New York Times*?'

Ordeleau and Boagland were old acquaintances, so the Senator agreed.

'Hi John,' said Ordeleau, 'What's up, then?'

'Harry, we're running a story tomorrow from our Moscow correspondent,' said Boagland. 'It details a secret diplomatic hiatus between Moscow and Washington over a Soviet claim to have uncovered a CIA plot to assassinate General Jaruzelski in Poland ... Harry, as chairman of the Senate Intelligence Committee can you confirm that there is such a row? ... Secondly, have you been notified of this CIA covert operation, and if so does it come within the new guidelines laid down by the President in December? ... Thirdly, if it doesn't comply, does your committee have any intention of initiating an investigation?'

It was a heavily loaded package of questions which caught the Senator off guard.

'I know nothing about it, I'm afraid John,' he answered unconvincingly. 'Perhaps you'll be kind enough to tell me your source?'

'Our source was off the record, I'm afraid, Harry. I can only tell you we've used him in the past, and everything he's said has been as reliable as you could ever hope it to be.'

'Well, the most I can tell you at the moment, John, is that it's all garbage. Call me back in a couple of hours.'

'Could I make it an hour?' insisted the newspaperman.

Ordeleau had to relent to avoid giving the impression he might have something to hide. The Senator didn't want to be drawn into a public row until he knew the full facts. Already his fury was rising. As chairman of the Intelligence Committee he had once again learned about important intelligence developments not from a CIA briefing but from the press.

First he phoned the staff director of the Intelligence Committee to see if the CIA or Casey's office had sent a formal notification of an intelligence alert. They hadn't and there was no message that any senior CIA official had been trying to contact him. Then Ordeleau asked his assistant to find Casey on the phone urgently.

The CIA director was in his armour-plated, mine-proof limousine driving down Connecticut Avenue. Ordeleau and Casey had been bitter political adversaries for years, and since Casey had taken over the CIA a year earlier both men had feuded openly. The Senator angrily challenged Casey with the little information he had gleaned from Robertson and Boagland about the assassination conspiracy.

'It's bollocks!' Casey mumbled defiantly down the phone. There was no love lost between the two Republicans. As chairman of the Intelligence Committee, Ordeleau was responsible for maintaining congressional control over all CIA activities. But with Casey running the CIA it was virtually impossible because the CIA director never disguised his contempt for the politicians on Capitol Hill – even old hands like Ordeleau.

'I know nothing about such a hare-brained plan. You're wasting my time, Senator.'

The devious Casey was, as usual, half-right. Having attended the National Security Council meeting he knew about the Soviet claims of a CIA plot, but as CIA Director he had not been party to authorising any such illegal operation and so far his staff had failed to uncover even the smallest trace of evidence to corroborate the allegations.

But Ordeleau did not believe him. He knew too much about Casey's passion for clandestine operations, which dated back to his involvement with the OSS in the Forties.

'Bill, you're a past master at evasion – you always say you never know anything, but in truth I know you're a stickler for detail and you know the tiniest fact about every CIA operation. If you don't tell me straight what's going on then I'll summon a special hearing and ensure my committee puts you in the dock just like we did last year ... Each time there's an alert like this, you assure me that the CIA knows nothing. Then six months later, confirmation of the CIA's active involvement leaks out in the press, and only then do we begin to find out that you and the Company's senior directors knew about it all along ... So you'd better tell me straight this time, Director. Or else!'

Casey's meagre patience evaporated. 'Harry, get this! If I say no, I mean no! Now get off my back!'

Casey hung up.

Such was Ordeleau's fury that he immediately dispatched a scathing handwritten letter by courier to the CIA Director.

Russell Building
Washington DC
28 April 1982

Dear Bill,

I can best describe my feelings on learning that the

478

CIA was involved in the Jaruzelski assassination conspiracy by saying 'I am pissed off.' Such blatant, overt deceit is no way to run your railroad.

The conspiracy violates both international law and the President's own Executive Orders. It is tantamount to an act of war. I don't see how on earth we are going to explain it. If you know please call me. You cannot expect any sympathy or understanding for your situation unless you are completely open with both me and the whole Intelligence Select Committee. I do not believe you have been. By law the CIA has to be fully accountable to the administration. I trust you will make sure that it *is* accountable and that there is no unauthorised covert action being actively contemplated within Poland or any other theatre of operations.

I also trust that in line with your duty and agreed procedures you will keep me informed of all relevant developments immediately they arise and that you will take a more constructive attitude to relations with me and my committee.

Yours, Harry.

By late afternoon the *New York Times* had contacted nine of the Intelligence Committee's fifteen members to check Fred Steele's story from Moscow. Each was asked if they could confirm a secret row between Moscow and Washington over a covert CIA assassination conspiracy against the Polish leader. But unlike Ordeleau, the other Committee members did not have to mislead. They knew nothing and therefore could confirm nothing. By five o'clock each of the nine Senators had contacted Ordeleau for clarification and advice, and the Senator's recommendation was unequivocal. 'Say nothing. Sit on it!' he told them all.

And for the moment they did.

Evidence of this escalating crisis reached Casey at half

past five in another heated phone call from Ordeleau.

'The *New York Times* have the story,' yelled the Senator. 'They're phoning every member of my Intelligence Committee for confirmation and they're going to publish tonight ... Bill, let me warn you again: you'd better have a good answer. You'd better be clean or I'll have your arse!'

Casey had a mind of his own. As usual, he did not bother to consult the President or the National Security Adviser about his next steps. Instead he made an unprecedented call to the Assistant Editor of the *Times* in New York.

'Who the hell are you working for?' Casey screamed at Boagland. 'I order you to kill the story and back off! By publishing these Soviet propaganda allegations you can hardly claim to be working for the interests of the United States – so I take it you're working for the Soviets. The most delicate matters of US national security are at stake.'

The Assistant Editor was outraged but unshaken. Once again a government official was trying to use the catch-all phrase 'a matter of national security' to suppress a legitimate piece of journalism which he did not like.

'Mr Casey, you don't mean it's a matter of national security. You mean it's another CIA screw up and that's why you want us to refrain from publishing, right?'

Casey didn't like anyone talking back at him. 'Don't be sucked blindly into the Soviets' game. I ask you to sit on the information. Let the storm pass ...'

'Mr Casey,' Boagland interrupted, 'I don't have to tell you that the United States has a Freedom of Information Act and a First Amendment which guarantees the freedom to publish, and that is what I intend to do. But perhaps, before I do, I can clarify one matter. I have a shorthand note of your remarks. Can I take it they were on-the-record? You did say "I order you to kill the story and back-off"?'

'No!', yelled Casey. 'And let me tell you that I have a battery of federal laws designed to protect national security, and some of them have never been used before. But when they are they'll guarantee you a place as a defendant in a court of law. I'm coming up to New York to talk you out of it in person.'

'You'll be wasting your time, Mr Casey.'

'I'll still get you shit-canned,' Casey told him before slamming down the phone.

Within minutes the CIA Director had telephoned both the President and National Security Adviser to alert them to the *Times*'s intention to publish.

Casey feared he had lost the fight. But then, as the *Times*'s first edition went to bed the Assistant Editor pulled Fred Steele's story from the paper. As he read and re-read the file, then consulted colleagues, Boagland felt uneasy at the lack of corroboration from at least one other source. Steele's story needed further authentication. Contacts in Washington had to be cross-checked thoroughly to ensure the Soviet allegation was fireproof against the wrath of the Reagan administration. Steele's article had to be right – absolutely right.

Late that Wednesday night, all those involved in Washington's new Polish crisis waited to read the text of Steele's story from the first edition of Thursday's *Times*. The US President waited. Senator Ordeleau, chairman of the Senate Intelligence Committee, waited. And in Moscow Chief Director Semenov and Director Zuyenko waited.

But in vain.

No one outside the newspaper knew why the story had not appeared. But in the office of the White House Chief of Staff there was no hiding the relief. On Capitol Hill, Senator Ordeleau was mystified. And in Moscow, Generals Semenov and Zuyenko began to get cold feet. Andropov's two senior KGB officers had dealt all their cards and now one of the most important tricks had failed to come good. Moscow Centre's carefully-conceived strategy had not taken into account the inscrutable reputation of one of America's most respected newspaper editors.

Amber Monkey had been rumbled.

20

On Rutkowskiego Street, a traffic-free shopping street in central Warsaw, an SB agent planted in the upper echelons of the Solidarity underground handed his latest intelligence to a plainclothes colleague as they both queued in the April drizzle for mushroom-burgers at a fast-food kiosk. Within thirty minutes the document sat on General Siwinski's desk at the Polish Interior Ministry.

Siwinski put other pressing work aside in order to read the first communique of the new provisional underground Solidarity leadership. It confirmed the rumour that the leaders of the illegal union who had not been interned, had evaded tight surveillance and security measures to meet in secret six days earlier, on 22 April. At the meeting they had agreed to call for a nationwide fifteen-minute strike on 13 May during which traffic would be halted at midday. The leaders believed the strike and demonstrations would be a test of the union's unity and strength after four months of martial law.

And with the communique, the SB 'wire' had also sent an urgent message that plans were well advanced for a huge Solidarity demonstration on May Day designed to outnumber the official Communist Party parade and embarrass General Jaruzelski and his officials.

The Deputy Interior Minister swore as he read the scrap of paper. 'Not only will the ministry have to devote manpower to tracking down Sulecki and protecting Jaruzelski,' he mumbled to himself, 'now we will have to deploy enormous additional forces to prevent a major threat to public order on the very day Jaruzelski wants to portray life in Socialist Poland as "normal".'

Siwinski was horrified by the prospect.

21

On the morning of Thursday 29 April, Washington's political crisis still remained a nervously guarded secret. Nothing of the turmoil and damage-limitation efforts at the White House had yet spread beyond the President's close band of loyal advisers.

In Warsaw, CIA Station Chief Jefferson knew nothing of Casey's frantic efforts to suppress the *New York Times* story. Instead he spent most of the day weighing-up his personal career options and wondering how best to hide his operational screw-ups. Jefferson eventually decided that his reply to Casey's cable should not arrive at Langley headquarters until early evening Washington time, after the end of the normal working day.

When completed, Jefferson's cable was a farrago of dishonesty which displayed all the ingenuity and deviousness expected by the CIA from its field agents. It reported in vague terms that after the CIA Director's urgent Tuesday night message, agents in Warsaw had made contact with 'a certain Magda Gajewska' and 'Bogdan Miskiewicz' – both described as 'acquaintances' of the alleged terrorist, Andrzej Sulecki. Jefferson detailed how Bogdan had followed Sulecki back to Poland as well as Theobold's analysis that Sulecki might be an undercover KGB Illegal planted in Solidarity in order to embarrass the CIA. Jefferson added that so far there had been no sightings of the Russian in Warsaw since Magda spotted him on Easter Sunday.

The final draft of Jefferson's cable was being enciphered in the communications room when Jeb Theobold returned at eleven o'clock, just as curfew began.

'What progress, Jeb?' demanded Jefferson. 'Did you find that broad, Gajewska?'

'No,' Theobold replied. 'She's gone.'

'Gone? Gone where?' the Station Chief barked angrily as if Theobold was to blame for her disappearance.

Theobold poured himself a whisky from Jefferson's bottom drawer then perched on the corner of the desk. 'I spoke to a neighbour ... Magda left her apartment key with him this morning. She was near to tears. She told him she was going to the country to her family's *domek*.'

'Where the hell's that?'

'The neighbour didn't know. But he remembered her talking once about a place sixty kilometres south of here.'

Theobold stepped across the office to the map of Poland hanging across most of one wall and pointed to a town south of Warsaw.

'That must make it somewhere near here. It's a small, downtrodden market town called Grojec. I went there for a couple of Solidarity demos last year.'

'Address?'

Theobold shrugged, swigged his whisky and shook his head. 'Didn't have it.'

Jefferson swore.

'Shee-it! Then we'd better start looking.'

22

Magda arrived at the *domek* in the Grojec forest just before three o'clock on Thursday afternoon, having stumbled for forty minutes down the muddy farm tracks from the bus-stop.

Inside, Sulecki sat in the kitchen clutching a mug of coffee and expecting no one. After fifty days of self-imposed isolation, the KGB Illegal had completed his final preparations for *Amber Monkey* and was about to leave for Warsaw. Around him, the bare floorboards, wood-panelled walls and flaking plaster ceilings looked just as Sulecki had found them seven weeks earlier, on 10 March. The *domek* had been swept clean, the fire in the cast-iron stove extinguished, all food and incriminating evidence of occupation buried in the forest, and all the household furniture and equipment returned to the exact positions from which Sulecki removed them in mid-March.

Sulecki's rural solitude was broken by a large steel key rattling in the front door, the unexpected sound echoing across the empty living room and past the mothballed furniture. The timber door squeaked open and he heard a woman panting outside on the wooden verandah, fol-lowed by successive heavy clunks against the grey stone walls outside as mud was knocked from footwear.

Sulecki still sat half-hidden behind the kitchen door. He listened and waited, the shining components of the dismantled Ruger and the nine specially prepared dis-integration bullets lying neatly positioned on the table alongside him. The sixty practice bullets supplied by Petrovsky were all spent, and test firings over the past two weeks had tuned the weapon to perfection.

Sulecki heard the woman step into the living room and close the front door. She was clearly alone, so he did not panic and rush to hide the Ruger or the bullets. Instead he stood up and walked boldly into the main room.

'Magda!'

Sulecki's deep voice boomed around the *domek*'s bare walls. Magda recoiled in astonishment and dropped her belongings.

'Andrzej . . ?'

As she ventured his name she realised beyond any doubt that in spite of the long, straggly hair, unkempt moustache, gangly beard and dirty ill-fitting suit, it had been Andrzej she had seen on Easter Sunday in Warsaw.

'Magda!' Sulecki's voice was distant and without emotion, betraying both his surprise at her sudden arrival and his indifference towards her. Magda approached him with her feelings uncoordinated. On the one hand she tried to work out how to confront her lover with what she now knew about his escape to Sweden, on the other hand she wanted to ignore Jeb Theobold's incredible conspiracy theories and just embrace the man she had not hugged for four months.

'How are you . . . darling Andrzej?' she asked hesitantly.

Sulecki's response continued to be remote and cold. 'As you see I'm well, but in this isolation I'm going a bit crazy. I've lost a lot of weight. I've spent every day running and getting fit. That's why I'm a bit too thin . . . and you?'

'I'm well too, but very tired. They released me from internment three weeks ago . . .'

'It was bad?'

'When I got home I couldn't sleep for days. I couldn't find anybody. I couldn't settle down at the apartment, so I came here to the *domek* to try and get my strength back. And look what I found . . . What a beautiful surprise . . .'

Magda's voice tailed off, cut short by Sulecki's brusque manner. Conversation did not come easily.

'Where did they keep you?' Sulecki asked her.

'Jaworze, then Goldap, and finally the horrors of Darlowo because they said I was too undisciplined . .

And you? What are you doing here, Andrzej? Why didn't you come to Warsaw to find out about me and the others in Solidarity?'

'I didn't dare risk it,' he lied. 'The longer I stayed here the harder it became to leave. I've been hiding here for weeks now. After the SB arrested us last December I was taken to Bialoleka for a few days. One night I escaped as they were transferring us by truck – it was somewhere in the east near the Soviet border. I came here because I thought this was the safest place to hide. You're the first person I've seen for months.'

Magda moved closer and clutched each of Sulecki's shoulders. 'You've only been here?' she enquired. 'You've never left the *domek*?'

'Never! Where else could I go without risking arrest? I was sure the apartment would be watched, and I was sure it was the same for our colleagues and friends. It was easier and safer here.'

Magda pushed her body hard up against Sulecki's. They looked closely into each other's eyes and she kissed his cracked lips.

'What about the village? Didn't you go to Grojec to get food?' she probed innocently.

'Oh yes! I went to Grojec a couple of times but never further – it was too risky.'

'Never to Warsaw or anywhere else?'

'No. Why bother? It was too dangerous,' he lied.

To Magda, Sulecki's glib answers only underlined his earlier deviousness. This cold figure was not the Andrzej she knew and remembered. Suddenly her initial determination to give her lover the benefit of the doubt and not to believe Theobold's conspiracy theory evaporated.

For several minutes Magda and Sulecki clutched each other without speaking or moving, each trying to calculate their escape.

'But Andrzej, I'm sure I saw you in Warsaw on Easter Sunday in Castle Square. You were getting on a bus full of peasant women. You were wearing the same badly-fitting suit as you're wearing now ... You had the same straggly hair and beard. I'm sure it was you. But when I shouted you didn't respond...'

Magda felt Sulecki's hands tighten and change position around her waist.

'Oh? Easter Sunday? No! I was here at the *domek*. I'm quite sure of that.'

He had badly misjudged what Magda suspected and how much she knew. For once, Sulecki was trapped.

'And Sweden?' she persisted. 'The escape on the little Antonov crop sprayer? Then the stay in a refugee hotel at Frostavallen and your smuggled return here by boat ... You still say you never left here?'

'Never!' Sulecki was shaken by the accuracy of what Magda knew, but he still responded as if none of her facts bore any relation to the truth. 'Where on earth did you get such crazy ideas, darling?'

Magda was determined not to be put off. 'Pictures in newspapers. Contacts ... Reliable friends who keep me informed...'

The KGB Lieutenant Colonel had been unmasked by his lover. 'So you came here to trap me with fantasy tales of where I might have been in the last four months? That's no way to treat the man you love,' he said with contrived conviction.

Magda gently shook her head as it rested on his shoulder, her face pressed against his dirty peasant jacket.

'No, I needed a break,' she said. 'I came here to get away from Warsaw, and I found you. It was nothing premeditated. Just pure chance.'

Behind Magda, the front door creaked noisily, blowing back and forth in the late afternoon breeze. Her eyes peered over Andrzej's shoulder and wandered around the familiar contours of the *domek* she had known since childhood. The empty fire grate reminded her of the evenings when she and Andrzej had frolicked naked and made love during the best moments of their relationship. Then her eyes ventured through the half-open kitchen door to the table where the shining, charcoal-grey barrel of a rifle glinted against the daylight. Alongside, she could

488

see the casings of nine bullets.

Magda fought to control the nervous stiffening of her body. At last she confronted the stark reality of the conspiracy she had always refused to accept. Still, however, she caressed Andrzej's back in the hope of winning a few more minutes in which to think.

Magda realised that everything was stacked against her. Sulecki had fitness, strength, KGB training, a high-powered weapon and well-laid plans. There was no point breaking away and running to the nearest neighbours because he would kill her.

As they embraced again, each of them silently finalised their own strategy to extricate themselves. It was the ultimate test of the individual cunnings which had made Magda a leading dissident and Sulecki a highly-decorated KGB agent.

By dusk, one of them would be dead.

23

On America's east coast it was half past four as John Boagland, the *New York Times'* Assistant Editor, sat on the chief sub's desk fingering Fred Steele's rewritten story from Moscow. During Thursday, Boagland had assigned six specialist reporters to cross-check the story with sources at the CIA, Pentagon, State Department and White House. Now he was satisfied there was enough collateral evidence to confirm the existence of high-level administration fears about CIA secret involvement in an illegal covert assassination operation in Warsaw.

'Front page. Lead story!' Boagland told his sub editors as he flicked Steele's file into the 'Out' basket.

Two hundred and twenty miles south of New York at CIA Headquarters in Langley, Operations Directorate finally received Jefferson's delayed cable from Poland. As Casey read the text of the Warsaw Station Chief's memorandum he was more determined than ever to halt the *Times* story. He knew the presses would roll at six-thirty so he had just thirty minutes to prevent publication.

Casey and John Stein, his Deputy Director for Operations, first spent fifteen minutes studying Jefferson's cable in order to clarify the extent of the KGB's Active Measures operation in Warsaw. They treated as fact, Jefferson's 'belief' that Sulecki might be a KGB plant inside Solidarity. At six-twenty Casey finally had the detail he needed for an urgent phone call to Boagland, hauling him out of a meeting of the newspaper's senior management in the process.

As before, Casey's telephone manner was abrasive. 'Boagland, in case you have any doubts, *this* conversation is off-the-record,' Casey mumbled. 'Now, get this, John.

I accept the reasons for your stand last night on the Moscow story. I didn't like it but your clear intention to publish was fair game. I have no idea why you didn't publish yesterday – that was your problem. Now I'm worried about tonight.'

There was a pause. Casey waited for Boagland's reply but did not really expect one. The CIA director tried again. 'After what I've heard from some of our agents who've been approached by your guys today, I assume you'll be publishing tomorrow, John. Correct?'

'We will.'

'I assume it's on the front page?'

'Right!'

'Well, kill it, John! Get it out of the paper. I can't tell you why for the moment and I can't yet give you chapter and verse ...'

Casey was sure that Boagland would not just submit to whatever the CIA ordered. He knew he must give a credible justification to kill the story.

'In the last fifteen minutes my agency has received reliable intelligence which confirms beyond doubt that your man Steele in Moscow had been fed Soviet dis-information designed to implicate the CIA in a Polish operation which in reality is nothing to do with us, but which is masterminded by the KGB.'

As usual, 'flapper-lips' Casey dealt in half-truths on the principle that any gaps in knowledge should not undermine the basic thrust of a legitimate argument.

'But how can I trust you, Mr Casey? After the President's new orders to control CIA activity, how do I know you're not making a desperate effort to prevent publication as the way to save your own arse and the agency's reputation?'

'You don't, John. You only have my word. But take it from me. I'll guarantee you receive the relevant briefing as soon as I have full details. But I truly believe that if you publish you will be doing just what Moscow wants. You will be adding credibility to a despicable operation which the KGB planned for their own internal

491

political reasons. You will also be alerting the world to a bullshit Soviet story wrongly implicating the CIA.'

Boagland was not insensitive to the reality of KGB disinformation in the United States and he appreciated the logic of Casey's apparent fears. The newspaperman's main doubt was about Casey's integrity and ulterior motives.

The deadline for the *Times*'s first edition pressed. it was no time for long and considered reflections.

'OK, it's on your word, Mr Casey,' said Boagland. 'But you made me a promise. You'd better make sure you get the gen, Director, or next time I'll have the story of your assurances in coloured lights on my front page before you even get the chance to pick up the phone and kill it.'

'I'm most grateful,' spluttered Casey complacently.

It was 6.28 on 29 April. *Amber Monkey* had suffered its first major setback.

For the KGB there was worse to come. Boagland began assigning correspondents at the White House, State Department and CIA to research the story of how the KGB planned to dupe the American people over Poland.

By mid-morning on Friday rumours of a CIA assassination plot had begun circulating among Washington's press corps, and spokesmen from the White House and State Department had to spend the day smothering the bushfires the moment they flared. At the State Department's routine noon briefing officials were pushed hard about the rumours but managed to dismiss them.

'To my knowledge no such Soviet allegations of a CIA operation in Poland have been made,' said the duty spokesman. 'If they had been made we would of course reject them in the strongest possible terms. I have nothing more to say.'

That afternoon the President himself was pressed by the White House press corps as he crossed the lawn to a Navy helicopter taking him to Camp David for the weekend. Against the usual background clatter of the helicopter rotors the President shouted a barely audible answer.

'Rumours? What rumours? And if they were true they would be the biggest Soviet cheap shot in a long time.'

The Administration's damage-limitation tactics seemed to be working. Alleged facts remained unsubstantiated, and rumours remained rumours. By Friday night the media in Washington had shifted their interest from Poland to Britain's predicament in the Falklands War.

The White House and State Department hid their relief. And so, for the moment, did Bill Casey's CIA.

24

Across the Atlantic and beyond the Iron Curtain, it was already late evening. At the KGB's First Directorate headquarters in Moscow, Deputy Chairman Semenov faced the four senior KGB Generals involved in *Amber Monkey*. Each had been urgently summoned from dinner for this unscheduled meeting, but this time there were no drinks or caviar canapés and no heady conspiratorial atmosphere.

'Comrade Generals, you are familiar with the success of *Amber Monkey* up to this morning, but this evening we face our first crisis of any significance since Sulecki disappeared in January. Washington has penetrated Comrade General Zuyenko's disinformation campaign. The CIA are no longer rejecting the intelligence discovered by their operatives in Warsaw last week. All the indications are that the CIA and White House now realise there is a KGB operation designed to implicate the CIA ... It means there are two pressing questions. Has our operational cover been destroyed, and what effect does this propaganda failure have on our strategy?'

The hesitation among the generals underlined the new difficulties.

'But is the evidence so clear cut, Dimitri Fedorovich? How can you be so sure?' asked General Mironenko.

Semenov's response was unequivocal. 'The disinformation planted this week by Comrade agent Timoshkin on the *New York Times* correspondent has not been picked up in America. The press failed to publish what we always assumed they would see as newsworthy allegations against Casey and the CIA. That means someone warned them off. Why? We must assume it's because the CIA somehow penetrated our strategy and made sure the press didn't publish.'

General Kulagin was not so convinced. 'Comrade General, I suggest that with such circumstantial evidence you are being over-pessimistic.'

'Never!' retorted Semenov, shaking his head. 'Prudence is vital in any operation like this. From the start we've known the dangers if the Soviet Union were ever to become implicated. If *Amber Monkey* is no longer seen as an operation carried out by Solidarity extremists backed by the CIA then every one of our operational goals will be neutralised. If *Amber Monkey* backfires it will undermine not the CIA and Reagan as we want, but the Soviet Union. Comrades, I ask you for your considered opinion. Should we still proceed?'

General Martynov, the head of the Illegals 'S' Directorate who was directly responsible for Sulecki, inhaled briskly on a cigarette.

'Comrade General, I suggest there is little to discuss. Frankly, it's too late to change our plans. By now Comrade Sulecki should be in place in Warsaw preparing for the assassination. He is operating under radio silence so we cannot contact him, and we have no idea where he is. Having got this far we have no alternative. We must be ready to live with the political fall-out. Let's not forget our main goal: to purge Poland of Jaruzelski and his deviationist policies, then to ensure that internal discipline is reimposed on the terms demanded by Comrade Chairman Andropov.'

Semenov tacitly invited further comments by slowly casting his eye around the faces of the other generals. None had anything more to say.

'Comrade Generals, if my understanding is correct, then we all agree there will be no changes. So, I should add, does the Comrade Chairman. ... Thank you for coming. We continue as planned.'

25

Before leaving the *domek* for Warsaw, Sulecki had made sure he arranged the evidence to conceal any trace of Magda's murder. He rapidly re-dressed her then carefully crumpled her body inside the front door and laid her shoulder bag alongside, her hand loosely gripping the handle so that when the body was eventually discovered all forensic evidence would point to a natural death by cardiac arrest – a fatal consequence of the rigours of internment.

As dusk had fallen at the *domek* the previous afternoon both naked lovers had lunged passionately on the dust sheets in the living room. Magda had considered trying to knock Sulecki out with one of the logs which lay at arms length in the fireplace, but the KGB Lieutenant Colonel had overpowered her first. As they lay together on the floor, with Magda's pallid body on top of Sulecki's, the KGB officer had knocked her semi-conscious with a swift upward glance of his shoulder against the base of her chin. Then while Magda lay comatose, Sulecki had pressed gently on her windpipe until she stopped breathing. It was a quick clinical way to remove her threat to *Amber Monkey*.

Now, twenty-four hours later, Sulecki was in Warsaw. It was 5 p.m. and the height of the Friday evening rush hour. The KGB Lieutenant Colonel was safe, but he cursed Magda for delaying his arrival in the Polish capital by a day.

For three hours, Sulecki had sat below the lofty, whitewashed plaster ceilings in the ground-floor public reading room of the Interpress state news agency on one corner of Unii Lubelskiej Square. He had chosen a seat facing the outside wall which allowed him to look through the tall window and across Bagatela Street towards the crumbling, brown-brick facade of number 15. To anyone around him who might be taking an interest – like the conspicuous SB man in the corner – Sulecki tried to make it seem he was whiling away his Friday afternoon reading the Soviet Bloc newspapers on display in the reading racks. But in reality Sulecki was quietly using the time to construct a mental map of the building in which he intended to hide.

Number 15 was a nine-storey block, one of five rundown apartment buildings overlooking the traffic lights and roundabout just south of the city centre. The square itself was one of the busiest traffic intersections in Warsaw, with trams and buses converging down the six streets which fed into it. To the right, diagonally across the central grass knoll, was a fire station, and to the left was the shabby glass structure of a large *Supersam* supermarket. From his research before martial law Sulecki knew that General Jaruzelski's daily motorcade usually passed through the intersection on its way to the Council of Ministers. He had to hope that tomorrow – May Day – would be no exception.

Sulecki had chosen 15 Bagatela Street because among its scores of residents was an American he believed the Polish authorities could readily accuse of being a CIA agent. She was Joanne Decker, Warsaw correspondent of an international American news agency. From his days at Solidarity headquarters, Sulecki remembered Joanne as better informed about the union than any other Western journalist. She also had some of the best contacts in Solidarity, which was why he was sure she would be sympathetic to receiving him.

Number 15 had only one entrance – a set of large black double doors set back a few metres from Bagatela Street in the shadow cast by a brick arch above the doorway. During his three hours in the reading room Sulecki had carefully watched the comings and goings into Number 15, and there was a clear routine. The residents let themselves in with their own keys, but visitors had to wait several minutes for the surly *concierge* to open one of the two gates, check their identity and then allow them through after paying a tip.

At six o'clock, the Interpress doorman began locking up the reading room. Sulecki walked a hundred metres down Pulawska Street to a public telephone booth where he dialled the American journalist's home number which he had memorised during his preparations at the *domek*. He listened to the ringing tone for two minutes but there was no reply. Then he phoned Joanne's tiny office in the *Agroma* building on Piekna Street not far away. As usual a pre-recorded voice reminded Sulecki that the phone line was 'controlled', then a female voice which he did not recognise answered in Polish. He assumed it was Joanne's Polish assistant, and Sulecki made an attempt to speak in broken English.

'Is Joanne there, please?'

'I'm afraid she's out on a story.'

'When will she be back?'

'She won't finish until about nine this evening. Joanne told me she will not come back to the office. She'll go straight home. Can I help you?'

'No thank you.'

The KGB Lieutenant Colonel's plans were delayed yet again. He had no option but to wait.

26

Deputy Interior Minister Siwinski sipped his tepid coffee, loosened his tie yet again and re-examined his operational police orders for May Day. He was under instructions to prepare the most thorough police operation possible, regardless of cost. The SB General ran his pen down the twenty sheets of paper and double-checked the details.

All leave cancelled. 180,000 functionaries of the security forces deployed across the country: including the crack *Tiger* paramilitary brigade, the ZOMO motorised riot police, MO and WOW Internal Defence Forces, the SB, plus, if needed, WOP Frontier Police and WSW Army Security Service. Full Red-Alert issue of nightsticks, batons, riot helmets and shields, rubber bullets, water dye, gas canisters and masks, percussion grenades and launchers. Every one of the 45,000 *Nysa* trucks, wagons, jeeps, armoured personnel carriers, water cannons and undercover cars assigned to specific tasks. Sharp-shooters have orders to shoot on sight any suspicious targets, especially in area of Victory Square. Official authorisation granted for 58 undercover agents to use Solidarity posters and banners in order to create the pretext for the police reprisals and clampdown planned for May 3.

Such intense security underlined that May Day 1982 would not be allowed to become a repeat of the free-wheeling informality of 1981, when leading Polish government and party officials had mixed openly with workers and foreign television crews on the crowded streets of central Warsaw.

Just before seven o'clock that evening Siwinski confidently handed his plan to Interior Minister Kiszczak.

499

The General scanned the document at high speed, then looked up.

'Comrade Wladek, I must make one thing clear. Comrade Jaruzelski insists there must be no confrontation tomorrow. He knows very well that the party hardliners want a battle as the excuse to get rid of our leader. General Milewski, for example, with his many years representing state security interests on the Politburo, thinks he has a god-given right to expect the toughest of crackdowns, the kind he knows his old KGB friends in Moscow want. But you must understand that the views of Comrade Jaruzelski override Milewski's. The key must be restraint. You must not succumb to any nonsense from the hardliners. Tomorrow must be the day to respect Polish workers, not to beat them up. Those are the Prime Minister's orders and they must be clearly understood by every one of your officers.'

No sooner had General Siwinski returned to his own office on the third floor than his phone rang. He recognised the throaty Russian accent of General Klimanov.

'So ... you are ready for May Day, Comrade Wladek?' asked the KGB liaison officer. 'I trust it will be trouble-free and there will be the fullest possible security operation. ... I suppose that all suspicious counter-revolutionary elements have been rounded up by now?'

Siwinski did not dare commit himself too far. 'I can assure you, Yevgenni Viktorovich, that round-the-clock surveillance has been mounted on all relevant American-occupied properties in Warsaw and all possible contingencies have been allowed for. Please convey to the Eleventh Department that I can guarantee Moscow Centre will not be unhappy with the security operation in Warsaw tomorrow ...'

But with Sulecki undiscovered and apparently still on the loose in Warsaw, Siwinski knew he had no grounds to give the KGB such sweeping assurances.

27

It was nine o'clock as Jeb Theobold sat across the desk from Jefferson in the main chancery block of the US embassy. The CIA station chief sat slumped in his swivel chair, his eyes closed and his mind drained. The usual, thumping Friday night beat from the disco in the Marine Bar drifted across the deserted embassy compound. Jefferson had already drunk four double whiskies, and he restrained himself from pouring a fifth. Instead he just stared blankly and longingly at his empty whisky glass.

'That KGB fucker Sulecki has beaten us, Jeb,' Jefferson snorted.

Theobold feared Jefferson was right. 'I have a theory, Frank . . . The kind of security our friends on Rakowiecka Street have been putting on outside the twelve American residences in the city centre is more than just routine harassment. You know what I mean – the MO wagons and SB cars parked by the front doors and the infra-red cameras across the street. Frank, that's a lot of expensive hardware just to make some obscure political point against the United States . . . There has to be a more basic reason.'

'So? What's your theory, Jeb?'

Such questions compounded Theobold's resentment of his station chief. Why was it always he and not his boss who came up with the ideas?

'I believe the SB *must* know as much about Sulecki's plans as we do,' said Theobold. 'I'm sure the Interior Ministry also suspect that Sulecki is going to use an American residence. The Sovs may have passed them disinformation. Who knows how the Poles know? The fact is that I'm sure they do.'

'You really think so, Jeb?'

With Washington now aware of the assassination plot,

Jefferson could no longer afford to reject Theobold's suggestion as 'whisky talk'.

'If I'm right,' Theobold continued, 'then the SB are doing our job of tracking down Sulecki for us and we shouldn't be *so* worried!'

Neither CIA agent had much respect for the hamfisted tactics of Poland's SB. But with just over twelve hours to go before the May Day parade, for once both Americans began to secretly wish their Polish counterparts good luck.

28

Bogdan could not face the bare plaster walls, solitary light bulb and empty apartment on Dzika Street for another moment. He felt like a condemned prisoner making the most of his final hours. To ease the monotony and pass the time after dusk he rashly decided to join Friday evening's rush hour queues. Even though he had no ID documents, he frittered away his remaining zlotys riding the trams aimlessly up and down Warsaw's main boulevard, Marszalkowska Street. Outside the tram windows the Friday evening traffic had thinned to a trickle, but the grey city was already packed with militia vehicles in preparation for May Day. The faces he saw were spiritless; the familiar haunts and cafés depressing and lifeless.

After two hours, Bogdan rode the rattling Number 12 tram four kilometres south to his old allotment hideaway on Raclawicka Street, walking first west past the eerie concrete stands of the Interior Ministry's football stadium, then on to the allotments he had known so well in the first days of martial law. The snow and the army road block had long gone, and even in the dark the garden plots seemed grubby and hardly recognisable as the weeds and spring undergrowth grew untended.

Bogdan squeezed himself through the broken fence and groped his way carefully towards the shed which had once been his Solidarity hideaway. The wooden door was open and the latch un-padlocked. As he pushed back the door the boards creaked and bent under his weight. Inside, the air was musty and unlived-in, the furniture still upturned and his armchair still in pieces on the floor. Several windows had been smashed and floorboard which had once hidden the printing press lay scattered around the shed. The photocopier itself had gone and the illegal electricity cable which had run to a nearby lamp-post lay shredded into short lengths.

Surveying the destruction, Bogdan concluded that Jurek had not abandoned the hideaway of his own free will. Instead, there were all the signs of a raid by the militia or SB which must have been designed to ensure that no Solidarity activist would ever bother to return. And Bogdan was sure no one had. As he sat defeated by Sulecki and watching the dust settle in the narrow beams of the orange street lighting, his mind drifted to the only new challenge which now seemed to matter – the returning to his family in Sweden.

Meanwhile, at the Interior Ministry two kilometres to the north, General Siwinski sealed the May Day orders for the security forces, then dispatched them to the signals room for immediate communication to every operational command. Across the city, behind the floodlit facade of the American Embassy, Jefferson and Theobold dozed in the half-light of a desk lamp. And in Washington, the CIA and State Department crisis teams waited and watched. Their satellite and signals intelligence had yet to produce any new evidence, so there were no new conclusions or recommendations to pass to the President or the National Security Adviser.

In Washington it was 4 p.m., and the traffic on the bridges over the Potomac crawled to a halt as the usual pre-weekend commuter rush-hour began to build up.

29

Joanne Decker arrived home more than an hour later
than expected. Sulecki watched the American journalist
wheel her bicycle up to the entrance of the apartment
block on Bagatela Street at ten minutes past ten. As she
looked for her keys, the KGB Lieutenant Colonel stepped
from the shadows and walked towards her.

'Joanne!' he called softly.

She looked up from rummaging in her bag. In the dark
Joanne had difficulty recognising Sulecki with his new
long hair and straggly beard.

'It's Andrzej – Andrzej Sulecki. I used to work the
telex machines at Mokotowska Street,' he said.

Joanne broke into a half-grin and greeted Andrzej
warmly. 'Andrzej! I didn't recognise you for a minute.
Great to see you! How are you?'

As an escaped internee still high on the security forces'
wanted list, Sulecki's immediate objective was to get
inside Joanne's apartment as fast as possible, then stay
there until tomorrow.

'I feel a little vulnerable here. Perhaps we could talk
inside, Joanne. You know what I mean?'

The American understood Sulecki perfectly. Since the
declaration of martial law, Joanne had been involved in
many clandestine meetings with underground activists.

'Of course. Follow me.' Joanne unlocked the gate and
pushed her bicycle into the dark, unlit courtyard followed
by Sulecki carrying his blue holdall containing the dismantled Ruger. Behind a small window to their left a
finger lifted the corner of a net curtain as the grumpy
concierge checked Joanne's identity. In the stairwell, she
and Sulecki both waited in the pitch void for the antiquated lift to clunk down and take them up to her sixth
floor apartment overlooking Pulawska Street.

Joanne lit the stove to boil water for her favourite Lapsang Souchong tea. She invited Sulecki to make himself at home in the sitting room which was stuffed with artefacts and memorabilia from every country to which she had been posted. The pictures, rugs, pottery and ikons revealed the habits of an international traveller who found comfort in the continuity of her most prized personal possessions.

As Joanne changed her clothes, the KGB agent related the details of his escape from internment and his four months on the run as what he called a 'courier between underground Solidarity cells' – four months during which he claimed to have stayed in no place longer than two nights at a time and usually for only one night.

'And what brings you to see me, Andrzej?' asked Joanne in her usual soft-spoken manner.

Sulecki had prepared his carefully-crafted story. . . . 'Today I came up from Grojec to deliver some printing stencils passed on to me by a courier from Krakow. At nine o'clock tonight I delivered them to an apartment just across the junction in Polna Street. But the people there said I couldn't stay because it was too unsafe – the SB have raided the apartment twice in the last six days. I didn't want to travel to another part of the city so close to curfew, so I tried to think of someone else I knew who lived in this area. But everyone I know has either disappeared underground or been interned. Then I remembered that you lived here . . . I came to two of your parties last year. I decided to try my luck. I phoned your office. Your assistant said you'd be home late, so I thought it worth the risk of waiting for you outside as a way to get at least somewhere to rest my head for the night.'

It was a plausible tale which made it virtually impossible for Joanne to throw him onto the streets. In any case, offering overnight sanctuary to Solidarity activists had become part of life under martial law – even for foreigners.

Joanne looked at her watch. It was 10.41.

'It's nineteen minutes to curfew. You're welcome to
ay, Andrzej, and we'll just have to hope I don't get
ided tonight!'

As they both laughed, the lift cage slammed shut on
e landing outside. The smiles instantly disappeared
om both their faces. Joanne and Sulecki braced them-
lves for the thump on the front door and the familiar SB
ll of 'Open up!' Instead, there was a furtive and barely
dible rap on the woodwork.

'Yes?' Joanne responded nervously.

'Joanne?' asked a whispering voice beyond the door.
's Dick – Dick Werner.'

Joanne boldly opened the door giggling.

'Dick, you old bastard! Come in. I thought you were
e SB coming to raid me! What the hell do you want at
is time? Warsaw's crawling with cops and, the night
fore May Day, if you don't get home before curfew
ey'll sure as hell have your arse in the slammer for
ntravening martial law regulations.'

The *Washington Post* correspondent did not need the
arning. He knew exactly the kind of risk he was running.

'I'll only be a couple of minutes. I was passing by on
y way home, Joanne. I need that Solidarity bulletin
om Katowice which I lent you at lunchtime. The desk
Washington are after me again. They want more detail
out the appalling conditions under military commissars
the Silesian coalmines.'

'Come through, Dick, and I'll get it.'

Joanne led Werner from the hall into the living room.

'Hi!' Werner threw a brief and uninterested greeting
the grubby long-haired man sitting at the table. Having
et Werner and asked him for weapons outside the Vic-
ia Hotel in December, Sulecki did not want to be
cognised. The lies he had just told Joanne about his
derground Solidarity activities would he discredited
mediately. But as he was Joanne's guest Sulecki
alised he could not just run away from Werner. Instead,
best protection was to remain silent.

Joanne rummaged through a pile of documents on her

507

desk. 'Oh excuse my rudeness, Dick. This is Andrzej Sulecki. You probably don't recogise him. He used to work Solidarity's telex machines at Mokotowska Street.'

Werner moved across to the table to shake hands.

'Hi Andrzej. How are you? But what a surprise! I thought you'd escaped to Sweden.'

The KGB agent screwed up his face in feigned disbelief, then half-laughed. He cursed Joanne. Now there was no way he could fudge his past: he had to confront it.

'Sweden? You must be mistaking me for someone else, Dick. What makes you say that I was in Sweden?'

'I'm not making a mistake. Andrzej? We met sometime before Christmas in Victory Square. I spent weeks trying to find you after that, but you'd disappeared. We thought you must have been arrested again and re-interned ... Then in the *Herald Tribune* in the middle of February there was a picture of a Polish crop-spraying aircraft which had escaped to Sweden. There were twelve refugees and I swear I saw your face among them. So did someone else in Warsaw who knows you.'

'Who was that?'

'Jeb Theobold at the American Embassy.'

With each word from Werner, Sulecki felt his security in Joanne's apartment becoming increasingly precarious.

'No, Dick, you've got it wrong,' Sulecki insisted with a voice of bewilderment. 'Since Christmas I've been dee underground working for Solidarity. As I told Joann just before you arrived, I've been a union courier. That why I'm here. In four months I've rarely spent more tha one night anywhere. I certainly haven't dared go back my apartment. I've spent a lot of time travelling outsid Warsaw which is probably why you weren't able to fin me.'

'And the photograph?'

The KGB Illegal shrugged. 'You must have confuse me with someone who looks similar? Perhaps it was a b picture? But I haven't been to Sweden, so it can't ha been me.'

508

Dick Werner had been a leading foreign correspondent for ten years. He had the self assurance to know that he rarely made elementary mistakes of identification. But more important, it was Jeb Theobold who had first seen the *Herald Tribune* picture and brought it to Werner's attention. Surely an experienced diplomat and an acclaimed journalist were not both wrong? Werner remained unconvinced by Sulecki, but for the moment he had other more pressing issues on his mind.

'Dick, it's almost eleven o'clock,' Joanne reminded him. 'Curfew starts in two minutes. You'd better go!'

'Shit! Thanks. Where's that damn underground bulletin?'

There was no time for Werner to discuss the matter further with Joanne nor to explain who Sulecki was or to warn her. Instead he grabbed a crumpled sheet of paper covered with closely-typed printing, and rushed from the apartment down the six flights of stone steps to his BMW for the brief journey home to Hoza Street.

Joanne and Sulecki talked until midnight. As they ate a late snack of cheese, yoghurt and raisins they chatted like two old Solidarity friends who had been out of touch for months. To the KGB officer's relief, Joanne seemed not to have registered Werner's claims about him having been seen in Sweden.

At 1 a.m. they both listened to the world news from the Voice of America and the BBC. The bulletins talked of Poland preparing for its first May Day under martial law and of yet more Soviet warnings of American-backed terrorism in Poland.

Joanne pulled blankets and a sheet sleeping bag from a drawer and tossed them on to the settee. 'You can sleep here, Andrzej.'

As he prepared the bedding, Sulecki's mind already focussed on his plans for the morning. 'What time will you be up tomorrow?' he asked.

'Half past six. I have to be in the office by half past ten to write the day-lead.'

Joanne's intentions dovetailed neatly with Sulecki's plans.

By ten past eleven Dick Werner had returned to his apartment-cum-office. For an hour he sat at the faded plastic keyboard of his battered Polish telex machine talking to his foreign desk in Washington and providing the extra details they wanted on the commissars in the Silesian mines. Only at midnight did he finally get a moment to telephone Jeb Theobold to advise him of his strange meeting with Sulecki earlier that evening.

Werner had no knowledge of Theobold's deep involvement in a secret CIA crisis hunt for Sulecki. But eight days earlier Theobold had insisted that Werner must call him 'at any time of the day or night' if he ever came upon new information relating to Sulecki's whereabouts. Werner first tried phoning Theobold's villa on Gymnastyczna Street. He let the phone ring for five minutes in case Theobold was asleep or in his sauna, but there was no reply. Then Werner tried the American embassy where the duty Marine connected him to Theobold's office. Again there was no reply.

Neither Werner nor the Marine had thought to try Jefferson's room where Theobold and his Station chief were both dozing during their all-night vigil.

It was 1 a.m.

30

Curfew ended at 5 a.m. Sulecki rolled from under the crumpled blankets on Joanne Decker's settee and padded in his underwear across to the tall windows overlooking the roundabout on Unii Lubelskiej Square. To his right, a rich red dawn hovered over Warsaw's eastern skyline, and below, the streets converging on the square were deserted.

For the next hour Sulecki watched Warsaw awake to seemingly endless columns of militia *Nysa* wagons, *Star* trucks, *Gaz* jeeps and water cannons heading up Marsz-alkowska Street, their headlamps blazing through the heavy black pall of belching diesel fumes. The Jaruzelski government's message was unequivocal: that at all costs Poland's security forces must ensure May Day was trouble-free. As a senior Soviet security officer, Sulecki would have been delighted to endorse such tough Polish policing were it not for the complications it now created for *Amber Monkey*.

At half-past six, Joanne Decker emerged from her bedroom dressed in a kimono. She wiped sleep from her eyes then shuffled across the polished wood floor to brew tea and prepare breakfast.

'The city's crawling with goons,' Sulecki told her.

'Yes. I heard them as I lay in bed,' she groaned.

By 6.50, Sulecki began willing Joanne to leave the apartment. To arrive at the news agency office by 7.30 she would have to leave by 7.20. He calculated that after she left he would need at least fifteen clear minutes to make his preparations.

'Joanne, I must thank you for your hospitality. You saved me from the streets, and I'm deeply grateful.'

Joanne began washing the breakfast crockery. 'It's the least I could do, Andrzej,' she shouted from the kitchen.

Sulecki laced up his boots. 'I know you have to leave for your office in a few minutes,' he said, 'but I wonder if you'd let me stay for another hour – until about half past eight? I've been asked to collect a package at 8.45 from a drop-off point in the Lazienkowski Park.'

Joanne did not give the matter a second thought. 'No problem Andrzej.' She walked to the front door and fiddled with the lock. 'All you have to do is flick this catch and pull the door closed. It'll lock behind you.'

The KGB Illegal had expected he would have to work harder to secure Joanne's agreement. As she returned to her bedroom and dressed, Sulecki paced the floor and tuned himself mentally for the climax of *Amber Monkey*.

Ten minutes later Joanne re-emerged, dressed casually in a loose-fitting jersey, check shirt and baggy jeans with her face lightly made-up and her dark hair held back by a bandanna. She grabbed a file of newspaper cuttings and threw her bag across a shoulder.

'Sorry to have to leave you like this, Andrzej.' She leaned across to shake Sulecki's hand, her mind already on the problems of reporting May Day. 'G'bye Andrzej Good luck. Hope to see you again some time.'

The Russian was determined to leave the most favourable impression on his hostess. 'And remember, I am most grateful to you, Joanne – most grateful.'

The front door slammed shut and Sulecki waited to hear the sound of the old lift clunking slowly downwards. From the living room window he watched Joanne emerge below onto Bagatela Street and begin cycling northward up Polna Street.

It was 7.18. Sulecki re-opened the front door and surveyed the tiny landing. Three apartment doors opened on to it and there was a time-switch which left the communal light burning for just twenty seconds. He retreated into Joanne's apartment, closed the door, then walked through the living room and into her bedroom. He stepped gingerly across a beautiful Afghan rug, then stood behind the floor-to-ceiling glass doors which overlooked Unii Lubelskiej Square and the broad expanse of Pulawski

Street coming from the south. Sulecki's months of planning and reconnaissance led him to expect Jaruzelski's motorcade in twenty-four minutes from now, at 7.50.

He wrenched the door knob firmly, then pulled back the top and bottom bolts and edged himself out onto the small wrought-iron balcony where he stood among the plant pots and studied the view across the two tram tracks and the six lanes of Pulawska Street. Although he was six floors up, the line-of-sight down the three city-bound carriageways was as clear and uninterrupted as the Lieutenant Colonel's calculations had predicted.

31

The early morning sight of flashing blue lights and cruising militia convoys reminded Bogdan of the first terrifying hours of martial law five months earlier. As the orange shafts of early sun burned through the broken windows of the allotment shed he stirred from his broken sleep and lay shivering on the dusty floor. The previous evening he had given up any idea of rushing back to Dzika Street to beat the curfew. Instead he had sat propped up in the broken armchair, reliving his efforts with Jurek to run the underground printing press. He vividly recalled the smell of ink, the all-night printing sessions and the struggle to find food. Then there had been the nerve-racking forays into Warsaw to gather information and deliver copies of their news sheet. They had been inspiring, passionate times and Bogdan was proud to have been a small part of that underground struggle, whatever the later cost in terms of torture and personal failure.

But their dream was dead. Bogdan tried to look to the future, and the prospects were distressing. After risking everything to return from Sweden, he had failed in his hunt for Sulecki and was now marooned in Poland as a non-person with no legal status and without any ID papers.

At 7.15 Bogdan lifted himself slowly and pathetically from the debris of his underground dream and began heading north back to his apartment on Dzika Street. Without glancing behind him he kicked the shed door shut and trudged slowly through the damp grass and untilled soil, with his long early-morning shadow walking behind him.

32

Warsaw crawled with militia as Jeb Theobold returned home to Gymnastyczna Street from the US Embassy, first to shave and change his clothes, then to collect orange juice and waffles for breakfast back in Jefferson's office.

As Theobold clutched the box of provisions and double-locked the front door his phone rang. He rushed back into the house and grabbed the receiver.

'Jeb? It's Dick Werner.'

'Hi, Dick. I'm under pressure. Make it quick.'

Werner chose his words carefully. 'Remember Sulecki? The guy who flew to Sweden? The guy you recognised in the *Herald Trib*? You told me to get in touch the moment I discovered anything about him.'

Theobold knew exactly what Werner meant. 'Yeah, of course. Tell me more,' he gasped breathlessly.

'Shall I give details on this line, Jeb? Or can it wait?'

'Oh fuck those niceties, Dick. I need what you've got now. Fast as you can.'

'Sulecki's in Warsaw.'

'How d'ya know, Dick?'

'Saw him last night.'

It was the break Theobold had long wanted. 'J-E-E-Z! When? Where?'

'He was at Joanne's. He was staying the night.'

'Joanne's? Joanne who?'

It was a few moments before Theobold realised Werner was referring to Joanne Decker, a fellow American journalist. Theobold remembered visiting her apartment for cocktails and dinner in September the previous year.

'Remind me Dick! She lives on Bagatela Street, right? What number? Which floor?'

'Number fifteen, sixth floor.'

For days Theobold had worked through the threads

which somehow linked Sulecki to a KGB assassination of Jaruzelski, and which in turn was designed to implicate Washington and show American support for terrorism in Poland. Now the disparate pieces clicked into place in a terrifying way. Sulecki must be using Joanne Decker's apartment to prove American collusion for his 'terrorist' operation.

'What was Sulecki doing at Joanne's?' asked Theobold.

'Staying the night,' said Werner, a little overcome by Theobold's impatience.

'Where's he now?'

'Still there, I guess.'

Theobold ignored any security worries. 'Shit, Dick! Why didn't you tell me last night?'

'I tried, Jeb, I called you at home several times, and then I called the embassy. The marine tried your office but there was no reply.'

Theobold could not waste time pursing the matter. It was his error. He had failed to tell the duty marine he was going to be in Jefferson's office all night. 'Where's Joanne now? Is she at her apartment?' he asked Werner frantically.

'Joanne said she'd be at the office by half seven this morning. She told me she'd be working early.'

'Thanks for the call, Dick. I'll explain everything later. Got to go. Bye!' Theobold slammed down the receiver, consulted his contacts book and dialled Joanne Decker's office on Piekna Street.

'Joanne? ... It's Jeb Theobold!'

'Hi Jeb. How yer doing? It's a bit early for you, isn't it?'

Joanne spoke against the clatter of her agency's antiquated teleprinters. Theobold interrupted brusquely.

'It's business. Urgent business, Joanne. There's no time to talk. Did you have a visitor last night? Surname beginning with S? Christian name A?' Theobold did not want to implicate Joanne too openly on the phone.

'Yeah, Jeb. But why the fuss?'

'I can't explain on this line, Joanne. Is he still there?'

'Yeah.'

'What time's he leaving?'

'What's all this, Jeb?'

'Don't ask questions, Joanne. Just tell me as a favour.'

'He told me he'd be leaving at around half past eight.'

'Thanks Joanne. Please excuse me. I can't say more. I'll be in touch later.'

Theobold rang off abruptly. Before Joanne had time to reflect on the brief yet intriguing phone call her attention was distracted by a transatlantic call from the news agency's night desk in New York.

It took several minutes for the SB's notes of Theobold's two bugged phone conversations to pass up the long chain of command to the duty major supervising surveillance of Western diplomatic phone lines that morning.

The name Sulecki was listed on a high priority SB alert, so the major starred the two calls to and from Theobold's residence for urgent examination, then sent the transcripts by messenger to an intelligence officer. It took ten minutes for him to compare notes from both calls and conclude that an American journalist named Werner had warned an American diplomat named Theobold that someone called 'Sulecki' would be at an apartment on the sixth floor of 15 Bagatela Street until 08.30 that morning.

The officer initialled his summary, marked it urgent, entered the time, then passed the text to his adjutant.

It was 7.41.

33

Theobold acted on impulse. There was no time to call Jefferson to tell him the news about Sulecki.

Instead the CIA agent sprinted across Gymnastyczna Street to his BMW, flung the breakfast provisions on the back seat and roared off through the mud. Allowing for traffic lights and congestion, Theobold calculated that the four-kilometre drive north to Joanne Decker's apartment on Bagatela Street would take about eight minutes. But after four hundred metres he found himself stuck in a queue of early-morning traffic waiting to turn left on to Komorowa Street.

As Theobold waited, his agitated mind wandered along the solemn faces queuing for a tram at the kerbside. The BMW's squealing brakes had already attracted the attention of a young man who now stared intently at the car in an effort to make out the driver's face. Immediately Bogdan recognised the face in the BMW as that of Theobold, the American diplomat he had met on Victory Square two weeks earlier. Bogdan pushed his way down the gutter between the pavement and the tram line, then wrenched open the nearside door. 'Any news?' he asked tensely.

'Yes,' yelled Theobold. 'Jump in !'

Bogdan ignored what might happen if the SB saw him getting into the car of a foreign diplomat. He threw himself in and slammed the door. Theobold revved the engine and began driving down the wrong side of the road in order to overtake the tailback of cars. 'Why the hurry?' Bogdan asked.

Theobold ignored his questions. 'It's lucky I saw you Bogdan – incredibly lucky. I've just had a tip off about Sulecki ... I just heard that he's in an apartment over looking Pulawska Street. That means he may be tryin to get at Jaruzelski on his way to the May Day parade.'

Both men spoke in a staccato shorthand.

'Where's the apartment?' asked Bogdan.

'Bagatela Street.'

'Whose is it?'

'An American journalist. Joanne Decker. You know her?'

'Only vaguely.'

Outside the prison halfway down Rakowiecka Street the militia had established a new roadblock.

'Keep away from that roadblock. I haven't got my ID papers,' warned Bogdan.

'Shit!' Theobold swore. Had it not been for Bogdan he could have passed through easily because of his diplomatic immunity. Instead, he swung the BMW hard right down Opoczynska Street. Then he tried to turn east again, but a militia column heading north on Niepodleglosci blocked the way.

'Doing all these back doubles means we're losing valuable time,' Theobold cursed.

It was 7.51. Theobold and Bogdan were stuck one-and-a-half congested kilometres from Bagatela Street.

34

As General Siwinski arrived in his office at the Interior Ministry, Klimanov already sat at the deputy Interior Minister's desk. But the KGB liaison officer scarcely acknowledged Siwinski's arrival. He was flicking through the bulky case files he had taken without permission from Siwinski's desk.

'You *still* haven't found the CIA terrorist,' Klimanov complained. 'Moscow Centre is already talking of a serious dereliction of duty by the Polish security forces – in particular you, Comrade General.'

Siwinski stood with his head erect, his jaw jutting forward. 'Yevgenni Viktorovich, just get out of my desk and leave my office,' he yelled. 'I have a critical May Day security operation to coordinate and by your presence you're preventing me from carrying out my duties. Please leave . . .'

Siwinski strode to the other side of the desk and towered over Klimanov. 'I will give you and Mironenko a full report in good time, Yevgenni Viktorovich. Tell Moscow Centre to be patient . . . now piss off!'

The KGB General was taken aback by Siwinski's response and, as he left, he showed it. The Polish Deputy Interior Minister angrily kicked his office door shut. He began checking through the documents he had seen Klimanov reading, then a phone rang. 'Yes?'

It was the commander of SB surveillance services. He reported to Siwinski the details of two phone calls which had been monitored in Warsaw twenty-five minutes earlier. Both had mentioned the name Sulecki, and both had been made to and from the residence of a suspected CIA agent named Jeb Theobold on Gymnastyczna Street.

'Thank you, Comrade Colonel.'

Siwinski threw his phone receiver into its cradle then snatched up another.

'Commander! It's Deputy Minister Siwinski. Listen carefully. Scramble 'Tiger' Brigade. I repeat, scramble 'Tiger' Brigade. Terrorist alert. Address is 15 Bagatela Street, sixth floor. Fuller details to follow. . .'

'Tiger' Brigade was the Polish militia's crack para-military unit which had been on 24-hour red alert since the first warnings of a terrorist threat against Polish interests several days earlier. Within one minute of Siwinski's alert the brigade's first *Gaz* jeep roared from the unit's temporary billet in the centre of Warsaw.

It was 7.59.

35

General Jaruzelski was a stickler for precision and promptness so this morning's delay was most unusual. Normally the Polish leader left his villa at 7.40 for the six-minute journey to the Council of Ministers but today it was already 7.50 and the General's dark-blue BMW still sat outside flanked by the usual two brown *Polonez* security cars with their long floppy aerials.

Inside his villa, the General had been delayed by a pair of urgent phone calls. The first came from the Interior Minister, General Kiszczak, one of Jaruzelski's longtime friends and army colleagues. Kiszczak reported how during the night SB intelligence had revealed an intended turnout of tens of thousands of Solidarity sympathisers for an illegal demonstration designed to upstage the official May Day celebrations.

'I want no trouble,' Jaruzelski ordered Kiszczak. 'The security organs must not be party to any provocation. I don't want the smell of tear gas or the sounds of helicopters and percussion grenades interrupting our official celebrations. The picture we must send today both to our fraternal friends in the East and our capitalist adversaries in the West must be one of calm, order and controlled normality.'

Jaruzelski had faith in his new Interior Minister. Having shone in military counter-intelligence, Kiszczak had been appointed by Jaruzelski several months earlier to reform the Polish security apparatus built up under the Old Guard regime of General Milewski, the extreme hardliner who had once worked for the Russian secret police and who subsequently ran Poland's internal security machinery with an iron hand.

Within two minutes of ending his call to Kiszczak, Jaruzelski had to face the full force of Milewski's hardline backlash. The Polish leader distrusted Milewski, but was still not in a position to exclude him from the Politburo because outside it the former Interior Minister would be an even more dangerous threat to his policies than he was inside.

'Wojciech!' Milewski bellowed down the phone. 'You're mad! There are thousands of counter-revolutionaries threatening to take to the streets to humiliate us and your orders are to do nothing? On May Day of all days? Wojciech! You're confirming the worst fears of our allies to the east. I beg you – for the sake of Poland and before it's too late. Be firm and be brave!'

Jaruzelski knew that Milewski ultimately represented the all-powerful KGB. But the Polish leader was renowned for his cool head, and he would not be railroaded by Milewski's emotive cocktail of dire warnings. With his lisping upper lip quivering gently, Jaruzelski courteously thanked General Milewski for his call but ignored his warnings.

'I'm very grateful to you for phoning, Comrade Mirek. I am firm and I am brave, but not perhaps in the way you would have liked. I see no reason to change the Interior Ministry's operational orders. I hope we'll meet later this morning at the May Day parade on Victory Square.'

Within himself the Polish leader bubbled with fury but, as usual, he revealed none of his emotions to outsiders. Instead the ramrod-stiff figure calmly donned his khaki scarf, military raincoat and peaked cap, then walked under armed escort the fifteen paces from his villa to the BMW. A minute later the three-car convoy sped out of Ikara Street past the roadblocks and headed north up the dual carriageway on Pulawska Street.

It was 7.55, fifteen minutes later than usual.

36

Sulecki returned to Joanne Decker's bedroom, opened the canvas holdall, then pulled out the four sections of the Ruger. As neatly and precisely as a waiter setting places for dinner he lay the weapon alongside the magazine and its six bullets.

Despite the first uncharacteristic sign of nerves, Sulecki took just twenty-two seconds to assemble the sniper rifle with the precision perfected during the lonely weeks of training at Magda's *domek*. He screwed the barrel into the breech, then the silencer into the barrel. Then he inserted the rotating bolt, snapped open the steel folding stock and fed the nine remaining 5.56 mm specially prepared disintegration bullets into the doctored 20-round magazine. Finally he laid his right eye on the stock and checked the barrel alignment from both ends. It was perfect.

By 7.44 – one minute sooner than planned – Sulecki was crouching on the balcony behind a screen of Joanne Decker's washing, the three-and-a-half kilos of Ruger finely balanced in the palm of his left hand and against his right shoulder. The KGB Lieutenant Colonel waited, the barrel aimed downwards to a point one hundred and fifty metres south at the upper end of Pulawska Street. He recalled the words of grumpy Yuri Fedorovich, his instructor at Balashikha: 'Remember, Andrei! A few short breaths will relax the muscles. No urgent gulps. Then a long, even rhythm, and remember to pull the trigger during inhalation, not when you're breathing out.'

It was already 8.01, and by Sulecki's reckoning the Polish leader was now eleven minutes late.

Six floors below, and around the corner on Bagatel Street, Theobold's BMW appeared after its zigzagging high-speed dash across southern Warsaw. The CIA officer steered the car over the wide pavement and screeched to a halt alongside the high double gates into the courtyard of number 15. Bogdan hung on the doorbell until the *concierge* appeared.

'No entrance this morning. By order of the militia,' insisted the stubborn and bad-tempered gatekeeper.

'*Prosze bardzo*!! Urgent!' Bogdan yelled breathlessly.

Theobold stuffed a crumpled ten dollar bill into the hand of the *concierge*. The two men shot through the archway, into the yard and across the cobbles towards the lift shaft. Bogdan looked up the dark stairwell. 'Come on! Come on!' he hissed, clenching his teeth impatiently as he pressed the button and the lift cage failed to move down towards them. 'Dammit. Someone must have forgotten to close the gate.'

Sulecki made every effort not to fidget as he knelt on Joanne Decker's balcony. The laundry pegged to the balustrade ruffled in a sudden wisp of light early morning wind. Jaruzelski was already fifteen minutes late. Would he come at all?

One floor below Sulecki, on the fifth-floor landing, Bogdan and Theobold stood panting as they studied the name plates on the doors. On the left *Saniewski*. In the centre *Radkiewicz*. On the right *Dudkowska*. Wrong floor! They scampered up the next flight and repeated their breathless examination of names. On the left *Konapacki*. On the right *Gorzewski*. In the middle *Tillet*.

'You're sure this is the sixth floor,' gasped Theobold.

'I'm sure.'

'Where's Decker then? Wait a minute! Tillet was a Third Secretary at our embassy two years ago. I think Joanne took over his apartment.'

They tried the door. It was locked from inside.

'We'll have to force it.'

The door was solid, but the lock loose. Both men crouched in the dark, each with one shoulder braced at the level of the handle. They pushed in unison. Once. Twice. It took eight thumps before the lock gave way and the door burst open to reveal Joanne Decker's silent, empty living room.

Bogdan and Theobold listened. There was nothing but the busy hum of Saturday morning traffic coming through a window. Bogdan and Theobold advanced slowly through the small lobby, then the sitting room and the kitchen. Still there was nothing. Before entering the apartment neither man had thought to discuss tactics. Both felt acutely vulnerable because neither of them had a weapon. For Theobold, possession of a pistol – even, for self defence – would have been out of the question anyway, because CIA regulations forbade the use of fire-arms on the territory of another sovereign state without express approval. It could never be contemplated that a CIA officer might become involved in a gun-battle, especially in a Communist country.

At the foot of the apartment block a squad of armed militia officers on Unii Lubelskiej Square periodically scanned the crumbling facades above, but none gave a second thought to the laundry fluttering from the balcony railings on the sixth floor.

'Red alert! Red alert ... Rakowiecka Street, Unii Lubelskiej Square ... Approaching! ... Approaching! ...'

The voice of the Warsaw militia commander crackled loudly on each officer's antiquated radio. A traffic police-man walked from his blue-and-white patrol car to thrust a small lollipop-shaped baton firmly at the oncoming traffic, which dutifully pulled into the kerb to leave the outside lane clear.

Sulecki read the slowing of traffic correctly. He stiffened his kneeling position, steadied the Ruger and aimed at a point on the tarmac outside the Moscow cinema.

37

Bogdan and Theobold stepped slowly around Joanne Decker's bed and across the Afghan rug. Ahead, the net-curtains billowed and the glass doors onto the balcony creaked in the light wind.

Bogdan's determination to stop Sulecki was now driven as much by vengeance as by a commitment to protect the name of Solidarity. Theobold, on the other hand, was driven by his determination to prove that he had been right and his Station Chief Jefferson had been badly wrong. But the CIA agent knew that by being here without Jefferson's authorisation he had taken a huge risk. While he gambled on trapping Sulecki and foiling the KGB's assassination plot, he also knew that if he was captured he would precipitate a diplomatic incident of incalculable proportions.

They both edged forward, Bogdan slightly ahead of Theobold. From the street below they heard a sudden commotion of voices on the militia radio and then a squealing of tyres. Through the net curtains Bogdan could make out the faint but solid outline of a crouching figure. It was not the time to ponder or calculate.

'*Andrzej*!' he yelled, '*Andrzej Sulecki*!'

Sulecki recognised the voice behind him but did not react. He now had Jaruzelski's dark blue BMW square in the Ruger's sights as the car sped towards him up Pulawska Street sandwiched between the two *Polonez* hatchbacks carrying his bodyguards.

Sulecki gritted his teeth. 'Steady, Andrzej, steady!' he told himself.

Bogdan lunged forward, ripping back the net curtains to stand breathless and shaking over Sulecki. 'You double-crossing bastard. You're a KGB agent!' he yelled.

Sulecki wanted to pump bullets into Bogdan but he couldn't afford to turn round because he knew every tenth of a second counted. In the Ruger's sights he watched Jaruzelski's BMW begin to slow to negotiate the roundabout. One hundred metres. Eighty metres. Through his telescopic sight, Sulecki could clearly see the general reading his copy of the daily Communist Party newspaper, *Trybuna Ludu*, in the front seat. With the ice-cool confidence that made him one of Moscow Centre's most highly-prized agents, Sulecki waited for the precise moment when the windscreen and the General's torso were square on to the Ruger. But as Sulecki's forefinger prepared to squeeze the trigger, Bogdan catapulted his bulky frame across Sulecki's back.

It was no brilliant, precisely executed strike, but a desperate move designed to knock the Russian off balance. Sulecki tipped slightly backwards and the Ruger barrel jolted upwards sending the first silenced burst of three bullets wide and wild. He tried a second three-shot volley, but the bullets narrowly missed the roof of Jaruzelski's car and sprayed the windows of a passing tram, sending screaming passengers and pedestrians diving for cover.

Six floors below, as Jaruzelski's BMW swept unobstructed through Unii Lubelskiej Square, militia guards ran towards the screams and shattered glass on the immobilised tram. Meanwhile, around the corner on Bagatela Street a *Gaz* jeep carrying a six-man platoon from the anti-terrorist 'Tiger' brigade roared into the courtyard of Number 15. Sulecki heard a militia radio reporting first details of the shooting. '440 ... *Come in 440 ... Urgent ... Urgent ... Shooting in Lubelskiej Square ... Firearm sighted ... Firearm sighted ...*'

The 'Tiger' commander acknowledged the alert. '*Copy 440 ... Location please ... Location please?*'

'*Bagatela ... Bagatela,*' came the reply.

The commandos, dressed in berets, black-grey camouflage fatigues and dark glasses, carried either pump-action sub-machine guns or Dragunov sniping rifles. 'Sixth floor,' the commander yelled as he pointed across the cobbles to the west wing.

As the sirens and blue lights of four militia wagons filled the square, Sulecki's priority was now his own survival. He kicked the Ruger to the far end of the balcony as Bogdan frantically tried to push his head between the railings. The Russian fought back, ruthlessly thumping Bogdan's head and back against the brick doorway. Bogdan's body went limp, his eyes rolled and he slumped senseless to the floor.

Even at this late stage of the failed operation Sulecki realised he could salvage a grain of honour. The KGB Illegal scooped up the Ruger before felling Theobold with a flying kick to the jaw as the CIA officer tried to enter the struggle. Sulecki clambered over the iron balustrade and lowered himself, agile as a monkey, until he hung by his fingertips. He swung himself in over the railings of the fifth floor balcony below and landed uncomfortably across an old bicycle wheel.

There was no time to discover whether or not the fifth floor apartment was occupied. The Russian wrenched open the glass doors and tiptoed across the darkened room to the main door where he pressed his ear against the timber panel to listen. From the sixth floor above he could hear the first muffled sounds of military boots and raised voices.

He waited fifteen seconds before inching open the door. On the highest step well above him, Sulecki could just see two pairs of black army-style boots. Their proximity was a threat, but he knew he had to take the opportunity to try to escape while he could. He swept a hand through his hair, hunched his back inside the old farmer's suit and raised the collar of his ragged coat.

'*Dziekuje bardzo* ...!' In a rough peasant accent he faked a 'thank-you' and 'goodbye' to an imaginary occupant of the apartment, then stepped onto the landing. He did not want to tempt fate by waiting for the lift so he set off at a carefully measured pace down the stairs. As he descended each cold concrete step the militia voices echoing from above became more distant and less threatening.

Within a minute Sulecki emerged onto Bagatela Street and disappeared among the May Day crowds.

38

By the time Jeb Theobold had recovered from the KGB officer's flykick and picked himself up from the bedroom floor he could see only Sulecki's fingertips clinging to the balcony. He made a rapid guess of Sulecki's intentions then scrambled back through the apartment to try to cut off the Russian's escape from the fifth floor landing.

Theobold might have succeeded had he not been halted by the sound of the stomping boots rising rapidly up the stairwell. The CIA agent guessed they could only signal the militia or SB. He knew he had no option but to retreat. His overriding concern was to avoid capture and prevent a major East–West incident. In a matter of seconds he slipped onto the landing and squeezed himself into the rubbish chute where he clung to a stinking parapet, held his breath and listened.

The boot of the leading 'Tiger' commando kicked the half-open door to Joanne's apartment hard against the wall. A second 'Tiger' leaped inside to crouch behind a brick stanchion and aim his weapon. A third rolled across the polished timber floor, then a fourth slithered along the bedroom skirting board. The American journalist's apartment was suddenly filled with pump-action weapons, paramilitary uniforms, clanking grenades, tear-gas cannisters and the smell of male sweat.

Bogdan sat dazed and bewildered, limply clutching the Ruger and slumped against the wall next to the balcony doors which swung gently in the breeze. Out of the corner of his right eye he was conscious enough to see a commando in dark glasses aiming the barrel of a semi-automatic rifle directly at his head. Bogdan braced himself for a fusillade of bullets.

'Don't fire!'

The voice came from an unseen officer somewhere in the hall.

'*Terrorist action foiled – terrorist action foiled ...*' one of the 'Tigers' radioed to his commander.

Bogdan had no will to resist. His pale face stared blankly ahead confirming his exhaustion, his incomprehension and his anger. Whatever the personal cost, he was proud to have foiled the assassination plot and to have helped preserve the honour of Solidarity.

A corporal and lieutenant picked Bogdan up brutally by his arms and dragged him backwards down six flights of stairs to the 'bitch' wagon in the courtyard. They threw him face-down and trussed him like an animal with his legs and hands tied behind his back. Within four minutes, the 'bitch' wagon squealed into the Wilcza Street Police Depot where word had already spread that the 'Tigers' had netted a prize catch.

Bogdan dreaded what lay ahead. He knew that in the minds of the SB he was already guilty, while the real perpetrators – the KGB and Sulecki – would never be called to account. With a suspect apparently caught red-handed, no officer would bother to question whether the Ruger might have belonged to anyone other than him. Bogdan knew that to the Polish security forces he personified the incontrovertible proof of Solidarity terrorism against the Polish state – proof which the security forces had long sought.

The van's rear doors crashed open and two 'Tigers' manhandled Bogdan out like prize venison shot by hunters in the forests of Mragowo. 'No health path this time, comrades.' The gruff voice of the commander cut through the melee. 'I want no marks on him. This one's too valuable to be bruised and battered.'

A commando prodded Bogdan towards the building and four militia officers surrounded him for 'protection', as the commander and his deputy led the small procession through a throng of plainclothes SB men and uniformed patrolmen blocking the dingy corridor.

'Remember,' Bogdan heard the commander say, 'he's

got to appear in court and on television. He must not be touched. But I want you to grind him down so he'll do anything for us ... The American weapon proves he's a CIA agent in the Solidarity underground.'

The deputy commander acknowledged his orders and swung round to face Bogdan.

'Name?'

'Miskiewicz ... Bogdan Miskiewicz.'

'You're not Andrzej Sulecki?'

The question stunned Bogdan. He shook his head.

'No!' he said despairingly as the deputy commander slammed the door of the interrogation room.

It was two hours before anyone returned.

'Ah! Comrade Miskiewicz!' It was an unpleasantly familiar voice which roused Bogdan. In the doorway stood the SB captain from the Mostowski Palace who had spent four days torturing him before Christmas. Bogdan made no sign of recognition.

'Comrade Miskiewicz, functionary of the *Sluzba Bezpieczenstwa* ... We have been searching for you for over four months. You let us down. You deserted your duties. Such dereliction carries a dreadful price.'

It was as if the last months of Bogdan's life had never happened; as if he had never escaped the SB's clutches in December and fled on the Antonov to Sweden.

He shuddered and braced himself to face the captain. 'I wish to make a statement ... I have been detained by the security services of the Polish People's Republic on suspicion of being party to an assassination conspiracy .. I, Bogdan Misckiewicz, from the Solidarity chapter of Warsaw steelworks, deny ...'

The captain stood up, kicked back his chair and interrupted furiously.

'How dare you feed me such impudent claptrap? You are a confirmed counter revolutionary and a dangerous threat to the Polish State.'

The captain leafed through the file. 'We have irrefutable evidence that for some three years you have been working undercover as a mercenary agent for the capitalist, destabilising forces of the American Central Intelligence Agency. You fled this country to Sweden earlier this year to undergo intensive subversive training by the Americans. You returned recently with money and arms to carry out your American-approved mission – an assassination against the most senior representative of the Polish government, General Wojciech Jaruzelski.'

The captain threw the bulky SB file onto the table. 'You see, it's all here – the evidence of your work for President Reagan and the CIA – all of it is fully documented and corroborated by our own sources.'

'But I've just saved the life of Comrade Jaruzelski!' Bogdan began. 'I saved him not from assassination by me, but by a senior KGB agent named ...'

The captain refused to let Bogdan finish. 'You're a poison, Misckiewicz – a counter revolutionary. And Poland must now be rid of you.'

Bogdan began to tremble. He sensed further protests would yield nothing. He knew that whatever the truth, all evidence against him would now be contrived by a committee of propagandists, disinformation experts and government lawyers in order to frame him.

Bogdan had lost the struggle to clear his name before it had begun.

39

By half past ten, 170,000 hand-picked party activists, war veterans and loyal factory workers had assembled on Grzybowski Square in the centre of Warsaw for the carefully choreographed May Day parade. The obedient delegates stood in their grey overcoats and brown anoraks dutifully clutching national flags and drab red banners, the boldly written words trumpeting the same old tired Party slogans.

As eleven o'clock approached, the drab procession moved forward, walking silently east along Krolewska Street led by General Jaruzelski and accompanied by his Politburo and government ministers. Last year's May Day parade had been a freewheeling and festive occasion when Solidarity members had helped organise what was for once a genuine 'workers' day'. This year's parade was distinguished not by festivity but by the solid lines of militia who laid siege to Victory Square. All official passes were checked at least three times and marksmen with binoculars watched from rooftops as General Jaruzelski's monotone voice tried to allay Moscow's fears that counterevolution was still flourishing in Poland. 'Poland is on the road to normalisation,' the general confidently promised the crowd and the television audience.

But even as the general spoke, vivid proof of the enormous chasm remaining between the government and the governed in Poland was massing less than a kilometre away. Among the cobbled streets of Warsaw's Old Town, thousands of Solidarity supporters were risking arrest by defying the security forces and showing their support for their banned union.

40

At the Interior Ministry, a series of crisis phone calls
summoned General Siwinski to a smoke-filled communications room in the basement, where four rows of
television monitors carried pictures from closed-circuit
cameras located on buildings and lamp-posts in central
Warsaw. Siwinski watched in alarm as first Castle Square
and then the warren of streets and alleys around St John's
Cathedral rapidly filled with wave upon wave of defiant
workers, students and farmers.

'Who's responsible for this?' Siwinski snapped furiously.

'Radio Solidarity!' said a militia colonel. 'They
managed to broadcast details last night before we could
cut their transmission.'

'How many people on the streets so far?'

'Twenty thousand and still rising.'

Siwinski watched Castle Square become a sea of jubi-
lant faces and illegal Solidarity banners which bloomed
like spring flowers among the denim jackets and V-signs.

'It's humiliation,' Siwinski mumbled. 'First, General
Jaruzelski stands on a rostrum in Victory Square and
claims that Solidarity has been destroyed, then within
minutes we have all this crap which martial law was meant
to get rid of. Commander! Why was this not prevented?'

'Our operational instructions from Minister Kiszczak
were not to break up such gatherings.'

As ceremonial guns fired their May Day salute across
the Vistula and the Solidarity supporters sang 'God
Return us a free Poland', Siwinski realised the commander was only obeying the orders which he himself
had drafted for the Interior Minister's approval.

'Let me hear what they're shouting!' Siwinski ordered
the radio officer, who raised the loudspeaker volume.

'*Free Walesa! Imprison Jaruzelski!* ... *Solidarity will win* ... *Free all political prisoners* ... *Down with the junta* ... *The police are with us!* ... *It's our holiday. Our holiday!* ...'

Siwinski turned away. 'Clever bastards! They know we'd never order a workers' demonstration to be broken up on May Day.'

Siwinski was apoplectic with rage. 'Just make sure your officers stay in their wagons and that this rabble is kept away from Victory Square. Block them off. They must have no chance to disrupt the official parade in front of the television cameras ... Your men must gather every piece of intelligence possible – pictures, names, plans, anything!'

'And then?'

'And then we'll get them. Our own wires inside Solidarity will stir things up and make sure the counter-revolutionaries are on the streets again. On Monday these vermin will pay the price for today ...'

'And tomorrow?'

'Tomorrow will be a day off!'

Across Warsaw at the Wilcza Street militia depot Bogdan's spirits were lifted by the chants and patriotic songs which he could hear drifting downwind from the Old Town. They proved he was not alone.

41

At the headquarters of the KGB's First Chief Directorate outside Moscow, Deputy Chairman Semenov and the three generals agonised over the silence from Warsaw. There was no news from Sulecki, but Polish television pictures confirmed that Jaruzelski had survived the May Day parade.

Semenov's weasel face leered at General Martynov, the thick glass of his spectacles lenses glowing like two searchlights as they reflected light from a desk lamp. Semenov began to search for the way to shift the blame for failure away from himself.

'Why, Vasili Pavlovich? Why such a humiliating failure?'

The four generals could only fret and speculate. Had Sulecki been captured or shot? Had he even made the assassination attempt?

No one at Moscow Centre knew.

Sulecki crossed the Polish-Soviet frontier in Terespol at dusk having slipped out of Warsaw five hours earlier on board the *Sovtransport* lorry parked as planned on Defilad Square and driven by Major Petrovsky.

Back on Soviet territory the KGB Lieutenant Colonel released weeks of tension by gorging *pampushky* jam doughnuts at a favourite cafe haunt in the garrison town of Briest. Only then did he brace himself to telephone 'S' Directorate in Moscow.

'I want you back here by midnight!' Martynov ordered him. 'I will ensure a jet is standing by at the Briest military airfield within an hour. I want a full explanation.'

It was a brief conversation. In failure the decorated KGB Lieutenant Colonel remained proud and loyal. But he could only dread what awaited him in Moscow.

42

In Washington the White House duty officer buzzed the State Department desk officer responsible for Eastern Europe. 'What news on Warsaw? Anything I need to pass on to the President's office?' he asked.

'Nothing, Bill – apart from the big demonstrations you already know about,' reported the bored State Department official.

The White House officer then buzzed CIA headquarters at Langley. 'Any news from Warsaw?'

'Nothing . . .'

The May Day assassination rumoured by Soviet leaks and feared by the Reagan administration had not happened. The White House staffer nonchalantly tossed into his 'Out' tray the file marked 'Poland – Risk Minimisation Strategy – 1 May 1982'.

In Warsaw, Jeb Theobold reappeared in Station Chief Jefferson's office at one o'clock, seven hours after he first left the US Embassy to get some breakfast provisions from his villa.

'Where the hell have you been, Jeb?' roared Jefferson in his Louisiana drawl. 'And where's my fucking breakfast? . . . And come to think of it, where was the May Day terrorist attack you promised?'

Theobold was determined to tell Jefferson what had happened. He insisted they seek the total security of the embassy's lead-lined, leakproof 'bell'.

Jefferson was visibly shaken as he heard Theobold's story: first the discovery of Sulecki's assassination attempt, then the CIA agent's four terrifying hours hidden in the rubbish shute at Bagatela Street while militia officers searched Joanne Decker's apartment.

'From what I overheard,' said Theobold, 'the Polish

authorities are convinced that Bogdan is in fact Sulecki the assassin. The Interior Ministry intends to charge him. They'll take no account of the fact that Bogdan was an innocent Solidarity worker who stopped the assassination. It's criminal. They're already talking of putting him on television as an example of American-sponsored terrorism in Poland. Frank, we have to make representations to halt this charade. I'll be prepared to provide independent evidence of Bogdan's innocence . . .'

'No way, Jeb!' snapped Jefferson. 'Perhaps Bogdan's predicament is a tragedy, but it's an internal Polish matter, and the American government – especially the Company – mustn't be seen to be involved. In any case, how the hell would we explain the presence of a US diplomat at the scene of an attempted assassination of the Polish leader? Confirming your presence in Decker's apartment would only add to the Polish claims of American complicity. Jeb, just be thankful you weren't picked up by the commandos. Imagine the repercussions if you had been. It's too terrible to think of.'

Reluctantly Theobold had to accept Jefferson's argument. As always, the CIA's undisputed priority was the protection of its own interests and those of America. Personal considerations and sympathy for victims were irrelevant.

'D'you want me to prepare a report, Frank?'

'No. All I want is silence, Jeb. As far as you and me are concerned we know nothing about Miskiewicz or Sulecki. And as for the assassination attempt – this morning's record will show that you were on routine surveillance duties elsewhere. One day I'll file a classified memorandum for records at Langley, but not yet. We have to let the dust settle.'

Jefferson wanted no more discussion. He stood up and ushered Theobold out of the 'bell'.

'So you're buying the beers Jeb, 'cos officially you're the one who got it wrong. Remember our deal? There was no assassination. There was no Sulecki, no Bogdan no Magda ... and I was right, eh?'

Theobold had to nod agreement. He despised his Station Chief more than ever.

43

As dusk turned to night, the Interior Ministry completed its investigation into the security forces' May Day humiliation by Solidarity. The acrimony of the meeting was more than compensated for by the heartening news reported by Siwinski at the end. He made no attempt to disguise his delight as he sat poring over the three-page report of the assassin's capture and interrogation. The sole suspect was Bogdan Miskiewicz and the evidence of American backing was incontrovertible. What else could explain how a Solidarity leader had been caught red-handed holding a high-precision American weapon in the home of a US citizen within minutes of an attempt on the Polish leader's life? Faced with such damning evidence, Siwinski forgot all his earlier fears of KGB complicity.

One floor above, Interior Minister Kiszczak buzzed his deputy and invited him upstairs.

'Congratulations on the operation, Wladek,' he beamed at Siwinski. 'But we came within a hair's breadth of disaster, didn't we? The Mostowski Palace screwed up badly by looking for a suspect called Sulecki while the real criminal, Miskiewicz, was under interrogation by the SB, and not just once, but twice! Wladek, this case has shown up serious dereliction of duty at many levels. Those responsible must be disciplined . . .'

'Of course,' said Siwinski, relieved that as a longtime friend of the minister, he personally seemed to be escaping Kiszczak's finger of blame. 'But what about the American journalist who lives in the apartment? We don't have any evidence of her complicity!'

'Never mind that. Expel her as a spy,' said the minister. 'Without revealing the whole story, that'll signal to Reagan and the CIA that we *did* uncover their plot.'

44

Bad weather meant the KGB's Tupolev-134 carrying Lieutenant Colonel Sulecki did not reach Moscow until 2 a.m. An official *Volga* rushed the haggard agent from the military airfield to the headquarters of the First Chief Directorate where Generals Semenov and Martynov were waiting to debrief him.

It was a solemn confrontation. A male stenographer took notes as Sulecki spent two hours detailing the climax of *Amber Monkey* and explaining how the operation had failed.

'Comrade Generals,' Sulecki concluded. 'May I suggest the situation is not one of total gloom. The KGB can still turn the incident to its advantage. Our propaganda can make good capital out of a grave Polish security lapse in which a Solidarity terrorist supported by the United States came close to murdering the Polish leader.'

Sulecki was a wily professional who knew how to turn disappointment to his advantage.

Semenov's heavy silver eyebrows glowered silently. 'Comrade Lieutenant Colonel, that seems out of the question because of information received from Warsaw this evening while you were flying here. Our liaison officer at the Interior Ministry says the Polish security forces will not even admit that an assassination attempt has taken place. So if officially there was no attempt to kill Jaruzelski, how can we make public capital out of *Amber Monkey*'s failure without revealing our level of knowledge and involvement throughout?'

With no further discussion and without a word of appreciation for his two-year undercover operation, Sulecki was asked to leave. The KGB officer pulled himself up from the chair and dragged his tired body down the long curving corridor outside. It was 4 a.m.

Before nine o'clock that morning General Semenov was at KGB headquarters on Dzerzhinsky Square padding down the well-worn route of deep-green carpets past the armed guards in the corridors leading to the KGB Chairman's office. As Semenov stood beneath a photograph of Lenin, Chairman Andropov's wiry fingers waved him to a seat in front of the main T-shaped desk. He noted how Andropov's diabetes and kidney disease were noticeably wasting his body. Shakily, the KGB Chairman adjusted his thick pebble spectacles before thumping his frail knuckles onto the desk.

'My disappointment at the failure must be obvious to you, Comrade General. Failure is not in the spirit of a true Chekist! I should really despatch you indefinitely to somewhere like Khabarovsk in the Far East as punishment. But now that I have eclipsed Brezhnev and my high ground is secure you are saved, my dear Dimitri Fedorovich. But just this once!'

Andropov said nothing more. As usual he did not have to.

In Sweden, Jola passed her seventy-seventh day of exile among the newly green forests of a late, damp spring at Frostavallen. She hungered for gossip or smuggled messages from her homeland across the Baltic. But there was still nothing, and still no news of Bogdan.

On Wilcza Street, Bogdan chewed a wedge of bread and a slab of lard as he shivered in the evening chill of the interrogation room. It was Sunday 2 May. In the last twenty-four hours no one had visited or questioned him. As during his detention before Christmas he assumed the SB were biding their time in order to weaken his resistance. And time was on their side because as far as the outside world was concerned, Bogdan was a non-person who had disappeared and no longer existed. No one knew of his sacrifice and no one knew of his fate.

A key turned in the door and a fresh-faced, plainclothes functionary in his late twenties poked his head around the door. The face was instantly familiar.

'Sorry, wrong room . . .!' said the functionary.

The voice too was familiar.

'Jurek! . . . *Jurek Kucharski* . . .!' yelled Bogdan without a second thought.

The door stopped moving, gripped by the hand of someone clearly undecided whether to disappear or push the door open again. Bogdan was sure he had not made a mistake. '*Jurek Kucharski* . . .!' he shouted again.

Was it possible? Was it really Jurek who for seven years had been his longstanding friend and fellow dissident activist in the foundry at the Warsaw steelworks? Was it really the trusted Solidarity colleague who had helped set up and run the underground printing press at the allotment shed on Rakowiecka Street?

Bogdan was too shaken to do anything. He stared at the hand still gripping the end of the door. He willed it to push the door open and reveal the face for a second time. But having waited for half a minute it crashed the door shut.

Bogdan slumped ashen faced into the chair and stared at the door. His stomach and bowels folded over themselves with the shock, pain and humiliation of what he had just discovered. Not only had Bogdan's underground cell been infiltrated by Sulecki, the KGB agent. For months – maybe years – Jurek too must have been a 'wire' for the SB. The Interior Ministry must have infiltrated wires into all levels of Solidarity, and nothing can have been safe from them.

Bogdan lunged across the room and tried to wrench open the door. It was too late.

The key turned.

Jola had been right. She would never know what had happened.

SUE GEE

Spring Will Be Ours

From the streets of Nazi-occupied Warsaw, through the lonely dreams of a little Polish boy growing up in Clapham in the fifties, to a candlelit vigil for Solidarity outside London's Polish Embassy – this is the tragic story of Poland seen through the fortunes of a single family.

Jan and Anna Prawicki survived Hitler's devastation of Warsaw, and fled, haunted by the past, to England. Through their own struggles, the memories of their parents and the developing lives and loves of their children, Jerzy and Ewa, we enter the terrors of war, occupation, repression and resistance, as individuals and a nation struggle for life and liberty. Sue Gee's magnificent novel evokes a country politically oppressed but burning still with courage and hope.

RICHARD COX

An Agent of Influence

When self-made millionaire Sir James Hartman's private plane disappears in Africa, his son Robert flies out to join the search.

His father's background – from lowly birth in Central Europe, to decoration for valour in the British Army and marriage into the British upper classes – is public knowledge. But Robert soon realises that there is much more to his father than was previously apparent. What really motivates Sir James and where do his loyalties lie? To the business empire he has built so brilliantly? Or to shadowy figures from his alien past?

JOHN TOLAND

Occupation

It is 1945, and Japan lies in ruins, crushed by the defeat in the Pacific and ravaged by the explosions at Nagasaki and Hiroshima. Now the Americans, led by their 'Shogun' Douglas MacArthur, have arrived, as an occupying force and to conduct the war trials which will reopen many half-healed wounds.

Seen through the eyes of two families, one American and one Japanese, *Occupation* evokes the extraordinary atmosphere of a country sustained by pride and tradition now brought to its knees by war and unconditional surrender. Deeply moving in its depiction of the human dramas, it makes a remarkable companion novel to John Toland's *Gods Of War*, and reveals a glimpse of the modern Japan waiting to be born.

BOB COOK

Questions of Identity

A leading bacteriologist is seized by Red Brigade terrorists who demand a highly sinister and deadly ransom deal. The CIA have just one lead to the kidnappers – the bright and radical student, Monica Venuti – but she is protected by her influential family connections. So it is left to Michael Wyman, Monica's Philosophy Professor and ex MI6 to probe her philosophical beliefs and to alert the anti-terrorist squad the moment his pupil is ready to leap from ideological theory to revolutionary practice. But the CIA are impatient. Raiding Monica's apartment, they attempt to seize her, but are in for a nasty surprise . . .

From the author of *Disorderly Elements*, *Questions of Identity* is a tense, slick, provocative and entertaining thriller with a wonderfully dry final twist.

JAMES FOLLETT

U700

The Royal Navy's secret weapon in World War II is pin-point accurate radio direction finding. But the German U-boats have an even deadlier weapon: the magnetic torpedo armed with the Wotan warhead. Detonating beneath the ship and breaking its back, it gives the Germans the ability to sink even battleships with a single torpedo. Such a weapon could change the outcome of the war.

For British Intelligence the goal is to capture a U-boat and learn its secrets. With the surrender of U700, success is within its grasp. But one man stands between them and U700 – a man branded a coward by the Fatherland, but who may still be a hero . . .

James Follett is also the author of *Mirage*, *Dominator*, *Swift* and *Churchill's Gold*, all available from Mandarin.

JAMES FOLLETT

Mirage

The masterly new thriller from the author of *Dominator* and *Swift* is based on extraordinary historical fact.

It is the late 1960s and General de Gaulle has cancelled Israel's order for fifty Mirage 5 jet fighters – a stunning body blow for the Israeli Air Force, depleted by SAM missiles after the Six-Day war.

Now de Gaulle springs another surprise, embargoing the five missile-carrying high-speed craft under construction for the Israeli navy.

Against this background, Daniel Kalen, an Israeli fighter pilot grounded after injury, has been given an extraordinary mission by Mossad: to steal the Mirage blueprints – all 250,000 of them – so that Israel can build her own version of the fighter.

So begins a joint operation of breathtaking audacity – the theft of the plans, hand in hand with the 'liberation' of the high-speed craft. Kalen, aided by American research student Raquel Gibbons, has more adversaries than he knows – not only the French but also the shady aircraft dealer Lucky Nathan, who has much to lose should the synchronised espionage mission succeed . . .

NICK TOSCHES

Cut Numbers

'THE NUMBERS' IS THE NAME OF THE GAME, THE MAFIA-RUN RACKET SO SUCCESSFUL THE GOVERNMENT HAD TO LEGALISE IT

In downtown New York all the bums have something to bet even when they're down to their last nickel. They just need luck.

Streetwise but middle-aged, Louie Brunelleschi is down on his. Left once more by his embittered girlfriend, he lives on the squalid fringes of organised crime – a loan-shark chasing debts in the seedy afterhours dives and gambling dens of the Lower East Side.

Louie's great-uncle John is the one man he trusts. Rumour has it that it was he who once perfected the scheme to rig the numbers; and who is now looking for one last score.

Following a week-long bender of drink, sex and self-destruction, Louie needs to sober up fast if he is to find richer pickings – or indeed, as vengeful rivals muscle in – to escape with his life . . .

'Tosches . . . strikes gold with a brutal, corrosively funny portrait of New York's penny-ante hoods and professional lowlifes . . . (his) prose crackles with violence'.

PUBLISHERS WEEKLY

'His people are meaner than a rusty nail through the foot, and the story's a jaw-clencher too'.

GEORGE V. HIGGINS

A Selected List of Fiction Available from Mandarin Books

While every effort is made to keep prices low, it is sometimes necessary to increase prices at short notice. Mandarin Paperbacks reserves the right to show new retail prices on covers which may differ from those previously advertised in the text or elsewhere.

The prices shown below were correct at the time of going to press.

☐	7493 0077 9	**The Country Gentleman**	Fiona Hill	£2.99
☐	7493 0033 7	**Doctors and Women**	Susan Cheever	£3.50
☐	7493 0009 4	**Larksghyll**	Constance Heaven	£2.99
☐	7493 0012 4	**The Falcon of Siam**	Axel Aylwen	£3.99
☐	7493 0018 3	**Daughter of the Swan**	Joan Juliet Buck	£3.50
☐	7493 0042 6	**Snow Storms in a Hot Climate**	Sarah Dunant	£3.50
☐	7493 0025 6	**Here Today**	Zoë Fairbairns	£3.50

TV and Film Titles

☐	7493 0101 5	**My Left Foot**	Christy Brown	£3.50
☐	7493 0055 8	**Neighbours I**	Marshall/Kolle	£2.99
☐	423 02020 X	**Bellman and True**	Desmond Lowden	£2.50
☐	7493 0056 6	**Neighbours II**	Marshall/Kolle	£2.99
☐	7493 0057 4	**Dealers**	Gerald Cole	£2.50

All these books are available at your bookshop or newsagent, or can be ordered direct from the publisher. Just tick the titles you want and fill in the form below.

Mandarin Paperbacks, Cash Sales Department, PO Box 11, Falmouth, Cornwall TR10 9EN.

Please send cheque or postal order, no currency, for purchase price quoted and allow the following for postage and packing:

UK   55p for the first book, 22p for the second book and 14p for each additional book ordered to a maximum charge of £1.75.

BFPO and Eire   55p for the first book, 22p for the second book and 14p for each of the next seven books, thereafter 8p per book.

Overseas   £1.00 for the first book plus 25p per copy for each additional book.
Customers

NAME (Block Letters) ....

ADDRESS ....

....